The Dividing *of* AMERICA

Lee McGarr

First Edition

PAGE PUBLISHING, INC.
Conneaut Lake, PA

First originally published by Page Publishing 2020

ISBN 978-1-6624-1005-5 (pbk)
ISBN 978-1-6624-1006-2 (digital)

Printed in the United States of America

CONTENTS

FIGURES LIST

FOREWORD

THE UNITED STATES of America is experiencing events that are different than any before. Our rule of law and our Constitution have been compromised! What started for me as a bad dream in 2011 ended in 2014 with a unanimous jury trial in my favor. When that unanimous jury verdict was overturned by the judge, that short-lived victory had become a nightmare and continues to be one. At the end of the trial after closing arguments were presented, I was shocked when asked to take the stand once again. My attorney stated, "Chris, will you explain to the jury how this experience has impacted you and your family?" I stated as bad as it was, I have also benefited because now I have a closer walk with Christ.

Over and over since this life-changing experience started in 2011 through today, things have happened that cannot be explained as coincidence but rather divine intervention by God.

Not only were twenty-eight movie videos and documents compiled in the basement of my church making this book possible, but I was also handed a copy of Lee McGarr's book *What Difference Does It Make* in the same basement. One of the members of our church handed me Lee's book and said "Here, I think you should read this." Once again, coincidence is not how I met Lee McGarr for it was part of a bigger plan.

Lee McGarr's most common statement is "Keep the faith," and faith is why we met. Not only do Lee McGarr and I share the love for flying, fishing, and hunting in common, but we have had our lives turned upside down by corruption. Lee McGarr and I realized that this is a big puzzle and Lee only had one-third of the pieces when he wrote his two previous books *What Difference Does It Make* and *Unfit*. After meeting, we realized that I had the other two-third of the pieces, allowing us to complete the picture.

Out of the many miraculous events that have occurred during this journey, there are two that are clearly obvious revealing who controlled them:

1. After the state of Oklahoma lost three of my applications to see an inmate named Robert Stone, I was granted access after hiring an attorney. Robert Stone said, "If you can get me out of here, I will give you several thousand emails that went through my computer server while I have been incarcerated." Upon his release shortly afterward, he did just that which gave Lee McGarr and I the puzzle pieces to complete this picture. Note: I did not even know Robert Stone prior to meeting him but felt an unrelentless push to not give up on meeting with him and getting him released.
2. After having my life and my family's lives threatened, I decided to write a book, compile documents, and produce twenty-eight movie videos, which I stored on a zip drive. The purpose of this labor-intensive exercise was for protection by duplicating the drive and giving copies to family, friends, and church members. In the event I lost my life, my story would still be told. The most important thing I did was let my adversaries know that if anything happens to either myself or my family, the world would know about my story and be able to view the evidence that backs it up. Within one of the twenty-eight videos, I stated that "if you stand up or fight back against these bullies you either get killed or go to prison." In January of 2018, I was arrested on a trumped-up felony charge of Home Repair Fraud and faced the possibility of ten years imprisonment as explained by the judge. Much to my surprise, while reviewing the evidence filed against me, I realized the homeowner provided the police with the zip drive on the advice of his attorney who had served two terms as a state senator. The zip drive

> was logged in as evidence within the Beckham County Oklahoma Courthouse, making it a public record. Do you think that was just a coincidence? I think *not*!

Prayer is a powerful tool in everything we do in life, especially when fighting Satan. Prayer and faith is why I met Lee McGarr.

Lee McGarr's talent as a writer, a dedicated American citizen, and his love for this great country made this book possible.

PREFACE

ATTORNEY ED PRITCHETT formed Chisholm Trail Construction and prepared the partnership agreement between Robert Stone and Terry Kutcher. Terry Kutcher is Jack Stuteville's close friend and bank customer. Terry had a large and old debt at First Capital Bank. Once, a large loan was issued to the newly formed Chisholm Trail Construction. Part of the money was used to pay off Terry Kutcher's old debt at the bank, making Robert Stone liable to pay it back. Robert Stone had a personal relationship with Carl Edwards Jr. and his father, Carl Edwards, which allowed Jack Stuteville the opportunity to be involved in Junction Development. By Jack Stuteville loaning all of this money to Robert Stone for a housing development in Columbia, Missouri, Stuteville could control him because of Stone's debt to Chisholm Trail Construction. Jack had his eye on the $60 million NASCAR USDA scam and needed Stone to pull it off.

Terry Kutcher lives in Cashion, Oklahoma, near Kingfisher. Attorney Ed Pritchett and his wife, Judge Susie Pritchett, lived nearby. Together, Jack Stuteville, Terry Kutcher, Ed Pritchett, and Judge Susie Pritchett worked together on many Ponzi schemes involving First Capital Bank. Judge Susie Pritchett signed the extradition and arrest warrant to bring Robert Stone back from Missouri to take the fall for Chisholm Trail Construction and the NASCAR development scam.

Judge Susie Pritchett is now deceased. After freeing Mr. Stone, we were able to obtain all the e-mails between Terry Kutcher and Robert Stone with his assistance, as they were partners in the housing development using money loaned by Jack Stuteville's bank in Kingfisher, Guthrie and Cordell. Since Robert Stone set up Terry

Kutcher's e-mail account in Missouri, that is how we obtained all of the e-mails. Those e-mails have implicated many people involved in the Ponzi schemes: Jack Stuteville, who used his connections with the following agencies to pull this NASCAR Development off; FDIC agent Greg Hernandez, who shut down First Capital Bank; State Representative Todd Russ, who admitted working with the FDIC to shut down First Capital Bank; FBI agents whose names are Agent Fairboux, Agent Celso Ramos——in the e-mails working with Joey Istre, whose claims are many, with murder-for-hire being the most notable; Terry Kutcher; Mike Fusselman the DA; and OSBI agent Steve Neuman, who worked closely with Mike Fusselman for Stone's prosecution. They collapsed Cornerstone Stone Finance and Premier Bank in Columbia Missouri with the Ponzi schemes.

And so begins what is now known as PCG!

CHAPTER I

Where Will It End?

Early in March 2011, a successful contractor in Western Oklahoma was contacted by a man named Perry Streebin from Search Engineering in Norman, Oklahoma. He was soliciting bidders for a project called the Kingfisher West Bottom Project located in Kingfisher, a town in Western Oklahoma. This was well within the scope of what the contractor could easily accommodate.

It was at around this same time that I was approached by the Department of Transportation Inspector General (DOT/IG) to voice my over seven hundred complaints regarding corruption within the FAA to a newly formed department there called Aviation Audit and Evaluation (AAE). I was employed with the FAA as an inspection pilot and had watched millions of dollars flow from the taxpayers to corrupt individuals.

Unbeknownst to either of us at the time, our lives would become so tightly wrapped due to the thriving corruption within the federal government that was actually sponsored and promoted by our elected and unelected federal and state officials. The ride that the two of us were destined to take would be a devastating but an essential ride to preserve this nation.

This new friend, a Mr. Christopher Poindexter, called me regarding my first book, entitled *What Difference Does It Make*. He, as well, was a pilot and was having his life turned upside down by corruption at all levels and a continued series of attacks. This, for the most part, replicated my life.

From my first encounter with him, I found his story was nearly the same as mine; simply change the mode of attack slightly, change the names, and the ride was the same, where I would have been killed in an aircraft—a popular method with the FAA and those who enjoyed flying—or through the old-fashioned method of simply hiring a hit man! The outcome is always the same!

Where this book will take you to is into a true story of the underworld/Deep State, now operated primarily by our government and lawful entities guised as helpful departments of federal, state, and local agencies. This venture will combine two tragic stories of theft, corruption, Ponzi schemes, narcotics and human trafficking, murder for hire, extortion, and fraud!

You will read in the coming chapters of those who got too far inside and became fall guys, those who testified and befell various accidents that ended, in some cases, not only the primary target but also their entire family and friends—and all in the form of the FAA's normal excuse, pilot error.

The story covers locally elected officials hiring a noted hit man as a "special process server." I suppose the process that he was to serve was not as one would normally think?

As was stated by my new friend, we are dealing with terrorists that use ink instead of bullets to take down our great nation. All information presented in this book is predicated on public documents and public court records. Nothing here is speculation or accusations but, instead, actual factual data available to all! (Fig 1)

Terrorists who use ink instead of bullets
A Sodbuster Series One by Haynes Berk
The story of a modest contractor from a community called Lone Wolf in western Oklahoma who found himself plunged into a vortex of lies and deceit after a simple bid on a half-million dollar storm water project for a nearby town. Christopher Poindexter won the bid but his life became a long and twisted journey into the international world of banking, oil and gas. Sometimes truth is stranger than fiction.

Figure 1-1s

Page 1 of 2

BECKHAM COUNTY SHERIFFS OFFICE / DETENTION CENTER
108 S. 3rd Street Sayre, Oklahoma 73662
(580)928-2121

BOOKING SHEET

PARTY INFORMATION

POINDEXTER, CHRISTOPHER Booking Number 18-0076

Submitted Date 1/22/2018 10:46

DOB	6/24/1966
Age	51
Sex	MALE
Race	WHITE
Hair	GRAY OR PARTIALLY GRAY
Eye	BROWN
Ethnicity	NOT HISPANIC ORIGIN
Height	5 11"
Weight	195 lbs.
Birth City	OKLAHOMA CITY
Birth Place	OKLAHOMA

Social Security Number 440805831

Scars, Marks and Tattoos
SCARS-ARM, LEFT UPPER-LONG SCAR FROM FRACTURE

HOME ADDRESS

Address	21014 E. 1450 RD
City	LONE WOLF
State	OK
Zip Code	73655
Phone	(580)399-5678

EMERGENCY CONTACT INFORMATION

Name	POINDEXTER, BARBARA	Relationship	WIFE
Address	21014 E 1450 RD LONE WOLF, OK 73655	(580) 399-5679	

BOOKING INFORMATION

Booking Number	18-0076	Booked Date	01/22/2018 10:50
Booked Type	FULL BOOKING	Cell Number	1-D-2D
Classification	MEDIUM SECURITY - D POD	Custody Status	
Medical Eligible	YES	Med. Eligible Start	01/22/2018 10:50
Inmate Status	CONFINED BUT NOT CONVICTED		
Booking Officer	CORNELL, ERICA		
Searched Officer	BLANKEN, NICK SEARCH CLOTHING, SEARCH PATDOWN		
Call Made	NO		

Inmate is an Immigration Alien ? NO

ARREST INFORMATION

Arrest Date	01/22/2018 10:51
Arresting Agency	BECKHAM COUNTY SHERIFFS OFFICE / DETENTION CENTER
Arresting Officer	WALK IN, WALK IN

http://beckhamso/PrintBookingSheet.asp?ShowPic2=no&Picture=http://beckhamso/ODISimages/POINDEX... 1/22/18

Figure 1-2s

IN THE DISTRICT COURT OF THE SECOND JUDICIAL DISTRICT OF THE STATE OF OKLAHOMA
SITTING IN AND FOR BECKHAM COUNTY

ISSUED
On 1-19-18
Donna Howell, Court Clerk
Deputy [signature]

THE STATE OF OKLAHOMA,

Plaintiff,

vs.

CHRISTOPHER POINDEXTER

ADDR: P.O. Box 426
Lone Wolf, OK 73655
SSN: 440-80-5831
DOB: 06/24/1966

Defendant(s).

Case No. CF-2018-14

FELONY WARRANT

STATE OF OKLAHOMA, COUNTY OF BECKHAM, TO ANY LAW ENFORCEMENT OFFICER:

YOU ARE HEREBY COMMANDED to forthwith arrest and take said **CHRISTOPHER POINDEXTER** into custody for the offense(s) of:

COUNT 1: HOME REPAIR FRAUD, a FELONY, 15 O.S. § 765.3.

and bring him before me or some other Magistrate having cognizance of the case, to be dealt with according to law. You are further directed to execute this writ or warrant either in daytime or nighttime.

Bond for the release of the above named defendant, to guarantee said defendant's appearance in all the Court's proceedings herein, be and the same is hereby fixed in the sum of $10,000, until the further Order of the Court.

☐ Defendant to have no contact with alleged victim as a condition of the bond.

Dated this 18 day of January, 2018.

[signature]
Judge of the District Court

Presenting Agency: Elk City Police Department

Agency Case Number:

Identifiers: Gender: Male
Height:
Weight: lbs.
DL #: 004064847 (OK)

Race: White
Eye Color:
Hair Color:
Markings:

Figure 1-3s

CHAPTER II

The Bid Is Won, and the Hook Is Set!

In March 2011, the bid for the Kingfisher West Bottom Project was awarded to Pridex Construction LLC, owned by Mr. Christopher "Chris" Poindexter. This is where the fun began. Shortly thereafter, Chris went to meet with the city manager, a Mr. Richard Reynolds, to see if a cash bond was acceptable. He contacted Jack Stuteville, the mayor of Kingfisher, to seek his approval. This was Chris's first meeting with these individuals and with a great deal of envy in hindsight if he could have only avoided this project and meeting. Chris had attempted to find out if a cash performance bond would be acceptable with the city but had not heard back from the engineering firm that told him about the bid.

At that time, Mr. Stuteville was the owner of First Capital Bank and the elected mayor of Kingfisher. Chris came prepared with a cashier check payment for a $24,000 bid bond when he submitted his bid. For this project that was approved and funded by the Department of Agriculture, Chris would also need to provide a performance bond that would cost approximately $19,000 which he had already been quoted through Farm Bureau Insurance. When all was tallied up, including the security deposit, he needed to come up with approximately $95,000 to begin.

Once Chris was assured he had the contract, he contacted another bank in the area and secured a loan for the full value of the job, or $476,936. Unaware at that time, it was later discovered that the banker and his own attorney, Clay Christensen, was also in on the scam. When the mayor heard that he had the money for a full cash bond, he was very interested and requested Reynolds to contact the city attorney, Jared Harrison, of the Harrison & Mecklenburg Law Firm. When Harrison heard the details and the issue of a cash bond, he told Chris that it would not be acceptable. Stuteville was quick to suggest a man named Steve Standridge in Arkansas that could set him up with a bond for the job. Seeing as how the job was approved by the Department of Agriculture, Chris was not thinking of any kind of a scam, as it was a government-approved project and funding was all backed by the federal government. An interesting fact is that all that were in on the scam were heavily tied to the OSU foundation.

At this time, the hook was set, so to speak, and now was the issue of reeling Chris in! Chris went to work getting the paperwork completed and faxed to a company in Arkansas that Steve Standridge owned that evening. He stated that he was a retired insurance agent when, in reality, he was forced out of the business when he lost his license. The following day, the fourth of April 2011, Chris received a call from a man who identified himself as Dr. Larry Wright of The Underwriters Group of Jacksonville, Florida. The two talked and covered the details of the project and the fact that Chris was fully capable to accomplish the job at hand. For the bond, Pridex was approved, and all seemed well and in order. All that The Underwriters Group required was a payment of $19,000 and a deposit of $50,000, which Chris immediately acquired. When all was set, they wanted Chris to wire the funds to Ironstone Bank with a swift code of IR OSU S31 in the wiring instructions. Chris did not want to wire the funds and insisted that the bank make out two cashier's checks and then overnight them to the Underwriters Group. Now, things started to get even stranger; the checks needed to be made out to a PS Trust!

Steve Standridge insisted that Chris make the checks out to a PS Trust rather than The Underwriters Group. Again, later, Chris would find out that a company called Ramphart had just filed a $7.1 million garnishment against The Underwriters Group. The company,

Ramphart Capital, will be discussed later in the book, and they are all together with Stuteville and company. (Fig. 2-1)

Over the next two weeks, Pridex Construction made great headway. One peculiar event that continued to transpire was that the mayor of Kingfisher continued to drive by and occasionally stop to talk to Chris. He even asked if Chris would sell his equipment to some of the mayor's friends. After Chris refused to sell, Stuteville had the city manager, Richard Reynolds, come by and advise Chris that his bond was no good and that they would have to give the contract to the next lowest bidder. That bidding company owned by Jeremy McDowell was Redlands Construction. While Chris's attorney, Clay Christensen, was arguing his case at the city council meeting, the attorney for Redlands construction, a Mr. Evan Gatewood, stated that if the city continued to allow Chris to hold the bid, then they would sue the city of Kingfisher. He stated the bonds issued by The Underwriters Group were no good!

Later, this same attorney would represent Larry Wright in a federal lawsuit that was held in the court of Robin Cauthron! Perhaps a conflict of interest or, more simply put, a setup!

While the abovementioned meeting was going on, unbeknownst to Chris or his brother Randy, one of the thugs that the mayor probably employed and was paid through PCG, was breaking all the windows out of the pickup truck owned by Randy Poindexter parked on city property. This was understood to be a threat and to let the brothers know that they were serious. This also showed exactly how cowardly this bunch was.

If we look back at all this, it is simply stated that the mayor was looking to steal the time and labor of Pridex and them kick them out when a fair portion of the work was complete. From here, Redlands Construction would not get the job, but rather a construction company owned within the family businesses of the city attorney and their law firm.

The mayor and the gang believed firmly that Chris would tuck his tail and leave once the windows were out and Evan Gatewood was threatening suit against the city and that they would walk off with the prize. Chris refused to cower to the threats!

The city later voted to give Pridex an additional ten days to acquire a bond, which, in reality, allowed the mayor and city manager—with the assistance of TMC Construction, the family owned business of the mayor and friends—to manipulate the bid so that only the family-owned company would qualify and then the bid would be awarded to TMC.

It might be noted that on Mike Monroney Aeronautical Center (MMAC), while parked on FAA property, in the beginning after testifying, all the windows were broken out of my vehicle and the seats were sliced. Perhaps this was standard operating procedure (SOP) for cowards!

FIRST MOUNTAIN BANCORP

Trust Receipt Guarantee No. PC04072011-2

IRREVOCABLE TRUST RECEIPT PERFORMANCE GUARANTEE

That Pridex Construction, LLC, PO Box 426, Lone Wolf, OK 73655 as Principal (hereinafter referred to as "Contractor") and

First Mountain Bancorp, 3070 Rasmussen Road, Suite 285, Park City, Utah 84098 as

Trustee (hereinafter referred to as "Trustee"), are held and firmly bound unto City Kingfisher, Oklahoma as Obligee (hereinafter referred to as "Owner"), in the amount of $476,464.00, to which payment Contractor and Trustee bind themselves, their heirs, executors, administrators, successors and assigns, jointly and severally, firmly by these presents.

WHEREAS, the above bounden Principal has entered into contract with Owner bearing date of April, 5, 2011, for

Project: West Bottom Storm Water System Improvements in accordance with drawings and specifications prepared by

City of Kingfisher, Oklahoma which said contract is incorporated herein by reference and made a part hereof, and is hereinafter referred to as the Contract.

NOW, THEREFORE, THE CONDITION OF THIS OBLIGATION is such that, if the Contractor shall promptly and Faithfully perform and comply with the terms and conditions of said contract; and shall indemnify and save harmless the Owner against and from all costs, expenses, damages, injury or loss to which said Owner may be subjected by reason of any wrongdoing, including misconduct, want of care or skill, default or failure of performance on the part of said Principal, his agents, subcontractors or employees, in the execution or performance of said contract, then this obligation shall be null and void; otherwise it shall remain in full force and effect.

1. The Contractor and the Trustee, jointly and severally bid themselves, their heirs, executors, administrators, successors and assigns to the Owner for the Performance of the Construction Contract, which is incorporated herein by reference.

2. The said Trustee to this Guarantee, for value received, hereby stipulates and agrees that no change or changes, extension of time or extensions of time, alteration or alterations or addition or additions to the terms of the contract or to the work to be performed thereunder, or the specifications or drawings accompanying same shall in any wise affect its obligation on this Guarantee, and it does hereby waive notice of any such change or changes, extension of time or extensions of time, alteration or alterations or addition or additions to the terms of the contract or to the work or to the specifications or drawings.

3. If pursuant to the contract documents the Contractor shall be declared in default by the Owner under the aforesaid Contract, the Trustee shall promptly remedy the default or defaults or shall promptly perform the Contract in accordance with its terms and conditions. It shall be the duty of the Trustee to give an unequivocal notice in writing to the Owner within twenty-five (25) days after receipt of a declaration of default of the Trustee's election either to remedy the default or defaults promptly or to perform the contract promptly, time being of the essence. In said notice of election, the Trustee shall indicate the date on which the remedy or performance will commence, and it shall then be the duty of the Trustee to give prompt notice in writing to the Owner immediately upon completion of (a) the remedy and/or correction of each default, (b) the remedy and/or correction of each item of condemned work, (c) the furnishing of each omitted item of work, and (d) the performance of the contract. The Trustee shall not assert solvency of its Principal as justification for its failure to give notice of election or for its failure to promptly remedy the default or defaults or perform the contract.

3070 Rasmussen Rd., STE 285, Park City, Utah 84098
Tel: (435) 658-4979 Fax: (435) 608-4455
http://www.firstmountainbancorp.com

PLAINTIFFS' TRIAL EXHIBIT 3 POINDEXTER

Figure 2-1a

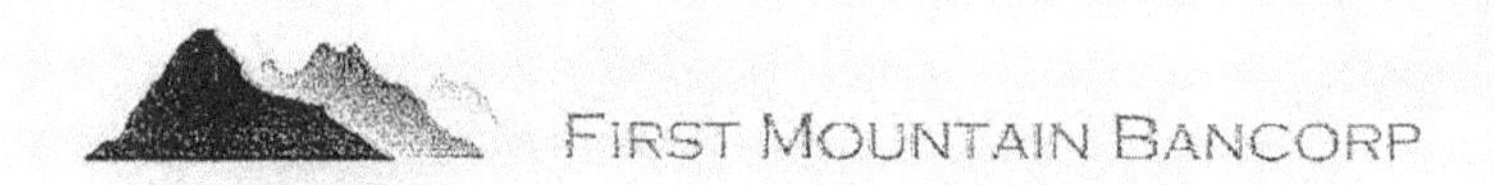

4. The Trustee agrees that other than as is provided in this Guarantee it may not demand of the Owner that the Owner shall (a) perform any thing or act, (b) give any notice, (c) furnish any clerical assistance, (d) render any service, (e) furnish any papers or documents, or (f) take any other action of any nature or description which is not required of the Owner to be done under the contract documents.

5. No right of action shall accrue on this Guarantee to or for the use of any person or corporation other than the Owner named herein or the legal successors of the Owner.

6. First Mountain Bancorp also declares that this ITR is an operating fully confirmed instrument and is subject to the Uniform Customs and Practice for Documentary Credits, International Chamber of Commerce (ICC) Publication No. 600 and engaged us in accordance with terms thereof.

Signed and sealed this 7th day of April, A.D. 2011

IN THE PRESENCE OF:

_______________________ (SEAL)
(Principal)

(Name/Title)

_______________________ (SEAL)
George Gowen, Trustee

FIRST MOUNTAIN BANCORP
TRUSTEE

3070 Rasmussen Rd., STE 285, Park City, Utah 84098
Tel: (435) 658-4979 Fax: (435) 608-4455
Email: ggowen@firstmountainbancorp.com http://www.firstmountainbancorp.com

PLAINTIFFS' TRIAL EXHIBIT 3 POINDEXTER 78

Figure 2-1b

FIRST MOUNTAIN BANCORP

furnishing and the Owner accepting this Guarantee, they agree that all funds earned by the Contractor in the performance of the Construction Contract are dedicated to satisfy obligations of the Contractor and the Trustee under this Guarantee, subject to the Owner priority to use the funds for the completion of the work.

7. Notice to the Trustee, the Owner or the Contractor shall be mailed or delivered to the address shown on the signature page. Actual receipt of notice by Trustee, the Owner or the Contractor, however accomplished, shall be sufficient compliance as of the date received at the address shown on the signature page.

8. The Trustee agrees that other than as is provided in this Guarantee it may not demand of the Owner that the Owner shall (a) perform any thing or act, (b) give any notice, (c) furnish any clerical assistance, (d) render any service, (e) furnish any papers or documents, or (f) take any other action of any nature or description which is not required of the Owner to be done under the contract documents.

9. No right of action shall accrue on this Guarantee to or for the use of any person or corporation other than the Owner named herein or the legal successors of the Owner.

10. First Mountain Bancorp also declares that this ITR is an operating fully confirmed instrument and is subject to the Uniform Customs and Practice for Documentary Credits, International Chamber of Commerce (ICC) Publication No. 600 and engaged us in accordance with terms thereof.

Signed and sealed this 7th day of April, A.D. 2011.

IN THE PRESENCE OF:

(SEAL)

(Principal)

Christopher Poindexter / Managing Member
Poindexter Construction LLC

(Name/Title)

George Gowen (SEAL)

George Gowen, Trustee

FIRST MOUNTAIN BANCORP TRUSTEE

3070 Rasmussen Rd., STE 285, Park City, Utah 84098
Tel: (435) 658-4979 Fax: (435) 608-4455
Email: ggowen@firstmountainbancorp.com http://www.firstmountainbancorp.com

PLAINTIFFS' TRIAL EXHIBIT 3 POINDEXTER 79

Figure 2-1c

AFFIDAVIT OF INDIVIDUAL SURETY
(See instructions on reverse)

OMB No.: **9000-0001**

Public reporting burden for this collection of information is estimated to average 3 hours per response, including the time for reviewing instructions, searching existing data sources, gathering and maintaining the data needed, and completing and reviewing the collection of information. Send comments regarding this burden estimate or any other aspect of this collection of information, including suggestions for reducing this burden, to the Regulatory Secretariat (MVA), Office of Acquisition Policy, GSA, Washington, DC 20405.

STATE OF
FL
COUNTY OF
St. Johns

SS. Ponte Vedra Beach

I, the undersigned, being duly sworn, depose and say that I am: (1) the surety to the attached bond(s); (2) a citizen of the United States; and of full age and legally competent. I also depose and say that, concerning any stocks or bonds included in the assets listed below, that there are no restrictions on the resale of these securities pursuant to the registration provisions of Section 5 of the Securities Act of 1933. I recognize that statements contained herein concern a matter within the jurisdiction of an agency of the United States and the making of a false, fictitious or fraudulent statement may render the maker subject to prosecution under Title 18, United States Code Sections 1001 and 494. This affidavit is made to induce the United States of America to accept me as surety on the attached bond.

1. NAME *(First, Middle, Last) (Type or Print)*
Lori Diaz

2. HOME ADDRESS *(Number, Street, City, State, ZIP Code)*
28197 Trigg Road
Hilliard, FL 32046

3. TYPE AND DURATION OF OCCUPATION
Individual Surety

4. NAME AND ADDRESS OF EMPLOYER *(If Self-employed, so State)*
151 Sawgrass Corners Drive
Suite 206
Ponte Vedra Beach, FL 32082

5. NAME AND ADDRESS OF INDIVIDUAL SURETY BROKER USED *(If any)* *(Number, Street, City, State, ZIP Code)*
NA

6. TELEPHONE NUMBER
BUSINESS - 904-412-6400

7. THE FOLLOWING IS A TRUE REPRESENTATION OF THE ASSETS I HAVE PLEDGED TO THE UNITED STATES IN SUPPORT OF THE ATTACHED BOND:
(a) Real estate *(Include a legal description, street address and other identifying description; the market value; attach supporting certified documents including recorded lien; evidence of title and the current tax assessment of the property. For market value approach, also provide a current appraisal.)*
NA

(b) Assets other than real estate *(describe the assets, the details of the escrow account, and attach certified evidence thereof).*
*****See Attached Irrevocable Trust Receipt*****

8. IDENTIFY ALL MORTGAGES, LIENS, JUDGEMENTS, OR ANY OTHER ENCUMBRANCES INVOLVING SUBJECT ASSETS INCLUDING REAL ESTATE TAXES DUE AND PAYABLE
NA

9. IDENTIFY ALL BONDS, INCLUDING BID GUARANTEES, FOR WHICH THE SUBJECT ASSETS HAVE BEEN PLEDGED WITHIN 3 YEARS PRIOR TO THE DATE OF EXECUTION OF THIS AFFIDAVIT.
No bonds other than the bond named herein has been pledged to the subject assets

DOCUMENTATION OF THE PLEDGED ASSET MUST BE ATTACHED.

10. SIGNATURE
Lori Diaz

11. BOND AND CONTRACT TO WHICH THIS AFFIDAVIT RELATES *(Where appropriate)* **PP04222011-PRI**
Concrete

12. SUBSCRIBED AND SWORN TO BEFORE ME AS FOLLOWS:

a. DATE OATH ADMINISTERED

MONTH	DAY	YEAR
April	22	2011

b. CITY AND STATE *(Or other jurisdiction)*
Ponte Vedra Beach, Fl.

Official Seal

c. NAME AND TITLE OF OFFICIAL ADMINISTERING OATH *(Type or print)*
Laura McDaniels

d. SIGNATURE
Laura McDaniels

e. MY COMMISSION EXPIRES
8/29/2013

AUTHORIZED FOR LOCAL REPRODUCTION
Previous edition is not usable

STANDARD FORM 28 (REV. 6/2003)
Prescribed by GSA-FAR (48 CFR) 53.228(e

LAURA McDANIELS
Notary Public, State of Florida
My comm. exp. Aug. 29, 2013
Comm. No. DD 906754

PLAINTIFFS' TRIAL EXHIBIT 4

POINDEXTER 1

Figure 2-2as

Bond# PP04222011-PRI

PAYMENT BOND (See Instructions on Reverse)	DATE BOND EXECUTED (Must be same or later than date of contract) 04/22/2011	OMB NO.: 9000-0045

Public reporting burden for this collection of information is estimated to average 25 minutes per response, including the time for reviewing instructions, searching existing data sources, gathering and maintaining the data needed, and completing and reviewing the collection of information. Send comments regarding this burden estimate or any other aspect of this collection of information, including suggestions for reducing this burden, to the FAR Secretariat (MVR), Federal Acquisition Policy Division, GSA, Washington, DC 20405.

PRINCIPAL (Legal Name and Business address)	TYPE OF ORGANIZATION ("x" one)
Pridex Construction, LLC PO Box 426 Lone Wolf, OK 73655	☐ Individual ☐ Partnership ☐ Joint Venture ☒ Corporation STATE OF INCORPORATION OK

SURETY(IES) (Name and business address)	PENAL SUM OF BOND			
Lori Diaz, Individual Surety 151 Sawgrass Corners Drive Suite 206 Ponte Vedra Beach, FL 32082	MILLION(S)	THOUSAND(S)	HUNDRED(S)	CENTS
	———	——476——	——464——.	———
	CONTRACT DATE	CONTRACT NO.		

OBLIGATION: CITY OF KINGFISHER

We, the Principal and Surety(ies) are firmly bound to the United States of America (hereinafter called the Government) in the above penal sum. For payment of the penal sum, we bind ourselves, our heirs, executors, administrators, and successors, jointly and severally. However, where the Sureties are corporations acting as co-sureties, we, the Sureties, bind ourselves in such sum "jointly and severally" as well as "severally" only for the purpose of allowing a joint action or actions against any or all of us. For all other purposes, each Surety binds itself, jointly and severally with the Principal, for the payment of the sum shown opposite the name of the Surety. If no limit is indicated, the limit of liability is the full amount of the penal sum.

CONDITIONS: SEE BACK OF AFFIDAVIT OF INDIVIDUAL SURETY

The above obligation is void if the Principal promptly makes payment to all persons having a direct relationship with the Principal or a subcontractor of the Principal for furnishing labor, material or both in the prosecution of the work provided for in the contract identified above, and any authorized modifications of the contract that subsequently are made. Notice of those modifications to the Surety(ies) are waived.

WITNESS:

The Principal and Surety(ies) executed this payment bond and affixed their seals on the above date.

PRINCIPAL

SIGNATURE(S)	1. (seal)	2. (seal)	3. (seal)	Corporate Seal
NAME(S) & TITLE(S) (Typed)				

INDIVIDUAL SURETY(IES)

SIGNATURE(S)	1. Lori Diaz (Seal)	2. (Seal)
Name(s) (Typed)	1. Lori Diaz	2.

CORPORATE SURETY(IES)

SURETY A	NAME & ADDRESS		STATE OF INC.	LIABILITY LIMIT $	Corporate Seal
	SIGNATURE(S)	1.	2.		
	NAME(S) & TITLE(S) (TYPED)	1.	2.		

AUTHORIZED FOR LOCAL REPRODUCTION
Previous edition is usable

STANDARD FORM 25A (REV. 10-98)
Prescribed by GSA – FAR (48 CRF) 53.228(c)

PLAINTIFFS' TRIAL EXHIBIT 4 POINDEXTER 2

Figure 2-2bs

Bond # PP04222011-PRI

PERFORMANCE BOND (See Instructions on Reverse)	DATE BOND EXECUTED (Must be same or later than date of contract) 04/22/2011	OMB NO.: 9000-0045

Public reporting burden for this collection of information is estimated to average 25 minutes per response, including the time for reviewing instructions, searching existing data sources, gathering and maintaining the data needed, and completing and reviewing the collection of information. Send comments regarding this burden estimate or any other aspect of this collection of information, including suggestions for reducing this burden, to the FAR Secretariat (MVR), Federal Acquisition Policy Division, GSA, Washington, DC 20405.

PRINCIPAL (Legal Name and Business Address)
Pridex Construction, LLC
PO Box 426
Lone Wolf, OK 73655

TYPE OF ORGANIZATION ("x" one)
☐ Individual ☐ Partnership
☐ Joint Venture X Corporation

STATE OF INCORPORATION
OK

SURETY(IES) (Name and business Address)
Lori Diaz, Individual Surety
151 Sawgrass Corners Drive
Suite 206
Ponte Vedra Beach, FL 32082

PENAL SUM OF BOND			
MILLION(S)	THOUSAND(S)	HUNDRED(S)	CENTS
----------	----476-----	----464----	--------

CONTRACT DATE	CONTRACT NO.

OBLIGATION: CITY OF KINGFISHER

We, the Principal and Surety(ies) are firmly bound to the United States of America (hereinafter called the Government) in the above penal sum. For payment of the penal sum, we bind ourselves, our heirs, executors, administrators, and successors, jointly and severally. However, where the Sureties are corporations acting as co-sureties, we, the Sureties, bind ourselves in such sum "jointly and severally" as well as "severally" only for the purpose of allowing a joint action or actions against any or all of us. For all other purposes, each Surety binds itself, jointly and severally with the Principal, for the payment of the sum shown opposite the name of the Surety. If no limit is indicated, the limit of liability is the full amount of the penal sum.

CONDITIONS: SEE BACK OF THE AFFIDAVIT OF INDIVIDUAL SURETY

The principal has entered into the contract identified above.

THEREFORE:

The above obligation is void if the Principal –

(a)(1) Performs and fulfills all the undertakings, covenants, terms, conditions, and agreements of the contract during the original term of the contract and any extensions thereof that are granted by the Government, with or without notice to the Surety(ies), and during the life of any guaranty required under the contract, and (2) performs and fulfills all the undertakings, covenants, terms conditions, and agreements of any and all duly authorized modifications of the contract that hereafter are made. Notice of those modifications to the Surety(ies) are waived.

(b) Pays to the Government the full amount of the taxes imposed by the Government, if the said contract is subject to the Miller Act, (40 U.S.C. 270a-270e), which are collected, deducted, or withheld from wages paid by the Principal in carrying out the construction contract with respect to which this bond is furnished.

WITNESS:

The Principal and surety(ies) executed this performance bond and affixed their seals on the above date.

PRINCIPAL

SIGNATURE(S)	1.	2.	3.	Corporate Seal
NAME(S) & TITLE(S) (Typed)	(seal)	(seal)	(seal)	

INDIVIDUAL SURETY(IES)

SIGNATURE(S)	1. Lori Diaz (Seal)	2. (Seal)
Name(s) (Typed)	1. Lori Diaz	2.

CORPORATE SURETY(IES)

SURETY A				
NAME & ADDRESS		STATE OF INC.	LIABILITY LIMIT	
SIGNATURES	1.	2.		Corporate Seal
NAME(S) & TITLE(S) (TYPED)	1.	2.		

AUTHORIZED FOR LOCAL REPRODUCTION
Previous edition is not usable

STANDARD FORM 25 (REV. 5-96)
Prescribed by GSA – FAR (48 CRF) 53.228(b)

PLAINTIFFS' TRIAL EXHIBIT 4 POINDEXTER 3

Figure 2-2cs

POWER OF ATTORNEY

(Federally approved alternate to Treasury listed, circular 570)

State of Florida >
>SS
County of St. Johns >

I, the undersigned being duly sworn, depose and say that I am one of the sureties to the attached bond, that I am a citizen of the United States (or a permanent resident of the place where the contract and bond are executed) and of full age and legally competent; that I am not a partner in any business of the principal on the Bonds on which I appear as surety that the information herein below furnished is true and complete to the best of my knowledge. The affidavit is made to induce the **City of Kingfisher,** to accept me as surety to the attached bond.

1. Attorney in Fact

Lori Diaz

Att.-In-Fact for
Lori Diaz, Individual Surety

2. Name of Agency

3. Business Address (No., Street, City, State, Zip Code)

151 Sawgrass Corners Drive, Suite 206
Ponte Vedra Beach, FL 32082

4. Telephone Numbers

Office: 904-412-6400

5. THE FOLLOWING IS A TRUE REPRESENTATION OF MY PRESENT ASSETS, LIABILITIES AND NET WORTH AND DOES NOT INCLUDE ANY FINANCIAL INTEREST THAT I HAVE IN THE ASSETS OF THE PRINCIPLE ON THE ATTACHED BOND.

Irrevocable Trust Receipt in the amount of $476,464.00 issued by PS TRUST

6. Signature

Lori Diaz

Lori Diaz, Individual Surety
Attorney-in-Fact

7.BOND AND CONTRACTOR TO WHICH THIS AFFIDAVIT RELATED (Where Appropriate)
BOND NUMBER: PP04222011-PRI

JOB NAME: **Concrete**

Sworn to and subscribed before me

DATE OATH ADMINISTERED City: State: Florida Notary Public:

This 22nd day of April, 2011 Ponte Vedra

SIGNATURE X Laura McDaniels

AUTHORIZED FOR LOCAL REPRODUCTION

LAURA McDANIELS
Notary Public, State of Florida
My comm. exp. Aug. 29, 2013
Comm. No. DD 906754

PLAINTIFFS' TRIAL EXHIBIT 4 POINDEXTER 4

Figure 2-2ds

SURETY ACKNOWLEDGMENT

State of Florida) SS:
County of St. Johns)

On this 22nd day of April, 2011, before me personally came Lori Diaz who, being duly sworn, did depose and say that she is Lori Diaz, Individual Surety, the individual surety described in and which executed the within instruments; that she is the individual of said seal, that the seal affixed to the within instrument is such seal, and that she signed the said instrument and affixed the said seal as Lori Diaz, Individual Surety, by authority of said individual surety.

Oath administered this 22nd day of April, 2011.

City of: Ponte Vedra Beach
County of: St. Johns

Notary Seal:

My commission expires:

X

LAURA McDANIELS
Notary Public, State of Florida
My comm. exp. Aug. 29, 2013
Comm. No. DD 906754

PLAINTIFFS' TRIAL EXHIBIT 4 POINDEXTER 5

Figure 2-2es

IRREVOCABLE TRUST RECEIPT

Date of Issue: April 22, 2011
Receipt Number: FB04222011-1
Name of Obligee: City of Kingfisher
Name of Contractor: Pridex Construction, LLC
Reference: PP04222011-PRI

The **PS TRUST**, a trust organized under the laws of the State of Florida (the "Trust"), does hereby issue this **Irrevocable Trust Receipt ("ITR") No. FB04222011-1 in the amount of USD $476,464.00.**

The Trust hereby certifies and confirms that at all times that this ITR is in effect, the Trust will be the beneficial owner cash and marketable securities (each in U.S. Dollars or readily convertible into U.S. Dollars if the securities are denominated in a currency other than U.S. Dollars) segregated and named below, at South Florida Trust & Title Escrow Acct# DMV-11-100.

This ITR shall remain in full force and effect for the Duration of the Contract.

Payment under this TRUST RECEIPT will be made to the Obligee upon receipt of an invoice stating that such amount represents funds owed to the Obligee and are to be used to repay amounts outstanding certified and conditioned by the Payment and Performance Bond criteria until exonerated by the Obligee. Said payment will be made within 45 banking days.

Upon the presentation of this ITR together with the certificate from the Obligee as set forth above, the Trust will cause the amount payable as set forth in the certificate to be paid from the assets segregated to secure this ITR.

The Trust represents and warrants that this ITR is its valid obligation enforceable against it in accordance with its terms. This ITR may not be amended, modified or waived, except by a written instrument duly executed by the Trust and the Obligee.

This ITR is subject to the Uniform Customs Practice for Documentary Credit (2007 Revision), International Chamber of Commerce (ICC) Publication No. 600 (the "ICC Publication").

To the extent not covered by the ICC Publication, this ITR shall be governed and construed in accordance with the laws of the State of Florida, without regard or reference to any of its conflict of law principles which require or could result in the application of the laws of another jurisdiction.

PLAINTIFFS' TRIAL EXHIBIT 4 POINDEXTER 6

Figure 2-2fs

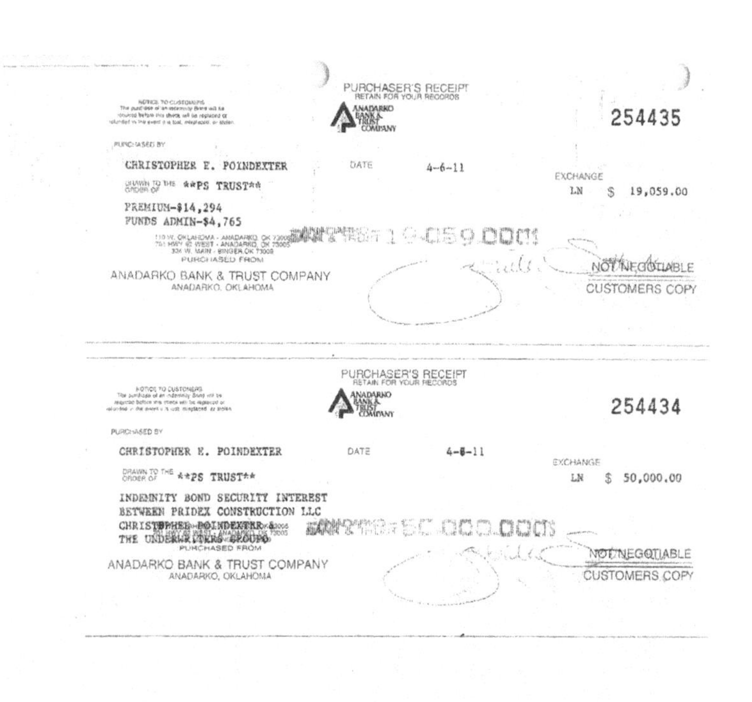

PURCHASER'S RECEIPT
RETAIN FOR YOUR RECORDS

ANADARKO BANK & TRUST COMPANY

254435

PURCHASED BY

CHRISTOPHER E. POINDEXTER

DATE 4-6-11

DRAWN TO THE ORDER OF **PS TRUST**

EXCHANGE LN $ 19,059.00

PREMIUM-$14,294
FUNDS ADMIN-$4,765

PURCHASED FROM

ANADARKO BANK & TRUST COMPANY
ANADARKO, OKLAHOMA

NOT NEGOTIABLE
CUSTOMERS COPY

PURCHASER'S RECEIPT
RETAIN FOR YOUR RECORDS

ANADARKO BANK & TRUST COMPANY

254434

PURCHASED BY

CHRISTOPHER E. POINDEXTER

DATE 4-6-11

DRAWN TO THE ORDER OF **PS TRUST**

EXCHANGE LN $ 50,000.00

INDEMNITY BOND SECURITY INTEREST
BETWEEN PRIDEX CONSTRUCTION LLC
CHRISTOPHER POINDEXTRR &
THE UNDERWRITERS GROUP

PURCHASED FROM

ANADARKO BANK & TRUST COMPANY
ANADARKO, OKLAHOMA

NOT NEGOTIABLE
CUSTOMERS COPY

POINDEXTER 25

PLAINTIFFS' TRIAL EXHIBIT 8

Figure 2-3s

CHAPTER III

Solyndra and the Ultimate Scams

If you don't recall the whole story of Solyndra, the company was to make tubular solar panels, and they were going to use a thin next-generation solar material and a lightweight racking system where the panels were to be installed. The company made their case that large power companies would pay a premium for its solar panels, partly because the panels could potentially save them money during the installation process. The Department of Energy accepted their logic completely and made the guarantee on the loan.

So why am I discussing a company that died away back in 2011? The reason is that it only died by name and is running full steam on our tax dollars!

The Solar thing just got a little more interesting…really!

The Tonopah Solar company and thirty-three others received in the vicinity of $80 billion in loan guarantees from the Department of Energy. Nearly two-third of all these have gone bankrupt.

This one project was to produce a 110-megawatt power system and employ forty-five permanent workers.

That's costing us just $16 million per job.

One of the investment partners in this endeavor is Pacific Corporate Group (PCG).

The PCG executive director is Ron Pelosi who is the brother to Nancy's husband.

Just move along, folks…nuthin' goin' on here.

With the $535 million from the loan, guaranteed by the Department of Energy (DOE), the new companies were up and ready to go with plenty of extra funds to attract even more monies. According to the DOE IG, "Solyndra officials were, at best, reckless and irresponsible or, at worst, an orchestrated effort to knowingly and intentionally deceive and mislead the Department."

From the death of Solyndra came the founders in a newly formed company, or was it just the rebirth of another Ponzi scheme, Performance Consulting Group (PCG)?

PCG immediately diversified and into PCG Worldwide, PCG Wind, and PCG Global. This is where this story gets really interesting. Let's begin by looking into the future by only a few years. An attorney by the name of Murray Abowitz represented PCG and as well American Energy Partners (AEP), Chesapeake, and a few others that are/were well-known. If you recall, the day that the CEO of Chesapeake and AEP ditched his security detail one morning and drove himself into a concrete viaduct under a bridge and was killed in the crash. That is the popular story. Suicide was not ruled out, but why was there so many questions! The accident occurred just one day after McClendon was indicted on conspiracy charges. The vehicle's data box showed that he was traveling at eighty-eight miles per hour five seconds prior to impact but had slowed to seventy-eight miles per hour upon impact. He had applied the brakes, but there were no skid marks. Three months later, the police said they have wrapped up their investigation and "have not found anything to lead us to believe Mr. McClendon's death is a suicide."

Just short of two years later, Chris Poindexter was having a discussion with the attorney for PCG and, at that time, was unaware that Murray Abowitz was named in some of the documents that he was showing the attorney, and after a lengthy meeting, he told Chris that he was unable to help him. About a week later, Chris called Murray, and Murray got very upset with him and all but hung up on him. Less than a week later, Murray had a heart attack and died. Was it really a natural heart attack, or was it induced?

So I believe that any conscientious individual could clearly see that the money shuffle from Solyndra to PCG to the current companies was there well and alive.

This grandiose hoax has been perpetuated across years, and neither McClendon nor Abowitz were welcomed as the messenger. Within a few hours of the McClendon accident, Chris received a phone call that clearly stated, "Did you hear what happened to McClendon?" The call was from an unknown caller who wished to remain anonymous and get his message across very clearly.

The monies from Solyndra, Tonopah Solar Energy ($737 milion), Solar Reserve LLC, and a host of other companies were involved in these questionable green energy projects. This, like the majority of these projects, failed, and the funds disappeared! All government backed loans that the Department of Energy / inspector general (DOE/IG) is still investigating.

Back shortly after Pridex had its initiation to these interesting folks, in 2011, a well-known individual to Chris Poindexter's told him he needed to stop as "he had no idea who he was dealing with, this goes all the way back to Solyndra!"

Really, this is phenomenally interesting. The same scammers are still stealing from us, the American taxpayers.

Page 1 of 1

t@ctc

From: <joeyistre@yahoo.com>
To: "Terry Kutcher" <terry@chisholmtrailconst.com>
Sent: Saturday, July 02, 2011 3:13 PM
Subject: Return trip

Dear terry. This is an FYI. When I return. It will be under the other company I own Elite International, Inc. Which I also provide investigative and protective services world wide. Due to the threats and corruption and intimidation that I personally, my administrative assistant, and Mr. Jody Jackson have suffered at the hands of Atty Dan Simon, Officer Todd Alber acting under color of law with columbia PD, The Edwards Family, and whoever else to protect the criminal actions and conspiracies under investigation involving robert stone, the following will happen; upon my return I will return with 6 men, myself included. Two 3 man teams with a lead investigator and two man security team for each investigator. No one will be armed but we don't need to be, enough said on that. Each of these men are equally qualified, trained, experienced, and are each a team lead IE supervisor who have volunteered for this. We can not return until we finish with the ongoing Federal trial in new orleans in which they are working to defend our brothers on trial for the Hurricane Katrina Danzinger bridge shooting in which our brothers are on trial for murder. Please understand that I am pleased that you wish to retain and keep me on board but I feel for your liability for our actions that this is done by "Elite" so there is no liability on the part of your company, Jack Stuteville on behalf of FCB, or Atty John Morris in his relations to you all and your cases. We will fly into Oklahoma City on an undisclosed date, rent two S U V 's and meet Mr Morris where Gungoll Jackson will be retained to represent Elite and its agents and Assigns as I will hold my teams harmless from any and all Liability for their actions as they are risking a lot. These men have served in the US Marine Corp with me, in law enforcement with men and have chewed some foreign dirt with me. Now they are each from Louisiana and after a conference call over my experience each highly excited to visit Columbia Month and Barney fucking Pfife. I leave you with this. It is not safe for you in Missouri and do not travel alone. Call a contact at a destination point if you do and set an arrival time with the arrival contact having my info incase u don't arrive. Plan ur routes, stops, and keep ur plans private. There are too many leaks and you are up against money, politics, law firms, and corrupt politicians and I have handled murder for Hire's and Homicides for much less. Please listen to these instructions as in my opinion your life may depend on it. Last. Please forward to all attorneys, dan simon via Tom Harrison, and any one you feel needs to know. Terry you are my client and now through time a friend and I fear for you. Joey
Sent on the Sprint® Now Network from my BlackBerry®

Figure 3-1

Stone charges dropped due to lack of witness credibility

ROBERT STONE JACK STUTEVILLE

▲ HIDE CAPTION

Robert Stone and Jack Stuteville mugs. - Online mugs

Figure 3-2as

Prosecutor drops charges against former Clark developer - Columbia Daily Tribune | Colu... Page 2

Stone says he was "not at all guilty" of any crimes in Oklahoma, but he declined to comment further. He says there is evidence that judges, attorneys and others in the legal system were manipulated by Kutcher and Jack Stuteville, former president of the now-defunct First Capital Bank in Kingfisher, Okla.

Sullivan said among the documents provided to Fusselman are emails between Kutcher, Stuteville, former Chisholm Trail Construction attorney Edd Pritchett and others that paint a picture of a conspiracy against Stone.

One email from December 2010 says, "By the way, the one thing that we all agree on is we need to get Stone out of the way."

In a mediation memorandum submitted to an Oklahoma judge, James Choate, an Oklahoma attorney representing Stone in civil cases there, outlined allegations that Kutcher and Stuteville made false allegations against Stone. "The allegations of fraud and embezzlement have been actively pursued in an attempt to mask the wrongdoing of Mr. Kutcher and others," Choate wrote.

Sullivan and Stone said the Oklahoma Attorney General's Office, the FDIC and others are investigating criminal complaints against Kutcher and Stuteville. Stone, who is currently working on construction projects in Oklahoma, said he is not the first victim to be blamed for their wrongdoing.

"I'm very happy that Mike Fusselman finally dismissed the charges," he said. "It's the right thing to do. It's just frustrating it took two years to get that accomplished. The real criminals in this are finally going to get what's due to them."

Figure 3-2bs

05/06/2012 09:54 5808462977 PRIDEX CONSTRUCTION PAGE 11/32

Case 5:12-cv-00031-F Document 48 Filed 05/10/12 Page 1 of 21

IN THE UNITED STATES DISTRICT COURT FOR THE
WESTERN DISTRICT OF OKLAHOMA

CHRIS POINDEXTER, et al.,	)	
	)	
Plaintiffs,	)	
	)	
vs.	)	Case No. CIV-12-0031-F
	)	
JACK STUTEVILLE, et al.,	)	
	)	
Defendants.	)	

ORDER

Five motions are before the court. They are: the motion to dismiss of Richard Reynolds, identified in the complaint as the city manager of Kingfisher, Oklahoma (doc. no. 24); the motion to dismiss of Jack Stuteville, identified in the complaint as the mayor of Kingfisher (doc. no. 32); the motion for partial dismissal filed by the City of Kingfisher (doc. no. 26); the motion to dismiss of Michael Mecklenburg and TMC Construction Company, Inc. (TMC) (doc. no. 29); and plaintiffs' motion to dismiss without prejudice claims alleged against defendants TMC and Michael Mecklenburg. (Doc. no. 40).

I. Motions Involving TMC and Mr. Mecklenburg
(Doc. Nos. 29 and 40)

Plaintiffs have filed a notice of dismissal without prejudice of claims previously alleged against Mr. Mecklenburg and TMC. (Doc. no. 47.) The notice was filed under Rule 41(a)(1)(A)(i), Fed. R. Civ. P. The notice effected dismissal of these defendants when it was filed on April 23, 2012.

Figure 3-3as

05/06/2012 09:54 5808462977 PRIDEX CONSTRUCTION PAGE 23/32

Case 5:12-cv-00031-F Document 48 Filed 05/10/12 Page 15 of 21

Based upon all of the factors relevant to a determination of continuity, the court finds no alleged continuing threat of racketeering activity. Accordingly, the complaint fails to allege a "pattern" of racketeering activity.

F. Element (4): (A Pattern of) Racketeering Activity.

Finally, RICO requires that the alleged pattern of activity be a pattern, specifically, of "racketeering activity."

The complaint alleges that defendants executed their scheme "by causing matters to be mailed and delivered by the United States Postal Service, and by causing sounds and electronic data to be transmitted by means of wire communications in interstate commerce." (¶ 5.) The complaint further alleges that "Defendants committed multiple acts of mail fraud, indictable under 18 U.S.C. §1341, which constituted 'racketeering activity' within the meaning of 18 U.S.C. § 1961(1), and all of which collectively constituted part of a 'pattern of racketeering activity' within the meaning of 18 U.S.C. § 1961(5)." (¶ 5.) Thus, the predicate acts alleged in the complaint are mail fraud and wire fraud.[5] *See*, 18 U.S.C. §1961(1) (defining "racketeering activity," and including mail fraud and wire fraud within the definition).

Identifying the predicate acts is just the beginning, however. A RICO claim must allege the predicate acts with particularity. *See*, Cayman Exploration Corp., 873 F.2d at 1362 (threat of triple damages and injury to reputation which attend RICO actions justify requiring plaintiff to frame pleadings in such a way that will give the defendant, and the court, clear notice of the factual basis of the predicate acts; Rule 9(b) particularity requirements apply in pleading RICO mail fraud and wire fraud).

[5]Later in the complaint, bid-rigging is also mentioned, without elaboration, as a possible predicate act. (¶ 57.) The allegation of bid-rigging as a predicate act is conclusory and insufficient for purposes of RICO.

-4-

Figure 3-3bs

To determine whether the RICO claim is sufficient, it is therefore necessary to review the elements of mail fraud and wire fraud, and the manner in which these predicate acts must be alleged.

To allege mail fraud under 18 U.S.C. §1341, a plaintiff must allege: 1) the existence of a scheme or artifice to defraud or obtain money or property by false pretenses, representations or promises, and (2) use of the mails for the purpose of executing the scheme. Tal v. Hogan, 453 F.3d at 1263. The elements of wire fraud are very similar but require that the defendant use interstate wire, radio or television communications in furtherance of the scheme to defraud. *Id.* The common thread among these crimes is the concept of "fraud." *Id.* Actionable fraud consists of (1) a representation; (2) that is false; (3) that is material; (4) the speaker's knowledge of its falsity or ignorance of its truth; (5) the speaker's intent it be acted on; (6) the hearer's ignorance of the falsity of the representation; (7) the hearer's reliance; (8) the hearer's right to rely on it; and (9) injury. *Id.* Failure to adequately allege any one of the nine elements is fatal to the fraud claim. *Id.* A plaintiff alleging mail fraud or wire fraud as predicate acts for a RICO claim must set forth the time, place and content of the false representation, as well as the identity of the party making the false statement and the consequences thereof. *Id.* In all averments of fraud, the circumstances constituting the fraud shall be stated with particularity; malice, intent, knowledge, and other conditions of mind of a person may be averred generally. *Id.* at n.20, quoting Rule 9(b).

The complaint's only specific allegations regarding use of the mails or wires are: that a day after having spoken with Mr. Stuteville by telephone, Mr. Wright advised Mr. Poindexter that The Underwriters Group would issue the bond (¶40); that on April 6, 2011, plaintiffs mailed funds to The Underwriters Group by overnight mail

-5-

Figure 3-3cs

05/06/2012 09:54 5808462977 PRIDEX CONSTRUCTION PAGE 24/32

Case 5:12-cv-00031-F Document 48 Filed 05/10/12 Page 17 of 21

(¶ 40); and that there were calls from Mr. Stuteville to Mr. Poindexter regarding the possibility of selling some of Pridex's equipment and Mr. Poindexter's confirmation that if the equipment were sold then Pridex would purchase updated equipment to complete the job. (¶ 37.)[6]

The gravamen of mail fraud or wire fraud is the fraud, and any use of the mails incident to effecting the fraud satisfies the mailing element. Bridge v. Phoenix Bond & Indemnity Co., 553 U.S. 639, 640 (2008). Nevertheless, it is noted that there are no allegations that any mail services or wire services were used to communicate a representation which was known to be false. Nor is there any allegation that Mr. Stuteville knew at the time he allegedly steered plaintiffs to The Underwriters Group that The Underwriters Group was not licensed to provide a bond in Oklahoma. In fact, there are no allegations that any defendant who was in a position to steer plaintiffs to The Underwriters Group did so despite personal knowledge that The Underwriters Group could not provide a proper bond.

The court concludes that the complaint fails to allege a pattern of racketeering activity.

G. Rulings Regarding the RICO Claim

The complaint fails to identify which subsection of §1962 plaintiffs' RICO claim is based upon. This renders the RICO claim insufficient under Rule 12(b)(6). Presuming that plaintiffs could amend their RICO claim to clarify that it is brought

[6]Plaintiffs' response brief attaches an affidavit (doc. no. 38, ex. 1) which the court does not consider for the purpose of determining the sufficiency of the RICO claim as alleged. The affidavit has been considered only for the limited purpose of determining whether amendment of the complaint to include the matters described in the affidavit would change any results. The affidavit states that the bond which was delivered to Mr. Poindexter from The Underwriters Group was delivered by use of a commercial carrier between Florida and Oklahoma. If included in the allegations, this fact would not change any results stated in this order.

-6-

Figure 3-3ds

CHAPTER IV

Sounded Like a Fiction Book to Me, You Know

In early January 2014, the trial of Jack Stuteville became a pivotal point for Pridex Construction and the owner, Chris Poindexter. When you read the following pages, you will come to clearly understand that Chris had walked into the lion's den and stepped on the lion's tail. From here, it was into a world of corruption and murder where our esteemed legal profession was up for sale and openly contracted murder (hits) on those that they could not browbeat into their ways of thinking or those that had become a total liability.

The first attachment (III-1) is a letter written to a law firm where the author clearly states that one of his many jobs in his forte is murder for hire!

So we begin with this trek at the trial of Jack Stuteville, who is being now sued for the monies that he unlawfully stole from Pridex Construction. The picture below is taken from the *Moberly Monitor-Index* (III-2). They are listed "Robert Stone and Jack Stuteville mugs." Additional interesting reading can be found on these topics by the *Arkansas Business Journal* and the magazine *ENR*.

In the opening to the trial, I would like to note that Judge William Friot, a federal judge is open to anything, whether lawful or? As stated in *Black Robe Fever*, these nonelected judges have become godlike creatures who make up whatever they may or may not see as lawful. I will elaborate in the following pages.

When the suit was filed, it first went into the federal court, as it was filed under the Racketeer Influenced and Corrupt Organizations Act (RICO) Statute and was assigned to Judge Friot's court, and he immediately threw it out. His order, in part, stated that "Upon review of the allegations as a whole, the court concludes that the complaint does not plausibly allege that any RICO defendant participated in the conduct of a RICO enterprise!" Apparently, he failed to read the suit or to even open the file! This behavior is not limited to only this judge or even this court. As you will see, the justice system is now a bought-and-paid-for competition elimination machine. Let's go back to my exemplary damage suit that was tossed out on a technicality that my attorney stated that we could have easily defeated. We did not file, as it only would have been run again and again.

Recall the phrase "by the people and for the people." It is no longer on the drawing board, as justice for the most part is a bought-and-paid-for service that goes to the highest bidder! I am certain that in some of these courts, if a serious review were conducted, the judges would not only be fired—they would be in prison!

When this case was tossed out of the federal court, Chris was forced to refile in a district court, in Kingfisher, Oklahoma, where all the problems began. The jury trial took place in front of Judge Paul Woodward, and to the surprise of all, after a unanimous jury verdict, the judge took it upon himself to overturn! One would most likely be inclined to ask why. In an article written by the *Kingfisher Times &Free Press*, Judge Paul Woodward granted the new trial in the lawsuit after a jury released the unanimous verdict against Stuteville, requiring him to pay $500,000 in total damages to Poindexter in January 2014.

There were many almost-humorous events that took place. On the opening morning of the trial (CJ-2012-52 January 27–30, 2014), we heard from the plaintiff's attorney, as Pridex Construction (Chris Poindexter) was attempting to get the money back from the city of Kingfisher. The city and a bogus bond company called The Underwriters Group had stolen a large sum of money from this company. As the attorney began, he stated, "So of course the City gives Chris's money back. Of course they don't." Now, mind you, that through a competitive bidding, Chris had won the bid and was the lowest bidder. He had come in with not only the bid bond but also the performance bond and was prepared to put up a cash bond on the project for the total of $476,936, and the mayor and the city manager were all interested in this and quickly contacted the city attorney, who stated that that wouldn't work; he would need a bonding company to write such. For those of us who don't understand this, the performance bond states nothing more than "I will do this job to specifications stated, and if not, you keep the bond." For Chris to go out to a bonding company, he would have paid nearly $70,000 for the bond, and with a cash bond, he would only have paid for the interest for the less than a month that he would use the bond—a major difference.

As briefly stated in chapter 2, the mayor quickly states that a friend of his, Steve Standridge in Arkansas, could assist. Stuteville failed to mention that this guy was prohibited from doing business in Oklahoma and Arkansas and that he owed the mayor a great deal of money. I'm certain that that was only an accidental oversight that he did not mention that to Chris.

Now, while on the witness stand in this trial, Mr. Stuteville actually responded to a question regarding this suit in his deposition that it was a "silly assed deal." Then in the actual trial, after being questioned on this point, he stated, "I don't think that's my exact…" He was then referred to line 40 of his deposition, and it read, "I think this case is a very silly-ass case, yeah." This was his opinion that Pridex Construction, Chris Poindexter, had lost approximately $150,000 due to their—Mr. Stuteville and his associates—corrupt actions.

Going back to when Pridex was awarded the job and the fiasco when one of the business associates of Jack Stuteville provided fake bonds, Chris was told to get busy as soon as possible, as the wheat harvest would be coming soon; and they, the city, would need the road open for trucks shortly. To go one better, completely across town, the city needed fill dirt at a city location, and he—the city manager, Mr. Reynolds—told Chris to dump there at that location to help the city. In being told to get started and where to dump the dirt, Chris unloaded sixteen semi loads of dirt across town for them at no additional charge. Seeing as there would additionally be trees to be removed, the city had the fire chief, Randy Poindexter, ensure that the dump was open for these trees to be dropped over the weekend. As stated earlier, Mr. Stuteville made numerous trips by the work site to see the progress. When he had seen the project to a point they wanted, the city stopped the project. Interestingly enough, now the bond was no good?

From here, the fight was on. As stated in the trial, the city would release the bonds if he, Chris, would sign a release for any other monies, like the fact that the project was slightly less than half done, and he would lose nearly $250,000 off the contract. As stated in the trial, he was welcome to go and would get his bond back but nothing else if he signed their release. This "silly-ass case" would net Stuteville in excess of $250,000 from work accomplished.

With Pridex now out of the mix and the need to simply tweak the specs for this project, the city reissued the bid, and strangely enough, a construction company owned by the city attorney's family, the mayor, and the city manager won the bid. This company, named TMC Construction, bid over $550,000 with nearly half of the work already accomplished. Realistically, this group walked off with over $300,000 in net profit and still kept the bonds that Pridex had paid.

An interesting fact that should be noted is that the bid initially seemed to have an immediate deadline and needed to be accomplished as soon as possible. The time frame that TMC was now on began in July 2011 and with a completion date of January 2012.

As this trial was drawing to a close and Mr. Stuteville was on the last round of questioning, a most interesting conversation transpired.

The attorney for the plaintiff: "You heard an opening statement in this case where there was allegation that Mr. Harrison, Mr. Mecklenburg, and other people and you conspired with regard to Pridex and Mr. Poindexter. Did you participate in any kind of a conspiracy along these things or anything in any way?"

Mr. Stuteville: "Sounded like a fiction book to me, you know."

As the trial drew to a close and the last witness was dismissed, the burden now fell to the jury. In approximately an hour, the jury returned a unanimous verdict that awarded Pridex Construction and Chris Poindexter $1,950,000 from Larry wright and $500,000 from Jack Stuteville. While the jury was in deliberation, the city settled with Chris Poindexter, paying him $50,000.

Much to everyone's surprise, on June 11, 2014, Judge Paul Woodward signed an order granting Jack Stuteville a new trial, thereafter overturning the unanimous jury verdict against Stuteville and dropping the awards.

Chris appealed to the Oklahoma Court of Appeals, and two and a half years later, the jury verdict was reinstated. Chris then filed a garnishment against Jack Stuteville's farm subsidy payments. The US attorney Mark A. Yancy called Chris and threatened him of what would happen if I did not retract the garnishment. When Chris refused, the US Attorney's Office pulled Chris's case out of Kingfisher District Court and put it in federal court, where the garnishment was dismissed and then sent back to Kingfisher District Court. Perhaps we need to see who is actually violating the RICO Statute as defined under 18 USC.

If we go back to the original trial where the jury awarded Mr. Chris Poindexter the unanimous verdict, I am quite certain most any citizen would have found it very sad and sick humor listening to Mr. Jack Stuteville.

Regarding the event of the broken windows noted earlier to Randy Poindexter's truck during the meeting of the lost bid at the city offices, the following exchange was noted and demonstrated the credibility of Mr. Stuteville.

When asked in the trial about going to Randy Poindexter's home and threatening him, he flatly denied any such action. When confronted with the actual recording, he simply stated, "Well, I guess I have"—a completely not credible witness.

"Sounded like a fiction book to me, you know."

CHAPTER V

What's the Connection? PCG and TMC

Most of those reading this book at this point are still asking, "Is this book fact or fiction?" A very dear friend of mine stated as she read each chapter after I had it completed, "I am still having difficulty believing that this is really happening in our country."

Much to the misfortune to most Americans, this is all true and will collapse our nation's economy if left unchecked.

PCG is an acronym that may stand for Performance Consulting Group whether Wind, Global, or Worldwide. If you noted in chapter 3, there is a major connection to a now-defunct company Solyndra, which absorbed $535,000,000 of your tax dollars in the form of guaranteed loans through the Department of Energy! Each of these companies shared a basic operating theory and the manufacture of fake (fraudulent) performance, bid, and construction bonds (Fig. 5-1). This can easily be traced back to a Dr. Larry Wright who had numerous convictions against him for fraud and yet continues to write these and is not forced to pay up! Even worse than that, he is protected by the US government. If you had to make a guess where the money is now, try hard! I'll provide you a hint—the management is now in the PCG world.

So how did we get to this point? We will join our story around the time that Pridex became associated and allow only chapter 3 to define the connection to PCG and the other assorted and absorbed acronyms.

If you recall at the time, Pridex Construction Company had its bond pulled by the City of Kingfisher and was told that they had ten days to secure a valid performance bond or lose the contract on the West Bottom Project. That was in the spring of 2011. While at that meeting, the windows of Randy Poindexter's (Chris's brother) pickup truck were busted out, apparently for the purpose of saying "Don't mess with us!" Shortly after this event, it became apparent that the resolution to the lost bid was a legal battle! As stated in chapter 4, Pridex prevailed and was awarded $2.45 million. When the legal battle was initially beginning, Chris received a text from Mike Mathews, who is associated with Jack Stuteville, that stated, "U better zip your lip, or I will do it for u." This macho mentality seemed to run rampant with the two Mathews brothers. With just a little research of Mike and Randy Mathews, I found that they owned a number of companies and were well acquainted with the oil business. Some of the companies that they operated in Kingfisher County were Titan Well Service, NASC Holdings, Laran Operating, Complete Well Service, Rig Tech, and P&B Auto Sales. In a more interesting find, according to a bankruptcy filing for PCG, Mike was receiving payments from the company Stuteville was an owner of. What the payments were for is a real mystery. It is interesting to see how these two individuals have slid into and out of felony charges and never convicted. It makes me think of another, but we will get to that later.

Things rolled along, and the Mathews brothers kept in touch with Chris as in such matters as trying to get him to write a slanderous article against Mr. Stuteville, and all the time, Chris declined their offer.

In March 2014, Chris could see many issues that were anything but right, and they seemed to be spiraling out of control as our justice system was failing greatly. Along with his brother Randy and Kingfisher County sheriff Dennis Banther, the three confronted the local district attorney, Mike Fields, and spelled it out to him that fraud, theft, murder, and public corruption at all levels was erupting all around him and that he and his office were greatly in question. That day, Mike Fields wrote a letter to the first assistant attorney general and recused himself of acting in his capacity. Along with this, a request was made of the Oklahoma State Bureau of Investigation (OSBI) to look into these allegations.

In September 2014, Randy Mathews was charged with three counts of wire fraud and two counts of false declaration. Each count of wire fraud was punishable of up to twenty years in prison and a $250,000 fine. The count of false declaration was punishable of up to five years and a $250,000 fine on each count. The reason that I bring this up is that even though he appeared to have sufficient monies to hire an attorney and the penalties were severe, he used a public defender. One could only ask the question why. The only logical reason is that he knew that he would be acquitted, and upon entering the federal court of Timothy DeGiusti, shortly, he was!

With all the fake bonds that were being used on the Air Force bases, the FAA, and a handful of other government agencies, the question was how this could continue.

On April 11, 2014, Randy Mathews's wife Kymberly was severely beaten by her husband. The apparent reason was due to her posting on Facebook some of the corruption that her husband and his brother was participating in along with Mr. Stuteville. Allegedly, the following week, she committed suicide and, again, allegedly, just prior to this event, she posted a note and a picture of her hand holding two .357 bullets asking which was better for the job of hunting? Really, and according to the *Kingfisher Times*, the OSBI accepted this and did not have an autopsy conducted. Seriously, a lady who has children is beaten one day and commits suicide the next week. Just the sheer fact that she was a woman and conducted a violent suicide is hard to swallow, but with the rest? It would have been so easy to simply check for powder residue on her hand that allegedly fired the gun. Also, the OSBI found that they were unable to get the Facebook posts all hushed away; why did they want them so badly? Why was there a questionable apology placed on Facebook—from whom, Mike Mathews or someone else?

With the thuggish behavior of the Mathews boys, why were they not questioned? Let's now turn the dial back a few years and look at the OSBI agent who was assigned to the case. Mr. Steve Neuman was tasked with such.

In 1998, there was an interesting event where Fred Wofford dropped his son at a ball game. When he left, he was never seen alive again. Nearly two weeks later, his body was found in his car with a "self-inflicted" gunshot wound to the back of the head. The same OSBI agent assigned to the Wofford murder was, at that time, having an affair with Mr. Wofford's wife. There had been a domestic disturbance at his home involving the agent a few weeks prior. Next in this string of bad luck for the Wofford family was this: his daughter, Bobby Lynn Wofford, in 1999, was murdered. A fourteen-year-old girl living in Kingfisher, Oklahoma, was killed, and the killer remained unidentified for thirteen years. This person was later identified as Tommy Lynn Sells, a convicted mass murderer. An interesting fact is that there are many questions about this conviction and how he was actually involved. Perhaps he wasn't at all.

The next association to this group is a very interesting individual named Joey Istre. He is an ex-Marine who has taken up some very unusual job attributes. He has done such things as bodyguarding and police/investigations and has even served as a special process server in Kingfisher County, Oklahoma. In his forte, he openly claims to have done murder for hire. His openly stated profession of hit man was well known to Judge Davis before hiring him for such as a so-called special process server! Another attorney, Ed Pritchett, had corresponded with Terry Kutcher, and in such, it was clearly stated that he, Joey Istre, did murder for hire and had done it less than they were paying him to work as a process server. I suppose that the citizens of Kingfisher County will be less than pleased when they find their tax dollars were being used to hire a hit man!

Later, Joey would run for Jefferson Parish sheriff in Louisiana. He lost and was later charged with second-degree rape. He is currently out on bail and has had the charge of second-degree rape raised to first-degree rape.

As we now look forward to TMC Construction, the company who successfully took over the West Bottom Project from Pridex Construction, I have found many great projects that they have done in and around the city of Kingfisher and are usually slightly higher than other comparable bids. In the case of the West Bottom Project, they were over $200,000 higher than that of Pridex. It seems to be a mystery as to why they would be higher than other bidders and still manage the award. Perhaps there is more to the tweaking the bid than meets the eye. Perhaps it is the City of Kingfisher attorney, Harrison, who is related to the Mecklenburgs who have the construction company or perhaps it is the city manager, Dave Slezickey, who took over for the departing city manager, Mr. Reynolds. Mr. Slezickey left the city of Anadarko, and prior to his arrival there, they had a rather large surplus of funds. When he left to go to work for the City of Kingfisher, they, the City of Anadarko, no longer had a surplus whatsoever, and I'm certain they would like to have it back. Along with his questionable accounting skills, he seemed to fit right in with the City of Kingfisher. An interesting fact is that Chris had initially filed his case under the RICO Statute and Judge Friot in the Western District of Oklahoma Federal Court but had a case discharged that clearly fell under the statute. It is not the discharge itself but the why that is very much in question.

FIRST MOUNTAIN BANCORP

Trust Receipt Guarantee No. PC04072011-2

IRREVOCABLE TRUST RECEIPT PERFORMANCE GUARANTEE

That Pridex Construction, LLC, PO Box 426, Lone Wolf, OK 73655 as Principal (hereinafter referred to as "Contractor") and

First Mountain Bancorp, 3070 Rasmussen Road, Suite 285, Park City, Utah 84098 as

Trustee (hereinafter referred to as "Trustee"), are held and firmly bound unto City Kingfisher, Oklahoma as Obligee (hereinafter referred to as "Owner"), in the amount of $476,464.00, to which payment Contractor and Trustee bind themselves, their heirs, executors, administrators, successors and assigns, jointly and severally, firmly by these presents.

WHEREAS, the above bounden Principal has entered into contract with Owner bearing date of April, 5, 2011, for

Project: West Bottom Storm Water System Improvements in accordance with drawings and specifications prepared by

City of Kingfisher, Oklahoma which said contract is incorporated herein by reference and made a part hereof, and is hereinafter referred to as the Contract.

NOW, THEREFORE, THE CONDITION OF THIS OBLIGATION is such that, if the Contractor shall promptly and Faithfully perform and comply with the terms and conditions of said contract; and shall indemnify and save harmless the Owner against and from all costs, expenses, damages, injury or loss to which said Owner may be subjected by reason of any wrongdoing, including misconduct, want of care or skill, default or failure of performance on the part of said Principal, his agents, subcontractors or employees, in the execution or performance of said contract, then this obligation shall be null and void; otherwise it shall remain in full force and effect.

1. The Contractor and the Trustee, jointly and severally bid themselves, their heirs, executors, administrators, successors and assigns to the Owner for the Performance of the Construction Contract, which is incorporated herein by reference.

2. The said Trustee to this Guarantee, for value received, hereby stipulates and agrees that no change or changes, extension of time or extensions of time, alteration or alterations or addition or additions to the terms of the contract or to the work to be performed thereunder, or the specifications or drawings accompanying same shall in any wise affect its obligation on this Guarantee, and it does hereby waive notice of any such change or changes, extension of time or extensions of time, alteration or alterations or addition or additions to the terms of the contract or to the work or to the specifications or drawings.

3. If pursuant to the contract documents the Contractor shall be declared in default by the Owner under the aforesaid Contract, the Trustee shall promptly remedy the default or defaults or shall promptly perform the Contract in accordance with its terms and conditions. It shall be the duty of the Trustee to give an unequivocal notice in writing to the Owner within twenty-five (25) days after receipt of a declaration of default of the Trustee's election either to remedy the default or defaults promptly or to perform the contract promptly, time being of the essence. In said notice of election, the Trustee shall indicate the date on which the remedy or performance will commence, and it shall then be the duty of the Trustee to give prompt notice in writing to the Owner immediately upon completion of (a) the remedy and/or correction of each default, (b) the remedy and/or correction of each item of condemned work, (c) the furnishing of each omitted item of work, and (d) the performance of the contract. The Trustee shall not assert solvency of its Principal as justification for its failure to give notice of election or for its failure to promptly remedy the default or defaults or perform the contract.

3070 Rasmussen Rd., STE 285, Park City, Utah 84098
Tel: (435) 658-4979 Fax: (435) 608-4455
http://www.firstmountainbancorp.com

PLAINTIFFS' TRIAL EXHIBIT 3 POINDEXTER

Figure 5-1a

FIRST MOUNTAIN BANCORP

4. The Trustee agrees that other than as is provided in this Guarantee it may not demand of the Owner that the Owner shall (a) perform any thing or act, (b) give any notice, (c) furnish any clerical assistance, (d) render any service, (e) furnish any papers or documents, or (f) take any other action of any nature or description which is not required of the Owner to be done under the contract documents.

5. No right of action shall accrue on this Guarantee to or for the use of any person or corporation other than the Owner named herein or the legal successors of the Owner.

6. First Mountain Bancorp also declares that this ITR is an operating fully confirmed instrument and is subject to the Uniform Customs and Practice for Documentary Credits, International Chamber of Commerce (ICC) Publication No. 600 and engaged us in accordance with terms thereof.

Signed and sealed this 7th day of April, A.D. 2011.

IN THE PRESENCE OF:

______________________ (SEAL)
(Principal)

(Name/Title)

______________________ (SEAL)
George Gowen, Trustee

FIRST MOUNTAIN BANCORP
TRUSTEE

3070 Rasmussen Rd., STE 285, Park City, Utah 84098
Tel: (435) 658-4979 Fax: (435) 608-4455
Email: gjgowen@firstmountainbancorp.com http://www.firstmountainbancorp.com

PLAINTIFFS' TRIAL EXHIBIT 3 POINDEXTER 78

Figure 5-1b

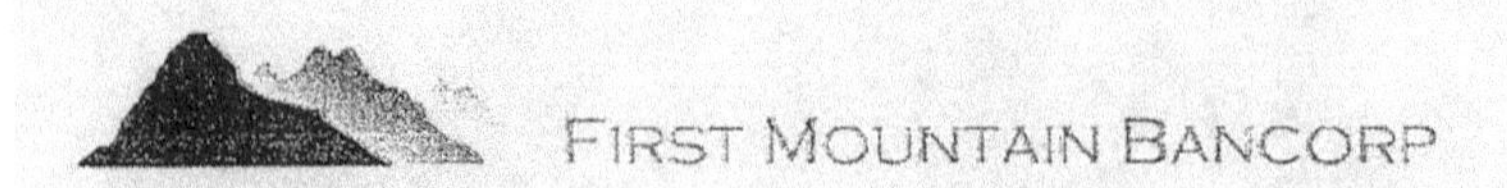

furnishing and the Owner accepting this Guarantee, they agree that all funds earned by the Contractor in the performance of the Construction Contract are dedicated to satisfy obligations of the Contractor and the Trustee under this Guarantee, subject to the Owner priority to use the funds for the completion of the work.

7. Notice to the Trustee, the Owner or the Contractor shall be mailed or delivered to the address shown on the signature page. Actual receipt of notice by Trustee, the Owner or the Contractor, however accomplished, shall be sufficient compliance as of the date received at the address shown on the signature page.

8. The Trustee agrees that other than as is provided in this Guarantee it may not demand of the Owner that the Owner shall (a) perform any thing or act, (b) give any notice, (c) furnish any clerical assistance, (d) render any service, (e) furnish any papers or documents, or (f) take any other action of any nature or description which is not required of the Owner to be done under the contract documents.

9. No right of action shall accrue on this Guarantee to or for the use of any person or corporation other than the Owner named herein or the legal successors of the Owner.

10. First Mountain Bancorp also declares that this ITR is an operating fully confirmed instrument and is subject to the Uniform Customs and Practice for Documentary Credits, International Chamber of Commerce (ICC) Publication No. 600 and engaged us in accordance with terms thereof.

Signed and sealed this 7th day of April, A.D. 2011.

IN THE PRESENCE OF:

____________________ (SEAL)
(Principal)

(Name/Title)

____________________ (SEAL)
George Gowen, Trustee

FIRST MOUNTAIN BANCORP
TRUSTEE

3070 Rasmussen Rd., STE 285, Park City, Utah 84098
Tel: (435) 658-4979 Fax: (435) 608-4455
http://www.firstmountainbancorp.com

PLAINTIFFS' TRIAL EXHIBIT 3 POINDEXTER 79

Figure 5-1c

AFFIDAVIT OF INDIVIDUAL SURETY
(See instructions on reverse)

OMB No.: 9000-0001

Public reporting burden for this collection of information is estimated to average 3 hours per response, including the time for reviewing instructions, searching existing data sources, gathering and maintaining the data needed, and completing and reviewing the collection of information. Send comments regarding this burden estimate or any other aspect of this collection of information, including suggestions for reducing this burden, to the Regulatory Secretariat (MVA), Office of Acquisition Policy, GSA, Washington, DC 20405.

STATE OF
FL
COUNTY OF
St. Johns

SS. Ponte Vedra Beach

I, the undersigned, being duly sworn, depose and say that I am: (1) the surety to the attached bond(s); (2) a citizen of the United States; and of full age and legally competent. I also depose and say that, concerning any stocks or bonds included in the assets listed below, that there are no restrictions on the resale of these securities pursuant to the registration provisions of Section 5 of the Securities Act of 1933. I recognize that statements contained herein concern a matter within the jurisdiction of an agency of the United States and the making of a false, fictitious or fraudulent statement may render the maker subject to prosecution under Title 18, United States Code Sections 1001 and 494. This affidavit is made to induce the United States of America to accept me as surety on the attached bond.

1. NAME *(First, Middle, Last) (Type or Print)*
Lori Diaz

2. HOME ADDRESS *(Number, Street, City, State, ZIP Code)*
28197 Trigg Road
Hilliard, FL 32046

3. TYPE AND DURATION OF OCCUPATION
Individual Surety

4. NAME AND ADDRESS OF EMPLOYER *(If Self-employed, so State)*
151 Sawgrass Corners Drive
Suite 206
Ponte Vedra Beach, FL 32082

5. NAME AND ADDRESS OF INDIVIDUAL SURETY BROKER USED *(If any)* *(Number, Street, City, State, ZIP Code)*
NA

6. TELEPHONE NUMBER
BUSINESS - 904-412-6400

7. THE FOLLOWING IS A TRUE REPRESENTATION OF THE ASSETS I HAVE PLEDGED TO THE UNITED STATES IN SUPPORT OF THE ATTACHED BOND:
(a) Real estate *(Include a legal description, street address and other identifying description; the market value; attach supporting certified documents including recorded lien; evidence of title and the current tax assessment of the property. For market value approach, also provide a current appraisal.)*
NA

(b) Assets other than real estate *(describe the assets, the details of the escrow account, and attach certified evidence thereof).*
*****See Attached Irrevocable Trust Receipt*****

8. IDENTIFY ALL MORTGAGES, LIENS, JUDGEMENTS, OR ANY OTHER ENCUMBRANCES INVOLVING SUBJECT ASSETS INCLUDING REAL ESTATE TAXES DUE AND PAYABLE
NA

9. IDENTIFY ALL BONDS, INCLUDING BID GUARANTEES, FOR WHICH THE SUBJECT ASSETS HAVE BEEN PLEDGED WITHIN 3 YEARS PRIOR TO THE DATE OF EXECUTION OF THIS AFFIDAVIT.
No bonds other than the bond named herein has been pledged to the subject assets

DOCUMENTATION OF THE PLEDGED ASSET MUST BE ATTACHED.

10. SIGNATURE
Lori Diaz

11. BOND AND CONTRACT TO WHICH THIS AFFIDAVIT RELATES *(Where appropriate)* **PP04222011-PRI**
Concrete

12. SUBSCRIBED AND SWORN TO BEFORE ME AS FOLLOWS:

a. DATE OATH ADMINISTERED

MONTH	DAY	YEAR
April	22	2011

b. CITY AND STATE *(Or other jurisdiction)*
Ponte Vedra Beach, FL

Official Seal

c. NAME AND TITLE OF OFFICIAL ADMINISTERING OATH *(Type or print)*
Laura McDaniels

d. SIGNATURE
Laura McDaniels

e. MY COMMISSION EXPIRES
8/29/2013

AUTHORIZED FOR LOCAL REPRODUCTION
Previous edition is not usable

LAURA McDANIELS
Notary Public, State of Florida
My comm. exp. Aug. 29, 2013
Comm. No. DD 906754

STANDARD FORM 28 (REV. 6/2003)
Prescribed by GSA-FAR (48 CFR) 53.228(e

PLAINTIFFS' TRIAL EXHIBIT 4

POINDEXTER 1

Figure 5-2as

Bond# PP04222011-PRI

PAYMENT BOND (See Instructions on Reverse)	DATE BOND EXECUTED (Must be same or later than date of contract) 04/22/2011	OMB NO.: 9000-0045

Public reporting burden for this collection of information is estimated to average 25 minutes per response, including the time for reviewing instructions, searching existing data sources, gathering and maintaining the data needed, and completing and reviewing the collection of information. Send comments regarding this burden estimate or any other aspect of this collection of information, including suggestions for reducing this burden, to the FAR Secretariat (MVR), Federal Acquisition Policy Division, GSA, Washington, DC 20405.

PRINCIPAL (Legal Name and Business address)
Pridex Construction, LLC
PO Box 426
Lone Wolf, OK 73655

TYPE OF ORGANIZATION ("x" one)
☐ Individual ☐ Partnership
☐ Joint Venture ☒ Corporation

STATE OF INCORPORATION
OK

SURETY(IES) (Name and business address)
Lori Diaz, Individual Surety
151 Sawgrass Corners Drive
Suite 206
Ponte Vedra Beach, FL 32082

PENAL SUM OF BOND

MILLION(S)	THOUSAND(S)	HUNDRED(S)	CENTS
-------	-----476-----	---464---.	------

CONTRACT DATE	CONTRACT NO.

OBLIGATION: CITY OF KINGFISHER

We, the Principal and Surety(ies) are firmly bound to the United States of America (hereinafter called the Government) in the above penal sum. For payment of the penal sum, we bind ourselves, our heirs, executors, administrators, and successors, jointly and severally. However, where the Sureties are corporations acting as co-sureties, we, the Sureties, bind ourselves in such sum "jointly and severally" as well as "severally" only for the purpose of allowing a joint action or actions against any or all of us. For all other purposes, each Surety binds itself, jointly and severally with the Principal, for the payment of the sum shown opposite the name of the Surety. If no limit is indicated, the limit of liability is the full amount of the penal sum.

CONDITIONS: SEE BACK OF AFFIDAVIT OF INDIVIDUAL SURETY

The above obligation is void if the Principal promptly makes payment to all persons having a direct relationship with the Principal or a subcontractor of the Principal for furnishing labor, material or both in the prosecution of the work provided for in the contract identified above, and any authorized modifications of the contract that subsequently are made. Notice of those modifications to the Surety(ies) are waived.

WITNESS:

The Principal and Surety(ies) executed this payment bond and affixed their seals on the above date.

PRINCIPAL

SIGNATURE(S)	1. (seal)	2. (seal)	3. (seal)	Corporate Seal
NAME(S) & TITLE(S) (Typed)				

INDIVIDUAL SURETY(IES)

SIGNATURE(S)	1. Lori Diaz (Seal)	2. (Seal)
Name(s) (Typed)	1. Lori Diaz	2.

CORPORATE SURETY(IES)

SURETY A	NAME & ADDRESS		STATE OF INC.	LIABILITY LIMIT $	Corporate Seal
	SIGNATURE(S)	1.	2.		
	NAME(S) & TITLE(S) (TYPED)	1.	2.		

AUTHORIZED FOR LOCAL REPRODUCTION
Previous edition is usable

STANDARD FORM 25A (REV. 10-98)
Prescribed by GSA – FAR (48 CRF) 53.228(c)

PLAINTIFFS' TRIAL EXHIBIT 4 POINDEXTER 2

Figure 5-2bs

Bond # PP04222011-PRI

PERFORMANCE BOND (See Instructions on Reverse)	DATE BOND EXECUTED (Must be same or later than date of contract) 04/22/2011	OMB NO.: 9000-0045

Public reporting burden for this collection of information is estimated to average 25 minutes per response, including the time for reviewing instructions, searching existing data sources, gathering and maintaining the data needed, and completing and reviewing the collection of information. Send comments regarding this burden estimate or any other aspect of this collection of information, including suggestions for reducing this burden, to the FAR Secretariat (MVR), Federal Acquisition Policy Division, GSA, Washington, DC 20405.

PRINCIPAL (Legal Name and Business Address)	TYPE OF ORGANIZATION ("x" one)
Pridex Construction, LLC PO Box 426 Lone Wolf, OK 73655	☐ Individual ☐ Partnership ☐ Joint Venture X Corporation STATE OF INCORPORATION OK

SURETY(IES) (Name and business Address)	PENAL SUM OF BOND			
Lori Diaz, Individual Surety 151 Sawgrass Corners Drive Suite 206 Ponte Vedra Beach, FL 32082	MILLION(S) ----------	THOUSAND(S) ----476----	HUNDRED(S) ----464----	CENTS -------
	CONTRACT DATE	CONTRACT NO.		

OBLIGATION: **CITY OF KINGFISHER**

We, the Principal and Surety(ies) are firmly bound to the United States of America (hereinafter called the Government) in the above penal sum. For payment of the penal sum, we bind ourselves, our heirs, executors, administrators, and successors, jointly and severally. However, where the Sureties are corporations acting as co-sureties, we, the Sureties, bind ourselves in such sum "jointly and severally" as well as "severally" only for the purpose of allowing a joint action or actions against any or all of us. For all other purposes, each Surety binds itself, jointly and severally with the Principal, for the payment of the sum shown opposite the name of the Surety. If no limit is indicated, the limit of liability is the full amount of the penal sum.

CONDITIONS: **SEE BACK OF THE AFFIDAVIT OF INDIVIDUAL SURETY**

The principal has entered into the contract identified above.

THEREFORE:

The above obligation is void if the Principal –

(a)(1) Performs and fulfills all the undertakings, covenants, terms, conditions, and agreements of the contract during the original term of the contract and any extensions thereof that are granted by the Government, with or without notice to the Surety(ies), and during the life of any guaranty required under the contract, and (2) performs and fulfills all the undertakings, covenants, terms conditions, and agreements of any and all duly authorized modifications of the contract that hereafter are made. Notice of those modifications to the Surety(ies) are waived.

(b) Pays to the Government the full amount of the taxes imposed by the Government, if the said contract is subject to the Miller Act, (40 U.S.C. 270a-270e), which are collected, deducted, or withheld from wages paid by the Principal in carrying out the construction contract with respect to which this bond is furnished.

WITNESS:

The Principal and surety(ies) executed this performance bond and affixed their seals on the above date.

PRINCIPAL				
SIGNATURE(S)	1.	2.	3.	Corporate Seal
NAME(S) & TITLE(S) (Typed)	(seal)	(seal)	(seal)	

INDIVIDUAL SURETY(IES)		
SIGNATURE(S)	1. Lori Diaz (Seal)	2. (Seal)
Name(s) (Typed)	1. Lori Diaz	2.

CORPORATE SURETY(IES)					
SURETY A	NAME & ADDRESS		STATE OF INC.	LIABILITY LIMIT	Corporate Seal
	SIGNATURES	1.	2.		
	NAME(S) & TITLE(S) (TYPED)	1.	2.		

AUTHORIZED FOR LOCAL REPRODUCTION
Previous edition is not usable

STANDARD FORM 25 (REV. 5-96)
Prescribed by GSA - FAR (48 CRF) 53.228(b)

PLAINTIFFS' TRIAL EXHIBIT 4 POINDEXTER 3

Figure 5-2cs

POWER OF ATTORNEY

(Federally approved alternate to Treasury listed, circular 570)

State of Florida >
>SS
County of St. Johns >

I, the undersigned being duly sworn, depose and say that I am one of the sureties to the attached bond, that I am a citizen of the United States (or a permanent resident of the place where the contract and bond are executed) and of full age and legally competent; that I am not a partner in any business of the principal on the Bonds on which I appear as surety that the information herein below furnished is true and complete to the best of my knowledge. The affidavit is made to induce the **City of Kingfisher**, to accept me as surety to the attached bond.

1. Attorney in Fact

Lori Diaz

2. Name of Agency

Att.-In-Fact for
Lori Diaz, Individual Surety

3. Business Address (No., Street, City, State, Zip Code)

151 Sawgrass Corners Drive, Suite 206
Ponte Vedra Beach, FL 32082

4. Telephone Numbers

Office: 904-412-6400

5. THE FOLLOWING IS A TRUE REPRESENTATION OF MY PRESENT ASSETS, LIABILITIES AND NET WORTH AND DOES NOT INCLUDE ANY FINANCIAL INTEREST THAT I HAVE IN THE ASSETS OF THE PRINCIPLE ON THE ATTACHED BOND.

Irrevocable Trust Receipt in the amount of $476,464.00 issued by PS TRUST

6. Signature

Lori Diaz

Lori Diaz, Individual Surety
Attorney-in-Fact

7.BOND AND CONTRACTOR TO WHICH THIS AFFIDAVIT RELATED (Where Appropriate)
BOND NUMBER: PP04222011-PRI

JOB NAME: Concrete

Sworn to and subscribed before me

DATE OATH ADMINISTERED

City: Ponte Vedra

State: Florida

Notary Public:

This 22nd day of April, 2011

SIGNATURE X Laura McDaniels

AUTHORIZED FOR LOCAL REPRODUCTION

LAURA McDANIELS
Notary Public, State of Florida
My comm. exp. Aug. 29, 2013
Comm. No. DD 906754

PLAINTIFFS' TRIAL EXHIBIT 4

POINDEXTER 4

Figure 5-2ds

SURETY ACKNOWLEDGMENT

State of Florida) SS:
County of St. Johns)

On this 22nd day of April, 2011, before me personally came Lori Diaz who, being duly sworn, did depose and say that she is Lori Diaz, Individual Surety, the individual surety described in and which executed the within instruments; that she is the individual of said seal, that the seal affixed to the within instrument is such seal, and that she signed the said instrument and affixed the said seal as Lori Diaz, Individual Surety, by authority of said individual surety.

Oath administered this 22nd day of April, 2011.

City of: Ponte Vedra Beach
County of: St. Johns

Notary Seal:

My commission expires:

X Laura McDaniels

LAURA McDANIELS
Notary Public, State of Florida
My comm. exp. Aug. 29, 2013
Comm. No. DD 906754

PLAINTIFFS' TRIAL EXHIBIT 4 POINDEXTER 5

Figure 5-2es

IRREVOCABLE TRUST RECEIPT

Date of Issue: April 22, 2011
Receipt Number: FB04222011-1
Name of Obligee: City of Kingfisher
Name of Contractor: Pridex Construction, LLC
Reference: PP04222011-PRI

The **PS TRUST**, a trust organized under the laws of the State of Florida (the "Trust"), does hereby issue this **Irrevocable Trust Receipt ("ITR") No. FB04222011-1 in the amount of USD $476,464.00.**

The Trust hereby certifies and confirms that at all times that this ITR is in effect, the Trust will be the beneficial owner cash and marketable securities (each in U.S. Dollars or readily convertible into U.S. Dollars if the securities are denominated in a currency other than U.S. Dollars) segregated and named below, at South Florida Trust & Title Escrow Acct# DMV-11-100.

This ITR shall remain in full force and effect for the Duration of the Contract.

Payment under this TRUST RECEIPT will be made to the Obligee upon receipt of an invoice stating that such amount represents funds owed to the Obligee and are to be used to repay amounts outstanding certified and conditioned by the Payment and Performance Bond criteria until exonerated by the Obligee. Said payment will be made within 45 banking days.

Upon the presentation of this ITR together with the certificate from the Obligee as set forth above, the Trust will cause the amount payable as set forth in the certificate to be paid from the assets segregated to secure this ITR.

The Trust represents and warrants that this ITR is its valid obligation enforceable against it in accordance with its terms. This ITR may not be amended, modified or waived, except by a written instrument duly executed by the Trust and the Obligee.

This ITR is subject to the Uniform Customs Practice for Documentary Credit (2007 Revision), International Chamber of Commerce (ICC) Publication No. 600 (the "ICC Publication").

To the extent not covered by the ICC Publication, this ITR shall be governed and construed in accordance with the laws of the State of Florida, without regard or reference to any of its conflict of law principles which require or could result in the application of the laws of another jurisdiction.

PLAINTIFFS' TRIAL EXHIBIT 4 POINDEXTER 6

Figure 5-2fs

CHAPTER VI

PCG Acquires Smart Water Technologies (SWT)

In the mid-2000s, PCG was growing, due in part to new acquired fortunes. At the same time, they were exploring more and more avenues and looking for as much money as they could possibly capture.

The questionable acquisition of Smart Water Technologies from Mr. Rick Webster brings out more questions than answers and shady dealing than anything that I have seen in a long time.

This union was accomplished before Pridex Construction was tossed into the mix, but it demands explanation. As previously described, PCG in this case stands for Performance Consulting Group. It also stands for PCG Wind, PCG Global, and PCG Worldwide.

Operating under these corporations, the owner of First Capital Bank, Jack Stuteville loaned his corporations over $8 million. As the primary owner of these corporations, he was able to make millions in doing nothing more than lending himself money. In testimony in federal court in the Western District of Oklahoma in the case of National Comtel vs. Ron Murray, some of the below facts were disclosed.

PCG employed a retired Air Force general to assist in the acquisition of bids on military instillations. He was given the title of CEO of PCG, who readily used the bonds provided by The Underwriters

Group, Larry J. Wright, even though just a few years earlier, the insurance commissioner in Oklahoma had banned this group from doing any kind of bonding business in Oklahoma. These bonds were used on the military installations by PCG with no lawful ability to use them.

Mind you, while this was occurring, Mr. Jack Stuteville was the primary banker for PCG and was also well aware of these bonds and the fact that they were completely fraudulent.

The operations manager was the named defendant in the suit, Mr. Ron Murray. For the most part, he covered the day-to-day operations of PCG. This was not the first legal difficulty that he had encountered. He was convicted of the rape of a nine-year-old girl in California years earlier. In looking back, he and Jack Stuteville had a long history in Oklahoma, as he was the primary owner of First State Bank when Leonard Briscoe purchased the bank and shortly made Jack Stuteville president. This same bank was later purchased by Stuteville around 1984 and renamed First Capital Bank.

During testimony, Ron Murray made the point that PCG was routinely overdrawn by $400,000 to $600,000 from their account at First Capital Bank. From his statement, at one point, an employee of PCG, a Mr. Jeff Foss, had leveraged his home and provided a bridge loan to keep PCG going on particular contracts at Tinker AFB and was promised that this note would be repaid as soon as the contract was completed. This never happened, and when pressed as to why this did not happen, he, Ron, stated that "You do not understand all money paid to PCG went straight to Jack (Stuteville) or he would shut us down."

Jeff Foss was convinced by a Mr. Robert Torres (Fig 6-1) that if he could arrange a bridge note to keep the company going that he would personally guarantee such. Mr. Torres was an employee of PCG as well the marketing manager for Titan Atlas Manufacturing (TAM) out of North Charleston, South Carolina, and he signed a personal note to guarantee Mr. Foss his money. Because of all the payments going directly to Mr. Stuteville and not into the company coffers, Mr. Foss was still concerned. Mr. Torres and a Mr. Joiner stated that they had information over on Stuteville and Murray that would ensure payment.

Two other men that were working on the contracts at Tinker AFB had previously been employed with Smart Water Technologies. They were brothers of Jack Joiner and all were now employed by PCG.

After this project was completed, Mr. Foss was never paid, but in a very odd turn of events, both Mr. Jack Joiner and Mr. Robert Torres died. Mr. Joiner "slipped" while in a bathroom in Frisco, Texas, and died of blunt force trauma on July 26, 2010, and then, while in the Carolinas, Mr. Torres committed suicide on June 30, 2011. It seems very odd that both men who knew something that would ensure payment from Stuteville were dead within a year of making this comment to Jeff Foss.

Mr. Foss sued PCG for the monies that he had contributed to the business and eventually ended up losing. Perhaps it was due to his attorney who had previously represented the opposition, and as he stated, they (the defendant) always seemed to know what we were going to do.

Transcripts of the trial revealed that indicated that John Joiner, a brother of Jack, was contacted in Plainview, Texas, by the Kingfisher County sheriff Dennis Banther. And he made the following statement: "After Lt. Col. Robert Torres' death from a reported suicide, his wife Wendy Torres contacted the two remaining Joiner brothers, Jeff and John, where she stated, they got Robert be careful they may be coming for you next."

Joey Istre became acquainted and was hired by Jack Stuteville while his company, Chisolm Trail Construction (CTC), was operating on a demolition contract in New Orleans on or about the first half of 2006.

Mr. Istre will come to play many roles in the future with Mr. Stuteville! He has a most colorful resume.

MURRAY,%20RONALD%20-%20Vol.%20I[1]

```
4        Q.   Were you acquainted with a person named Robert L.
5   Torres?
6        A.   Yes.
7        Q.   And what was the nature of your relationship with
8   Mr. Torres?
9        A.   It was two natures.  One, we were friends and,
10  two, we were business associates.
11            (Plaintiff's Exhibit No. 2 marked)
12       Q.   Mr. Torres is no longer a witness, is he?
13       A.   He's dead.
14       Q.   He's dead.  He worked for PCG for a while, did he
15  not?
16       A.   He was our National Sales Director.
17       Q.   And then, at some point, he left, or was fired,
18  or laid off, or something?
19       A.   He was fired.
20       Q.   What was he fired for?
21       A.   For sabotaging our company and diverting funds
22  out of our company to another company.
23       Q.   Really?
24       A.   Yes.
25       Q.   Approximately, what year was that?
0013
 1       A.   2009, approximately.
 2       Q.   He diverted funds to another company he owned?
 3       A.   Yes.
 4       Q.   What was the name of the company?
 5       A.   I'm not sure I remember that.
 6       Q.   But it was an entity that he wholly owned?
 7       A.   I understand he and Jeff Foss owned the company,
 8  and that's -- at the time, those documents that indicated
 9  that were discovered and he was fired by Rita Murray.
10       Q.   And he had actually diverted funds or was just
11  trying to?
12       A.   He did.
13       Q.   In what denomination?
14       A.   We don't know exactly, but we believe at least a
15  million dollars.
16       Q.   How did he accomplish this?
17       A.   He took our contracts that he was responsible
18  for, he and Jeff Foss were responsible for, and gave them
19  to other companies.
20       Q.   Is this at a time when Jeff Foss was employed by
21  you?
22       A.   Yes.
23       Q.   So Foss was there for only a few months, it seems
24  like to me.  Do you recall the length of his --
25       A.   No.
0014
 1       Q.   Certainly, less than a year, wasn't it?
 2       A.   It was about a year.
 3       Q.   And explain to me.  They took contracts, what,
 4  that should have gone to PCG?
 5       A.   Yes.  If you want to know the details of that,
 6  you can talk to Murray Abowitz.  He's the one that
 7  responded to the lawsuit.  And he has the details on that.
 8       Q.   He represented PCG?
 9       A.   Yes.
10       Q.   Was there a motion filed --
11       A.   Yes.  Foss sued us for funds, and Jim Priest was
12  the other attorney that was involved on our behalf.
13       Q.   Okay.  And you think there was a counterclaim
14  involved in that?
```

Page 6

Figure 6-1as

MURRAY,%20RONALD%20-%20Vol.%20I[1]

15 A. No, it wasn't that. They were suing us because
16 -- they sued us for the $200,000.
17 Q. Okay. Explain to me, if you can, how Foss and
18 Torres allegedly were taking contracts.
19 A. They had direct access to all of our records, as
20 the executives in the company. They had direct access to
21 our enormous network of customer bases.
22 Q. These would be people that would be buying and
23 doing business with PCG?
24 A. Yes. And they had total access to our
25 prospective contracts and our contracts in place. So they
0015
1 were diverting those to other companies.
2 Q. And that was because all the prospects and
3 prospective prospects were a part of the electronic
4 records of PCG?
5 A. They were paper documents.
6 Q. And what is the alleged extent of this piracy?
7 How many contracts are you talking about?
8 A. It's been since 2009 since all this happened. I
9 don't remember the exact number of contracts or amounts.
10 But, at the time, those contracts that they were diverting
11 were discovered on their desks, and that's when they were
12 fired.
13 Q. Okay. And do you recall any of the companies
14 they were going to?
15 A. No.
16 Q. But you're sure they were going to a corporation
17 or an entity that was owned by Torres and Foss?
18 A. Oh, sure.
19 Q. Do you know the name of it?
20 A. CCG or CSG, something like that. They were using
21 the acronym or the letters that sounded like PCG, which
22 was, like, CCG or CSG, or something. And that's what they
23 were using to take our customers to that company.
24 Q. And what kind of service were they going to
25 perform for your customers?
0016
1 A. They were similar services that we were providing
2 in the energy services.
3 Q. Could you give me an example of what type of
4 service?
5 A. Sure. We upgraded lighting projects, like, in
6 this building. We had various kinds of technologies that
7 we had acquired or used. Smart water technologies, for
8 example, is a water technology. We had a number of air
9 conditioning technologies that we would upgrade various
10 buildings to make them more efficient.
11 Q. And you said these contracts were existing or --
12 A. They were either existing or in the process.
13 Q. And they would have contacted the customers?
14 A. Yes.
15 Q. And asked them to switch over to their company?
16 A. Yes. And not only that, while they were working
17 for us, they went to our other employees that were -- we
18 had offices around the country, and tried to hire them
19 into their company.
20 Q. Can you give me the names of these employees?
21 A. No.
22 Q. Even one of them?
23 A. Tom Hicks.
24 Q. Tom H-I-C-K-S?
25 A. Uh-huh.

Page 7

Figure 6-1bs

CHAPTER VII

Joey Comes to Town

IN THE SPRING of 2006, Chisolm Trail Construction (CTC), a Jack Stuteville company, had engaged in a project in New Orleans, Louisiana, to provide demolition services on what was known as the Twi-Ro-Pa site.

A gentleman by the name of Donald K. Swanzy had been contracted to accomplish some of the maintenance on equipment that was in use at this site as well as general demolition of the site. Another gentleman had been contracted to move the equipment to Mr. Swanzy's garage/shop to accomplish the required maintenance when necessary. Apparently, there was a series of bills that were sent to Mr. Stuteville for work accomplished, and he failed to pay, even after an attorney attempted to collect for Mr. Swanzy, to receive payment. At the end of this, Mr. Swanzy under Louisiana law, filed and took possession of the equipment. What would follow was allegations of theft that led to court and Joey Istre (as referenced in the prior chapter) working for Jack Stuteville, as Jack had paid him ten to twelve thousand for "services rendered" prior.

Looking back just a brief time, we saw where Jack Stuteville had agreed to pay a Mr. Jeff Foss for monies ($200,000) lent to PCG to complete a project. And finally, Mr. Foss had to sue to get his investment returned. As it appears here, it is evident it was a one-way street for funds to Mr. Stuteville.

This time frame appears to be when Joey Istre became acquainted with Jack Stuteville and a Mr. Terry Kutcher, a partner and friend of Jack Stuteville. The pair found that they could make a little extra money by turning on their contractor, Mr. Swanzy, with a small expense that was noted above, by adding a little muscle.

In the summer of 2007, Robert Stone was introduced to Terry Kutcher by his cousin Ray Smith from Clark, Missouri. Smith had known Kutcher for several years and had literally done a few horse trades with him. Kutcher said that after the meeting, he and Stone were almost instant friends and almost as quickly formed a business partnership.

In October 2007, Stone showed Kutcher a financial statement that listed Stone's assets at more than $3.3 million. More discussions of land and heavy equipment followed, and shortly, with a handshake and a smile, Kutcher signed over 50 percent of Chisolm Trail Construction (CTC) to stone. Stone had told them that he owned the Fairhaven property and showed them the Jenne Hill Townhomes development near the junction of Route B and Highway 63 in north Columbia, Missouri.

In late 2008 to early 2009, Stuteville was looking for a new Ponzi scheme that would have a substantial payout. For the above-mentioned reasons, his mind set in on the area of Columbia, Missouri, and a gentleman named Robert Stone. Mr. Stone was a developer who had constructed numerous homes and commercial projects in that area of Columbia, Missouri, and was well known in the area. An important part of this package was that he had made friends with a gentleman by the name of Carl Edwards Sr., whom you may know has a son who is a famous NASCAR driver and would add to the chances of getting something like the NASCAR Complex constructed in Missouri at the intersection of Highway 63 and Highway 22 (Fig. 7-1). This complex would engulf an area near Sturgis, Missouri, and would tremendously boost the economy of the area. The proposed complex would contain seating for 7,500. The track, hotel, restaurants, and all that would be required to make this a profitable venture. It was initially stated at around $45 million, but once Stuteville and Kutcher got into this, it grew to just over $60 million. In his usual mode of operation, Jack was able to secure guaranteed loan financing by the use of federally backed lending.

As time went on, Mr. Stone provided a financial statement so that they could get the backing they needed. A target was cited, and Mr. Stone complied. Little did he know or understand at the time that this was a normal scam for Stuteville, and it would take him down a road to complete failure and prison.

At this point, I want to take a short look backward and see that this was just another scam of this kind for the nth time. Prior to this, Mr. Stuteville had accomplished this type of scam that imprisoned Jack Logsdon for twenty-nine years, Donald Swanzy (as previously discussed), and before that, Robert Thompson. The common element to each of these is Jack Stuteville.

In the case with Robert Stone, monies that were received from the USDA guarantee was transferred to Mr. Stuteville's First Capital Bank and used to pay off old debt of his friend and partner, Terry Kutcher, and charged to Robert Stone.

Along this time frame, Joey was sent to visit Jack Joiner in Frisco, Texas, where, after his visit, Mr. Joiner (one of two that had told Mr. Foss they held something over on Stuteville that would ensure repayment of his loan to PCG) was found dead in the bathroom. Noted cause of death was blunt force trauma. Then less than a year later, the second who had told Foss of the guarantee, Mr. Robert Torres, committed suicide?

Here is the interesting conclusion of this: a string of e-mails that were each coded with "Terry Istre" in the subject line. The following individuals were on this e-mail chain that discussed Istre's ventures and stated that "I have got to get this stopped, if there is a way to do so. Istre is leaving a lot of damage in his trail." (June 30, 2011 at 1:30PM. Less than three hours after Lt. Col Robert Torres "Committed Suicide"?) [Attorney's, Dan Simon to Tom Harrison]

(June 30, 2011 12:58PM) "Are you just about done with your trip to, and investigation in, Missouri for now, so I can tell him that you are leaving?" [Attorney John Morris to Joey Istre]

It is important to assimilate the dates and times that this was occurring. Where was Joey really, and why were these e-mails coded? The evidence lies in the e-mails! (Fig. 7-2)

New lawsuit sheds light on alleged wrongdoing of Robert Stone | Saturday Business | colu... Page 3 of 12

Kit Doyle
The site of the former Collier's truck stop was supposed to be part of an auto racing and entertainment venue at the junction of Highways 63 and 22 near Clark between Columbia and Moberly. The project never got off the ground, and Robert Stone, the ringleader of the plan, is now in jail in Oklahoma.

Jodie Jackson Jr.   Apr 6, 2013

STURGEON — A flock of redwing blackbirds noisily gather among the gnarled, thorny branches of a contorted black locust tree at the edge of an overgrown 40-acre lot on the western border of the Sturgeon fairgrounds. A few mounds of dirt and leaning white pipes that stood erect five years ago, marking sewer locations, are the only evidence of what was to be the Fairhaven subdivision.

A mile and a half to the northwest, just across the Boone County line at the junction of Highways 22 and 63, rust continues to consume the former Collier's truck stop, while a tractor kicks up a small cloud of dust in a field on a wide, flat expanse parallel to Highway 63, within sight of the old truck stop.

Figure 7-1

Page 1 of 1

t@ctc

From: <joeyistre@yahoo.com>
To: "Terry Kutcher" <terry@chisholmtrailconst.com>
Sent: Saturday, July 02, 2011 3:13 PM
Subject: Return trip

Dear terry. This is an FYI. When I return. It will be under the other company I own Elite International, Inc. Which I also provide investigative and protective services world wide. Due to the threats and corruption and intimidation that I personally, my administrative assistant, and Mr. Jody Jackson have suffered at the hands of Atty Dan Simon, Officer Todd Alber acting under color of law with columbia PD, The Edwards Family, and whoever else to protect the criminal actions and conspiracies under investigation involving robert stone, the following will happen; upon my return I will return with 6 men, myself included. Two 3 man teams with a lead investigator and two man security team for each investigator. No one will be armed but we don't need to be, enough said on that. Each of these men are equally qualified, trained, experienced, and are each a team lead IE supervisor who have volunteered for this. We can not return until we finish with the ongoing Federal trial in new orleans in which they are working to defend our brothers on trial for the Hurricane Katrina Danzinger bridge shooting in which our brothers are on trial for murder. Please understand that I am pleased that you wish to retain and keep me on board but I feel for your liability for our actions that this is done by "Elite" so there is no liability on the part of your company, Jack Stuteville on behalf of FCB, or Atty John Morris in his relations to you all and your cases. We will fly into Oklahoma City on an undisclosed date, rent two S U V 's and meet Mr Morris where Gungoll Jackson will be retained to represent Elite and its agents and Assigns as I will hold my teams harmless from any and all Liability for their actions as they are risking a lot. These men have served in the US Marine Corp with me, in law enforcement with men and have chewed some foreign dirt with me. Now they are each from Louisiana and after a conference call over my experience each highly excited to visit Columbia Month and Barney fucking Pfife. I leave you with this. It is not safe for you in Missouri and do not travel alone. Call a contact at a destination point if you do and set an arrival time with the arrival contact having my info incase u don't arrive. Plan ur routes, stops, and keep ur plans private. There are too many leaks and you are up against money, politics, law firms, and corrupt politicians and I have handled murder for Hire's and Homicides for much less. Please listen to these instructions as in my opinion your life may depend on it. Last. Please forward to all attorneys, dan simon via Tom Harrison, and any one you feel needs to know. Terry you are my client and now through time a friend and I fear for you. Joey
Sent on the Sprint® Now Network from my BlackBerry®

Figure 7-2as

t@ctc

From: <joeyistre@yahoo.com>
To: "Terry Kutcher" <terry@chisholmtrailconst.com>
Sent: Thursday, June 30, 2011 7:17 PM
Subject: Fw: First Capital Bank/Chisholm Trail/Terry Istre
Sent on the Sprint® Now Network from my BlackBerry®

From: joeyistre@yahoo.com
Date: Fri, 1 Jul 2011 00:17:13 +0000
To: John Morris<Morris@GungollJackson.com>
ReplyTo: joeyistre@yahoo.com
Subject: Re: First Capital Bank/Chisholm Trail/Terry Istre

Tell him I am getting fingerprinted for my missouri agency license and being hired by an undisclosed law enforcement agency that has made me an offer on a temporary basis and I am renting a house and changing my residency for now. I have to meet the fbi and U S secret service for one last federal heraring in fulton county GA. Then I am here for atleast one year or as long as these criminal cases take. Please forward to dan simon and tell him that I don't need a fucking job. I will take the paycut and I don't give a fuck about any civil cases that he is worried about. I am a new resident of none other than Columbia Missouri and my louisiana drivers license and voters registration will be changed to missouri. And if anyone fucking thinks that I will be threatened. Intimidated. Bullied as the good citizens of missouri have. They have lost their mind. Not me. And the beauty of being independantly wealthy is I can come and go as I please. Maybe I will have a few select individuals who have my credentials move up here with me being jody jackson was the only one with enough nuts to stand with me. And john one last thing. The only ones bitching are the ones who don't want to get caught. Certainly not all the good people I have statements and evidence from. And last. I am going to the bar with facts and proof of their violations of any cannon they may violate. Please forward to ALL u choose

Sent on the Sprint® Now Network from my BlackBerry®

From: "John Morris" <Morris@GungollJackson.com>
Date: Thu, 30 Jun 2011 12:58:24 -0500
To: Joey Istre<joeyistre@yahoo.com>
Cc: <jstuteville@fcbanker.com>; Douglas L. Jackson<jackson@GungollJackson.com>
Subject: FW: First Capital Bank/Chisholm Trail/Terry Istre

Joey:

Please see the e-mail from Dan Simon to me, below. Are you just about done with your trip to, and investigation in, Missouri for now, so that I could tell him that you are leaving?

Thanks.

John

John R. Morris
Gungoll, Jackson, Collins, Box & Devoll, P.C.
3030 Chase Tower
100 North Broadway

Figure 7-2bs

Page 1 of 1

t@ctc

From: "John Morris" <Morris@GungollJackson.com>
To: <joeyistre@yahoo.com>
Cc: "Terry Kutcher" <terry@chisholmtrailconst.com>; "Tom Harrison" <tom@vanmatre.com>; "Mike Fusselman" <fuss@mcmsys.com>
Sent: Saturday, July 02, 2011 4:11 PM
Subject: RE: Thoughts (CTC)

Joey:

I do not see a need for you to go to the Carolinas - at least not yet.
And please remember that I am not counsel for CTC, but rather consulting with you on behalf of my client, First Capital Bank.

Thanks.

John

John R. Morris
Gungoll, Jackson, Collins, Box & Devoll, P.C.
3030 Chase Tower
100 North Broadway
Oklahoma City, OK 73102
Phone: (405) 272-4710
Fax: (405) 272-5141
E-mail: morris@gungolljackson.com

This e-mail contains PRIVILEGED AND CONFIDENTIAL INFORMATION intended only for the use of the recipient(s) named above. If you are not the intended recipient of this e-mail, or the employee or agent responsible for delivering it to the intended recipient, you are hereby notified that any dissemination or copying of this e-mail is strictly prohibited. If you have received this e-mail in error, please immediately notify us via e-mail and delete this e-mail from your system. Thank you.

-----Original Message-----
From: joeyistre@yahoo.com [mailto:joeyistre@yahoo.com]
Sent: Saturday, July 02, 2011 3:53 PM
To: Terry Kutcher; John Morris; Tom Harrison; Mike Fusselman
Subject: Thoughts

Terry. We have been so busy in Missouri. Correct me if I am wrong but JR also resides in the carolinas. Stone lived in the carolinas and stones sister was arrested and extradited from carolinas to missouri when she was convicted and did time. And Santini air also has a business in carolinas. And the colliseum that is modeled in the junction development group packet is in the carolinas. And I can visit Cherry Point and Camp LeJune while I am there. Question. Do u want me to take one team to carolinas and follow up when I am finished with my appointments w govt agencies in Atlantas fulton and Bartow counties before me and the boys come back. John Morris and Tom Harrison please respond as counsel for CTC. Important. And Mr. Fusselman. If there is any info that would assist you in your cases I will surrender upon return Sent on the Sprint(r) Now Network from my BlackBerry(r)

Figure 7-2cs

Page 1 of 4

t@ctc

From: <joeyistre@yahoo.com>
To: "Terry Kutcher" <terry@chisholmtrailconst.com>
Sent: Thursday, June 30, 2011 7:39 PM
Subject: Fw: RE: RE: First Capital Bank/Chisholm Trail/Terry Istre
Sent on the Sprint® Now Network from my BlackBerry®

From: joeyistre@yahoo.com
Date: Fri, 1 Jul 2011 00:39:20 +0000
To: John Morris<Morris@GungollJackson.com>
ReplyTo: joeyistre@yahoo.com
Subject: Re: RE: RE: First Capital Bank/Chisholm Trail/Terry Istre

And mr morris. By the way. Who is dan simon worried about. His own ass. I don't care about any civil suit. I care about justice and none of you have sat and listened to ladies tremble in fear over the corruption and damage done to their families that may never recover from while robert stone has continuously repeatedly defrauded individuals of not only their dreams and hopes but their hard earned money. Tell dan simon that he and the edwards have woken a sleeping giant. I will forward a final bill. Resign my contract w mr kutcher and I will legally pursue the remainder pro bono for my new clients who have been wronged at the hands of all aforementioned. And please forward to dan simons that calling a off duty policeman and conspiring to falsely imprison me. My associate. Or jody jackson is a felony in his state. Then the act caught on tape proves the act and substantiates the conspiracy. Tell dan to call a professional next time. Not barney pfife who tapes himself. After being stabbed. Shot at. Hospitalized numerous times in the line of duty and subject to a few explosions at the hands of the taliban. This fat prick thinks he scares me. I think jody jackson has more balls than every fucking one of them and he got a threatening harassing call from none other than jr himself. Are they that fucking bold. That overconfident that they can violate anyones rights and keep doing it. I got but one thing left to say and the facts are what they are. The coonass is here to stay. I kind of like this amish area. Joey istre. Please forward to dan simons. Tom harrison and anybody they fucking please. The giant is awake.

Sent on the Sprint® Now Network from my BlackBerry®

From: "John Morris" <Morris@GungollJackson.com>
Date: Thu, 30 Jun 2011 13:41:39 -0500
To: Joey Istre<joeyistre@yahoo.com>
Cc: <jstuteville@fcbanker.com>; Douglas L. Jackson<jackson@GungollJackson.com>
Subject: FW: RE: RE: First Capital Bank/Chisholm Trail/Terry Istre

Joey:

Please call me ASAP.

John

John R. Morris
Gungoll, Jackson, Collins, Box & Devoll, P.C.
3030 Chase Tower
100 North Broadway
Oklahoma City, OK 73102

Figure 7-2ds

t@ctc

From: "Tom Harrison" <tom@vanmatre.com>
To: "Terry Kutcher" <terry@chisholmtrailconst.com>; "e. Edd Pritchett" <eddpritchett@msn.com>
Sent: Wednesday, July 27, 2011 6:48 AM
Subject: FW: FW: Joey Istre/Carl Edwards II

We need to discuss this.

From: John Morris [mailto:Morris@GungollJackson.com]
Sent: Tuesday, July 26, 2011 10:24 PM
To: Tom Harrison
Cc: E. Edd Pritchett
Subject: RE: FW: Joey Istre/Carl Edwards II

Tom:

Thanks for your e-mail.

I had hoped that an informal meeting between Mr. Istre, Dan Simon, myself, and Carl Edwards, II could conclude (1) whatever is going on in Missouri, and (2) the efforts of my client, First Capital Bank, to work with CTC in trying to resolve its remaining indebtedness to the Bank. However, it appears from Dan's e-mail that this will not be possible. Thus, I shall discuss the matter with my client to determine its preferred course of action involving CTC. In the meantime, please be advised that, effective immediately, First Capital Bank will no longer be responsible, directly or indirectly, for paying your firm's legal fees for services rendered to CTC.

Finally, with regard to Mr. Istre, please allow me to clarify that he has not been retained by me, my law firm, or my client with regard to his investigation in Missouri. My understanding is that he is rendering his services to CTC in connection with its lawsuit against Robert Stone in Kingfisher County, Oklahoma, for which the deposition of Carl Edwards, II was taken earlier this year. My client did advance the funds necessary for Mr. Istre to complete his work for CTC, just as it advanced funds to pay your legal fees for services rendered to CTC as well as funds to pay the court-approved accounting firm working on the Kingfisher County case (Gillispie & Ogilbee, P.C., CPAs) for services rendered to CTC. We trust that, in all three instances, these funds will be reimbursed by CTC at or before the conclusion of its lawsuit against Mr. Stone.

John

John R. Morris
Gungoll, Jackson, Collins, Box & Devoll, P.C.
3030 Chase Tower
100 North Broadway
Oklahoma City, OK 73102
Phone: (405) 272-4710
Fax: (405) 272-5141
E-mail: morris@gungolljackson.com

This e-mail contains PRIVILEGED AND/OR CONFIDENTIAL INFORMATION intended only for the use of the recipient(s) named above. If you are not the intended recipient of this e-mail, or the employee or agent responsible for delivering it to the intended recipient, you are hereby notified that any dissemination or copying of this e-mail is strictly prohibited. If you have received this e-mail in error, please immediately notify us via e-mail and delete this e-mail from your system. Thank you.

From: Tom Harrison [mailto:tom@vanmatre.com]
Sent: Tuesday, July 26, 2011 3:50 PM
To: John Morris

8/25/2011

Figure 7-2es

Turrentine Jackson Morrow Obituaries | Page 1 of 2

Life is Worth Celebrating

Planning a Funeral | Resources | Life Insurance

Obituaries | Contact Us | Home

Jack Allen Joiner

March 5, 1968 - July 26, 2010
McKinney/Allen/Plano

Email to a friend | Add a Memorial | Print

OBITUARY

Mr. Jack Allen Joiner, age 42, of McKinney, Texas passed away July 26, 2010. He was born March 5, 1968, in Sherman, Texas to Jim and Frankie (Gant) Joiner. Jack grew up in Plano, Texas. He attended Plano Sr. High School, where he was a member of the baseball and football teams. On May 3, 1997, he married Andrea Logsdon in Dallas, Texas. Jack was an avid golf player, and loved to hunt and fish. He was also actively involved with his children's sports activities. He is survived by his wife, Andrea and children, Mason and Jax of McKinney, Texas; parents, Jim and Frankie Joiner of Ft. Collins, Colorado (formerly of Plano); brothers, Jeff Joiner of Ft. Collins, Jon Joiner and wife, Kristy of Plano, and Joel Joiner of Austin, Texas; sister, Joni Bowick and husband, Jeffrey of Ft. Collins; and numerous other loving relatives and many friends. Jack was preceded in death by sister, Jinger Joiner and both maternal and paternal grandparents. A memorial graveside service will be held at 10:30 a.m., Saturday, July 31, 2010, at Ridgeview Memorial Park in Allen, Texas with Pastor Don Garner officiating. Arrangements are under the direction of Turrentine-Jackson-Morrow Funeral Directors. The family would like to express that through the tragic death of Jack, he was able to save lives by being an organ and tissue donor. Memorials may be made to the American Heart Association, 7272 Greenville Avenue, Dallas, Texas 75231, www.heart.org or the Juvenile Diabetes Research Foundation International, 26 Broadway, 14th Floor, New York, New York 10004, www.jdrf.org.

We have loved Jack since we met some 30 years ago in our PSA activities. He blessed us with a unique personality and gave back to us the love that we shared with him. He is already missed and God please hold him close in your loving arms. Don and Janiece

Don and Janiece Caple, July 28, 2010

We have too many to write down..........

Jimmy & Wendy Herring, July 28, 2010

I had a limited contact with Jack through work. He was always very pleasant and friendly. I know he will be missed by those who knew him.

Michael Martin, July 28, 2010

James has always thought so much of Jack for so many years - it is such a shock. We are just so saddened for your loss and pray that God will watch

http://www.turrentinejacksonmorrow.com/obituaries/jack-joiner-45879 | 3/6/2014

Figure 7-2fs

CHAPTER VIII

NASCAR Comes to Sturgis?

As NOTED EARLIER in this book, Robert Stone and Terry Kutcher had been connected through probably one of the worst unions in history! It is unclear who was actually attempting to scam who, if either. Mr. Stone was interested in putting forth a very exaggerated financial statement, which he did in October 2007, and Mr. Kutcher was interested in capturing this wealth by offering half of Chisolm Trail Construction (CTC) with its questionable value. This all transpired by the fall of 2007. Mr. Stone's financial statement showed an exaggerated net worth in the vicinity of $3.3 million. Stone claimed to own the forty-acre parcel that was Fairhaven property along with a number of other noteworthy assets.

The initial target for Kutcher appeared to be the Fairhaven subdivision, but this was shortly shed for a much larger target. Soon after their introduction, Mr. Stone was half owner of CTC, and construction would begin almost immediately on this subdivision. They would first need to obtain a $1.5 million line of credit for the construction project from First Capital Bank of Guthrie, owned by none other than Jack Stuteville. Strangely enough, the line of credit was approved almost instantly, and the Ponzi scheme was up and running. What would seem to be a missed red flag was the offering on both sides of the fence. Why, unless each was out to capture the other!

Once the line of credit was secured, it was game on! In passing conversation, probably to embellish himself, Stone identified that he was friends with Carl Edwards Sr., whose son was Carl Jr., the NASCAR driver and celebrity. Additionally, Stone identified himself as the contractor that had accomplished the Jenne Hill development. All this, from the Fairhaven to the Jenne Hill to a truck stop he claimed was owned by him, was all fraudulent.

In a complementary business, the Junction Development Group LLC, in the late 2000s, was formed to build the target scam, the entertainment and industrial area at the intersection of Highways 63 and 22. The complex was initially going to be endorsed by the local NASCAR racer Carl Edwards Jr., who was, at one time, believed to be the namesake of a 240,000-square-foot coliseum on the completed area.

With the new partners, the price tag jumped from the $45 million to a whopping $60 million. The complex would be home to the racetrack, hotel, night club, etc.

With the ground barely being broken, Stone went on a spending spree, printing checks on an office printer using the company account for properties, a new Corvette, etc. From first glance, it would appear that Stone was the perpetrator, and he was found guilty in Oklahoma's Kingfisher and Logan Counties. But now, not so fast!

Robert Stone, a Missouri resident, was charged with four class B felony counts of theft/stealing property or services valued at $25,000 or more, one class C felony count of theft/stealing property or services valued between $500 and $25,000, and five class C felony counts of forgery in Randolph County.

A district attorney in Randolph County, Missouri, named Mike Fusselman said that the aforementioned forgery and theft charges stemmed from Stone's part as a member of another partnership—Chisholm Trail Construction, with Oklahoman Terry Kutcher—in which Stone, for his part, presented a fraudulent financial statement to Oklahoma First Capital Bank (FCB) so that he could secure a line of credit to develop the racetrack project. The statement showed that Stone owned the Fairhaven Subdivision and the former Collier's truck stop at 63 and 22—neither of which he did at that time. Instead, Stone is said to have begun using money from the credit line two days after it was granted by the bank to purchase those two properties. Stone also allegedly used a dot matrix printer (without Kutcher's knowledge) to produce business-related checks to make purchases "that didn't go for [the business] at all," Fusselman said. When these checks were discovered by Kutcher, he brought law enforcement in to investigate. This led to the filing of forgery and stealing charges.

Now that you have that under your belt, it was noted that the checks he had written did not clear and were bogus. However, shortly after this occurred, Jack Stuteville had his bank foreclosed on and shut down by the FDIC by an agent named Hernandez. This agent will appear later in the book as he reappears like a bad dream to the American taxpayer.

As was being stated, First Capital Bank (FCB) was being closed due to insolvency. The question needs to be asked is, where did the money go? The checks that Stone was writing were bad, but CTC had a line of credit for $1.5 million, and if one tallies the total that Stone spent, it was nowhere near what was available. Granted, what he did spend, for the most part, was not a legitimate construction expense. The FDIC charged Stone with $2.2 million, but the line of credit was $1.5 million? Now comes the real clincher: where did the money go? It was guaranteed by FDIC. The money that Stone wrote, for the most part, was not there and available but was guaranteed?

The bank, FCB, became insolvent and was closed!

In mid-November 2013, Fusselman moved to take the Stone case to trial between the dates of March 13–14, 2014.

As if this story couldn't get stranger, on Friday (Feb. 21, 2014), Fusselman dismissed Stone's case outright. Mind you that Stone had already served more than a year in an Oklahoma prison. Initially, Stone was handed a three-year sentence in Logan County, Oklahoma, for writing a bad check for $200,000 and convicted of filing false financial statements in Kingfisher County, Oklahoma, and was forced to pay restitution for the line of credit he used. "He got out around Christmas [2013]," Fusselman said.

If you have not at this time noted, the witnesses who had gotten Stone convicted were now themselves embroiled in a maze of prosecution of lying, embezzlement, extortion, and fraud.

These witnesses had been communicating with this prosecutor, Fusselman, at hours on the back side of the clock on how to convict

Stone on Fusselman's private e-mail account, and comments such as this from an Oklahoma law firm stated, "We have got to get Stone out of the way"! (Fig. 8-1)

Why?

Prosecuting attorney Fusselman of Randolph County, Missouri, said that he received an e-mail from Stone's attorney, Connie Millican Sullivan, of Columbia, Missouri, about three weeks prior, requesting that he contact the sheriff of Kingfisher County, Oklahoma, Dennis Banther, about "an investigation into...Jack Stuteville."

Jack Stuteville—one of Fusselman's key witnesses in the trial against Robert Stone. He was once the chairman and CEO of First Capital Bank—the one that Stone is said to have presented the fake financial statements to and the former mayor of Kingfisher, Oklahoma.

According to FOX 25 KOKH-TV in Oklahoma City, Oklahoma, the former Mayor Stuteville was embroiled in a scandal involving the misappropriation of nearly $4 million in flood prevention bonds into a buyout program for his city that included property that he personally received $277,000 for from the state of Oklahoma's taxpayers. At least one of the properties in the city purchased by taxpayer buyout dollars is an abandoned office building.

A successful recall petition removed Stuteville from office, and he was not reelected in the election of February 11, 2014, where his name appeared on the ballot.

Based on Sheriff Dennis Banther's reports to Fusselman and more recent correspondences with the defendant's (Stone's) attorney, there are credibility issues with respect to Mr. Stuteville that make it difficult to go forward with the case. It might be noted that Mr. Terry Kutcher and Mr. Stuteville have been longtime friends and business associates.

In closing, Mr. Stone has been freed with his comment that "he was not at all guilty" of any crimes in Oklahoma but declined to comment further. He says that there is evidence that judges, attorneys, and others in the legal system were manipulated by Kutcher and Jack Stuteville, previous president of the now-defunct First Capital Bank of Kingfisher, Oklahoma.

Page 1 of 1

t@ctc

From: "Webb, Jim" <Jim.Webb@mcafeetaft.com>
To: "'Terry Kutcher'" <terry@chisholmtrailconst.com>; "E. Edd Pritchett" <eddpritchett@msn.com>
Sent: Thursday, December 16, 2010 12:26 PM
Subject: RE: STONE

By the way, the one thing that we all agree on is we need to get Stone out of the way.

Jim Webb
McAfee & Taft A Professional Corporation
Tenth Floor, Two Leadership Square
211 N. Robinson
Oklahoma City, Oklahoma 73102
Direct Phone: 405-552-2246
Direct Fax: 405-228-7446
www.mcafeetaft.com

- **Caution**: Message contents may be subject to attorney-client privilege and/or the litigation work product doctrine. This message is intended solely for the addressee(s) identified above.

From: Terry Kutcher [mailto:terry@chisholmtrailconst.com]
Sent: Thursday, December 16, 2010 12:19 PM
To: Webb, Jim; E. Edd Pritchett
Subject: STONE

We still need to meet and discuss the conference call yesterday. I really didn't say much because it would not of done any good! I want to do what's best for CTC,LLC but I also need to do what's in my best interest. Jack has brought on FCB personnel to put the pressure on as you could probably tell. His men have done some going around my back that I will need to address and will! I have not brought on a personal attorney but with Jack's and my relationship didn't feel it was necessary until maybe yesterday. First Capital Bank has only asked me to sell the Colliers Truck Stop and I have done everything possible to do just that and hopefully getting closer. I did not get a real good read on what FCB attorneys want or what advantages or dis-advantages to me personally. Jack really couldn't tell me after the meeting either. It is my thought that we need to be on the January docket to get my equipment back for non-payment as we had intended to do in December but were tricked by FCB attorneys not to. I will be leaving soon for Missouri in hopes of meeting with Dave Babel and starting the environmental clean-up of Colliers Truck Stop and Fairhaven Sub-division and then going on to Iowa for X-mas.
Please let me know if its possible to meet
Thanks for your help

1/24/2011

Figure 8-1

CHAPTER IX

Pridex Elevates Its Complaint

As discussed in chapter 4, Pridex went into a trial in Kingfisher County in January 2014 after the federal case was tossed out of federal court in May 2012. At this time in 2014, as you saw in the last chapter, a lot of events were transpiring for the Stuteville Mob. The court case of Pridex received a unanimous jury verdict that Stuteville was guilty of what was being accessed, and the jury awarded a full settlement holding both him and a fake bond salesman, Larry Wright, liable for their actions, and to this date, Pridex is still waiting for a complete settlement. Again, as discussed, Judge Woodward overturned a unanimous jury verdict and gave Stuteville a new trial. It was shortly after this time in March that Chris Poindexter, his brother Randy Poindexter, and the Kingfisher County sheriff, Dennis Banther, went to the district attorney for District 4 (which included Kingfisher, Grant, Blaine, Canadian and Garfield Counties), came into his office, and laid it on the line. They made allegations of wrongdoing and criminal conduct by several people. These allegations include (among others) fraud, theft, murder, and public corruption at all levels of the government (city, state, and federal). Shortly after this, Mr. Fields recused himself from any prosecution! Seems like that may have hit a little too close to home for him, or, as the saying goes, they hit a nerve!

Let's look at when Mr. Poindexter had the seven-thousand-plus e-mails that were recovered from the server that Robert Stone had set up as a courtesy to Terry Kutcher delivered to Mike Fields, the DA. The DA then stood up Mr. Poindexter at a scheduled meeting because he did not want to look at the evidence. In a phone conversation, the call got heated, and Poindexter was telling him of all the criminal activities going on in his district; and an assistant district attorney (ADA), Mr. Brian Slabosky, the OSBI, and local businessmen, stated that they did not appreciate Poindexter talking to him like that. Chris said, "If that's the way you see it, you can hang up now, and I will simply have the families of these dead people come and see you personally." He didn't like that and became very humble very quickly.

Now is when the tide gets deep and the undercurrents become nearly overwhelming! As I had said, Judge Davis had knowingly hired a noted hit man as a "special process server" and paid for it with the tax dollars from the good citizens of Kingfisher County.

The same day that this letter was written to recuse himself from the prosecution as it included him and his office, he, Mike Fields, requested that the OSBI open an investigation as to the allegations against him and his office. But now, recall that the OSBI agent in this area was Steve Neuman, and there are numerous allegations against him, so an unbiased investigation from him was doubtful. Let me see, Mr. Fox, have you noted any missing chickens?

Finally, as things drew on and on, in August 2014, Chris Poindexter received a command to appear before the state's attorney general for a State of Oklahoma Multicounty Grand Jury (Fig. 9-1) to testify as a witness. You could only imagine the relief of finally getting a chance to call this mob on the carpet. Recall my earlier comment on the lion's tail? Well, here we go.

Another district attorney named John Wampler set up Poindexter for this fake grand jury and knew it early on. What was to occur was beyond even a science fiction writer's wildest dream. Upon arrival to the Oklahoma state attorney general's office for the purpose of testifying, Chris was given this document to sign (Fig. 9-2). Note that before the grand jury convened, Chris was ordered to sign the order (9-2), and if he did not agree, he would see prison time for violation of this agreement—an order directing nondisclosure. That's correct; he was not allowed to tell the grand jury what was going on! Mr. E. Scott Pruitt, the state's attorney general, did not want anyone to know and to keep all that is in this book a secret and more! I'm quite certain that most out there are saying, "Perhaps it was only a single isolated event for Mr. E. Scott Pruitt." Again, not so fast; you recall that in 2017, he became the secretary of the EPA, and then a short time later (the same year), he resigned (was evicted) from that position. Let's look into an article written by the Investigative Fund.

> EPA Administrator Scott Pruitt is the most corrupt administrator in the history of the EPA. Since taking office in 2017, he has spent hundreds of thousands of taxpayer dollars on luxury travel, absurd security measures and countless expensive perks for himself and his friends. (Friends of the Earth)

Recall we are speaking of the previous attorney general of Oklahoma. Now, be sure and read what a witness was mandated to sign to "provide information" for this multicounty grand jury (9-2). In hindsight, perhaps the security measures weren't so absurd after all—well, from his perspective anyway.

The letter in effect states that you will sit there, sit on your hands, and keep your mouth shut! Strangely enough, at the conclusion of the grand jury, was there sufficient evidence to declare that there was any criminal activity? Better yet, was there any report at all? There was not even a note that said "Thanks for your time." Surprised?

Look back to 2008, when the State of Oklahoma issued a cease and desist order against Larry Wright from the Underwriter Reinsurance Company.

> Oklahoma Insurance Commissioner Kim Holland has ordered Underwriter Reinsurance Co., also known as The Underwriter Group, to refrain from selling unlicensed, unauthorized insurance in her state. The Oklahoma Insurance

> Department reported that an investigation found The Underwriter Group, headed by Dr. Larry Wright and M. Shane Dickens, provided an unauthorized business performance bond to an Oklahoma entity seeking to secure a bank loan. (Claims Journal, August 19, 2008)

Under the watchful eye of the attorney general of Oklahoma, Dr. Larry Wright and Mr. Jack Stuteville went right back to what they were ordered not to be doing in Oklahoma—selling fake bonds—and in a big way! These fake bonds—recall the bonds that Pridex Construction purchased—were now being used on military bases in Oklahoma and many others. Many such as myself had no idea what these bonds were or meant. In basic language, they guarantee that you will do what you say you would do in a construction project or similar so that a bank will loan you money to proceed. If you do not complete the job, the bank or lending institution is paid for the project you failed to do. In this case, these bonds may as well be written on small helium-filled balloons, as they are worthless and simply float away.

Let's see, Chris Poindexter elevated his complaints to the top law enforcement in the State of Oklahoma and you have seen where it went. The complaints were not difficult to comprehend but were severe in nature. Armed with numerous examples to back up his allegations, any law-abiding citizen could see the issues at hand. Why could our top law dog in the state of Oklahoma not understand? The answer lies in the way he assigns controls and ensures that civil and criminal law is applied or, in this case, not applied. Do you recall the three monkeys'? That is what Mr. E. Scott Pruitt is doing—hear no evil, speak no evil, and see no evil! The entire escapade is to hide, conceal, and destroy any evidence of what is occurring. On the bottom of the citizen complaint form, it clearly states that the attorney general may not respond at all! So why is he hired and paid for a job he does not do?

Now that we have broken the egg open, chapter 10 will take us into the dark, shadowy world of a lawless society and uncover the axis of evil that plagues our system and the government that is to be by the people and for the people.

●●●○○ AT&T 4G 6:00 AM 32%

 Camera Roll **1,769 of 2,129**

)espite unanimous verdict in favor of 'oindexter, district judge orders retrial

From Kingfisher Times and Free Press

Editor's note: The following ry appeared in a recent edi- n of the Kingfisher Times and ee Press.

It concerns Lone Wolf resi- nt Chris Poindexter and his mpany Pridex's unanimous y verdict against Kingfisher's mer mayor Jack Stuteville.

Poindexter told the Democrat- if he has filed a motion for an lanation of why the new trial ordered.

)istrict Judge Paul Woodward ted former Kingfisher mayor Stuteville's motion for new , effectively throwing out a ty jury's unanimous verdict nst him which awarded),000 in damages to Pridex struction.

Voodward's decision does not t the more than $1 million ctual and punitive damages ury awarded Pridex from a er Florida bond underwriter his now defunct company he $50,000 settlement that resulted in the dismissal of the city of Kingfisher and former city manager Richard Reynolds as co-defendants.

Stuteville, who was in the midst of his second term as mayor when the lawsuit was filed, has since been the subject of a successful recall petition.

He was defeated in the subsequent recall election by current Mayor Steve Richards, who will serve the remainder of Stuteville's term.

Woodward's order was issued last Thursday, after months of legal wrangling among Tulsa attorney Charles Wilkins, representing Pridex and owner Chris Poindexter, and Oklahoma City law firm Lester, Loving and Davies, representing Stuteville.

In the weeks following the January verdict against Stuteville, Andrew Lester filed a motion seeking either an order of judgment notwithstanding the jury's verdict which would have had the effect of resolving the lawsuit in favor of the mayor.

Alternatively, the motion sought a new trial or "remittitur" (a judicial reduction or elimination of the damage award as being excessive).

Lester argued in support of the motion that evidence presented at trial was not legally sufficient to prove the required elements of the allegations that Stuteville conspired against Pridex, and through fraud and deceit, prevented the company from getting the bonds required by the city in order to be awarded a drainage improvement contract in Kingfisher's West Bottom.

The motion also argued that the judge's instructions presented to the jury before deliberations began contained "fundamental errors" that prejudiced Stuteville's defense.

In addition to the written brief and responses from Stuteville's attorney, both sides also presented oral arguments earlier this month before Woodward took the matter under advisement.

In his written order filed Thursday, Woodward did not state a basis for his decision, which also overruled the motion for judgment notwithstanding the verdict and declared the request for remittitur as moot, based on his order for a new trial.

The ruling halts all ongoing efforts by Pridex to collect the $500,000 judgment against Stuteville, but doesn't necessarily spell the end of the lawsuit.

According to state court procedure laws, Pridex has 30 days to appeal the decision to the state Supreme Court or begin the process to retry the case with Stuteville as the sole defendant.

Figure 9-1as

OKLAHOMA ATTORNEY GENERAL
E. SCOTT PRUITT

CITIZEN COMPLAINT FORM
Website: www.oag.ok.gov

Your Contact Information			
Name	Christopher E Poindexter	Phone Number	580-399-5678
Street Address			
City, State, Zip	Lone Wolf OK 73655	County	Kiowa

By completing this form you are filing a formal complaint against an individual or entity. In order to investigate your complaint, you must provide sufficient information to properly investigate your complaint as well as a summary of evidence available to you at this time to support your claim. Please note that an investigation must be based on facts or circumstances that you personally observed or heard. If you do not have any personal knowledge of a fact or circumstance, you must provide sufficient information to permit us to contact the individual who does have such evidence.

Complaint Information			
Date of Incident	April 6, 2011	Place of Incident	Kingfisher OK
If your complaint is against a public entity, give the name of the agency and any specific individuals within that agency who are connected to the incident.	City of Kingfisher		
If your complaint is against an individual, give their name and relationship to you.	See Case No. CIV-12-31-M		
Describe in detail the incident, any injuries you received and how the Attorney General can aid you in resolving your issue.			
See Federal Court Case No. CIV-12-31-M			

(Please continue on other side)

Figure 9-1bs

List any evidence you can provide to support your complaint	
Name, Address and Phone Numbers of Witnesses	Brief summary of evidence to be provided by the witness
1. See Attached	
2.	
3.	

List any documents available to you or to any witnesses	Copies are attached	
1. See Federal Case # CIV- 12-31-M	Yes ☒	No ☐
2. See Case no CV-2012 - 3 Kingfisher	Yes ☒	No ☐
3. County	Yes ☒	No ☐

Please attach additional pages if needed.

Have you filed a complaint with any other agency or organization? Yes ☒ No ☐

If yes, identify the organization. Oklahoma Insurance Department

What action was taken? Underwriters Group Inc Dr. Larry Wright was issued a cease + desist order in 2008. OID verified they have no License to conduct Business in Oklahoma.

I understand that the false reporting of a crime is a criminal offense pursuant to Title 21 O.S. § 589.
I swear or affirm the above statement is true and accurate to the best of my knowledge?

Your signature is required: [signature] Date: 2-10-12

The Attorney General does not guarantee an investigation or inquiry. Furthermore you must understand that the Attorney General is not your private attorney. Oklahoma law prohibits us from giving legal advice or opinions or acting as your personal attorney; therefore, if you desire legal advice, we suggest you consider contacting a private attorney to discuss you complaint.

RETURN TO:

OFFICE OF ATTORNEY GENERAL
313 N.E. 21st Street
Oklahoma City, OK 73105

FOR OFFICE USE ONLY

OAG Unit: ____________ **Referred to:** ____________

Disposition of Complaint:

☐ Investigation ☐ Inquiry ☐ Referred to another agency ☐ No action taken

Figure 9-1cs

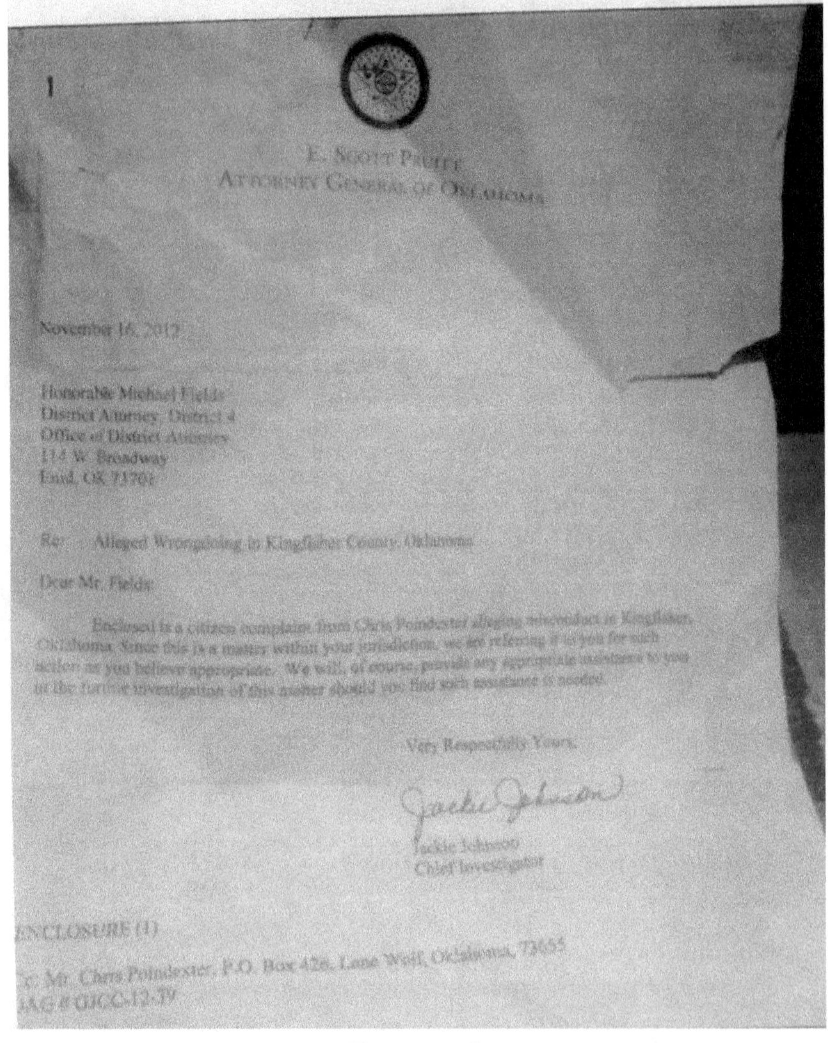

E. Scott Pruitt
Attorney General of Oklahoma

November 16, 2012

Honorable Michael Fields
District Attorney, District 4
Office of District Attorney
114 W. Broadway
Enid, OK 73701

Re: Alleged Wrongdoing in Kingfisher County, Oklahoma

Dear Mr. Fields:

Enclosed is a citizen complaint from Chris Poindexter alleging misconduct in Kingfisher, Oklahoma. Since this is a matter within your jurisdiction, we are referring it to you for such action as you believe appropriate. We will, of course, provide any appropriate assistance to you in the further investigation of this matter should you find such assistance is needed.

Very Respectfully Yours,

Jackie Johnson
Chief Investigator

ENCLOSURE (1)

Cc: Mr. Chris Poindexter, P.O. Box 426, Lone Wolf, Oklahoma, 73655

Figure 9-1ds

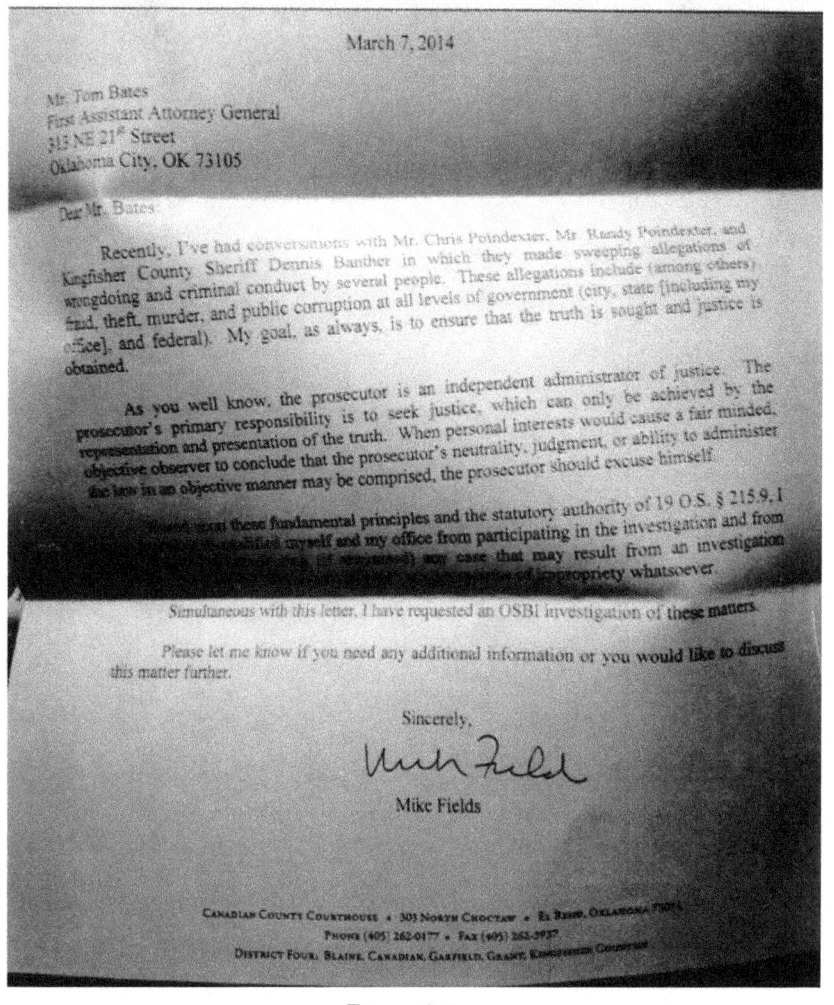

March 7, 2014

Mr. Tom Bates
First Assistant Attorney General
313 NE 21st Street
Oklahoma City, OK 73105

Dear Mr. Bates:

Recently, I've had conversations with Mr. Chris Poindexter, Mr. Randy Poindexter, and Kingfisher County Sheriff Dennis Banther in which they made sweeping allegations of wrongdoing and criminal conduct by several people. These allegations include (among others) fraud, theft, murder, and public corruption at all levels of government (city, state [including my office], and federal). My goal, as always, is to ensure that the truth is sought and justice is obtained.

As you well know, the prosecutor is an independent administrator of justice. The prosecutor's primary responsibility is to seek justice, which can only be achieved by the representation and presentation of the truth. When personal interests would cause a fair minded, objective observer to conclude that the prosecutor's neutrality, judgment, or ability to administer the law in an objective manner may be comprised, the prosecutor should excuse himself.

Based upon these fundamental principles and the statutory authority of 19 O.S. § 215.9, I [illegible] myself and my office from participating in the investigation and from [illegible] (if requested) any case that may result from an investigation [illegible] impropriety whatsoever.

Simultaneous with this letter, I have requested an OSBI investigation of these matters.

Please let me know if you need any additional information or you would like to discuss this matter further.

Sincerely,

Mike Fields

Canadian County Courthouse • 303 North Choctaw • El Reno, Oklahoma [illegible]
Phone (405) 262-0177 • Fax (405) 262-[illegible]
District Four: Blaine, Canadian, Garfield, Grant, [illegible] Counties

Figure 9-1es

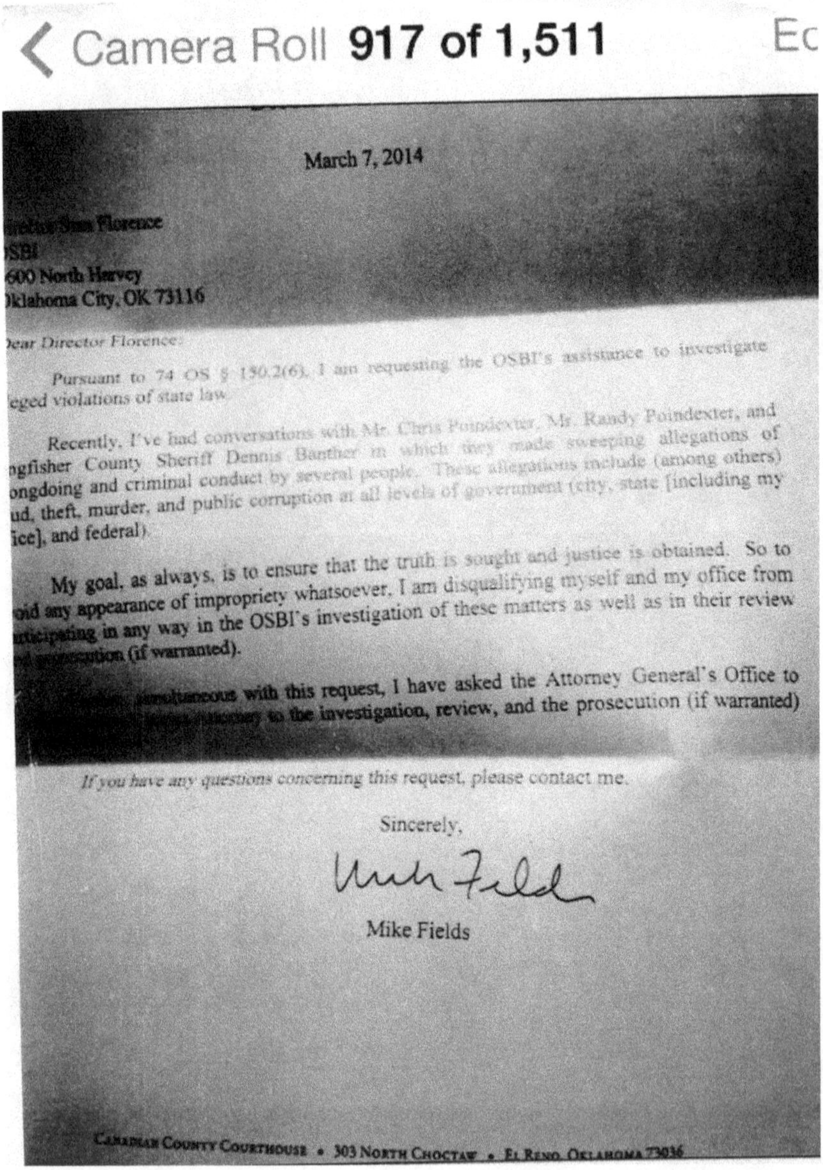

Camera Roll **917 of 1,511** Ec

March 7, 2014

Director Stan Florence
OSBI
6600 North Harvey
Oklahoma City, OK 73116

Dear Director Florence:

Pursuant to 74 OS § 150.2(6), I am requesting the OSBI's assistance to investigate alleged violations of state law.

Recently, I've had conversations with Mr. Chris Poindexter, Mr. Randy Poindexter, and Kingfisher County Sheriff Dennis Banther in which they made sweeping allegations of wrongdoing and criminal conduct by several people. These allegations include (among others) fraud, theft, murder, and public corruption at all levels of government (city, state [including my office], and federal).

My goal, as always, is to ensure that the truth is sought and justice is obtained. So to avoid any appearance of impropriety whatsoever, I am disqualifying myself and my office from participating in any way in the OSBI's investigation of these matters as well as in their review and prosecution (if warranted).

... simultaneous with this request, I have asked the Attorney General's Office to ... attorney to the investigation, review, and the prosecution (if warranted)

If you have any questions concerning this request, please contact me.

Sincerely,

Mike Fields

Canadian County Courthouse • 303 North Choctaw • El Reno, Oklahoma 73036

Figure 9-1fs

BEFORE THE OKLAHOMA WORKERS' COMPENSATION COMMISSION

FILED
WORKERS' COMPENSATION COMMISSION
STATE OF OKLAHOMA
July 5, 2016
Norma McRae
COMMISSION CLERK

COMPLIANCE DEPARTMENT WCC Employee-Claimant	)))	Commission File No.
PRIDEX CONSTRUCTION LLC Employer-Respondent	)))	CM-2016-00277Y
NO INSURANCE Insurer	)))	Claimant's Social Security Number: ssn

ORDER ENTERING JUDGEMENT AND PENALTY ASSESSMENT

Hearing before Administrative Law Judge T SHANE CURTIN on JUNE 2, 2016, in Oklahoma City, Oklahoma.

Claimant appeared by counsel, STEVEN A BARKER.

Respondent appeared by counsel, JAMES A CHOATE.

I. BACKGROUND

Pursuant to 85A O.S. § 40 (B) (1) a Proposed Judgement and Penalty Assessment was issued against Pridex Construction, LLC. Pridex Construction, LLC submitted its notice of appeal and the matter was set for hearing.

The Commission contends Pridex Constuction, LLC failed to have a policy of Workers' Compensation Coverage for employees for a period of time between September 23, 2015 to December 17, 2015. The penalty assessment requested is $1,000.00 per day for a total of $86,000.00.

Counsel for Pridex Construction requested a continuance of the hearing indicating the respondent is attempting to obtain a policy of workers' compensation insurance, but has been unable to find a carrier. The request for continuance was denied and the penalty for the period of non-compliance was considered.

II. FINDINGS AND CONCLUSIONS

Having considered the record, and being well and fully advised in the premises, I find:

1. Based on admissions of respondent, they had employees and failed to have in place a policy of workers' compensation coverage from September 23, 2015 to December 17, 2015; therefore, they were non-compliant with the statutory requirement and subject to penalty for the period of non-compliance.

Figure 9-1js

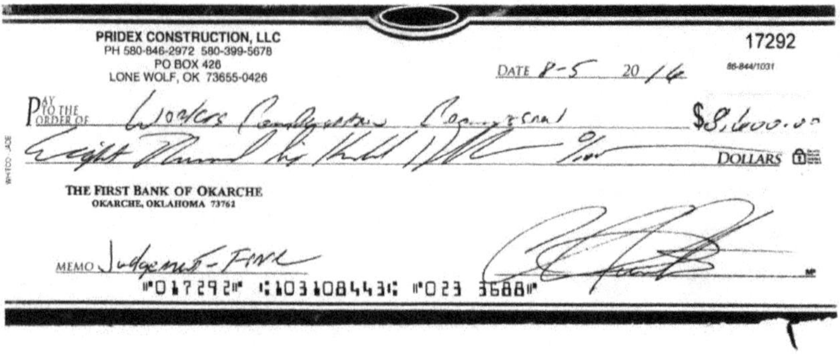

PRIDEX CONSTRUCTION, LLC
PH 580-846-2972 580-399-5678
PO BOX 426
LONE WOLF, OK 73655-0426

17292

DATE 8-5 20 16

86-844/1031

PAY TO THE ORDER OF Workers Compensation Commission $8,600.00

Eight Thousand Six Hundred Dollars 00/100 DOLLARS

THE FIRST BANK OF OKARCHE
OKARCHE, OKLAHOMA 73761

MEMO Judgment - Fine

"017292" :103108443: "023 3688"

RECEIVED
RECEPTIONIST
AUG 05 2016
ATTORNEY GENERAL

Figure 9-1ks

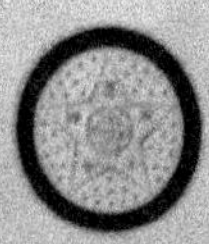

Office of Attorney General
State of Oklahoma

November 16, 2016

Pridex Construction, LLC
21014 E 1450 RD
Lone Wolf, OK 73655

10 DAY COMPLIANCE NOTICE

Dear Employer,

Please be advised that this office represents the Compliance Department of the Oklahoma Workers' Compensation Commission. On June 20, 2016, Administrative Law Judge T. Shane Curtin entered an order requiring Pridex Construction, LLC, to obtain Workers' Compensation insurance coverage immediately. My office has been advised that although Pridex Construction has paid the assessed civil penalty, it has not yet acquired insurance coverage for its employees, despite several notices and reminders.

Please provide the Compliance Department of the Workers' Compensation Commission a certificate of proof of coverage no later'than **December 5, 2016.** If Pridex Construction has not obtained coverage by that date, my office will seek an injuction from the District Court of Kiowa County to compel your compliance with the Order.

Should you have any questions, please feel free to contact me directly.

Sincerely,

R. Mitchell McGrew
Assistant Attorney General

313 N.E. 21st Street • Oklahoma City, OK 73105 • (405) 521-3921 • Fax (405) 521-6246

Figure 9-1ls

I'm proud to be part of the recently announced water rights settlement agreement among the state of Oklahoma, the Chickasaw and Choctaw nations and Oklahoma City.

By choosing cooperation and collaboration over conflict and litigation, this historic agreement strengthens governmental relationships based on the common interests of the state and the Choctaw and Chickasaw nations.

Having a sufficient, reliable supply of water is essential for life, economic development, manufacturing, recreational activities, and important industry sectors like agriculture and energy.

The settlement, which will be presented to Congress for final approval, will resolve long-standing questions over water rights ownership and regulatory authority over the waters of the Choctaw and Chickasaw nations' historic treaty territories, an area that spans approximately 22 counties in south-central and southeastern Oklahoma.

Under the agreement, the state will continue to exercise its authority to manage and protect water resources in Oklahoma.

This way, existing uses of water remain secure, and it provides certainty for future development.

The agreement also gives the Choctaw and Chickasaw nations a voice in specific proceedings addressing water resources within their treaty territories.

They rightly will play a role in significant water allocation and management evaluations within the settlement area.

This agreement is an important first step in all Oklahomans coming together to address the wise use and protection of our shared water resources.

It also fully resolves the state's debt to the federal government for the construction of Sardis Lake, ensuring Oklahoma City has a reliable water supply while providing a standard to protect lake levels in Sardis, which we all agree is very important.

A mechanism is in place to collaboratively address any possible out-of-state water use

With this agreement, the rural communities and recreational and ecological values of south-central and southeastern Oklahoma are preserved and protected.

And Oklahoma City has a path to obtain access to sufficient water to secure the economic posterity of central Oklahoma for generations to come.

Without this agreement, existing water rights -- for urban, agricultural, industrial uses -- and development for future uses and needs would remain uncertain.

When finalized, the agreement will protect existing rights and provide certainty for the development of future uses both in and outside southeastern Oklahoma.

After the agreement is signed by all parties, it must be approved by federal legislation and executed by the secretary of the U.S. Department of the Interior.

We will be asking our Congressional delegation to spearhead legislation that will:

Approve the transfer of the state's Sardis storage to the city of Oklahoma City.

Approve the transfer of the state's financial obligations to the city.

Forgive and waive all future use debt associated with Sardis because Sardis storage associated with future use will remain in the lake for recreation and wildlife purposes. It will not be used directly for drinking water supply.

Direct the U.S. Army Corps of Engineers to approve an amended storage contract transfer agreement between the state and the city, transferring all of the state's rights and obligations related to Sardis, including waiver of the debt related to future use storage.

More information about the agreement can be found by visiting www.waterunityok.com

I appreciate all sides working diligently to find common ground to reach this agreement.

It strengthens governmental relationships based on the common interests of the state and the Choctaw and Chickasaw nations.

And I applaud the determination and visionary leadership

The required number [illegible] (1,277 voters), which amounted to 320 signatures. The Council was to discuss the matter at the September 3 meeting. Vanderveer did not have an exact number of signatures as of Tuesday afternoon but she said she didn't see a problem in obtaining the required number. Petitions were located at Van's Book Store, Joy Jean, Hinds Drug, Don Cannon Auto, Glasscock Motors, Inc., and Bill's Restaurant.

Two Cordell City Council members had thrown their hats into the ring for the mayor's race. Max Cunningham and Robert Guenther, both of whom were elected to the council in April, were the only two candidates to have filed by 5 p.m. Tuesday. The filing period was to close at 5 p.m. on Wednesday.

City Administrator John Haynes reminded Cordell utility customers that as of September 1 they were to place all after-hours emergency calls to the Cordell Police Department. City employees would not be allowed to respond to calls made to their homes, Haynes said.

The Oklahoma State Department of Health had advised the Town of Rocky that water from its public water supply be boiled vigorously for 20 minutes before using. The boil advisory was issued after water samples submitted for routine analysis indicated the presence of fecal coliform bacteria.

Phil Kliewer of Cordell had been selected to participate in the current year's class of Leadership Oklahoma. He was to join 5[illegible] other leaders from communities across Oklahoma.

Seventy-two people registered at the Red Cross Blood Drive. Those donating included: Sarah Foust, Romeo Berard, O.R. Williams, Eddie Holt, Mary Cook, Joanne Long, Carol Maynard, Ralph Cunningham, Anthony Schmidt, Scott Fry, Judy Hardin, Julie Slinkard, Rollan Steigman, Lisa Davis, Kenny Waugh, Charlie Greene, Dennis Slaughterback, Ronnie McKee, Gary Maynard, Teresa Grimsley, Leah Jones, Dudley Simpson, Carol Hoefer, Terry Patton, Richard Parrish, Tena Arganbright, Shannon Taylor, Freda Dudgeon, Terrance Dudgeon, Gary Coburn, Evelyn Jackson, [illegible], Tom Barker, Chuck Davis, Beulah Gregg, Della Allen, Bob Taylor, [illegible], Virginia Walker, Michelle Ainsworth, Sherrill Morris, David Hamilton, Darla Gibler, Jerry Price, John Dudgeon, Rebecca Gilchrist, Tony Hileman, George Williams, DeDe Feldman, Jennifer Wedel, Nolan Russell, Chris Baird, George Francis, James Gambrell, Larry Leppke, Jack Ettis, Waldo Emerson, Nita Ettis, Virginia Kissner, Cindy Ramsey, Andrea Waller, Emily Flores, Charles Kremeier, Carol Halford, Athena Halford, Curtis Rorick, Kristie Fry, Norma Parsons, Wesley Parsons, Mike Stowers, and Lonnie Smith.

50 Years Ago

(August 25, 1966)

Cordell schools were to open Monday, August 29, for the 1966-67 term. Charles Mitchell, superintendent, stated buses would run their regular routes Monday and all school cafeterias would be in operation. Cordell teachers assigned to senior and junior high school included: Allen Zisman, high school principal; Mrs. Maxine Sewell, home economics; Mrs. Thelma Johnson, business; Mrs. Joanne Long, business and speech; Mrs. Hazel Walters, mathematics; Frank Harris, bookkeeping and history; Melvin Williams, mathematics and athletics; Jim Payne, science; Ted Fariss, agriculture; Mrs. Lorene Hull, French and Spanish; Mrs. Eilee[n] Leeper, English and history; Waldo Emerson, Counselor; Mrs. P[...] Emerson, business and secretary; T. J. Loafman, physical educa[...]tion; Fred L. French, junior high principal; Jim McPherson, ban[d;] Wylie Johnson, social science; Orville Long, shop and athletic[s;] Joe Martin, mathematics and athletics; Mrs. Virginia Dunkleber[g]er, junior high economics; Mrs. Margaret Chung, English; M[...] Lavada Parrish, English; Mrs. Mabel French, assistant librari[an;] Paul Vogt, shop and history. The Lincoln elementary school sta[ff] included: Melvin Krewall, principal and sixth grade; Mrs. Ma[...] Emma Hann, fifth grade; Mrs. Edith Sears, fourth grade; Mrs. R[...] Sims, third grade; Mrs. Altabelle Tucker, second grade; and M[...] Flo Williams, first grade. J. T. Myers was principal and sixth gra[de] instructor at the Washington elementary school. Other teache[rs] were Mrs. Elsie Beauchamp, fifth grade; Mrs. Ruth Quine, four[th] grade; Mrs. Florence Marshall, third grade; Mrs. Edith Bond, se[c]ond grade; and Mrs. Susie Akers, first grade. Teachers at Jeffe[r]son elementary school included: Sid Johnson, principal and sixt[h] grade; Mrs. Leah McBride, fifth grade; Mrs. Ellen J. Olsen, fourt[h]

Figure 9-1ms

IN THE DISTRICT COURT OF OKLAHOMA COUNTY
STATE OF OKLAHOMA

MULTICOUNTY GRAND JURY SUBPOENA GJ-2012-1

STATE OF OKLAHOMA)
OKLAHOMA COUNTY) ss.

THE STATE OF OKLAHOMA
MCGJ-12-2099

TO: Chris Poindexter
P.O. Box 426
Lone Wolf, Oklahoma 73655

GREETINGS - Upon application of **E. SCOTT PRUITT**, the Attorney General of the State of Oklahoma, or his duly appointed Assistant Attorney General, you are Hereby Commanded to appear and testify as a witness before the State of Oklahoma Multicounty Grand Jury at the Office of Oklahoma Attorney General, 313 N.E. 21st Street, Oklahoma City, Oklahoma, on the **20th day of August, at 9:00 a.m.** and remain in attendance on and call of said Multicounty Grand Jury from day to day and term to term until lawfully discharged.

Dated this 6th day of August, 2014.

E. SCOTT PRUITT, ATTORNEY GENERAL
By: ____________________
Assistant Attorney General

IN WITNESS WHEREOF, I have hereunto set my hand and affixed the seal of the District Court of Oklahoma County this 8 day of August, 2014.

TIM RHODES, Court Clerk
By Renee Marquardt, Deputy

(SEAL)

It appearing that the within named witness is a material witness for the grand jury and the attendance of the witness being shown to be required by the affidavit of **ATTORNEY GENERAL E. SCOTT PRUITT** or his duly-designated Assistant Attorney General, the witness is hereby ORDERED to appear and give testimony on the date set forth above on the within subpoena. **FURTHER, THE WITNESS IS HEREBY ORDERED TO REFRAIN FROM DISCLOSING THE EXISTENCE OF THIS SUBPOENA TO ANY OTHER PERSON FOR A PERIOD OF SIX (6) MONTHS FROM THE ABOVE APPEARANCE DATE,** provided the witness may privately consult with the witness' attorney, who also must then likewise refrain from disclosing the existence of this subpoena to any other person other than this Court or the grand jury's legal advisors.

Signed this 8th day of August, 2014.

Barbara Swinton
PRESIDING JUDGE

Figure 9-2a

IN THE SUPREME COURT OF THE STATE OF OKLAHOMA
IN THE DISTRICT COURT OF OKLAHOMA COUNTY

IN THE MATTER OF THE MULTICOUNTY) Case No. SCAD-2014-70
GRAND JURY, STATE OF OKLAHOMA) D.C. Case No. GJ-2014-1

ORDER DIRECTING NON-DISCLOSURE

This matter coming on for hearing upon the application of the Attorney General, as legal advisor to the Fifteenth Multicounty Grand Jury and pursuant to 22 O.S. § 355(c), and the Court being fully advised upon the premises finds as follows:

Witness Chris Poindexter appeared before the Fifteenth Multicounty Grand Jury and offered testimony in an ongoing investigation.

The Assistant Attorney General advises the Court that disclosure of information regarding the ongoing investigation in which the witness testified could adversely impact the progress of the ongoing investigation. For this reason, the Court finds good cause has been shown and the Court orders the witness not to disclose to third parties, the subject or nature of the questions posed to the witness nor the answers given. The Court further orders that the witness may, however, discuss his/her testimony with his/her legal counsel.

IT IS HEREBY ORDERED, ADJUDGED AND DECREED that the herein named witness appearing before the Multicounty Grand Jury shall refrain from disclosing any question directed to him or her by the Grand Jury or its legal advisor and shall refrain from disclosing his or her testimony before the Multicounty Grand Jury to any person other than his or her personal attorney, with whom such witnesses may disclose his or her testimony in confidence for the purpose of receiving legal advice.

-1-

Figure 9-2b

IT IS FURTHER ORDERED, ADJUDGED AND DECREED that any attorney appearing with the herein named witness as the witness' legal advisor before the Multicounty Grand Jury shall refrain from disclosing any questions directed to the attorney's client by the Grand Jury or its legal advisor, shall refrain from disclosing the content or existence of anything shown the witness by the Grand Jury or its legal advisor, and shall refrain from disclosing the testimony of the attorney's client to any other person.

IT IS FURTHER ORDERED, ADJUDGED AND DECREED that this Order for non-disclosure shall bind such witness and/or such witness' attorney until the Fifteenth Oklahoma Multicounty Grand Jury is excused from further service, or until such witness' testimony is required in a Court of law or until such witness is relieved from the force of this Order by a Court of law.

IT IS SO ORDERED. WITNESS MY HAND this 13th day of May, 2015.

DONALD L. DEASON
PRESIDING JUDGE OF THE
MULTICOUNTY GRAND JURY

-2-

Figure 9-2c

CHAPTER X

Oklahoma Representative Todd Russ

CONSERVATIVE. HONEST. QUALIFIED. RESPECTED.
OKLAHOMA BORN. OKLAHOMA PROUD.
As your State Representative I will always make certain that the people of House District 55 are well represented at the State Capitol. I believe I understand the issues that concern the people in my district and I know that I hold the same conservative values as the vast majority of the people in our area. I know the value of hard work and the importance of standing for Godly values and honest leadership in government. Please contact me anytime if you would like to know more about my views or my campaign, or if I can assist you in any way.

Todd Russ was first elected to the legislature in 2010. Since that time, Todd has proven to be an effective leader in the Republican-led State House of Representatives.

He is chairman of the House Banking and Financial Services Committee. He also serves on several other key committees: Appropriations and Budget, Insurance, Administrative Rules, and the Joint Committee on Appropriations and Budget.

Todd graduated from Sentinel High School in 1979 where he was active in Future Farmers of America receiving the State Farmer degree his senior year. Todd worked as a welder to help fund his college education. He then attended Southwestern Oklahoma State University, obtaining a degree in Finance.

Todd was founder of the Burns Flat-Dill City Educational Foundation and a member of Leadership Oklahoma.

Conservative. Honest. Qualified. Respected

The above is copied from Representative Russ's reelection website. What you will find in the following chapters may not only amaze you but also perhaps make you want to return to old Western justice! Let's begin with something that he stated at the beginning of this chapter: "I know the value of hard work and the importance of standing for Godly values and honest leadership in government."

I would like to break this statement down by segments. "Honest leadership in government"—in 2011, while Pridex was losing a contract and money due to the criminal activity that has been condoned even after Kim Holland, the Oklahoma insurance commissioner ordered Larry Wright to cease and desist in 2008 in selling any more fake bonds in the state. Mr. Poindexter made Mr. Russ more than aware of this, and the actions that he took will not only shock you but also make you realize that his own pocketbook overruled any and all citizens within District 55. Larry Wright continued to sell the fake bonds. Jack Stuteville was a major bond salesman here in the state of Oklahoma.

Now, Mr. Russ being made aware of this, nothing happened from him. What became even more evident was when he was busy going to Missouri on a state-owned and -operated aircraft, an OSBI agent was flying it for the purpose of "we have got to get Stone out of the picture" and helped close banks in Missouri. When confronted as to his reasons, read the text exchange below:

From Randy Poindexter—12/22/2013 08:24

Now I know why you have avoided me! How was Missouri trip on November 23rd 2010? I was told you were an honest man!

Response, Todd Russ—12/22/2013 09:57

You need to ask FDIC about it. I have absolutely nothing to hide. I just can't talk about information that us under confidentially. Surely you understand.

Response, Randy Poindexter—12/22/2013 10:29

I completely understand, I never knew a representative from the FDIC would go look at a land development in another state for a bank!

Response, Todd Russ—12/22/2013 18:42

Chris. Sometimes I'm not sure how to take the tone of a text or e-mail. If you were joking about me being an honest man, it left me wondering. If you were serious about me avoiding you, I'm even more surprised. I have been more than reasonable in trying to accommodate you when you've asked to meet with me. I admit that sometimes my ability to communicate with all my constituents as much as they would like is limited but I do the best I can. As far as your discovery of some new document that relates to any of your communication, you have known from the beginning that I was involved in banks of Jack's on a contract basis. I assumed you knew the rest of the details but, it appears you don't. Your welcome to anything you can find. It just won't be coming from me for legal reasons. I am in no way hiding anything. I'm just fulfilling my legal obligation to confidentiality. To me that's called honesty. I hope you will see it the same. I hope you success and happiness in your life.

Response, Randy Poindexter—10/22/2013 18

This is not Chris this is Randy Poindexter the one who has honestly tried to contact you & the FDIC over a man that you contracted with in his banks. I'm the one who got fired as fire chief for being honest.

Response, Todd Russ—10/22/2013 18

I did try to call you twice for Chris. No one answered. I recommend you contact Mike Sanders. He is in your district.

Response, Randy Poindexter—10/22/2013 18

Thanks

Reviewing this exchange, here are the items that are out of place—he was on a state-owned aircraft in Missouri, and it is most apparent that he was not doing business for the people—"involved in banks of Jack's"! This is a case of possible fraud, as the citizens of Oklahoma are paying his travel to and from and for what reason? Also, this association with Stuteville was just after the investigations were running rampant, and Stuteville was "not a credible witness"!

As we have seen, the FDIC, Greg Hernandez, was busy closing banks that had accepted Larry Wright's fake bonds. Now, we have an Oklahoma state representative in Missouri assisting in the closure of two banks for Jack after the same bonds that cost Pridex the $468,000 contract! At this point, I have to ask exactly what Oklahoma state function Mr. Russ was completing in Missouri.

If you look in this time frame, Mr. Robert Stone was also being unlawfully convicted of fraud and on and on. Apparently, Mr. Russ was assisting in "getting him out of the way" (Fig. 10-1). Mr. Todd Russ knew very well that Robert Stone was nothing more than a fall guy and was innocent but allowed him to take the fall. It's interesting that after the two banks in Missouri and FCB in Kingfisher, Cordell, and Guthrie, Oklahoma, fell, Mr. Russ came in and bought the FCB building from Jack Stuteville in Cordell just in time to lease it to the county while the Washita County Courthouse was being remodeled. What a coincidence!

Not to exclude that in 2019, the FDIC went to the bank in Burns Flat, Oklahoma, in which Todd Russ was the previous owner and still a stockholder. They then pulled the loans of Pridex Properties and proceeded to review then. After leaving the bank, the examiners went straight to the bank in Okarche and went directly to the Pridex loans at that bank. The first statement by the examiners was "This is not the same Chris Poindexter as the Poindexter at Burns Flat?" Even though his accounts were current and not in a collection status after their review of the loan files, the bank was ordered to write off $90, 000 in old debt and no longer issue any operating loans. At that point, they wrote off the debt and made it impossible for Pridex to obtain any loans to grow or maintain his businesses. This is the same congressman who claims "the importance of standing for Godly values and honest leadership in government." This particular congressman cherishes his relationship with his wallet over his own neighbors and constituents.

We the people need to ignore our politicians' advertisements and look at their past and ambitions.

CHAPTER XI

John Doak Oklahoma Insurance Commissioner (2011 to 2019)

John Doak assumed his office in January 2011 following Kimberly Holland, who, in 2008, had issued a cease and desist order on the fake bonds that Dr. Larry Wright was peddling here in Oklahoma as well as a number of other states. To the last count, there were more than five states that prohibited use of these bonds.

A few months after Mr. Doak had assumed office, Chris Poindexter ended up purchasing some of these fraud insurance bonds. Finding that Dr. Wright had been ordered to stop selling in Oklahoma, he believed that this would need to be reported, so he called the commissioner's office to come and discuss what had happened with the new commissioner.

Mr. Doak had two of his underlings put up sufficient interference and prohibited Mr. Poindexter from having a meeting or even displaying what had been done. Mr. Poindexter notified Mr. Doak's office that he was willing to drive to Oklahoma City or Tulsa or wherever he needed to go to meet.

One of these agents was a man by the name of Rick Wagnon and the other a Robert E. Lee (and from what I can understand, nothing like his namesake). Apparently, he had worked for the state of Oklahoma in the Oklahoma State Bureau of Investigation (OSBI) and had retired from that state job. He next went to work again for the same state, drawing a full salary. You understood this correctly—drawing a retirement from the state and a full salary. He did, however, still pack his pistol and his badge. The first thing Robert E. Lee did was send Chris Poindexter to the attorney general's office to file a citizen complaint form on February 10, 2012. As seen in chapter 9, that happened. Nine months later, E. Scott Pruitt, attorney general of Oklahoma, issued a letter regarding alleged wrongdoing in Kingfisher County to Honorable Michael Fields, district attorney, District 4. This letter was dated November 16, 2012. One year and four months later, district attorney Mike Fields responded by issuing a letter dated March 7, 2014. This letter was issued to Mr. Tom Bates, first assistant attorney general, and Stan Florence, director of OSBI (11-1). After this event when all this information became public knowledge via the arrest of Chris Poindexter for home repair fraud, Stan Florence, on January 20, 2018, submitted his resignation from the OSBI. Again, I wonder why—perhaps because of this large amount of information showing significant criminal activity on the part of the director and persons that he worked with.

Mr. Rick Wagnon had made it perfectly clear that anything that he (Chris) wanted to get to John Doak would go through him with no exceptions. "Insurance Commissioner John Doak will not be able to visit with you!"

Mr. Robert E. Lee stated, "We can do nothing further due to the fact that Dr. Larry Wright with The Underwriters Group does not hold a license to sell insurance in the State of Oklahoma." Say for instance we had a bank robber and the information of such. If this robber was not licensed in the state to rob banks, we have no need to know about him? In this case, we do have a bank robber, and they should be jumping through hoops to get this person or group corralled and stopped! But they are not interested in the least. The big question is why. Even though Dr. Larry Wright and The Underwriters Group was issued a cease and desist order in 2008, they still continued to sell bogus bonds within the state of Oklahoma. Its business as usual!

Why would someone selling fraudulent bonds in the state without a license not be of interest to the state's insurance commissioner?

Let's digress for a minute; at the FAA, why would employees stealing from the American taxpayer not be of interest to the inspector general? That's still a question that begs to be answered. Forget the problem; lets shoot the messenger so we don't hear the message!

The drill seemed to be the same; Chris Poindexter would call in or go into the office to meet with Mr. Doak, and he would be greeted by one of two underlings. They would postpone and delay him for an hour or more, then deny him access to one of our state civil servants.

> The many times I went to the Insurance Commissioner was to see Robert E. Lee to make him do something. He sent me to the AG's office and even made my appointment but as time went on every time, I went to see him he became more aggravated. After Rick Wagnon wanted to know everything from me and I was not getting anywhere I started calling John Doaks office directly both in OKC and Tulsa. Then Rick Wagnon contacted me and told me I was not going to be able to see John Doak and any communications would have to go through him. (Chris Poindexter, 2020)

It became very apparent that Mr. Doak simply did not want to hear the news about what was again happening in his state—seems like we are again back to the three monkeys!

In 2008, after Kim Holland issued the cease and desist order due to the fraudulent bonds being sold to First National Bank of Davis, the Underwriters Group continued selling bonds within Oklahoma. The bond sold to First National Bank of Davis was part of a multimillion-dollar USDA-backed government guarantee loan called the Honey Washita. This was a very carefully orchestrated play involving the following groups and individuals: the Caddo Indian Tribe; the US Department of the Treasury; Dub Moore, president of the First National Bank of Davis (he was the fall guy and received a twenty-four-month sentence in El Reno, Oklahoma); the

Indigenous Nations Buffalo Charter individuals; Dr. Larry Wright and the Underwriters Group; the USDA; and many lessor persons that conspired to make this happen.

To the time in 2019 when John Doak left office, he had not done anything to bring Dr. Larry Wright and the Underwriters Group to Justice. Why?

If you look at the list of those who accepted these bonds, you will find the list is lengthy and includes many private and government projects: Altus AFB, Tinker AFB, CSR Nationwide, Aduddell Roofing, the FAA, Fountains of Canterbury (a retirement center), USDA, and the list goes on! Most of these were sold by none other than Jack Stuteville and bankers such as Representative Todd Russ and the fraud insurance salesman from Arkansas, Steve Standridge.

The fraudulent bonds are in the hundreds of millions of dollars that it has stolen from the tax coffers. Another of many of these scams that have been perpetuated on the citizens of Oklahoma and this nation was a power plant on Fort Cobb Lake designed to purposely steal millions and wire the loan proceeds out of the country through the West Norman Bank of America location.

There was a special put-on by Oklahoma City FOX 25 Television, "Waste Watch," where they interviewed the Department of Agriculture Director here in Oklahoma, Mike Thrawls, where there was $25 million on flood buyout properties and special projects in both Kingfisher and Caddo Counties. The money was not used for the projects that it was approved for. After this story aired, Mike Thrawls was replaced as the director! It really makes one wonder why. To positively conclude this chapter, if that is possible, Steve Standridge (another fall guy) was sent to prison in Arkansas for sixty months concerning insurance fraud. The projects that I have named in this chapter are only a slim example of the hundreds that have stolen millions of dollars from the nation.

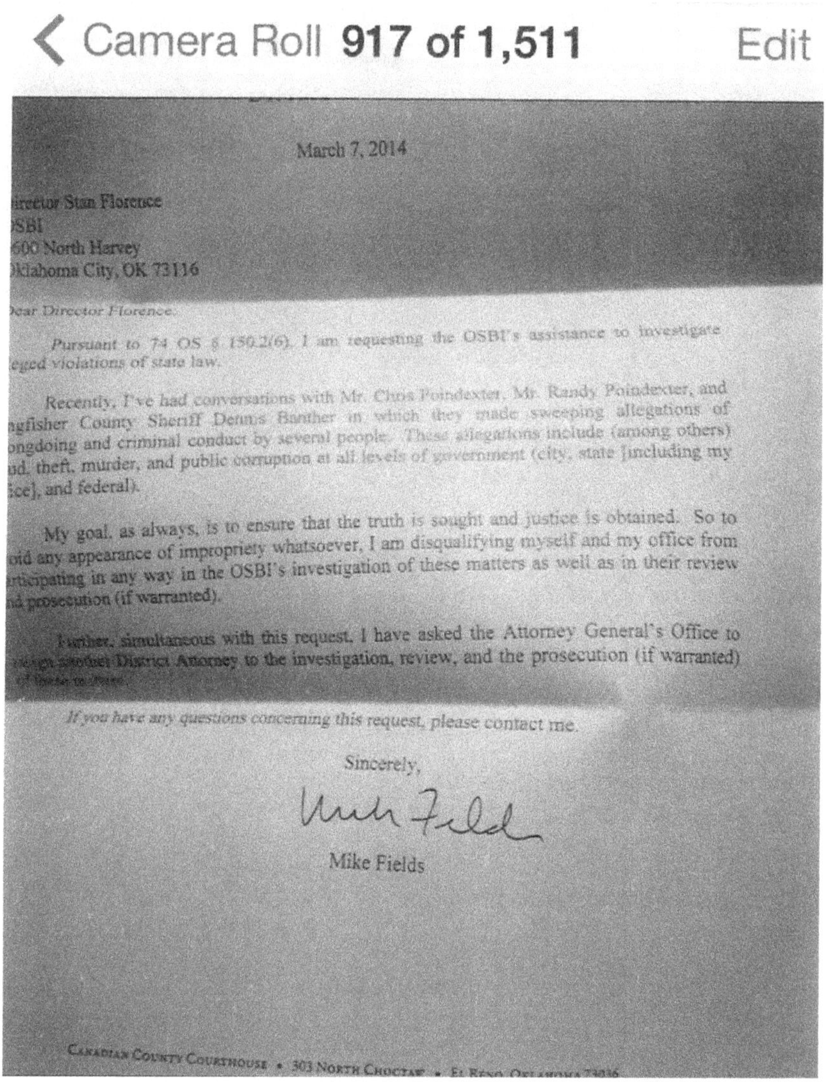

‹ Camera Roll **917 of 1,511** Edit

March 7, 2014

irector Stan Florence
SBI
600 North Harvey
Oklahoma City, OK 73116

ear Director Florence:

Pursuant to 74 OS § 150.2(6), I am requesting the OSBI's assistance to investigate leged violations of state law.

Recently, I've had conversations with Mr. Chris Poindexter, Mr. Randy Poindexter, and ngfisher County Sheriff Dennis Banther in which they made sweeping allegations of ongdoing and criminal conduct by several people. These allegations include (among others) ud, theft, murder, and public corruption at all levels of government (city, state [including my fice], and federal).

My goal, as always, is to ensure that the truth is sought and justice is obtained. So to oid any appearance of impropriety whatsoever, I am disqualifying myself and my office from rticipating in any way in the OSBI's investigation of these matters as well as in their review nd prosecution (if warranted).

Further, simultaneous with this request, I have asked the Attorney General's Office to ssign another District Attorney to the investigation, review, and the prosecution (if warranted) [illegible]

If you have any questions concerning this request, please contact me.

Sincerely,

Mike Fields

CANADIAN COUNTY COURTHOUSE • 303 NORTH CHOCTAW • EL RENO, OKLAHOMA 73036

Figure 11-1

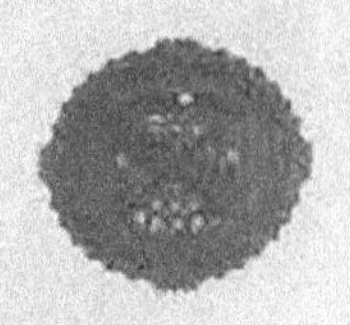

Oklahoma State Bureau of Investigation

STAN FLORENCE
Director

CHARLES D. CURTIS
Deputy Director

February 9, 2018

Mr. Mike Boring, Chairman
OSBI Commission
6600 N Harvey
Oklahoma City, Ok 73116

Dear Mr. Boring,

Effective February 20, 2018 at the close of business, I will resign as OSBI Director. In accordance with Title 74 Section 150.8(D), I seek reinstatement into classified service without any loss of rights, privileges or benefits upon my completion of the duties as Director.

I want to thank you and the other OSBI Commission members for your support and service to the agency. Your oversight and sacrifices are truly appreciated.

My service as agency director for over seven years has been rewarding and I have enjoyed my role in providing oversight of this great agency. I look forward to my continued service with the OSBI and stand ready to serve in the capacity assigned to me.

Respectfully,

Stan Florence
Director

Figure 11-2

CHAPTER XII

Loose Ends

As WITH ANY project, there are always loose ends that need to be covered. Looking at our federal and state governments, the same applies. In this case, when our officials, as you have seen, are trying to overthrow our democratic society, one can only imagine how tight the level of security must need to be. As you have seen early in the book, the levels of government will employ some very precarious people to do all kinds of jobs, like the hit man as a special process server, and send old partners to prison to cover their actions and allow the money to flow. One thing that I find interesting about these "government" operations is, they always begin with a bribe or at least an attempted bribe!

What it seems to begin with is the promise of great wealth and an easy ride that ends in prison, death, dead family members, or a variety of lawsuits that are always looking for retribution and repayment.

In the early 1980s, as were most years, one of the most important issues in Oklahoma was the Sooners being number 1 in football. That was not working out so well then; however, even though it was having its worst year in sixteen years, Oklahoma became number 1 in the largest kickback scandals in US history. Over 250 county officials, contractors, and suppliers across the state either pleaded guilty, had been found guilty, or agreed to plead guilty to federal charges (usually income tax–related) in an investigation that centered on kickbacks in the purchase of roadbuilding and repair equipment.

You're probably wondering how this applies to the corruption at hand. As you have seen along with the banks, bankers, assistant district attorneys, district attorneys, Oklahoma State Bureau of Investigation (OSBI) officials, county, state, and federal judges are all on board as well as FBI agents.

As you have seen in previous chapters, there are a number of individuals unlawfully imprisoned, very interesting "suicides" that were confirmed by the OSBI, and deaths that just seemed to happen. In this and the following chapters, I will be going through each of these and how the same banking officials and "civil servants" always seem to be involved but the money always seemed to go into the same pockets.

One major implicating factor that will allow this entire money folly to succeed is currently heading to the US Supreme Court. The case is, an individual named Patrick Dwayne Murphy, a member of the Creek Nation, argues that the state could not prosecute him for murder, as the murder occurred on an American Indian reservation rather than state-controlled land.

Does this ring any bells? "A house divided against itself, cannot stand" (Abraham Lincoln, 1858).

Now, let's start with an interesting series of events around the time that Pridex lost their contract on the West Bottom Project in Kingfisher, Oklahoma, in 2011. As you recall, Jack Stuteville had Chris Poindexter call this guy in Arkansas named Steve Standridge about getting his bonds for the West Bottom Project. It is a well-established fact that the three people involved—Standridge, Stuteville, and Larry Wright—were longtime business partners. At the time that Stuteville had Chris Poindexter contact Standridge, Standridge owed Stuteville a good deal of money. I believe in this; it was a matter of stealing from Peter to pay Paul. Standridge would eventually end up going to prison on a number of felonies and was in the hotseat in Arkansas. Likewise, Stuteville was feeling the heat, which could very well lead back to his door!

Just prior to Pridex getting involved with The Underwriters Group, Steve Standridge and Jack Stuteville had events that were unraveling across Oklahoma, Texas, and Arkansas. As I had referenced, Steve Standridge was drawn into a legal entanglement that would lead to his demise. With him may very well go others should they testify for or against him.

In a series of at first seemingly unrelated events, two bankers in Russellville, Arkansas, had their lives abruptly ended. The first was William John Clement on June 2, 2012, and the other was Thomas Edward Bullock on June 11, 2012. He was only forty-eight years old. An interesting fact on this was that in the dark of night, he ran his car into his bank building and the pistol that he carried accidently went off and shot him in the head! Mr. Clement had gotten involved in the commercial and personal insurance business shortly after retiring from the bank. The third man and his wife and another couple were killed in an accident on June 13, 2010. Michael Hunt, his wife, Terri, and friends Carl and Carolyn Davis. For them, one would think it just a horrible accident. But looking at the connections and the means of the accident, you will find it highly irregular.

The next in this series of unusual deaths was a forty-six-year-old pilot, Dr. Edward Cooper; his sixteen-year-old daughter, Mary Cooper; his fourteen-year-old daughter, Elizabeth Cooper; and fifty-six-year-old Dr. Martin Draper. They all came from hot springs, and the wreckage of their A36 Beechcraft Bonanza was located in Northwest Arkansas. It is rumored that he had loaned Steve Standridge a few million dollars and Standridge had just paid him back. Presumably before the check was cashed, he perished.

Next, a man discussed earlier in this book, Jack Joiner, met his fate. On July 26, 2010, in a restroom at a restaurant in Allen, Texas. A very healthy and fit individual in his midforties "accidentally" fell and was killed by blunt force trauma?

A gentleman by the name of Lt Col. Robert Torres "committed suicide" on June 30, 2011. He was employed at that time by Titan Atlas Manufacturing (TAM) and had previously worked for PCG in Norman, Oklahoma. As you recall from a previous discussion, he and Mr. Joiner knew something—or should I say—he had something over on one of the owners of PCG, a Mr. Jack Stuteville that would force him to pay Mr. Jeff Foss back for the $200,000 he had lent to PCG to complete a project on Tinker Air Force Base. Coincidently, the Kingfisher County special process server just happened to be in North Charleston, South Carolina, at the same time that he committed suicide. Robert Torres's widow warned Jack's brother John to beware, "They may be coming for you next!" This information was later provided to the Kingfisher County sheriff Dennis Banther when he spoke to John Joiner.

Gregory Hunt was employed by his construction company and used these bonds from Standridge from time to time on his projects. In the eastern district of Arkansas, an indictment against Standridge followed pleas of guilty to an information by Danny Wood of Idabel, Oklahoma, and Gregory A. Hunt of Russellville, Arkansas. On March 2, 2012, Wood pleaded guilty to aiding and abetting bank fraud. On July 6, 2012, Wood was sentenced to thirty months' imprisonment. On June 6, 2012, Hunt pleaded guilty to aiding and abetting bank fraud. Hunt was sentenced on October 31, 2012, to thirty-three months' imprisonment.

Throughout the period outlined in both indictments, Standridge owned, operated, and/ or managed various independent insurance agencies in the state of Arkansas. Through these companies, Standridge provided various types of insurance policies and bonds to his customers including Danny Wood and Gregory A. Hunt.

The indictment against Standridge filed in the eastern district of Arkansas alleged that Standridge conspired with Wood and Hunt to commit bank fraud.

Mr. Hunt was allegedly preparing to testify with Standridge and, in doing such, implicate Stuteville and Larry Wright of The Underwriters Group. On February 25, 2013, Gregory Hunt had a massive heart attack, survived for hours, and was conscious and talking to his parents at the hospital when two female guards came in and told his parents they had to leave. That was the last time they saw their son alive. It was very curious his passing almost immediately after his parents were pushed out the door!

Last on our list of fatalities of this one cover-up is a young lady who is very difficult to comprehend! Her name was Kymberly Marie Hatler-Mathews. She was going through a great deal of marital issues and unrest. She decided to begin to post issues on Facebook of all that was going on, including her husband and his brother's business dealings. With this came an old, familiar name, Jack Stuteville. After being severely beaten one day by her husband, Randy, she posted that "everyone, for some reason backs down to the Matthews. I NEVER WILL!" The following day, she committed suicide after asking "What type shell would be best for shooting, might go shooting tomorrow?" It is strange, as no autopsy was ordered by the OSBI, Steve Neuman. Additionally, almost immediately, her posts were taken down. This same agent who was involved earlier was now perpetuating exceedingly odd events.

If we now look at only those that we know of, a total of thirteen deaths all surrounded this one event. We are not counting those who are or were in prison as fall guys! Each one has a direct connection to these fake bonds and the sales team!

CHAPTER XIII

The Money Game

While most of us go through our lives trying to save our money and make some investments to prepare for our retirement, others are trying to figure a way to take it. However, there are those who would prefer the honest American to be pushed into a camp and left to die. This, with a noncorrupt government, would never work well. The overall result of an honest government is a thriving economy and a wholesome, happy population.

What you will see ahead is what happens to those who attempt to bring to light to a very organized and corrupt financial and government system. Like cockroaches, this bunch runs from the light of justice; unlike cockroaches, they attempt to retaliate in most every form possible. The preferred method is to simply kill the whistleblower as you saw in chapter 12 and in my new book, *Unfit*. When this fails, next comes the discrediting and, if possible, financial ruin. For Mr. Poindexter, I'm quite certain that their initial plan was to scare him off. That, as I stated earlier in the book, was the broken windows in his brother's pickup while they were attending a meeting with Stuteville and the city fathers of Kingfisher. For me, in the FAA, the same strategy was pushed to that and many other levels.

I feel certain that the only reason that they have not attempted to eliminate Chris is because of the flash drive that was entered into evidence when he was wrongly arrested for home repair fraud.

When this all began, it was only a civil case for the homeowner Alan Beck's refusal to pay for the work done on his house. At first, Wells Fargo would not release his insurance funds so Pridex could keep working. To complete, Pridex borrowed $52,000 after Mr. Beck had Wells Fargo contact Pridex's bank to let them know they would release funds upon completion. When the home was completed and a bill was given to Mr. Beck, he told Chris from Pridex to go f—k himself! At this point, as there was no other avenue, Pridex filed a lien against Alan Beck's house. Because no action was taken by Alan Beck to settle the debt, Pridex was forced to foreclose on their lien. Chris Poindexter told the ADA Lynn Lawrence that Alan Beck had violated the Oklahoma Construction Trust Fund Act by putting insurance funds intended to rebuild his house into his pocket and not using the funds for the intended purpose. ADA Lynn Lawrence said, "Do you think you know the law better than I do? There may be a warrant for your arrest next!" Approximately a week later, she issued a warrant for the arrest of Chris Poindexter for home repair fraud. I'm certain that it was only a coincidence, her earlier comment and the warrant?

What started as a civil case initiated by Pridex with a lien against Beck's house has now ended up as a criminal case against Chris Poindexter for home repair fraud. After hiring two criminal attorneys who were working for Stuteville, Ed Blau and Laura Deskin to babysit Ed, either directly or indirectly, Chris was forced to switch attorneys when they did not show for a pretrial hearing nor contact him. After spending over $40,000 for criminal attorneys, a motion to quash was granted, which proved that Chris was a victim of malicious prosecution and he should never have been arrested.

Trumped-up charges that all knew were a lie were allowed to perpetuate. Strangely enough, the assistant district attorney, Lynn Lawrence, was fired almost immediately after she unwittingly preserved all the damning evidence against the county and state officials on the zip drive that Chris had provided to an Alan Beck. It is oh so interesting how the truth shall set one free!

Now for our happy-go-lucky banker, Dwight Waugh. Apparently, in the years past, he had worked for Jack Stuteville at the First Capital Bank. Now, in his official capacity as president of BancFirst in Hobart, he one day had a meltdown and began screaming at Chris Poindexter, as Chris had converted a nursing home into an apartment complex and spent slightly more in the process than the initial note. The loans on his construction projects were current and ahead of schedule. In an open-door meeting, he proceeded to attempt to disgrace Chris for issues that were not! Does one think that there may be a connection here since there was nothing incorrect with the loans on the construction projects? Additionally, he had told a bank customer at his bank that Chris was going bankrupt. This was step 1 in attempting to drive an honest businessman out who would not go along with the thug mentality.

For good reason, killing Mr. Poindexter was bad for their business interests, not to mention bad for Chris. Like with the FAA and myself, when they feared what information may have leaked out on their plans, they resorted to plan B!

Plan B was to make him appear untrustworthy and no-account. With Chris, they began to unlawfully foreclose on his loans and repossess properties they did not have claim to.

Now came the real crown jewel! They, the Stuteville Mob, employed a gentleman whom Pridex Construction as previously discussed had done repair work on his home, and then they had him file home repair fraud. This person, Alan Beck, had talked to Chris while the work on his home was ongoing, and during one of these chat sessions, Chris mentioned to him that Judge Woodward had overturned a unanimous jury verdict in Kingfisher County. Alan stated that such did not happen. Chris stated that such did happen and that he had written a book about that and many other issues. Alan stated that he wanted to read the book, and Chris gave Alan a copy of the Zip drive to prove his case. Alan gave the Zip drive to his attorney, Tom Ivester—coincidentally a two-time state senator—who told Alan to take the drive to the police department in Elk City, Oklahoma, which he did. The case was filed against Chris by the abovementioned ADA, and Chris was arrested. Recall her statement "There may be a warrant for your arrest next!" It gets very interesting here, as just before this, Alan was arrested on a DUI and spent the night in jail around the first of July 2017. Now, the interesting part is, the arrest and concurrent jail time was all purged from the court record. As a matter of fact, had it not have been for Chris quickly pulling public records, all of this event would be gone forever. Note the attached documents. You, the book holder, have the proof! I wonder if the judge still has her copy.

How does that work unless one happens to be close friends with a judge or close friends with those who are close friends with the judge that may be on the take as well? Perhaps the said judge doesn't like the publishing of a book that tags her for what she really is.

The worst thing in the world, as Chris believed, ended up being the best thing in the world. With the zip drive and book being logged in as evidence, it was now a public document and therefore could be used and written about by writers such as myself.

Months after the fact, Chris was preparing for the trial, and in the deposition, he noted that the one who had perjured him, Alan Beck, introduced him to his attorneys at the deposition. So the question begs to be asked, Did this guy file a felony charge and hire these attorneys? One must look to see who has the banking systems tied up and who is benefitting!

What you are seeing is not justice for hire; it is for sale. By doing to Chris as they have done to me, they simply run a person who sought the truth out of money so that they cannot represent themselves or, should I say, afford such.

By having county, district, state, and federal representatives, judges, and district attorneys all on the payroll, one could easily state that the deck was stacked!

FILED
AUG 23 2017
DONNA HOWELL COURT CLERK
BY ______ DEPUTY

IN THE DISTRICT COURT OF BECKHAM COUNTY
STATE OF OKLAHOMA
COURT MINUTE

8-23-17

State of Oklahoma, Plaintiff,

Case No. CM 17-151

vs.

Alan Dale Beck
Defendant.

Defendant appears (with) (without) counsel P. Albert for sentencing and after being advised of his rights and of the possible punishment, enters a plea of guilty (nolo contendere). The State appears by Assistant District Attorney Lueck Court Reporter ______

✓ This matter is a plea agreement and it is approved by the Court.

SENTENCE IMPOSED

✓ Count 1
✓ Sentencing is deferred to 8-21-19 at 1:30
______ in the custody of (County Jail) (DOC)
______ All is suspended.
______ With ______ to serve ______ suspended.
✓ Court costs: 35.00 VCA: 500.00 Fine

✓ DNA fee
______ D.A. Drug fee
______ Drug Ed. fee
______ Lab fee
______ OIDS fee

______ Count 2
______ Sentencing is deferred to ______
______ in the custody of (County Jail) (DOC)
______ All is suspended.
______ With ______ to serve and ______ suspended.
______ Court costs: ______ VCA: ______ Fine

______ Waives his right to remain in the County Jail 10 days.

______ Count 3
______ Sentencing is deferred to ______
______ in the custody of (County Jail) (DOC)
______ All is suspended.
______ With ______ to serve and ______ suspended.
______ Court costs: ______ VCA: ______ Fine

______ Prosecution fee ordered $40.00 per month for ______ months.

______ If checked, defendant may substitute treatment for jail time. Defendant must begin serving jail time or must begin inpatient treatment by ______

______ Pre-Sentence investigation ordered.

______ Sentencing continued to ______

______ If checked, defendant may serve jail time on days off. If so, defendant is admonished to schedule his jail time with the Sheriff in Beckham County.

______ Credit for time served if checked here.
______ Concurrent if checked here.
______ List any other cases this case relates to: ______

______ A review is set for ______

✓ **Conditions of probation:** Good behavior, payment of all fines, fees and costs.

______ Obtain an evaluation by ______ with proof of completion by ______ AND
Follow rules of evaluation and provide proof to DA's office or Probation and Parole.

______ Attend 12 step meetings ______ Random UA's ordered
______ Attend VIP by ______ ______ Attend DUI school by ______ with proof of completion by ______

✓ Probation is supervised/unsupervised. (D.O.C. / D.A.)
✓ $40.00/month Probation fee is ordered.

______ Pay restitution: $ ______ Restitution hearing scheduled for ______

______ Although the defendant appears without counsel the court finds defendant has knowingly and voluntarily waived his right to court appointed counsel.
______ Appear for a Rule 8 hearing (today) (prior to release) (within 30 days of release).

Michelle Kirby Roper
Michelle Kirby Roper, Associate District Judge

Figure 13-1

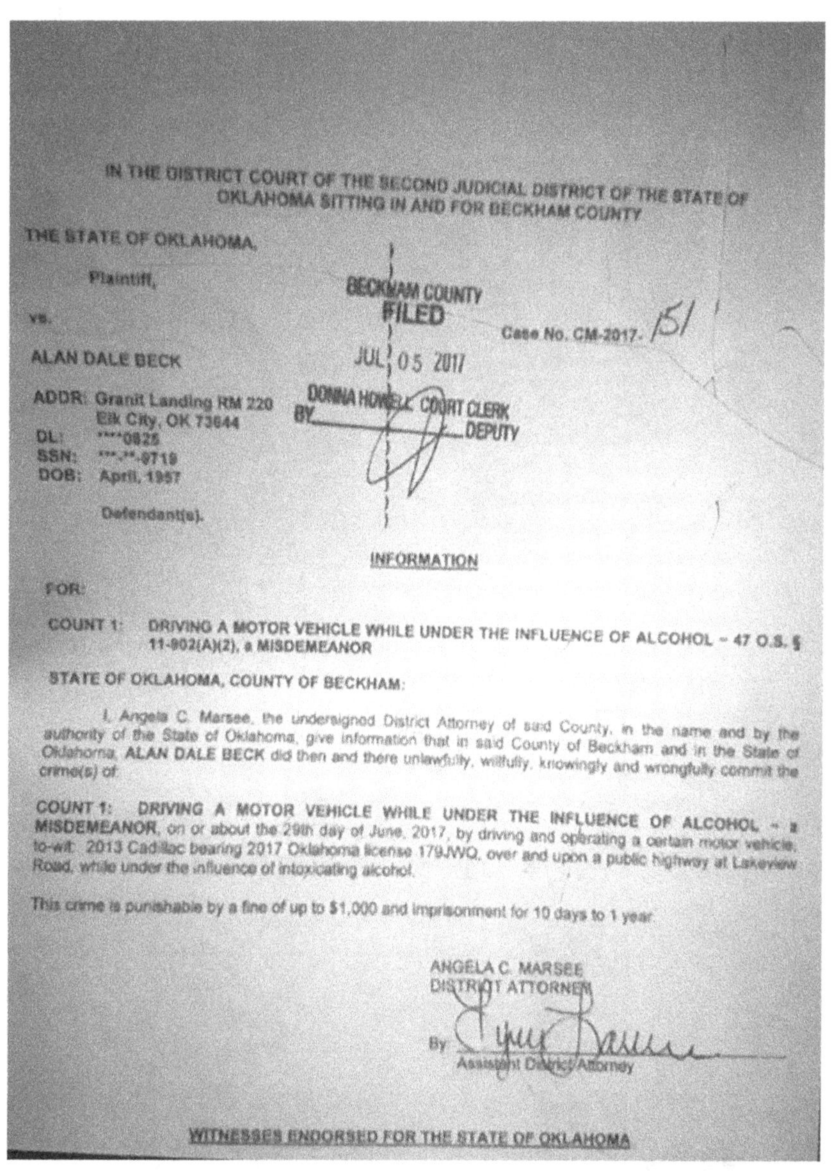

IN THE DISTRICT COURT OF THE SECOND JUDICIAL DISTRICT OF THE STATE OF OKLAHOMA SITTING IN AND FOR BECKHAM COUNTY

THE STATE OF OKLAHOMA,

Plaintiff,

vs.

ALAN DALE BECK

ADDR: Granit Landing RM 220
Elk City, OK 73644
DL: ****0825
SSN: ***-**-9719
DOB: April, 1957

Defendant(s).

BECKHAM COUNTY
FILED
JUL 05 2017
DONNA HOWELL COURT CLERK
BY ____ DEPUTY

Case No. CM-2017-151

INFORMATION

FOR:

COUNT 1: DRIVING A MOTOR VEHICLE WHILE UNDER THE INFLUENCE OF ALCOHOL – 47 O.S. § 11-902(A)(2), a MISDEMEANOR

STATE OF OKLAHOMA, COUNTY OF BECKHAM:

I, Angela C. Marsee, the undersigned District Attorney of said County, in the name and by the authority of the State of Oklahoma, give information that in said County of Beckham and in the State of Oklahoma, **ALAN DALE BECK** did then and there unlawfully, willfully, knowingly and wrongfully commit the crime(s) of:

COUNT 1: DRIVING A MOTOR VEHICLE WHILE UNDER THE INFLUENCE OF ALCOHOL – a MISDEMEANOR, on or about the 29th day of June, 2017, by driving and operating a certain motor vehicle, to-wit: 2013 Cadillac bearing 2017 Oklahoma license 179JWQ, over and upon a public highway at Lakeview Road, while under the influence of intoxicating alcohol.

This crime is punishable by a fine of up to $1,000 and imprisonment for 10 days to 1 year.

ANGELA C. MARSEE
DISTRICT ATTORNEY

By ____
Assistant District Attorney

WITNESSES ENDORSED FOR THE STATE OF OKLAHOMA

Figure 13-2

SPECIAL CONDITIONS: (Check only those that apply) The probationer will initial each item checked to acknowledge full understanding of the special conditions imposed by the Court:

___ A. COUNT(S) 1 Judgment & Sentence is Deferred to 8-23, 20 18 at 1:30 p.m. **DEFENDANT MUST APPEAR IN COURT ON THAT DATE.**

___ B. COUNT(S) ______ Defendant is hereby sentenced to ______ in the Beckham County Jail, with all of said time suspended except for ______ days. Jail time to begin in the Beckham County Jail beginning ______

___ C. Pay restitution through the District Attorney's Office per attached schedule in the sum of $ ______

X D. Pay a $40.00 per month District Attorney's Probation Fee DUE ON 20TH OF EACH MONTH OF PROBATION (Must be paid monthly OR in ONE lump sum at D.A.'s Office during first month of probation). D.A's Office/ UPF, P.O.Box 36 Arapaho, OK 73620 or in person at Beckham County Courthouse, D.A's Office. Payable by Cashier's Check or Money Order. Also Debit/Credit Card, at GovPayNet (888) 604-7888 using code #8764. Include *Defendant's name, case number, and County on payment.*

X E. Perform 15 Community Service hours with a non-profit organization that benefits the community and provide written proof of completion to the D. A.'s office by ______

< F. Defendant shall obtain a DAvg's Alcohol evaluation and provide a copy to the D.A.'s office within 30 days of sentencing and provide proof of completion of all requirements set out in that evaluation by 8-23-17

✓ G. Attend a certified 10 hour ADSAC/DUI course and provide written proof of completion to the District Attorney's Office by 8-23-17

X H. Said Defendant is to participate in the Victim's Impact Panel and provide written proof of completion to the District Attorney's Office by: 8-23-17

___ I. Attend ______ Self Help meetings per week and provide proof of attendance monthly to the District Attorney's Office.

___ J. Sign Deferred Prosecution Agreement with the D.A.'s Office for all bogus checks currently on file with the D.A.'s Office, and pay in full within the terms of probation.

___ K. Attend Anger Management or Domestic Abuse Counseling and provide proof of completion to the D.A.'s Office, and attend Review Hearing ______

X L. You are to submit to random urinalysis at the direction of the District Attorney's Office and provide the results of that UA to the D.A.'s office.

___ M. Serve ______ days in the Beckham County Jail beginning ______

___ N. Other: ______

Signed this 23 day of August, 2017

IT IS HEREBY ORDERED THAT THE PROBATIONER OBEY AND COMPLY WITH ALL OF THE RULES AND CONDITIONS OF PROBATION ABOVE.

JUDGE OF THE DISTRICT COURT

Defendant's Signature

P.O. Box 2469
Defendant's Mailing Address

Elk City OK 73648
City State Zip

580-247-8881
Phone number

Attorney for Defendant

Assistant District Attorney

Figure 13-3

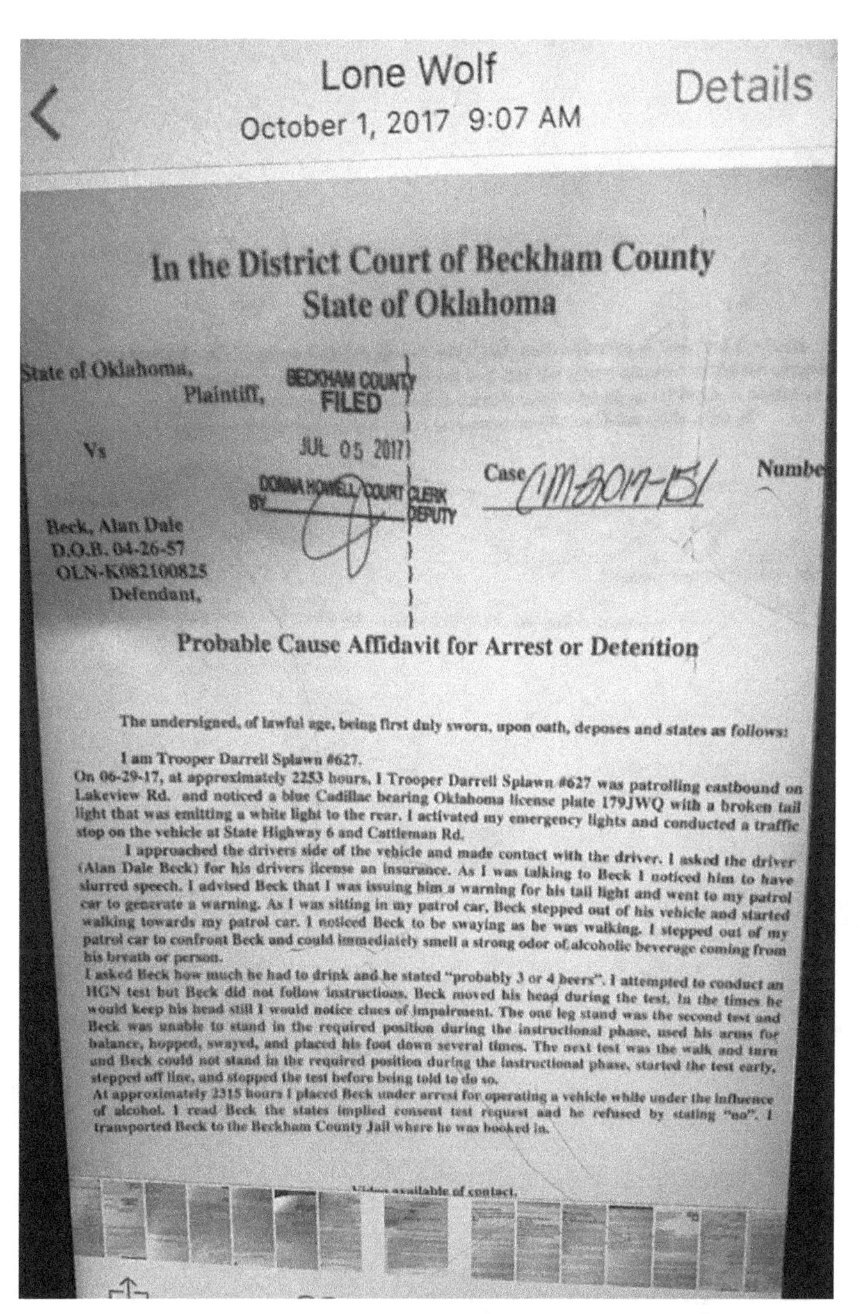

In the District Court of Beckham County
State of Oklahoma

State of Oklahoma,
Plaintiff,

BECKHAM COUNTY
FILED
JUL 05 2017
DONNA HOWELL, COURT CLERK
BY DEPUTY

Vs

Case Number CM-2017-151

Beck, Alan Dale
D.O.B. 04-26-57
OLN-K082100825
Defendant,

Probable Cause Affidavit for Arrest or Detention

The undersigned, of lawful age, being first duly sworn, upon oath, deposes and states as follows:

I am Trooper Darrell Splawn #627.
On 06-29-17, at approximately 2253 hours, I Trooper Darrell Splawn #627 was patrolling eastbound on Lakeview Rd. and noticed a blue Cadillac bearing Oklahoma license plate 179JWQ with a broken tail light that was emitting a white light to the rear. I activated my emergency lights and conducted a traffic stop on the vehicle at State Highway 6 and Cattleman Rd.

I approached the drivers side of the vehicle and made contact with the driver. I asked the driver (Alan Dale Beck) for his drivers license an insurance. As I was talking to Beck I noticed him to have slurred speech. I advised Beck that I was issuing him a warning for his tail light and went to my patrol car to generate a warning. As I was sitting in my patrol car, Beck stepped out of his vehicle and started walking towards my patrol car. I noticed Beck to be swaying as he was walking. I stepped out of my patrol car to confront Beck and could immediately smell a strong odor of alcoholic beverage coming from his breath or person.

I asked Beck how much he had to drink and he stated "probably 3 or 4 beers". I attempted to conduct an HGN test but Beck did not follow instructions. Beck moved his head during the test. In the times he would keep his head still I would notice clues of impairment. The one leg stand was the second test and Beck was unable to stand in the required position during the instructional phase, used his arms for balance, hopped, swayed, and placed his foot down several times. The next test was the walk and turn and Beck could not stand in the required position during the instructional phase, started the test early, stepped off line, and stopped the test before being told to do so.

At approximately 2315 hours I placed Beck under arrest for operating a vehicle while under the influence of alcohol. I read Beck the states implied consent test request and he refused by stating "no". I transported Beck to the Beckham County Jail where he was booked in.

Video available of contact.

Figure 13-4

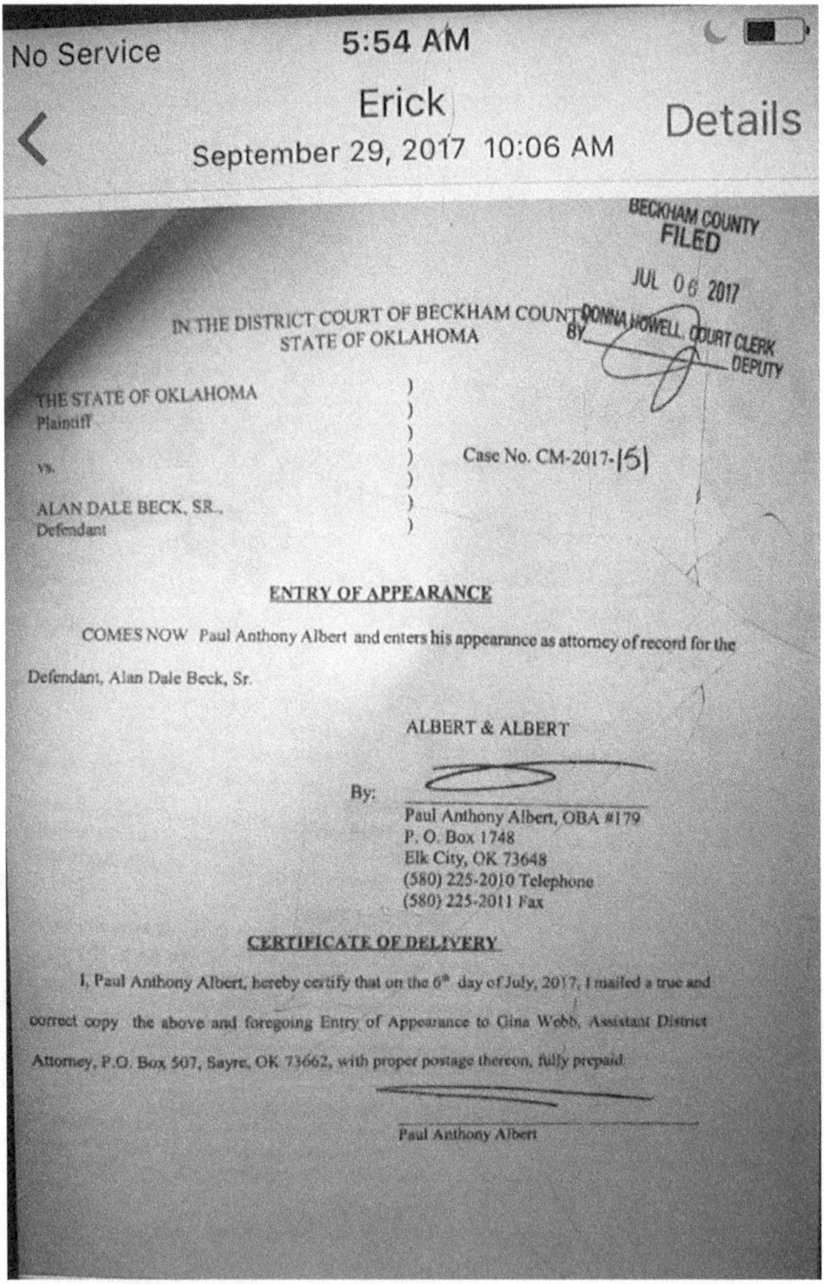

BECKHAM COUNTY
FILED
JUL 06 2017
DONNA HOWELL, COURT CLERK
BY ________ DEPUTY

IN THE DISTRICT COURT OF BECKHAM COUNTY
STATE OF OKLAHOMA

THE STATE OF OKLAHOMA)
Plaintiff)
)
vs.) Case No. CM-2017-151
)
ALAN DALE BECK, SR.,)
Defendant)

ENTRY OF APPEARANCE

COMES NOW Paul Anthony Albert and enters his appearance as attorney of record for the Defendant, Alan Dale Beck, Sr.

ALBERT & ALBERT

By: ________________
Paul Anthony Albert, OBA #179
P. O. Box 1748
Elk City, OK 73648
(580) 225-2010 Telephone
(580) 225-2011 Fax

CERTIFICATE OF DELIVERY

I, Paul Anthony Albert, hereby certify that on the 6th day of July, 2017, I mailed a true and correct copy the above and foregoing Entry of Appearance to Gina Webb, Assistant District Attorney, P.O. Box 507, Sayre, OK 73662, with proper postage thereon, fully prepaid.

____
Paul Anthony Albert

Figure 13-5

CHAPTER XIV

Sue the Judge

"One thing I have learned through the years about 'cowards' is that by in large they all seek positions of POWER as the more power a coward receives the SAFE the coward feels. And once a coward gets power the coward will become a bully. So, when dealing with a judge or anyone else and they are being a bully we know we are dealing with a 'coward'…!" (Black Robe Fever)

After numerous runs through the court systems, it had become an issue of, if Judge Paul K. Woodward did not like what a superior court ruled, whether Appeals or Supreme Court on his ruling. He was a godlike creature who would simply do again what he had been instructed to not do. As stated by his majesty himself, "In my courtroom, I make the rules." Should this not work, he would simply stay the case until the plaintiff gave up or was out of money! This, from all appearances, goes directly against the judicial system and a standard of equal application of the law. By doing what he wants, he is violating the exact job that the people of the county elected him to accomplish.

Perhaps to avoid a lot of this kind of clannish behavior, the United States needs to mandate that no attorney can function as a judge or official in an area where he or she has ties and a history with the local clientele. We are seeing that judges, attorneys, and elected officials seem to have connections, as here in Oklahoma, to the Oklahoma State University (OSU) Foundation! We will discuss this issue in great length in coming chapters.

Now that we have established this base to work from, we shall proceed back to March 2011, when Pridex was awarded the contract for the West Bottom project. You have seen how at first this case was filed under the RICO Statute and was summarily dismissed, for " it doesn't qualify under the statute." Now why on earth would it not qualify? I feel that we have a real mystery here. Perhaps unless Al Capone is involved, it doesn't meet the requirements? At any rate, Pridex was forced to file in the Oklahoma District Court in the county (Kingfisher) where this entire mess began. So here we go again, a complete redo of the case and then wait for another year or two.

So forward we go to a trial. In January 2014, the case finally went to trial, and Pridex Construction LLC was awarded $2.4 million in a unanimous jury verdict. That was a sweet yet short-lived victory. On May 26 of the same year, Pridex had only received a token payment that came from the City of Kingfisher and nothing else, then came one of the biggest shocks that anyone could possibly imagine—the judge, Paul Kent Woodward, signed an order granting Jack Stuteville a new trial that essentially overturned the unanimous jury verdict. Correct me if I am mistaken, but I don't believe the phrase reads "by a jury of your peers," which does not include "unless the judge doesn't like it." Where did this exception come from? Finally, in May 2016, the Oklahoma Court of Appeals reinstated the original jury verdict. Finally, this mess was over—or so all involved thought. Well, that was excluding district court judge Paul Kent Woodward, who again removed the reversal by simply staying the case.

At this point, it was up to Pridex to file under lis pendens so as to retrieve the monies that had been awarded and then reestablished by the appellate court here in Oklahoma. Even though the Stuteville Mob put up a vigorous defense, it was to no avail until—you guessed it—it went back to his majesty's court!

What was going on with this judge? Was he oblivious as to what was going on, or were his interests best served by stopping this truthful verdict? What may have had a major impact with his decision-making was that immediately prior to this decision, he received a donation of $1,100 for his campaign for reelection from the defendant's counsel in this case! One can only assume that such a timely donation would sway the good judge's opinion on such events. Perhaps I am only jumping to conclusions here.

In a short time later, Jack Stuteville filed with the Oklahoma Supreme Court under certiorari so that this court would take one last look to see if the finding would stand. The petition for certiorari was denied, and the bill stood! When this was accomplished and Stuteville was found to still have to pay, he had only one last unlawful direction to go—he must plead for his majesty's grace, and then they would simply stay the case.

Looking back at the lis pendens and all the properties that was beginning to affect the cash flow of the Stuteville Mob, the counsel for the defense would simply go to his majesty's court with a pleading and request that he make another ruling so that Stuteville would not be held in compliance of a higher court's lawful ruling and then back to business as usual. As you have seen here and if you so desire, beyond the trace of the court findings and orders apparently meant nothing to Lord Woodward and again, "in my courtroom, I make the rules!"

CHAPTER XV

Lord Woodward Reigns over the Land

As one recalls in the days of old, the feudal lords were the law—if one wished to call it such—over the land. They would make rulings over things that only benefited themselves. By all rights, it appears that in the Northern and Western District of Oklahoma, we may be back to the feudal system.

As you saw briefly in the last chapter, an individual company had won a unanimous jury verdict, and the judge stepped in and overturned that verdict. The ruling was next sent to the appellate court, and again, the jury verdict was returned; and again, the judge stayed the case. "It is an abuse of discretion for a trial court to grant a new trial when a jury's verdict is supported by competent evidence."

For those of us who are not familiar with the term *lis pendens*, the following is the definition that applies here within the United States of America: "Lis pendens is a written notice that a lawsuit has been filed concerning real estate, involving either the title to the property or a claimed ownership interest in it. The notice is usually filed in the county land records office. Recording a lis pendens against a piece of property alerts a potential purchaser or lender that the property's title is in question, which makes the property less attractive to a buyer or lender. Once the notice is filed, the legal title of anyone who nevertheless purchases the land or property described in the notice is subject to the ultimate decision of the lawsuit."

The good judge next vacated the notice of lis pendens: "Order expunging notice of Lis Pendens was illegally filed by Judge Paul K. Woodward on April 15, 2015." That then complicated or removed the petitioner's ability to collect the award that was awarded from the jury. "By signing and filing order expunging notice of Lis Pendens District Judge Paul K. Woodward made the case less about the plaintiff & Defendant & more about him."

Next, the defendant filed with the State Supreme Court for a review of certiorari, a "writ or order by which a higher court reviews a decision of a lower court," which took another two full years and was then denied.

During this time, the defendant, Stuteville, filed a lawsuit against Chris Poindexter and his attorney and represented himself (Prose) or so he claimed. However, the process server was from the Gungoll-Jackson Law Firm and was paid to be the process server by Gungoll-Jackson Law firm. Strange—that is the same firm that worked for Stuteville and represented him throughout all the above proceedings. Probably just a coincidence?

Our good judge, Lord Woodward, again stayed the case of collecting and stated that he will simply stay the case to next year. And, I might add, what comes after this year? And so on and so on!

Next, the judge took some extraordinary measures. In March 2018, the plaintiff, Chris Poindexter, on a trumped-up charge of home repair fraud was arrested in Beckham County. The judge denied payment due to an accusation—note, *no conviction!* What happened to that old adage "innocent until proven guilty"? Here, it gets really sticky—the person who is claiming this unexplainably had a DUI and the night in the crossbar motel removed from his record. Recall this a few chapters back. There is no legal reason how this event would set off or terminate the required payment, except in Lord Woodward's court!

The last event in this series of fiascoes was when they, our good Lord Woodward, had Chris Poindexter come to Enid, Oklahoma, for a settlement discussion. They told him if he did not accept the $629,000 ($500,000 plus $129,000 in interest) payment, the case would continue to be stayed until January 2019. In effect, take it or lose it!

Stand back for a minute and let's get a good overview of what is occurring. Larry Wright had the insurance commissioner and the state's attorney general providing a cover of protection, so to take down Larry Wright would take away the cash flow. Recall that Chris Poindexter repeatedly requested to talk to John Doak, the State of Oklahoma insurance commissioner, to advise him that Larry Wright was doing business in the State of Oklahoma after the previous insurance commissioner, Kim Holland had issued a letter to Larry Wright to cease and desist any further insurance activity whatsoever in the state.

Take one look at this and the answer is obvious. When the state's attorney general, E. Scott Pruitt, and the state's insurance commissioner, John Doak, would not even listen to a recipient of these fake bonds that Larry Wright was selling in the state and is strictly prohibited, there had to be a really good reason. Any guesses as to who may have been paid?

When Larry has over $540 million in a bank account in Clayton, Missouri, and doesn't have to pay what he has for judgments against him, there exists a problem. For the state's attorney general to not enforce what has been levied against him, you must ask yourself, What good are these smiling politicians that we the people are paying for?

He is protecting those who are protecting him from being lynched. When the word gets out as to the fraud bond market, it's all over! The old Wild West lynchings may well return to this country. Let's look at how our legislature gives themselves raises, lifetime salaries, and do nothing! We are seeing a complete and absolute sham of our justice system, and justice no longer applies to those with the money or have stolen the money. Welcome to the two-tier system!

CHAPTER XVI

The Medal of Valor

This honor, the Public Safety Officer Medal of Valor, is awarded by the president of the United States and is awarded to a public safety officer who has exhibited bravery above and beyond to save the lives of citizens. This medal is comparable to the military's Medal of Honor.

Every day, public safety officers risk their lives to protect America's citizens and communities. To honor such a commitment, Congress passed the Public Safety Officer Medal of Valor Act of 2001, which created the Public Safety Officer Medal of Valor, the highest national award for valor by a public safety officer. The medal is awarded annually by the president or vice president to public safety officers who have exhibited exceptional courage, regardless of personal safety, in the attempt to save or protect human life.

In qualifying for such an honor, Randy Poindexter, the fire chief of Kingfisher, Oklahoma, hung from the skid of a helicopter to save an elderly couple who would have shortly drowned in raging floodwaters. All this transpired on August 19, 2007. Above and beyond the call of duty, Randy hung to the skid while getting the elderly couple from their flooded pickup to safety. In doing such, Randy exhibited exceptional courage, extraordinary decisiveness, and presence of mind. Due solely to his actions and unusual swiftness regardless of his personal safety, he attempted to and saved two lives.

All was going quite well for Randy; he received his medal from former Vice President Joe Biden (Fig. 16-1). Shortly thereafter, the city of Kingfisher voted in an annual Randy Poindexter Day Celebration to honor their fire chief—a substantial honor for a great citizen and, in this writer's mind, well deserved.

Now, in early 2011, as you have seen, Chris Poindexter came to a major disagreement with the City of Kingfisher or, should I say, the Stuteville Mob. As you recall, they could not accept a cash bond for a contract that he had won, as he was the low bidder and was shuffled off to a Steve Standridge, who got him set up with Larry Wright and the fake bond market.

The Mob fully expected for Chris to tuck his tail and run when he was warned that this bunch went all the way back to Solyndra (chapter 3) and the major sham that they had pulled on this country to the tune of $535 million. Chris refused and the fight was on!

Now, mind you, Randy was a local hero, and all who knew him respected him for the great job he did for his community. Well, maybe not all! One fine day in early 2011, after the fraud bond business had reared its ugly head, the City of Kingfisher chief of police, Dennis Baker, contacted the county sheriff, Dennis Banther, and told him that he had been ordered to "dig up all the dirt" on the fire chief Randy Poindexter because he had to be terminated.

As you can imagine, not only was this very troublesome for Randy but also for our good mayor as well, Jack Stuteville. When this came out, the citizens of the city were up in arms. Shortly, a recall petition for the good mayor was circulated and, when the required number of signatures met, filed.

While all this was occurring, the mayor had instructed the new city manager, Dave Slezickey, to put together charges and terminate the fire chief.

You may recall dear Mr. Slezickey from the earlier discussion where he left the city of Anadarko, Oklahoma, and around that exact time, the large cash reserve that the city had disappeared? Gee, I wonder where it went. Okay, lest I digress!

One fine morning, Mr. Slezickey appeared in the Kingfisher fire chief's office and visited for some time. With him, he had six and a half pages of directives to cover. Within these, he had documented that contracting with an employee was a misdemeanor and that he had already consulted with the assistant district attorney (ADA) Brian Slabotsky about filing charges on the fire chief. Apparently, the fire chief had purchased needed accessories for the brush truck (a truck used for fighting brushfires that was a four-wheel drive and lighter than a standard fire engine) from an employee and, in so doing, saved the fire department approximately $4,400 for something that they needed badly. I'm certain at this time you are thinking, *How anyone could be so foolish and wasteful as to do something this serious and save money?* But wait, what was this guy thinking! Now comes the real proverbial straw. The chief went out on his own and purchased from a surplus store a cardiac monitor for one of the three ambulances the city had (the other two already had such equipment) and saved the city $27,475. The going price for such was $27,500! But since he paid for it out of his own pocket, he actually saved the city the full amount. Not to mention he was on his own time and did it for the single reason that perhaps this small piece of equipment may save the life of a single citizen sometime in the future. Well worth the price!

Why, this foolhardy fire chief had actually put the cardiac monitor on the maintenance contract for the fire department. This meant that it was an approved purchase for the county, not the city. What on earth was this civil servant thinking, actually looking out for the citizens. We shall not allow such a good deed to go unpunished.

The fire chief was forced to hire an attorney to defend his good deeds from the soon-to-be-terminated mayor. The attorney that he hired immediately went to the county commissioners and obtained sworn statements that the funds that paid for the parts for the brush truck were county funds that the chief had prior approval to purchase. The funds were not even from the city, therefore making it impossible for the City to charge the chief with any type of crime.

The legal expenses that the chief incurred totaled $7,500, but as the chief stated, it was worth it to clear his good name!

Unfortunately, the battle did not stop there, as the city manager, Dave Slezickey, terminated the fire chief shortly thereafter on more bogus charges.

FOX 25 out of Oklahoma City reported the following:

> The former fire chief for the city of Kingfisher is fighting to get his job back. The city manager fired Chief Randy Poindexter earlier last month (August 2013). Now Poindexter has filed an appeal to be put back in charge of the town's fire department."
>
> In a letter to city board of commissioners, Poindexter's attorney, Matt Smith, writes the termination was "an orchestrated farce intended only to discredit a faithful public servant and hero."
>
> "City Manger Dave Slezickey says he cannot comment on a pending personnel action but says he did send multiple memorandums to Poindexter that 'provided guidance and direction.'" He says Poindexter had ample notice to the reasons he was to be terminated that ended with a twelve-minute hearing. "He did not request additional time; he demanded that he would not meet at this time unless given more time, Slezickey told Fox 25."
>
> Matt Smith, Poindexter's attorney says there was a request for additional time to prepare for the hearing, and up until the final notice of termination, the city failed to provide enough specifics about the reasons for his firing. "Chief Poindexter was railroaded into being terminated, a 12-minute hearing was conducted by city manager Dave Slezicky; he fired Chief Poindexter for basically doing his job." According to documents provided by Poindexter, one of Slezickey's concerns was Poindexter working outside his scheduled duty shift. However, the three specific days mentioned in his termination memorandum

were times when Poindexter was responding to emergencies. Including a time when emergency crews made a wrong turn and Poindexter was first on the scene to provide emergency CPR to a dying man.

"I think you can ask his widow and she's very thankful that Randy Poindexter didn't call Dave Slezicky first and ask permission before he showed up at her house that night to try and save her husband," Smith told Fox 25.

"I had never heard that, but any employee that accrues compensatory time requires prior approval," Slezickey said. Slezickey said he did not know the details of the incidents that Poindexter worked without his approval.

Slezickey also wrote Poindexter failed to get permission to go on a trip to the nation's capital. Though, Poindexter did write a memo to Slezickey requesting that permission, but never heard back from the city manager. In that memo Poindexter wrote he was paying for the entire trip himself and the purpose of the annual trip was to lobby for federal firefighting funds for Oklahoma, along with training from the National Fire Academy. Poindexter says his self-funded trips over the past six years have resulted in nearly $500,000 in federal funds for the city of Kingfisher.

"He's going to get federal funds for Kingfisher?" Slezickey asked when we showed him the letter Poindexter wrote to him. Slezickey says he never knew the purpose of the trip was to lobby for federal funds for the city. He refused to say if he thought such a trip was appropriate for the city's fire chief to take citing the ongoing personnel action.

> "Randy wants the city of Kingfisher to know that he did his job correctly and still wants to be their fire chief," Smith said.

We are, however, very thankful that the case did not go before his Majesty's court, as there would have been a risk of the death penalty!

Source: http://okcfox.com/archive/medal-of-valor-fire-chief-fighting-for-his-job

Medal of valor fire chief fighting for his job

By Phil Cross Wednesday, October 9th 2013

Figure 16-1as

KINGFISHER — The former fire chief for the city of Kingfisher is fighting to get his job back. The city manager fired Chief Randy Poindexter earlier last month. Now Poindexter has filed an appeal to be put back in charge of the town's fire department.

In a letter to city board of commissioners, Poindexter's attorney Matt Smith writes the termination was "an orchestrated farce intended only to discredit a faithful public servant and hero." It was just three years ago when Poindexter attended a ceremony in Washington D.C. where he was awarded the President's Public Safety Officer Medal of Valor for his efforts to save people during the 2007 floods in Kingfisher.

City Manger Dave Slezickey says he cannot comment on a pending personnel action, but says he did send multiple memorandums to Poindexter that "provided guidance and direction." He says Poindexter had ample notice to the reasons he was to be terminated that ended with a 12 minute hearing. "He did not request additional time; he demanded that he would not meet at this time unless given more time," Slezickey told Fox 25.

Poindexter's attorney says there was a request for additional time to prepare for the hearing and up until the final notice of termination the city failed to provide enough specifics about the reasons for his firing.

Chief Poindexter was railroaded into being terminated, a 12 minute hearing was conducted by city manager Dave Slezicky; he fired Chief Poindexter for basically doing his job," Smith said.

According to documents provided by Poindexter, one of Slezickey's concerns was Poindexter working outside his scheduled duty shift. However, the three specific days mentioned in his termination memorandum were times when Poindexter was responding to emergencies. Including a time when emergency crews made a wrong turn and Poindexter was first on the scene to provide emergency CPR to a dying man.

"I think you can ask his widow and she's very thankful that Randy Poindexter didn't call Dave Slezicky first and ask permission before he showed up at her house that night to try and save her husband," Smith told Fox 25.

"I had never heard that, but any employee that accrues compensatory time requires prior approval," Slezickey said. Slezickey said he did not know the details of the incidents that Poindexter worked without his approval.

Slezickey also wrote Poindexter failed to get permission to go on a trip to the nation's capital. Though, Poindexter did write a memo to Slezickey requesting that permission, but never heard back from the city manager. In that memo Poindexter wrote he was paying for the entire trip himself and the purpose of the annual trip was to lobby for federal firefighting funds for Oklahoma, along with training from the National Fire Academy. Poindexter says his self-funded trips over the past six years have resulted in nearly $500,000 in federal funds for the city of Kingfisher.

Figure 16-1bs

"He's going to get federal funds for Kingfisher?" Slezickey asked when we showed him the letter Poindexter wrote to him. Slezickey says he never knew the purpose of the trip was to lobby for federal funds for the city. He refused to say if he thought such a trip was appropriate for the city's fire chief to take citing the ongoing personnel action.

"Randy wants the city of Kingfisher to know that he did his job correctly and still wants to be their fire chief," Smith said.

Figure 16-1cs

CHAPTER XVII

The Chickens Are Coming Home to Roost

Our economy depends upon honest and fair dealing rather than deceit and fraud. In the case of Steve Alan Standridge, he carried out several schemes to defraud, resulting in multimillion-dollar losses to companies and individuals across the state of Arkansas and many others. On July 2, 2014, Mr. Steve Alan Standridge of Mount Ida, Arkansas, plead guilty to one count of wire fraud from a twenty-three-count indictment that was issued by a federal grand jury in the Western District of Arkansas and to one count of money laundering from a twelve-count indictment issued by a federal grand jury in the Eastern District of Arkansas, which was transferred to the Western District of Arkansas.

On December 5, 2014, he was sentenced to sixty months in prison followed by three years of supervised release and victim restitution totaling $7,096,417.35 for money laundering and wire fraud.

Steve Standridge had used his longtime business and connections in his hometown and state to deceive and defraud individuals and banks out of millions of dollars.

This scheme did not end in the state of Arkansas, as two of his longtime associates and friends were right here in Kingfisher, Oklahoma, and the other in Jacksonville, Florida. You guessed it correctly; they were Jack Stuteville in Oklahoma and Larry Wright in Florida. If you recall, in an earlier chapter, Jack Stuteville had Pridex contact Steve Standridge in early 2011 and then the link to Larry

Wright. More fraudulent bonds! The question begs to be asked; where is our law enforcement and all our criminal investigators while this is going on? I will attempt to answer that exact question in the next twelve chapters.

In effect, some of these criminals have grown so large that they now incorporate elements within our government. We are going to focus initially on a few of those that are within the body count or, should I say, in part responsible for.

Mr. Gregory Hunt was a construction contractor who had done business with Steve Standridge for years. On the average, he and his brother Michael would annually spend $300K to $400K on premiums for their construction business. In 2009, the construction business was slowing down, and it was becoming an issue to keep working in Arkansas as well as the United States overall. With the economy sliding downhill, things were looking somewhat grim, and bankruptcy was on the horizon.

Steve Standridge appeared to come to the rescue of the Hunt brothers and instigated a falsified financial statement. He had Gregory Hunt sign it to state it was accurate, whereas he would receive a loan that he could put in an interest-bearing account and it would be paid off at the completion of the job. One major problem was that by that time, Gregory Hunt was in prison and the money had vaporized into an account maintained by Standridge. In reality, Standridge needed to show he had the funds available to shore up Wright's fraud bond market so they could continue to peddle fake bonds.

According to the Arkansas Business Journal, Steve Standridge had taken out $6.7 million dollars in premium finance loans from the Chambers Bank in Danville, Arkansas. Multiple banks and multiple loans were made from these falsified financial statements not only in Arkansas but also in Missouri. Premier Bank and Cornerstone Finance in Columbia, Missouri, was also on their target list. Recall our state representative from Oklahoma, Todd Russ, who was "helping the FDIC" at these facilities, and they were both soon closed down! Interesting how these chickens all seem to focus on various destinations. I would say buzzards, but they were closing in on the kill, not on the already dead.

When a gentleman was speaking with the family of Gregory and Michael Hunt, they were asked if they had ever heard of a man named Jack Stuteville, they responded to the positive and stated that he was the banker who called all the time asking to verify that we owed Steve Standridge $4 million. They, the family, had been told by Standridge to just go along with whatever Jack Stuteville said. As you recall, Michael, his wife, and another couple were killed in a plane crash shortly after one of these calls on June 13, 2010! There were no reported eyewitnesses; however, a witness reported hearing a low-flying airplane followed by the sound of an impact. The description and the cause indicated by the FAA/NTSB do not agree!

Gregory A. Hunt, Michael's brother of Russellville, Arkansas, pleaded guilty to aiding and abetting bank fraud on March 2, 2012. Hunt was sentenced on October 31, 2012, to thirty-three months' imprisonment.

While he was in prison, he had agreed to testify in behalf of Steve Standridge, and in return, he was to receive a greatly reduced sentence. On February 25, 2013, he had a massive coronary event and was rushed to the hospital. He was revived and coherent and was speaking with his parents and his other brother. Two female guards from the prison came in and forced the parents and his brother from the room. That was the last time that they saw their son alive. Coincidence? Doubtful!

While Standridge was on his money capturing rampage, another that was listed in the "loose ends" chapter had personally lent him a few million dollars, and strangely enough, the repayment arrived just after his death and was never cashed! How convenient!

In each of these accident events, it appears that only one individual was the target, yet each case has yielded three for collateral damage. So to sum this up, six people died as nothing more than being collateral damage, and all had only one common thread! They were with someone who had done business with Steve Standridge, the Stuteville Mob, and/or the good reverend Dr. Larry Wright. I suppose that we should also include within all this the federal government swamp that was trying to and still is trying to overthrow our democracy!

Steve Standridge was trying to corner the insurance market, or that is what he was professing to his friends and clients in Arkansas. However, if one looks closer, that was not it at all. He was accruing funds, if one can call these unlawful actions accruing for the sole purpose of keeping Larry Wright and Stuteville in the business of syphoning funds off federal guarantees and guaranteed loans. The single purpose of collapsing our economy is a takeover, as we have seen from inside the government. Standridge stated that he was borrowing monies such as from the Hot Springs Corporation $2.7 million dollars to buy insurance agencies. That was never his reason nor did he purchase one new agency!

I have heard the expression "Bread lines are a good thing." We know people are getting fed. Honestly, is that a good thing? You grow up in a capitalistic country and the harder you work, the more rewards are earned by that person. What this bunch is doing is trying to remove this from our country forever. It's the same old story; take what you can, then steal all you can carry.

Steve Standridge was the fall guy and promoted the Stuteville Mob, which includes the good reverend Dr. Larry Wright. Don't forget; the good doctor has millions of dollars of legal judgements against him that he is not paying a single red cent on. Why is the US government, or factions within, covering for him as the overthrow plan looms on? That is some of what Gregory Hunt was about to testify to when he was killed! The old saying "Silence is golden" for the mob—that's their goal!

CHAPTER XVIII

The RICO Statute

In 1970, the Racketeer Influenced and Corrupt Organizations Act (RICO) became a federal law designed to combat organized crime in the United States. It allows prosecution and civil penalties for racketeering activity performed as part of an ongoing criminal enterprise. Such activity may include illegal gambling, bribery, kidnapping, murder, money laundering, counterfeiting, embezzlement, drug trafficking, slavery, and a host of other unsavory business practices.

> To convict a defendant under RICO, the government must prove that the defendant engaged in two or more instances of racketeering activity and that the defendant directly invested in, maintained an interest in, or participated in a criminal enterprise affecting interstate or foreign commerce. The law has been used to prosecute members of the mafia, the Hells Angels motorcycle gang, and Operation Rescue, an anti-abortion group, among many others.

A gentleman by the name of Jack Logsdon was wrongly imprisoned for a period of over ten years under the above statute in part due to a lying, self-serving DA named Charles Rogers and a greedy banker and head of the Stuteville Mob, Jack Stuteville, who needed a fall guy and the fraud DA to assist in the fall!

Here, this story takes a real sharp left turn. Recall that Judge Friot, the federal judge in the Western District of Oklahoma, just could not see clear to allow a suit under the RICO Statute to proceed in the case of Pridex where there were multiple patrons taking part in a fraud upon a single contractor/bond user.

Now, this DA Rogers floats these charges past a court, and it prosecuted only one person and none of the coperpetrators who signed his checks and were in on the act. The defense attorney needs to equally be investigated, as the deals she made for her client was effectively holding the leash on the way to the slaughter platform.

As I am learning more about all this, there is a document called District Attorney's Narrative (DAN) that each occupant of the Department of Corrections (DOC) has written about the incarcerated person or, should I say, about their case if they are to be incarcerated for greater than two years. From my understanding, each detainee is owed this DAN and has the right to see and to read such. As you will see, Mr. Jack Logsdon was deprived of this right until he had been a guest of the DOC for over seven years! The question that each of us should ask is why. Why would the DA fail to complete his job? Was he overworked, or was there a more precarious reason for this lack of attention to his job?

After nearly two years, Jack Logsdon had been told of such and by three different case managers and the Logan County Courthouse that such never existed; however, he found nearing year five that it did. According to State Statute 19215.39, I should have received it and had the opportunity to respond to this. As it would appear, nearly everyone wants nonviolent offenders out of the DOC within seven years, Mr. Logsdon included. Well, that was excluding the Logan County Courthouse.

As Mr. Logsdon stated, he had dismissed the conspiracy theory long ago, but perhaps he had dived off that diving board a bit premature. It appears that the Attorney General's Office and the DA for Logan County were being supported by Stuteville and his banking operations. So one must assume, since he profited from Logsdon being the fall guy, that he may have pushed this prosecution theory in that direction. Why else would the DAN be held for such a long period of time and even disavowed that such existed? At one point, there was a new case manager for Jack Logsdon, Mrs. Welcher, and she had requested the DAN if it could be located. She stated that she would get it for Jack Logsdon on Monday. He went in on Monday, and she stated, "Here it is!" She was called out about that time, and she said, "Take it to Mr. Lee, and he will make a copy of it for you." When he did such and showed it to Mr. Lee, he looked at it briefly and said, "Sure, I will get you a copy." Then he read it briefly, looked at it in dismay and disbelief, and stated, "You cannot have this." Unfortunately, Jack had not had time to read it and see what it said. Jack asked why and said that he was entitled to it. He stated the only way that Jack could get this was to have his attorney subpoena it or sequester it from the court. Mind you that this document (DAN) should have been provided to Jack within the first month that he was incarcerated.

It is very curious how Mr. Logsdon was prosecuted and convicted under the RICO statute. As a matter of fact, he was unaware that he was being prosecuted under such until his conviction! He then had to research what it was and try to figure out whom he had conspired with. He did find out, by Mr. Lee, that there were eight witnesses that had testified against him, and he was unable to find out who or what they had said.

For that matter, he was not allowed to have any of his witnesses testify on his behalf or even himself. Do you think that perhaps his defense attorney may have been in on the hit? According to Mr. Logsdon, he continued to wait for the judge to call him, and that never happened. With no voice on his behalf, he was hauled off to jail for a nonviolent crime that he never did! Accused and convicted of conspiring in organized crime, and yet only he went to prison? Again, why and how did this happen?

The next big question is, why was the trial transferred to Payne County? Here is a very interesting fact: the alleged fraud took place in Logan County, Oklahoma, and they, Mr. Logsdon's attorneys, managed to convince him that he could not receive a fair trial in Guthrie (Logan County), Oklahoma, so it would be necessary to move the case to Stillwater (Payne County). The reason was that most of his "victims" were from in and around Guthrie. In reality, the bought-and-paid-for judge and the DA, as is noted later, were on the payroll of the bank, and they were doing nothing more than leading the lamb to slaughter.

Perhaps if a serious audit of Charles Rogers, Rob Hudson, and his boss, Drew Edmonson, the attorney general of Oklahoma were accomplished, an answer could be found! Also, we would need to audit the source of these funds that would be essential! As a side note, Rob Hudson was on the bank board and received a monthly stipend and received contributions for his election. I don't suppose that would have a tendency to influence his discretion or attitude toward anyone being prosecuted? Even perhaps if the bank owner were lending and sending clients to Mr. Logsdon's businesses, the one being prosecuted? No, I'm certain they could not be swayed by a few measly dollars.

Let's take a quick look at this; Stuteville lends money to close clients to invest in businesses of Mr. Logsdon and strongly suggests that they will get a great return! Be certain that you tell your friends to invest their monies. Of course, he most likely would not lend the other folks' money to invest. Wait a minute; there is a word that describes this process—let me see—Ponzi Scheme maybe? Let's take a look at this by definition: "a form of fraud in which belief in the success of a nonexistent enterprise is fostered by the payment of quick returns to the first investors from money invested by later investors." It was a classic Ponzi scheme built on treachery and lies.

You know, this seems to exactly fit the crime by exact definition. The only part missing is where Stuteville lent clients of his money to go invest, suckered monies from later investors, collapsed the scheme, and walked away. But also, by definition, if one Mr. Jack Logsdon was charged and convicted under the RICO statute, Stuteville would have to be. Now there is some food for thought!

Looking diligently at the standards of the RICO statute, it appears that the prosecution of certain sectors of the banking business that have been working in Oklahoma and a few other states may be an open and closed case!

CHAPTER XIX

The Wright Protection

THROUGHOUT THIS BOOK, from time to time, I have referred to an individual named Larry James Wright. I have referred to him in usually less-than-sterling terms. As in most of the cases, he is and/or was the defendant in a number of lawsuits where he has written fake bonds for various reasons and then pocketed the premiums for the bond that simply did not exist. In brief, in 1986 and 1988, Wright was convicted of filing false SF28 (affidavit of individual surety), and then again in 1995, he was convicted of grand theft and sentenced to a federal prison in Jessup, Georgia. Along with these, he was convicted of similar charges in the 1980s, 1990, and 1993.

We will now start our most current escapade around the 2011 time frame when Larry James Wright had over $540 million in a bank account in Clayton, Missouri. Now, I'm certain that most of us happen to have an extra $540 million lying around, so we can understand the dilemma he was in. Unfortunately, I'm not one of them and see no reason why he didn't just pay the judgement against him.

In 2004, Special Agent Hamblin of the Army's Criminal Investigation Division (CID) opened an investigation on our man Larry Wright for fraudulent issuance of bogus individual surety bonds to the US government. In March, Hamblin issued a criminal alert notice (CAN) number 0006-04-CID274. The CAN stated that individuals George Gowen, Edward C. Scarborough, and you guessed it, Larry James Wright, were issuing their fake bonds on

DOD contracts. The purpose of the CAN was to warn DOD officials of the possible fraudulent activity of the individual sureties and to collect information that would be useful to investigators.

On October 7, 2011, a press release was issued that stated "Florida CFO Jeff Atwater Announces Arrest of Jacksonville Man for Grand Theft." Let's take a look at this: Larry James Wright was arrested for selling surety bonds without a license and pocketing the premiums. Reflecting back, he was ordered to no longer conduct business in Oklahoma in 2008 for the same issue when Kim Holland recognized his activities and expelled him from doing business in Oklahoma. In 2011, Kim Holland was replaced by John Doak, and you saw his earlier statement. And he would not do anything to the fake bond salesman, as he wasn't licensed to sell his bonds (fake or not) in Oklahoma.

Larry James Wright allegedly sold a bid bond to a Massachusetts construction company without a valid license and kept the premiums of some $180,000. The department issued a cease and desist order and booked Wright into the Florida Duval County Jail. If convicted, he could see fifteen years behind bars.

This is where it begins to get really interesting or fuzzy, if you will. The United States government filed charges against this group that included Larry James Wright and the bunch. The bunch then filed a suit against the Army, DOD, and the Small Business Administration (SBA) for multiple violations of the Privacy Act, and they prevailed. Pay no attention to the fake bond issue and letting others know what they were up to. The Army put out truthful information, and that was illegal? From here on, it's a crazy world. The Oklahoma Kiowa County Sheriff requested the DA John Wampler to write out an arrest warrant for Jack Stuteville, Lori Diaz, and Larry Wright—he refused! Why and how could this be occurring?

As you recall from an earlier chapter, Pridex Construction was awarded a unanimous jury verdict that listed Mr. Wright to pay a settlement of now over $2 million. At the time of this writing, he still has refused to pay this judgement and many others. With $540 million in the bank, why can't he just pay this one judgement? Now the question is this, who is protecting him and, more importantly, why?

On March 5, 2014, Chris Poindexter met with the Kiowa County Oklahoma sheriff Mr. Bill Lancaster as referenced above. After a thorough briefing, the Sheriff wrote out a request for the district attorney John Wampler to sign an arrest warrant for none other than Larry James Wright, Jack Stuteville. And the assistant to Wright, a Lori Diaz (Fig. 19-1). The next surprise was that John Wampler would not sign and issue an arrest warrant. Let's look a little deeper; Kim Holland had recently been promoted/had taken a job that moved her from her current position of insurance commissioner. John Doak came in and forgot about the cease and desist order issued against Wright and his company and even refused to investigate when evidence was produced to show Wright was doing business in Oklahoma.

What good are public officials when they openly refuse to do their jobs? (*Makes one think a little about the FAA and "the Regulations Do Not apply to Us."*) I believe the answer is exactly nothing.

So now with the insurance commissioner and the DA in District 4 aware of it—the state's attorney general's assistant should be aware of this—one can only make the assumption that the attorney general, at that time E. Scott Pruitt, was aware of it, and no one even lifted a finger to stop this madness.

Boldly stated from Mr. Larry Wright was the fact that his company, The Underwriters Group, does business routinely with the FAA Southwest Region, the USDA, and many other government agencies.

With the alert notices from CID and the criminal past, still, this group sells their wares on military installations and pretty much anywhere a government-backed loan exists.

Apparently, there are a lot of our civil servants and the "swamp" that have their hands dirty on this one and have no intention of stopping this train and probably not realizing the buck will stop here!

Page 1 of

KIOWA COUNTY SHERIFF
301 S Jefferson Hobart, Oklahoma 73651
(580)726-3265

INCIDENT REPORT

Report Number	0003521	NCIC Number
Reported On	03/05/2014 11:20	
Incident Date / Time	04/01/2011 08:00 **and** 01/30/2014 17:00	
Type of Report	PROPERTY	
Arrestee		
Suspect	DIAZ, LORI	
Suspect	STUTEVILLE, JACK	
Suspect	THE UNDERWRITERS GROUP, INC	
Suspect	WRIGHT, LARRY JAMES	
Report Person		
Originate Officer	LANCASTER, BILL	
Location of Offense	100 East Main Street	
IBR	26A FRAUD - FALSE PRETENSES/SWINDLE/CONFIDENCE GAME	
Charge Description	2 O.S. § 5-62.9(A)(6) • Making a misrepresentation for the purpose of defrauding.	
Case Status	OPEN	
Investigator Assigned		
Date Assigned		
Date Cleared		
Clearance Type		
Clearance Disposition		

4/1/201

Figure 19-1as

Page 2 of

KIOWA COUNTY SHERIFF
301 S Jefferson Hobart, Oklahoma 73651
(580)726-3265

INCIDENT REPORT

ADMINISTRATIVE • Send this report to OSBI as a part of SIBRS ? NO					
Case Number	0003521	**Report Date**	03/05/2014 11:20	**Case Approved**	NO
Occured Between	04/01/2011 08:00 **and**	01/30/2014 17:00		**Case Sensitive**	NO
Type of Report	PROPERTY				
Case Status	OPEN	**Clearance Type**			
Clear Disposition				**Date Assigned**	

OFFENSE(S) INFORMATION		
1	**26A FRAUD - FALSE PRETENSES/SWINDLE/CONFIDENCE GAME**	
	Charge From	DISTRICT ATTORNEY
	Charge Desc.	2 O.S. § 5-62.9(A)(6) • MAKING A MISREPRESENTATION FOR THE PURPOSE OF DEFRAUDING.

PARTY INFORMATION

1 **POINDEXTER, CHRISTOPHER**

Party Type VICTIM

DOB	6/24/1966	**Age**	47
Sex	MALE	**Race**	WHITE
Hair	BROWN	**Eye**	BROWN
Height		**Weight**	
Ethnicity	NOT HISPANIC ORIGIN		
SSN			
DL	004064847		

Home Address

Address	P.O. Box 426
City	Lonewolf
State	OK
Zip Code	73655
Phone	(580)846-2972

2 **THE UNDERWRITERS GROUP, INC.**

Party Type SUSPECT

DOB		**Age**	
Sex		**Race**	
Hair		**Eye**	
Height		**Weight**	
Ethnicity			
SSN			
DL			

3 **WRIGHT, LARRY JAMES**

Party Type SUSPECT

DOB		**Age**	
Sex	MALE	**Race**	WHITE

4/1/201.

Figure 19-1bs

Page 3 of

KIOWA COUNTY SHERIFF
301 S Jefferson Hobart, Oklahoma 73651
(580)726-3265

INCIDENT REPORT

PARTY INFORMATION

3 WRIGHT, LARRY JAMES

Hair	GRAY OR PARTIALLY GRAY	Eye	
Height		Weight	
Ethnicity	NOT HISPANIC ORIGIN		
SSN			
DL			

Home Address
Address 13936 Atlantic Blvd
City Jacksonville
State FL
Zip Code 32225
Phone (904)551-1975

4 DIAZ, LORI

Party Type SUSPECT

DOB	1/7/1975	Age	39
Sex	FEMALE	Race	WHITE HISPANIC
Hair	BROWN	Eye	BROWN
Height	5' 4"	Weight	160 LBS.
Ethnicity	HISPANIC ORIGIN		
SSN			
DL	H620524755070		

Home Address
Address 28197 Trigg Rd
City Hillard
State FL
Zip Code 32046
Phone

5 STUTEVILLE, JACK

Party Type SUSPECT

DOB	9/21/1947	Age	66
Sex	MALE	Race	WHITE
Hair		Eye	
Height		Weight	
Ethnicity			
SSN			
DL	K080666007		

Home Address
Address 1009 Park Plaza
City Kingfisher
State OK
Zip Code 73750
Phone (405)368-7713

6 LANCASTER, BILL

Party Type OFFICER

4/1/201

Figure 19-1cs

Page 5 of

KIOWA COUNTY SHERIFF
301 S Jefferson Hobart, Oklahoma 73651
(580)726-3265

INCIDENT REPORT

SUSPECT(S) INFORMATION

3	**DIAZ, LORI**
	Medical Problems
	Surgery
	Broken Bones
	Other Description
4	**STUTEVILLE, JACK**
	Victim Of Offender N/A

VICTIM(S) INFORMATION

1	**POINDEXTER, CHRISTOPHER**	
	Victim Type	INDIVIDUAL
	Type of Injury	NONE
	NCIC Number	
	Location of Injury	
	Injury Location Code	

PROPERTY INFORMATION

1	**COPY OF BOGUS BOND**		
	Names	POINDEXTER, CHRISTOPHER	FINDER
		THE UNDERWRITERS GROUP, INC,	OWNER
	Seized / Recovered	04/22/2011 18:00	
	Descripiton Code	Documents/Personal or Business	
	Loss Code	Evidence	
	Quantity	1 Dosage Units/Items	
	Brand		
	Description	COPY OF BOGUS BOND	
	Total Value	$0.00	
	Entered NCIC	NO	
	NCIC Number		

NARRATIVE(S) INFORMATION

1 **LANCASTER, BILL** • Report this narrative to OSBI ? **NO**

On March 05th, 2014 I met with Chris Poindexter in reference to receiving a bogus bond via mail.

Poindexter was awarded a bid for a construction job by the City of Kingfisher in April 2011. He was told he needed to obtain a performance bond by bid specifications. Poindexter was referred to, The Underwriters Group, Inc AKA Underwriters Reinsurance Company, LTD by the City Mayor Jack Stuteville.

Poindexter contacted an individual named, Steve Standridge about obtaining a bond. Standridge then put Larry James Wright in contact with Poindexter.

Wright told Poindexter he had been approved for a bond and that he needed to send the money to, The Underwriters Group, Inc at 8777 San Jose Blvd Jacksonville, FL 32257. At the last minute Poindexter was informed to write the checks payable to PS Trust. It is believed this was done based on a judgement against The Underwriters Group Inc. The check was sent via Fed Ex to the address above from Anadarko bank and Trust in April 2011.

4/1/201

Figure 19-1ds

Page 6 of

KIOWA COUNTY SHERIFF
301 S Jefferson Hobart, Oklahoma 73651
(580)726-3265

INCIDENT REPORT

NARRATIVE(S) INFORMATION

1 **LANCASTER, BILL** (Continued)

On April 22, 2011 an Affidavit of Individual Surety was signed and notarized by a, Lori Diaz (Harris). It was notarized by a Laura McDaniels in the State of Florida. It was then sent to Poindexter via UPS Overnight.

Poindexter received this bogus bond at his store, CJ's Convenient Store 100 East Main Street Lone Wolf, Kiowa County, Oklahoma 73655. Randy Poindexter then took the bogus bond to the City of Kingfisher and turned it over to Bill Tucker City Clerk for the City of Kingfisher.

Poindexter was informed by Kingfisher City Manager Richard Reynolds that the bond was not valid/bogus. Therefore Poindexter lost the contract to complete the job he was hired to do.

On January 30th, 2014 Poindexter was awarded a civil judgement in Kingfisher County, Oklahoma.

2 **LANCASTER, BILL** • Report this narrative to OSBI ? **NO**

On March 31st, 2014 I met with Poindexter at approximately 0930. At this time he gave me a video/DVD of depositions of Larry Wright and Tina Lyles. I did review this video that evening at 2215 hours.

I scheduled a meeting with Poindexter at 1000 hours on Tuesday, April 01, 2014 to see if I could further assist him with his case.

3 **LANCASTER, BILL** • Report this narrative to OSBI ? **NO**

On April 01st, 2014 I met with Poindexter at 1000 hours in reference to the DVD/video he provided me on 03/31/2014. After reviewing the DVD I did see and understand that Larry Wright admits to conversations with the former Mayor of Kingfisher (City) Jack Stuteville about providing a bond for Pridex Construction LLC. He (Wright) says that Stuteville informs him that the bond Pridex needs is the same as the two prepared for a previous contract (CSR Nationwide) and this will satisfy the cities needs.

Tina Lyles was also deposed on this video. She answers questions about Wright's fraudulent bonds. Lyles says that she began to believe that Wright was involved wrong doing in 2008. Her words were, the walls were closing in after the IRS and other agents came to her home. She also reviews e-mails covering that a refund is due to Pridex Construction and that she had forward these emails to Wright. And that was the end of her involvement.

At this point in the investigation I see that Larceny under 21-1711 is a possible charge to be filed in this case. Robert E. Lee, Oklahoma Insurance Commission provided Sheriff Banther with this information as a possible charge. Chris Poindexter pointed this information out to me.

At this time I have asked Poindexter to seek DA John Wampler opinion prior to requesting a warrant.

IT IS UNLAWFUL TO FALSELY REPORT A CRIME.
WILL YOU PROSECUTE: (Y/N) _______

REPORTED BY	DATE	REPORTING OFFICER	DATE	REVIEWED OFFICER	DATE

4/1/201

Figure 19-1es

Page 6 of 6

KIOWA COUNTY SHERIFF
301 S Jefferson Hobart, Oklahoma 73651
(580)726-3265

INCIDENT REPORT

IT IS UNLAWFUL TO FALSELY REPORT A CRIME.
WILL YOU PROSECUTE: (Y/N) Y

C. Poindexter	03/05/14	B. Lancaster	03/05/14		03/05/14
REPORTED BY	DATE	REPORTING OFFICER	DATE	REVIEWED OFFICER	DATE

Figure 19-1fs

Page 4 of

KIOWA COUNTY SHERIFF
301 S Jefferson Hobart, Oklahoma 73651
(580)726-3265

INCIDENT REPORT

PARTY INFORMATION

6	LANCASTER, BILL

SUSPECT(S) INFORMATION

1 **THE UNDERWRITERS GROUP, INC.**

Victim Of Offender	POINDEXTER, CHRISTOPHER	Victim was Otherwise Known
Last Seen Date		
Last Seen Location		
Last Seen With		
Clothing Description		
Amputations		
Artificial Limbs		
Medical Problems		
Surgery		
Broken Bones		
Other Description		

2 **WRIGHT, LARRY JAMES**

Victim Of Offender	POINDEXTER, CHRISTOPHER	Victim was Otherwise Known
Last Seen Date		
Last Seen Location		
Last Seen With		
Clothing Description		
Amputations		
Artificial Limbs		
Medical Problems		
Surgery		
Broken Bones		
Other Description		

OFFENSE 1

Victim of Offense	POINDEXTER, CHRISTOPHER
Charge From	DISTRICT ATTORNEY
Charge Description	2 O.S. § 5-62.9(A)(6) • MAKING A MISREPRESENTATION FOR THE PURPOSE OF DEFRAUDING.
Warrant Number	
Offense	COMPLETED
Location of Offense	100 EAST MAIN STREET
Geographic Loc.	CONVIENCE STORE~LONE WOLF~73655
Premise Type Name	CONVIENCE STORE
Premise Type	CONVENIENCE STORE
IBR Code	FRAUD - FALSE PRETENSES/SWINDLE/CONFIDENCE GAME

3 **DIAZ, LORI**

Victim Of Offender	POINDEXTER, CHRISTOPHER	Victim was Otherwise Known
Last Seen Date		
Last Seen Location		
Last Seen With		
Clothing Description		
Amputations		
Artificial Limbs		

4/1/201

Figure 19-1gs

Page 1 of 6

KIOWA COUNTY SHERIFF
301 S Jefferson Hobart, Oklahoma 73651
(580)726-3265

INCIDENT REPORT

Report Number	0003521	NCIC Number
Reported On	03/05/2014 11:20	
Incident Date / Time	04/01/2011 08:00 **and** 01/30/2014 17:00	
Type of Report	PROPERTY	
Arrestee		
Suspect	DIAZ, LORI	
Suspect	THE UNDERWRITERS GROUP, INC	
Suspect	WRIGHT, LARRY JAMES	
Report Person		
Originate Officer	LANCASTER, BILL	
Location of Offense	100 East Main Street	
IBR	26A FRAUD - FALSE PRETENSES/SWINDLE/CONFIDENCE GAME	
Charge Description	2 O.S. § 5-62.9(A)(6) • Making a misrepresentation for the purpose of defrauding.	
Case Status	OPEN	
Investigator Assigned		
Date Assigned		
Date Cleared		
Clearance Type		
Clearance Disposition		

Figure 19-1hs

Page 2 of 6

KIOWA COUNTY SHERIFF
301 S Jefferson Hobart, Oklahoma 73651
(580)726-3265

INCIDENT REPORT

ADMINISTRATIVE • Send this report to OSBI as a part of SIBRS ? **NO**

Case Number	0003521	**Report Date**	03/05/2014 11:20	**Case Approved**	NO
Occured Between	04/01/2011 08:00 **and**		01/30/2014 17:00	**Case Sensitive**	NO
Type of Report	PROPERTY				
Case Status	OPEN	**Clearance Type**			
Clear Disposition				**Date Assigned**	

OFFENSE(S) INFORMATION

1 **26A FRAUD - FALSE PRETENSES/SWINDLE/CONFIDENCE GAME**
Charge From DISTRICT ATTORNEY
Charge Desc. 2 O.S. § 5-62.9(A)(6) • MAKING A MISREPRESENTATION FOR THE PURPOSE OF DEFRAUDING.

PARTY INFORMATION

1 **POINDEXTER, CHRISTOPHER**
Party Type VICTIM

DOB	6/24/1966	**Age**	47
Sex	MALE	**Race**	WHITE
Hair	BROWN	**Eye**	BROWN
Height		**Weight**	
Ethnicity	NOT HISPANIC ORIGIN		

SSN
DL 004064847

Home Address
Address P.O. Box 426
City Lonewolf
State OK
Zip Code 73655
Phone (580)846-2972

2 **THE UNDERWRITERS GROUP, INC.**
Party Type SUSPECT

DOB		**Age**	
Sex		**Race**	
Hair		**Eye**	
Height		**Weight**	
Ethnicity			

SSN
DL

3 **WRIGHT, LARRY JAMES**
Party Type SUSPECT

DOB		**Age**	
Sex	MALE	**Race**	WHITE

Figure 19-1is

KIOWA COUNTY SHERIFF
301 S Jefferson Hobart, Oklahoma 73651
(580)726-3265

INCIDENT REPORT

PARTY INFORMATION

3 WRIGHT, LARRY JAMES

Hair	GRAY OR PARTIALLY GRAY	Eye	
Height		Weight	
Ethnicity	NOT HISPANIC ORIGIN		

SSN
DL

Home Address
Address 13936 Atlantic Blvd
City Jacksonville
State FL
Zip Code 32225
Phone (904)551-1975

4 DIAZ, LORI

Party Type SUSPECT

DOB	1/7/1975	Age	39
Sex	FEMALE	Race	WHITE HISPANIC
Hair	BROWN	Eye	BROWN
Height	5' 4"	Weight	160 LBS.
Ethnicity	HISPANIC ORIGIN		

SSN
DL H620524755070

Home Address
Address 28197 Trigg Rd
City Hillard
State FL
Zip Code 32046
Phone

5 LANCASTER, BILL

Party Type OFFICER

SUSPECT(S) INFORMATION

1 THE UNDERWRITERS GROUP, INC,

Victim Of Offender POINDEXTER, CHRISTOPHER Victim was Otherwise Known

Last Seen Date
Last Seen Location
Last Seen With
Clothing Description
Amputations
Artificial Limbs
Medical Problems
Surgery
Broken Bones
Other Description

2 WRIGHT, LARRY JAMES

Victim Of Offender POINDEXTER, CHRISTOPHER Victim was Otherwise Known

Figure 19-1js

Page 4 of 6

KIOWA COUNTY SHERIFF
301 S Jefferson Hobart, Oklahoma 73651
(580)726-3265

INCIDENT REPORT

ARRESTEE(S) INFORMATION

2 **WRIGHT, LARRY JAMES**

Last Seen Date
Last Seen Location
Last Seen With
Clothing Description
Amputations
Artificial Limbs
Medical Problems
Surgery
Broken Bones
Other Description

OFFENSE 1

Victim of Offense	POINDEXTER, CHRISTOPHER
Charge From	DISTRICT ATTORNEY
Charge Description	2 O.S. § 5-62.9(A)(6) • MAKING A MISREPRESENTATION FOR THE PURPOSE OF DEFRAUDING.
Warrant Number	
Offense	COMPLETED
Location of Offense	100 EAST MAIN STREET
Geographic Loc.	CONVIENCE STORE~LONE WOLF~73655
Premise Type Name	CONVIENCE STORE
Premise Type	CONVENIENCE STORE
IBR Code	FRAUD - FALSE PRETENSES/SWINDLE/CONFIDENCE GAME

3 **DIAZ, LORI**

Victim Of Offender POINDEXTER, CHRISTOPHER Victim was Otherwise Known

Last Seen Date
Last Seen Location
Last Seen With
Clothing Description
Amputations
Artificial Limbs
Medical Problems
Surgery
Broken Bones
Other Description

VICTIM(S) INFORMATION

1 **POINDEXTER, CHRISTOPHER**

Victim Type	INDIVIDUAL
Type of Injury	NONE
NCIC Number	
Location of Injury	
Injury Location Code	

PROPERTY INFORMATION

1 **COPY OF BOGUS BOND**

Names	POINDEXTER, CHRISTOPHER	FINDER
	THE UNDERWRITERS GROUP, INC.	OWNER

Figure 19-1ks

CHAPTER XX

PCG Spells Ponzi Scheme

In the late 1990s, a company came into existence named Performance Consulting Group (PCG). It was formed by a most interesting group of bankers and ex-bankers! Before we get too deep into this chapter, if you were like me, you really do not know how a Ponzi scheme was set up or, for that matter, exactly what one was prior to beginning this investigation.

So to ensure each of us is on the same sheet of music, the below is a definition of exactly what a Ponzi scheme is:

> A Ponzi scheme is a form of fraud that lures investors and pays profits to earlier investors with funds from more recent investors. The scheme leads victims to believe that profits are coming from product sales or other means, and they remain unaware that other investors are the source of funds. (Wikipedia)

Let us look back to what our fathers most likely told us early in life: "If it looks too good to be true, it probably is." There are lots of people who are always looking for that magic suitcase in the attic that Howard Hughes left there in the late '60s (even though the house was constructed in the '90s). My point is that people who set up this kind of trap know that there are ones out there that will fall for this. Recall Bernie Madoff? Okay, you have the picture.

As stated, in the late '90s, Jack Stuteville set up Performance Consulting Group (PCG) as well as PCG Wind, PCG Global, and PCG Worldwide. Now that he had set this up, he, via First Capital Bank, loaned his companies over $8 million. What this means exactly is that he loaned himself over $8 million. Don't forget that First Capital Bank (FCB) is FDIC insured! I really wonder which hat he was wearing when PCG filled out the loan application and which hat he was wearing when FCB approved the loan.

As I discussed earlier in the book, Jeff Foss had lent PCG around $200,000 to complete a project on Tinker AFB in Oklahoma City and ended up having to sue PCG to get his money back. His company, National Comtel, lost the suit, and even with a note signed by Robert Torres (see chapter 12, Loose Ends) that guaranteed repayment, he lost his case. Mr. Foss had hired an attorney named John Collero who happened to represent Steve Standridge. He stated after his loss, "I could never figure out why they were always one step ahead of me all the time."

It was stated that each time they were paid during the project on Tinker AFB, the checks went directly to Stuteville. It is important to note that Jack Stuteville, Larry Wright, and Steve Standridge were busy using The Underwriters Group's bogus bonds on the military installations that the CID investigator Hamblin had cautioned DOD about. PCG was the principal contractor, so they had free reign to pillage the village, so to speak! The work was completed, and unless there is a surprise, all was well with the fake bonds.

While all this was going on, Jack Stuteville introduced or, should I say, matched his next two victims—a Mr. Chris Coryell and Mr. Tim Aduddell, who set up a company, CSR Nationwide, who then soon ended up going bankrupt. In the filings, they owed millions to a number of banks including FCB, and additionally, Mr. Aduddell owed one bank alone $5 million in an unsecured note. It is suspected that Mr. Aduddell disappeared to Dubai and stayed there for seven years plus after the bankruptcy—I suppose one could say—in hiding?

As you might almost expect, PCG filed for bankruptcy in January 2012, and our old friend and attorney, Douglas Jackson, appointed the receiver or, should I say, requested a certain receiver in Logan County. As you might expect, FCB would be reimbursed by the FDIC. It must be great to loan yourself $8 million, go bankrupt, and get your money paid back to you by the FDIC. Over the next three years, each of the other PCG Groups would file for bankruptcy protection, and very similar results would be had by the owners of the company.

One might ask how this could get better—well, it does! On the sixteenth day of March 2011, Jack Stuteville's bank, FCB, sued his company, Performance Consulting Group LLC. I suppose this is one way to ensure that you will win or also guarantee that you will lose. With all this, you can rest assured that the only loser in this deal was the American taxpayer!

So what would be the dynamics of this escapade? Recall now that the two men who told Jeff Foss that they had something over on Stuteville that would ensure that he would get the money he loaned to PCG returned. Shortly after, Jack Joiner allegedly fell in a bathroom and died, and the other committed suicide. I really wonder if there was any assistance from the special process server. If it were just a suicide, why did Wendy Torres, Robert Torres's wife, contact the other two Joiner brothers and state, "They just got Robert, be careful, they may be coming for you next"?

As it appears, if there is a way to take monies, this group will find a way to steal it, embezzle it, or kill you and take it!

There are thousands of pages of documents that composed this chapter; however, I believe that you can see from here a glimpse of how our economy is teetering. Our recourse as a nation is to demand honesty and integrity from those we choose to represent us. It matters not what your political affiliation is—just honesty and integrity!

CHAPTER XXI

Which Came First?

I'M QUITE CERTAIN that most of us have heard the age-old expression "Which came first, the chicken or the egg?" Along with that comes the age-old argument that you have to have the chicken to get the egg. But the chicken comes from the egg, so the egg had to have come first. In this case, which came first, the deposit or the power of attorney?

The discussion here is nearly as complicated but with the far-reaching consequence for one individual, Clifford Newberry, who lost both his father and grandmother in an auto accident. On August 6, 2012, the father and grandmother were hit in an intersection by a Federal Express truck. The father was severely injured, and the grandmother killed. Clifford's father, for the remainder of his life, was a quadriplegic. He ended up dying in the coming four years in a major part due to the accident.

In the fall of 2012, an attorney from California, Stephen Bell, a private investigator named Kenny Burrell, who was a friend of Robert Newberry, and Robert's sister Andrea had a meeting with Clifford's stepmother, Sharon Newberry. Mr. Bell had come to Oklahoma to explain the contingency fee, potential litigation, settlement, and the contours of the possible lawsuit. It is believed that the group sought the approval of Sharon Newberry and she eventually agreed and signed the representation agreement. This seems to be where this plot may have hatched (no pun intended) to take over all of the settlement by Andrea. One very serious question is, why wasn't Clifford's father at this meeting? Apparently, the aunt did not want any intervention from her brother at that time.

In August 2015, FedEx came to a settlement of an undisclosed amount in the millions for the two in the car plus a few issues like expenses. The money was deposited to Robert Newberry's account, and Andrea Newberry, his sister, managed to get her name on the account as joint tenancy and power of attorney (POA). This occurred on August 26, 2015, and most interestingly, the POA was fraudulently signed August 30, 2015. The bank accepted this as it was even on the bank's stationary!

It wasn't very long after she signed a contingency fee agreement, on February 17, 2013, that Clifford's stepmother, Sharon Newberry, passed away in the hospital. Apparently, she suffocated; and there was no one there to come to her rescue, and she died of oxygen deprivation. No autopsy was conducted at the request of her daughter, Rhonda Bourland! Clifford, her stepson, was not made aware of her passing for nearly two days.

With the two needing round-the-clock care, the only child, Clifford, accepted the help offered by his aunt Andrea, his fathers' sister, and her friend Sue Livermore. Not suspecting that his aunt would attempt anything, things began to get quite precarious.

On March 17, 2014, a mortgage was executed by Andrea Newberry, Claud Newberry, Robert Dean Newberry, and BancFirst in Hobart, Oklahoma. Even though it was Robert Dean Newberry's property, there was no evidence of his signature. In that space, where his signature should have been, there was a line drawn above the X and nothing else. It was notarized by a JoAnn Campbell in Cleveland County, Oklahoma, some one hundred miles away on March 18, 2014. The statement of the notary (# 03006314) read, "For the state of Oklahoma, before me, the undersigned, in and for the State on this 18th day of March 2014, personally appeared before me Robert Dean Newberry, a single person"! Robert Dean Newberry was not physically capable to travel that distance!

Shortly thereafter, the caregiver, Sue Livermore, was able to get Robert Newberry to loan her on February 24, 2016, $10,000 (ck.

Number 191) to put down on a property for herself. This was made with the understanding that she would pay the money back. Clifford was made aware of all this. Since she had made no payments on the money lent to her, Clifford went to Chris Poindexter to request if he could assist. Chris first went to the county assessor's office and found that the property was in both Clifford's father's name and Sue Livermore. He also found that Sue Livermore had tried numerous times to have Robert Newberry's name removed. Next, Chris went to the bank for a copy of the check, and they, the bank, refused to provide him a copy. Chris was told that the account belonged to Andrea, Clifford's aunt, and they could not provide a copy. Next, Chris went to the attorney and found that Clifford was a trustee of the estate, and the bank would have to provide such. Later that same day, the bank called and told him the checks were ready—not one but three (Fig. 21-1). Apparently, she had elected to write two more on her own, one for $5,000 (ck. Number 196) dated March 4, and a third for $30,000 (ck. Number 195) also on March 4, 2016. Looking at the checks for $5,000 and for $30,000, the signature was forged, as it is very obvious the signer of the first check for $10,000 was not the signer of the other two. The caregiver had decided that paying off the property was a better idea since it wasn't her money to begin with.

With this action, the focus now began to shift to the attorney David L. Cummins and the bank, BancFirst.

Another very strange event after is that Clifford's father, who was a quadriplegic, was allegedly bounced around in the back of a van and then dropped nearly four feet. It was then more than twenty-four hours later when he was taken to the hospital in late October. Following this series of physical events, a day later, he passed away on October 30, 2016. The death record is a most interesting and deceiving document! (Fig. 21-2)

Viewing the death record, Clifford's aunt also did not request an autopsy and also had the body cremated. He had passed away in Altus, Oklahoma, and was cremated in Choctaw, Oklahoma, some 155 miles from where he passed. Correct me if I am wrong; she was not the next of kin but made a decision to disconnect Clifford's father's life support. She claimed to the hospital that she had the power of attorney to make such a decision. She did not! It appears that she, too, was attempting to tie up loose ends.

I would think that most people, such as myself, are saying, "What does the will say?" Interestingly enough, the will that Robert Newberry had had prepared conveniently disappeared. All this was done before Clifford was notified! It was nearly twenty-four hours before Clifford knew that his father was in the hospital. By the time he arrived, his father had had his life support disconnected!

This left dear aunt Andrea fraudulently in charge of the account of millions of dollars at BancFirst, a local bank in Oklahoma under now just her name. The monies were distributed into various investment accounts operated by BancFirst. In June 2019, dear Aunt Andrea spent over $200,000 for a new home from an account that she had acquired under fraudulent means, and the bank assisted here in that endeavor!

Clifford had begun his quest to discover what amount was paid to his family in the accident, as all had disappeared shortly thereafter. He employed an attorney named David Cummins in Hollis, Oklahoma, to assist him, as it was not remotely close to Hobart. The line below is his internet listing and his areas of expertise:

> David L. Cummins, Hollis, Oklahoma (OK) Lawyer, Attorney—Banking & Finance Law, Business & Commercial Law, Criminal Law.

Here the twists and turns get even wilder. On August 23, 2017, Clifford paid David L. Cummins $5,000 to represent him and to recover his family's assets. Mr. Cummins stated in a contract that he would charge Clifford 40 percent to accomplish the task. What he was not prepared for was that for nearly three years, the attorney did essentially nothing—well, nothing other than spend the $5,000 or gain interest off the money. At that time, Clifford was running short of most everything, including patience. He had been working with Chris Poindexter and knew that Chris was known for his desire to assist people who had come on hard times. He again contacted Chris and asked if he could assist him, as the attorney had done nothing for nearly three years in reacquiring his money and properties.

Upon the review of all that Clifford had that Chris had already found and saw, there was a serious need to fire the attorney Cummins. Cummins was a mudhole in the interstate. We will discuss Mr. David L. Cummins more in the coming chapter, as he seems to have an affliction with taking monies to represent and then doing nothing whatsoever.

The one thing that we can see is that he allegedly hired another law firm to take care of this issue for Clifford, and nothing was accomplished there either.

After he was fired, he refused to withdraw, which forced Chris and Clifford to drive the long distance to Hollis to confront him and get his withdrawal. Chris had called his office prior to departing on the trip, and he was open. Upon arrival, the door to his office was locked, and the lights were out. After a long afternoon waiting in front of his office for him to reappear, a guy who was not Cummins came walking by, got in Cummins's truck, and sped away. I suppose they should take that as a sign that he didn't wish to talk to them. I wonder why.

There appears to be a lot of interesting clues that have yet to be turned over. Apparently, the bank, BancFirst, was quite thrilled to accept money and allow others to withdraw without any verification. I'm certain you caught the four-day lapse in having a power of attorney. That also happened to be on BancFirst's letterhead, and they considered it good enough to go? Equally as interesting is, the attorney who accepts money to accomplish a job and then does nothing whatsoever and after fired, refuses to withdraw, stating he needs his final payment. In the coming chapter, we will see more of his requirements for payment in addition to him being a criminal attorney with the inability to file an appeal.

So after all of this, are we now quite certain which came first? Perhaps it was the pack of wolves that came first!

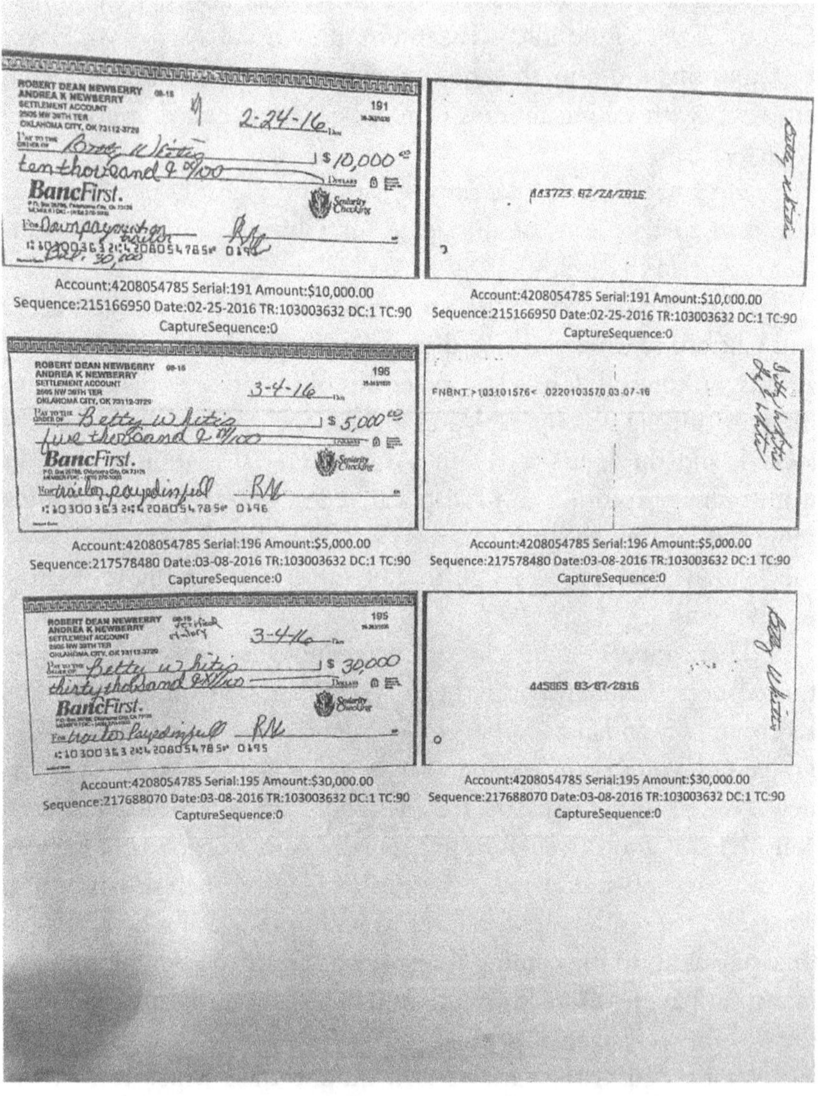
ROBERT DEAN NEWBERRY
ANDREA K NEWBERRY
SETTLEMENT ACCOUNT
2505 NW 36TH TER
OKLAHOMA CITY, OK 73112-3729

191

2-24-16

Pay to the order of Brett Whitis $10,000.00
ten thousand & 00/100 Dollars
BancFirst.
For Down payment on trailer 30,000

Account:4208054785 Serial:191 Amount:$10,000.00
Sequence:215166950 Date:02-25-2016 TR:103003632 DC:1 TC:90
CaptureSequence:0

443723 02/24/2016

Account:4208054785 Serial:191 Amount:$10,000.00
Sequence:215166950 Date:02-25-2016 TR:103003632 DC:1 TC:90
CaptureSequence:0

ROBERT DEAN NEWBERRY
ANDREA K NEWBERRY
SETTLEMENT ACCOUNT
2505 NW 36TH TER
OKLAHOMA CITY, OK 73112-3729

196

3-4-16

Pay to the order of Betty Whitis $5,000.00
five thousand & 00/100 Dollars
BancFirst.
For trailer paid in full

Account:4208054785 Serial:196 Amount:$5,000.00
Sequence:217578480 Date:03-08-2016 TR:103003632 DC:1 TC:90
CaptureSequence:0

FNBNT >103101576< 0220103570 03-07-16

Account:4208054785 Serial:196 Amount:$5,000.00
Sequence:217578480 Date:03-08-2016 TR:103003632 DC:1 TC:90
CaptureSequence:0

ROBERT DEAN NEWBERRY
ANDREA K NEWBERRY
SETTLEMENT ACCOUNT
2505 NW 36TH TER
OKLAHOMA CITY, OK 73112-3729

195

3-4-16

Pay to the order of Betty Whitis $30,000
thirty thousand & 00/100 Dollars
BancFirst.
For trailer paid in full

Account:4208054785 Serial:195 Amount:$30,000.00
Sequence:217688070 Date:03-08-2016 TR:103003632 DC:1 TC:90
CaptureSequence:0

445865 03/07/2016

Account:4208054785 Serial:195 Amount:$30,000.00
Sequence:217688070 Date:03-08-2016 TR:103003632 DC:1 TC:90
CaptureSequence:0

Figure 21-1

2016040030746

STATE OF OKLAHOMA

CERTIFICATE OF DEATH

STATE FILE NUMBER 2016-030746

1. DECEDENT'S LEGAL NAME (First, Middle, Last, Suffix): ROBERT DEAN NEWBERRY
1a. LAST NAME PRIOR TO FIRST MARRIAGE:
2. SEX: MALE
3. SOCIAL SECURITY NUMBER: 443-46-2280
4. EVER IN US ARMED FORCES? NO
5a. AGE-Last birthday (years): 72
5b. UNDER 1 YEAR: Months / Days
5c. UNDER 1 DAY: Hours / Minutes
6. DATE OF BIRTH (Mo/Day/Yr): AUGUST 10, 1944
7. BIRTHPLACE (City and State or Foreign Country): SENTINEL, OKLAHOMA
8a. RESIDENCE-State: OKLAHOMA
8b. RESIDENCE-County: KIOWA
8c. RESIDENCE-City or Town: LONE WOLF
8d. RESIDENCE-Zip Code: 73655
8e. RESIDENCE-Inside City Limits? NO
8f. RESIDENCE-Street and Number: 20456 E. 1410 ROAD
8g. RESIDENCE-Apt. Number:
9. MARITAL STATUS AT TIME OF DEATH: ☐ Married ☐ Never Married ☒ Widowed ☐ Divorced ☐ Married, but separated ☐ Unknown
10. SURVIVING SPOUSE'S NAME (If wife, give name prior to first marriage):
11. FATHER'S NAME (First, Middle, Last): CLIFFORD ALONZO NEWBERRY
12. MOTHER'S NAME PRIOR TO FIRST MARRIAGE (First, Middle, Last): GLADYS MARIE MAYES
13. DECEDENT OF HISPANIC ORIGIN? NO, NOT SPANISH/HISPANIC/LATINO
14. DECEDENT'S RACE: WHITE
15. DECEDENT'S EDUCATION: HIGH SCHOOL GRADUATE OR GED COMPLETED
16. DECEDENT'S USUAL OCCUPATION (Indicate type of work done during most of working life. DO NOT USE RETIRED): IRON WORKER
17. KIND OF BUSINESS / INDUSTRY: BUILDING INDUSTRY
18a. INFORMANT'S NAME: ANDREA KAY NEWBERRY
18b. RELATIONSHIP TO DECEDENT: SISTER
18c. MAILING ADDRESS (Street and Number, City, State, Zip Code): 2505 N.W. 39TH TERRACE, OKLAHOMA CITY, OKLAHOMA 73112
19. METHOD OF DISPOSITION: ☐ Burial ☒ Cremation ☐ Donation ☐ Entombment ☐ Removal from state ☐ Other (specify)
20. PLACE OF DISPOSITION (Name of cemetery, crematory, other place): ADVANCED CREMATION CARE CENTER
21. LOCATION – City, Town and State: CHOCTAW, OKLAHOMA
22. NAME AND COMPLETE ADDRESS OF FUNERAL FACILITY: PEOPLES COOPERATIVE FUNERAL HOME, INC. - LONE WOLF, 1400 W. MAIN, LONE WOLF, OKLAHOMA 73655
23. FUNERAL HOME DIRECTOR OR FAMILY MEMBER ACTING AS SUCH: ESSIE M SMITH
24. FH ESTABLISHMENT LICENSE # 1156ES

To be completed by the Funeral Home

25. PLACE OF DEATH (Check only one: see instructions)
IF DEATH OCCURRED IN A HOSPITAL: ☐ Inpatient ☒ Emergency Room/Outpatient ☐ Dead on Arrival
IF DEATH OCCURRED OTHER THAN IN A HOSPITAL: ☐ Hospice Facility ☐ Nursing home/Long term care facility ☐ Decedent's home ☐ Other (specify)
26. FACILITY NAME (If not institution, give street & number): JACKSON CO MEMORIAL HOSPITAL
27. CITY OR TOWN, STATE AND ZIP CODE OF LOCATION OF DEATH: ALTUS, OKLAHOMA, 73521
28. COUNTY OF DEATH: JACKSON
29. DATE OF DEATH (Mo/Day/Yr): OCTOBER 30, 2016
30. TIME OF DEATH: 11:06
31. WAS MEDICAL EXAMINER CONTACTED? YES
32. WAS AN AUTOPSY PERFORMED? NO
33. WERE AUTOPSY FINDINGS AVAILABLE TO COMPLETE THE CAUSE OF DEATH?

CAUSE OF DEATH (See instructions and examples)

34. PART I. Enter the chain of events- diseases, injuries or complications – that directly caused the death. DO NOT enter terminal events such as cardiac arrest, respiratory arrest or ventricular fibrillation without showing the etiology. DO NOT ABBREVIATE. Enter only one cause on a line. Add additional lines if necessary.

IMMEDIATE CAUSE (Final disease or condition resulting in death) → a. PARAPLEGIA, TRAUMATIC SEQUELA (SEPSIS) — Approximate interval Onset to death: UNDETERMINED
Due to (or as a consequence of):
Sequentially list conditions, if any, leading to the cause listed on line a. b.
Due to (or as a consequence of):
Enter the UNDERLYING CAUSE (disease or injury that initiated the events resulting in death) LAST. c.
Due to (or as a consequence of):
d.
1605500

35. PART II. Enter other significant conditions contributing to death but not resulting in the underlying cause given in PART I: CONGESTIVE HEART FAILURE; PACEMAKER; CHRONIC URINARY TRACT INFECTION; DECUBITUS ULCERS

36. MANNER OF DEATH: ☐ Natural ☐ Homicide ☒ Accident ☐ Suicide ☐ Pending Investigation ☐ Could not be determined
37. IF FEMALE: ☐ Not pregnant within past year ☐ Pregnant at time of death ☐ Not pregnant, but pregnant within 42 days of death ☐ Not pregnant, but pregnant 43 days to 1 year before death ☐ Unknown if pregnant within the past year
38. DID TOBACCO USE CONTRIBUTE TO DEATH? ☐ Yes ☐ No ☐ Probably ☒ Unknown
39. DATE OF INJURY (Mo/Day/Yr): UNKNOWN
40. TIME OF INJURY: UNKNOWN
41. PLACE OF INJURY (e.g., Decedent's home; construction site; wooded area): ROADWAY
42. DESCRIBE HOW INJURY OCCURRED: MOTOR VEHICLE
43. INJURY AT WORK? NO
44. LOCATION OF INJURY: State: OKLAHOMA City or Town: LONE WOLF Zip Code: 73655 Street & Number: UNKNOWN Apartment Number:
45. IF TRANSPORTATION INJURY, SPECIFY: ☐ Driver/Operator ☐ Passenger ☐ Pedestrian ☐ Other (specify)
46. CERTIFIER (Check only one)
ATTENDING PHYSICIAN: ☐ Physician in charge of the patient's care ☐ Physician in attendance at time of death only
To the best of my knowledge, death occurred at the time, date, and place, and due to the cause(s) and manner as stated.
☒ MEDICAL EXAMINER On the basis of examination, and/or investigation, in my opinion, death occurred at the time, date and place, and due to the cause(s) and manner stated.
Certifier: CHAI CHOI, MD
47. NAME, ADDRESS AND ZIP CODE OF PERSON COMPLETING CAUSE OF DEATH (Item 34): CHAI CHOI, MD, 901 NORTH STONEWALL, OKLAHOMA CITY, OKLAHOMA 73117-1218
48. LICENSE NUMBER: 14139OK
49. DATE DEATH CERTIFIED (Mo/Day/Yr): NOVEMBER 4, 2016
50. REGISTRAR'S SIGNATURE: Kelly M Baker
52. DATE RECEIVED BY STATE REGISTRAR (Mo/Day/Yr): NOVEMBER 7, 2016

REVISION 2013 V3.154

Monday, November 07, 2016

Figure 21-2

CHAPTER XXII

The Cummins Factor

In April 2014, an English high school teacher resigned from her position due to her own actions. No one spoke to her, reprimanded her, or even knew of what had just occurred. She realized what she had just done was completely unacceptable, and the thoughts of such gave her great unrest.

Just over a year earlier, she had gotten divorced from a ten-year loveless marriage and felt she was not worthy of any other human on this earth. Birthdays, Christmases, and any other special occasion was met with the same; there was not even a card telling her that she was appreciated. The feeling was deeply depressing and was a great weight on her shoulders. She had, at that time, a five-year-old son.

Teaching high school English, she had a wide variety of students and never even considered that one of these students would find her in the least way attractive until a fifteen-year-old boy made an approach to her and complimented her. Something such as this was bound to happen and finally did. With her mental state of believing that she was of no value to anyone, she was caught off guard by the flirtatious behavior. One thing lead to another, and before you-know-what transpired, it had happened. Having done such, she immediately resigned from teaching.

In the coming months, with great assistance from the young man's father, she believed that she had truly found love, and perhaps she had. The boy's father, for whatever reason, promoted the relationship and would even go to the extreme of picking Jennifer up and driving her late at night to his house to be with his son. Later, as you will see, the father perjured himself under oath and stated he knew nothing of what was going on. Police reports that were filed by neighbors validated that he definitively lied under oath. It appears that his attempt to make his son happy was short-lived and had a price tag.

The young man's mother had taken him to Mississippi, and Jennifer felt that she had to be with him and followed. Based upon notes that she had written, she went there to see the young man that she may have mistakenly believed she was in love with or perhaps actually was. There, she was arrested for having sex with a minor and a plethora of other related crimes. Her feeling of value diminished even further. Now, on top of all that had transpired, she had numerous legal problems to overcome.

A friend of a friend recommended that she contact a David L. Cummins to represent her and steer this sinking ship into calm waters. What was about to be orchestrated by this less-than-reputable attorney would turn out to be the ride for her life.

Imagine if you can that a defense attorney would actually set his client up to go on national television and discuss before the entire country what had happened. That is exactly what happened, and most of us at this point are wondering why and what would prompt anyone to do such. The answer is simple, and I can provide about thirty thousand reasons!

As you recall, in the previous chapter, there was a discussion about this attorney named David L. Cummins. Through some horrid event, Jennifer Caswell was provided his contact information to assist her after her arrest in Mississippi.

What was coming at her could only typically be written about in a fictional novel! It appears that after taking a retainer to represent her in this mess, this attorney actually suggested that she appear on the Dr. Phil show and sell her soul—and for what reason? The reason becomes rather clear, as the fee paid by the daytime dirt show would go directly to the attorney—some $30,000! That he would eventually hand some of the money back to her parents was of little comfort.

After the Dr. Phil show interview, which took place in a hotel in Oklahoma City, Oklahoma, on her way back to Granite, Oklahoma, Jennifer began to have substantial doubts as to what had just transpired. Upon arriving at home, she decided to call the producer back and cancel the show—"DO NOT AIR THIS SHOW!" It was originally set to go on the air only after she had been sentenced, but what would happen next was shocking. The week prior to her sentencing, the show was aired. We can only guess why, but an educated guess is this—the producer called the attorney who set this up. Realizing that the $30,000 would be delayed or, in the first case, cancelled, Mr. Cummins okayed the release, as the attorney had an issue going on that he would need some cash to get his stepson out of his fourth DUI (of which two had mystically disappeared from the court records); and at this time, he caused an auto accident, backed up and hit the other vehicle a second time, then left the scene of the accident. Here is an interesting fact: the county commissioner for Harmon County, Oklahoma, Mr. Nicky Boone, is the boy's biological father, and it is well known in that county that he tells the judges how they will rule in certain cases. I suppose that I must have misunderstood the word judge at some point in time. Additionally, as I was told by residents, Cummins is very influential in the town of Hollis and gets his way. Since it is fair to say that Cummins knows the commissioner as he is married to the commissioner's ex-wife, I'm certain that there was a level of collusion in Jennifer's case.

The show aired just prior to her sentencing, and the issue of a fair trial was thrown out the window. In another strange turn of events, the district attorney, the one prosecuting her, actually attempted to stand up for Jennifer and keep her sentence short. When they, Cummins and his client, were preparing for trial, Cummins actually steered her away from a jury trial and told her not to take a plea deal offered by the district attorney. He stated to her that juries were unreliable and couldn't be trusted! Why? Good idea if you are betting on a hanging! It might be noted that the stepson of Cummins who was scheduled for a hearing the very same day was let off scot-free. You read that correctly—four DUIs, leaving the scene of an accident, and not even a swat on the back of his hand!

As one works through the history of this escapade it is almost like a comedy routine with no punchline! Nearing the end of the sentencing, the judge states that she has no prior history of any run-ins with the law and lived a clean life up to that point. Therefore, he hits her with the maximum penalty allowed by law. Thank God she didn't have a parking ticket; she would have been on the gallows by sundown.

The father of the young man Jennifer had an affair with stated under oath that he knew nothing about the affair. Really! What about the times that he brought Jennifer to see his son and helped the two of them get together at his home? One pesty little detail was his neighbors who called the cops for what they saw going on numerous times! For some unknown reason, I feel that such would count as knowledge that there was something going on since he told the police, "What I do in my house was none of their business." He had also told the pair, Jennifer and his son, not to answer the door or the phone in times when he was absent from the house.

The boy and his father sued Jennifer Caswell and the small Western Oklahoma school district of Hollis in 2015 over the inappropriate relationship, which included sex in her classroom one time. Do you think that perhaps the dollar signs blinded his honesty and good judgement? It is rumored that there was a great deal more money than was published that exchanged hands over this, and it included the attorney Cummins.

Through one means or another, this case was now elevated to the federal court, probably as the young lady crossed state lines to see her friend. She is now serving time—fifteen years in a state penitentiary—and a federal judge stacked an additional $1 million fine to her sentence just for good measure. All this seems almost surreal. It is my understanding that the prison time and penalty is to rehabilitate the individual; her parents said that she has no incentive, as when she does get out of prison, she will never be able to build a future. As for her to pay off the fine, she will grow old prior to that happening.

As an interesting side note, at the time of her sentencing hearing, a man and his girlfriend were caught drugging a thirteen-year-old girl and selling her into prostitution. One would think that both of these two would be hung by the neck until dead, looking at the sentence that Jennifer received. Well, not so; the girlfriend was given a five-year sentence, and four years was suspended. The man slightly more but was less than one-third of Jennifer's sentence. It needs to be noted that the same Judge Darby oversaw both cases and sentencing.

So where is the good news at the conclusion of this chapter? Well, Cummins's stepson got off from his second(?) DUI and leaving the scene of an accident, and Cummins also got paid. I would like to add that on occasion, the attorney does write up sentence modification requests, which are all summarily dismissed, but he always remembers to bill Jennifer's parents! Mr. Cummins filed several sentence modifications that her parents paid handsomely for and none were accepted. This always remained the same and left this young lady to the wolves.

From an old Southern joke—"Well, how nice!"

CHAPTER XXIII

The Golden Gin

Out in Western Oklahoma in the thriving metropolis of Lone Wolf, their cotton gin was getting a bit antiquated and somewhat run-down, so the management increased the insurance coverage and then it burned down. A local ex-banker and his pal, the attorney from Enid, Oklahoma, decided that they could help resolve the issue with a new one. The planning (or should I say plotting and scheming) began almost immediately.

First, let's get a handle on what a cotton gin is. Some years back, there was a gentleman named ElI Whitney who came up with just an award-winning idea, literally. In 1794, US-born inventor, Eli Whitney (1765–1825), patented the cotton gin, a machine that revolutionized the production of cotton and greatly sped up the process of removing seeds from cotton fiber. By the mid-nineteenth century, cotton had become America's leading export. Despite its success, the gin made little money for Whitney due to patent-infringement issues. Interesting—there seemed to be folks way back when that would steal from their neighbors like they do today.

Anyway, this device nonetheless completely changed the process and made it substantially more productive and less labor intensive. Now thousands of bales could have all seeds removed in a short time period versus only a few pounds a day with a large manual labor workforce doing the cleaning.

Since the time of ElI Whitney, cotton gins have been in existence. Price ranges vary now from a couple hundred thousand dollars to ten or maybe twelve million dollars, with a few possibly going for maybe double that.

What we have here is a most unusual gin! Perhaps it is in what it does? As far as we know, it still does no more than separate cotton fibers from the cotton seeds. Currently, our gin here is passing the $26 million mark with no end in sight! We have located that the guaranteed monies on the gin is now at $37,700,000. (Fig 23-2) We recalled that the original construction of the facility was around $4 million. So here, one has to start asking why. Exactly why has the cost of this skyrocketed when the construction is still not complete?

Perhaps the cost of the actual components of the gin have gone completely out of sight? Looking into this, that is not the case, as we found that most of the components are not new at all. The components were all salvaged parts from two gins that had been closed down—one in Tennessee and the other in Arkansas. That destroys our theory as to where are the dollars going. This also means the folks out in Western Oklahoma are apparently buying a pig in a poke.

So, here we go, follow the money! Apparently, the construction job went to a well-known individual who had been around cotton gins all his life and is well respected in that particular industry. Consolidated Construction is, from all that I can see, a five-star gin construction company. So it would be unlikely that he would be driving the cost up after building a very strong business. With numerous recommendations and foundation that is rock solid, that would be very unlikely.

Now comes the electrical portion. As one might imagine, there are lots of motors and components continually drawing power. This portion of the construction went to an electrical construction contractor in Lubbock, Texas. That seemed to be a little unusual but still nothing enough to drive the construction costs up over 600 percent. I did find that several local workers who had done a great deal of the services and some repairs to the previous gin were led to believe that they could well get the job at hand on the new one. Many people in the area were of the thoughts that they may see work on this new gin, but nothing came to fruition. A particularly interesting note is that around the same time that this was going on, a similar-sized gin was constructed in Pampa, Texas, that could accommodate over two hundred thousand bales a year of cotton whereas the one now North of Hobart, Oklahoma, did only twenty-eight thousand bales and was constructed of used equipment. The one in Pampa was all new and state of the art; both the one in Pampa and the one near Hobart are the same physical size. Pampa has all-new equipment and cost a total of $25 million.

Looking at the Planters Co-op, from as far back as I could see, Doug Jackson has provided the legal representation for the group. For whatever the reason, after the original gin burned to the ground, the new facility changed its name to Western Planters LLC and moved five miles North of Hobart, Oklahoma. It has been noted that all of the shareholders' stock has been frozen, and they cannot receive dividend payouts for their shares as always before. Another really interesting fact is that the new cotton gin (Western Planters, LLC) has zero debt—nope, not one penny of the $37.7 million debt. However, the Planters Gin that burned to the ground and its member shareholders bear 100% of the $37.7 million debt! This is a very interesting and possibly detrimental bill to the co-op members who could be stuck servicing the entire debt while the new one operates debt-free! It might be noted that the original cotton gin that burned to the ground is about 2,400 feet from the convenience store in the community of Lone Wolf, which is owned by Chris Poindexter, and that is where the fake bonds were received from Larry Wright back in 2011. That, my friends, is what one would call a fun fact.

Here is where we start to see a commonality with other cases that we have looked at. There is a case where Mr. Jackson was representing another client. He continually used the word *we* in reference to the client. Perhaps the *we* went much deeper than most took it for at that hearing.

I believe that if we look at another adventure where Mr. Jackson represented a company called High Plains Bank, we will begin to see the truth in such statements. We need to recall that High Plains Bank is listed as a creditor in the PCG Bankruptcy that was filed by Doug Jackson! PCG is owned by Jack Stuteville.

You may recall from earlier discussions a Mr. Jack Stuteville and a few of his dealings. At one point in time, he owed High Plains Bank $1.3 million on land notes. A company named Hopkins AG Supply also at that time banked with High Plains Bank. Mr. Stuteville was coming down to the wire and needed to make a large payment on his land of approximately $300,000 to keep his land current. A company in Kansas called Advanced Trading took delivery of a large quantity of wheat from Hopkins and paid with a bogus $25,000 check and a fake Larry Wright (The Underwriters Group) bond. The wheat valued at $300,000 was quickly shipped to Turkey. Advanced Trading received payment, and somehow, Mr. Stuteville made payment on his land to the High Plains Bank. Doug Jackson represented Advanced Trading, and our old friend Evan Gatewood represented Larry Wright in federal court in Judge Robin Cauthron's court. Doug Jackson did not appear in court, as he and his client reached an agreement with Hopkins AG Supply prior to trial. Recall now the *we* earlier in this discussion? High Plains Bank got the payment that Stuteville owed, and then with the assistance from Bank 7, he moved the accounts away from High Plains Bank.

In a later case where lis pendens was filed on Stuteville Properties and assets in an attempt to collect on a verdict that was awarded to Pridex and Chris Poindexter, according to the transcript, Doug Jackson continually referred to *we* in such items as "We can't do anything because Mr. Poindexter has filed this lis pendens," "We need this filing vacated," "We can't sell lots," "We can't do an oil and gas lease!" We, we, we—sounds like something from your childhood story, doesn't it? The point is, these two seem to always work together!

In leading up to the trial, Larry Wright used another company name, Phenix, and his reasoning for this was, simply stated, legal counsel advised that due to the number of lawsuits against him (The Underwriters Group), should not use The Underwriters Group.

Doug Jackson arranged a settlement for a total of only $48,500 for Advance Trading. A man named Troy Rigel spent some time in jail for the hot check of $25,000 payable to Hopkins AG Supply, and that was it.

So to conclude this discussion, part of the *we* (this part) has no idea where the millions of dollars of this gin have disappeared to; however, I feel certain that the other part of the *we* may know exactly where it has gone!

This entire cotton gin fiasco has been financed by CoBank, which is an associated bank with BancFirst. The healthy sum is of $37.7 million, which is all held by a lien on Planters Coop, not Western Planters LLC. Western Planters has no associated debt for the new construction, and all debt has fallen or has been assigned to the original Planters Coop. Just a pleasant reminder—the original bid to construct the gin as a turnkey operation was approximately $4 million.

I-2019-000446 Book 0830 Pg 552
03/25/2019 10:10 am Pg 0552-0580
Fee: $ 69.00 Doc: $ 0.00
Nikki Dodd - Kiowa County Clerk
State of Oklahoma

MORTGAGE TAX
PAID $5,602.46 REC.# 232
MTG. TXFEE 5.00
DATE 3-25-19
DEANNA (BEAMON) MILLER
KIOWA COUNTY TREASURER
DEPUTY

After recording, return to:
CoBank, ACB
Legal and Loan Processing
6340 S. Fiddlers Green Cir.
Greenwood Village, CO 80111
(800) 542-8072

AMENDED AND RESTATED
REAL ESTATE MORTGAGE

Made By

PLANTERS COOPERATIVE ASSOCIATION
(a/k/a Planters Cooperative Association, Lone Wolf, Oklahoma, a/k/a Planters Cooperative Association of Lone Wolf, Oklahoma, a/k/a Planters Co-Operative Association, Lone Wolf, Oklahoma, a/k/a Planters Co-Operative Gin Company, of Lone Wolf, Oklahoma, a/k/a Planters Cooperative Association Lone Wolf Oklahoma, a/k/a Planters Cooperative Assosication, Lone Wolf, Oklahoma, a/k/a Planters Co-op Ass'n., Lone Wolf, Oklahoma, a/k/a The Planters Cooperative Association, a/k/a Planters Co-op Assn., a/k/a Planters CoOperative Association of Lone Wolf, Oklahoma, a/k/a Planters Co-Operative Association, Lone Wolf, Oklahoma)
as Mortgagor

in favor of

COBANK, ACB
as Mortgagee

Dated as of
March 22, 2019

A POWER OF SALE HAS BEEN GRANTED IN THIS AMENDED AND RESTATED REAL ESTATE MORTGAGE. A POWER OF SALE MAY ALLOW THE MORTGAGEE TO TAKE THE MORTGAGED PROPERTY AND SELL IT WITHOUT GOING TO COURT IN A FORECLOSURE ACTION UPON DEFAULT BY THE MORTGAGOR UNDER THIS MORTGAGE.

THIS INSTRUMENT CONSTITUTES AN AMENDED AND RESTATED MORTGAGE COVERING BOTH REAL PROPERTY AND FIXTURES AND IS TO BE CROSS INDEXED IN ALL INDICES IN WHICH ARE RECORDED LIENS, MORTGAGES, OR OTHER ENCUMBRANCES AGAINST REAL PROPERTY AND FIXTURES.

PURSUANT TO ARTICLE II, THIS INSTRUMENT CONSTITUTES A LIEN ON ALL AFTER ACQUIRED PROPERTY OF THE MORTGAGOR.THIS INSTRUMENT CONTAINS FUTURE ADVANCE PROVISIONS.

Figure 23-1

I-2019-000446 Book 0830 Pg: 580
03/25/2019 10:10 am Pg 0552-0580
Fee: $ 69.00 Doc: $ 0.00
Nikki Dodd - Kiowa County Clerk
State of Oklahoma

2. The Original Notes as described in the second WHEREAS clause above are:

Promissory Note No.	Note Date	Principal Amount
RIE20S01	August 8, 1995	$2,700,000.00

3. The "Obligations" as described in the Definitions section above include without limitation the "Original Notes" as well as the following additional promissory note(s):

Promissory Note No.	Note Date	Principal Amount
19400322S01-D*	____________, 2019	$30,000,000.00
19400322T07-B	____________, 2019	$5,000,000.00

*Amends and restates note No. RIE20S01 shown above, as subsequently amended.

Figure 23-2

I-2019-000446 Book 0830 Pg: 566
03/25/2019 10:10 am Pg 0552-0580
Fee: $ 69.00 Doc: $ 0.00
Nikki Dodd - Kiowa County Clerk
State of Oklahoma

IN WITNESS WHEREOF, each of **PLANTERS COOPERATIVE ASSOCIATION**, as Mortgagor, and **COBANK, ACB** as Mortgagee, has caused this Amended and Restated Real Estate Mortgage to be signed in its name and by its officers thereunto duly authorized, all as of the day and year first above written.

PLANTERS COOPERATIVE ASSOCIATION,
Mortgagor

3-22-19
CJN

By: Paul Kruska
Name: Paul Kruska
Title: President

STATE OF Oklahoma)
)
COUNTY OF Kiowa)

This instrument was acknowledged before me on the date of 3·19·19 by Paul Kruska as President (title) of Planters Cooperative Association.

JEANNE BLACK NOTARY PUBLIC IN AND FOR STATE OF OKLAHOMA KIOWA CO.

SEAL (if any)

Jeanne Black
Notary Public

My commission expires: 11·20·20

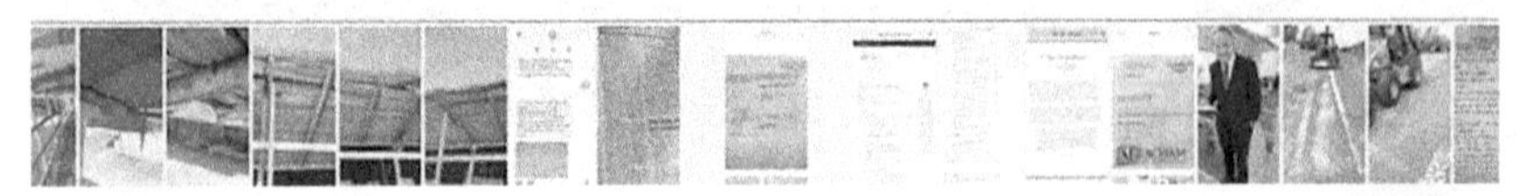

Figure 23-3

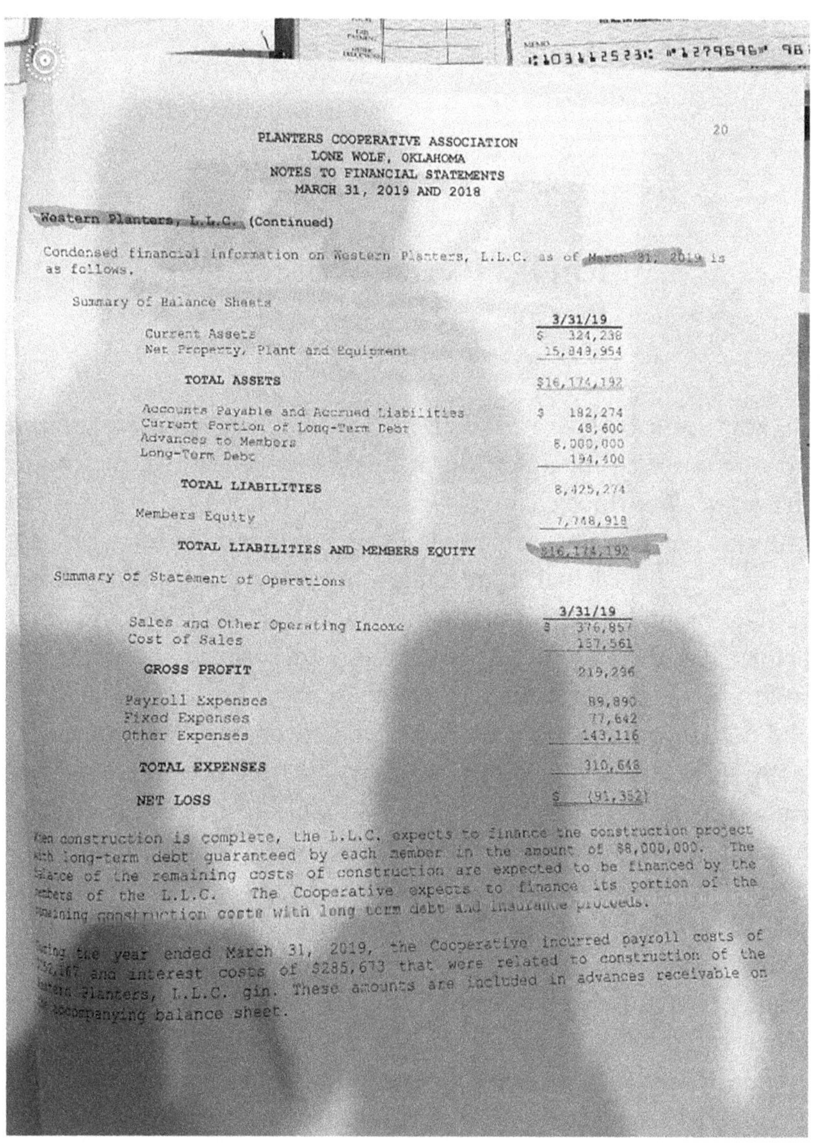

20

PLANTERS COOPERATIVE ASSOCIATION
LONE WOLF, OKLAHOMA
NOTES TO FINANCIAL STATEMENTS
MARCH 31, 2019 AND 2018

Western Planters, L.L.C. (Continued)

Condensed financial information on Western Planters, L.L.C. as of March 31, 2019 is as follows.

Summary of Balance Sheets

	3/31/19
Current Assets	$ 324,238
Net Property, Plant and Equipment	15,849,954
TOTAL ASSETS	$16,174,192
Accounts Payable and Accrued Liabilities	$ 182,274
Current Portion of Long-Term Debt	48,600
Advances to Members	8,000,000
Long-Term Debt	194,400
TOTAL LIABILITIES	8,425,274
Members Equity	7,748,918
TOTAL LIABILITIES AND MEMBERS EQUITY	$16,174,192

Summary of Statement of Operations

	3/31/19
Sales and Other Operating Income	$ 376,857
Cost of Sales	157,561
GROSS PROFIT	219,296
Payroll Expenses	89,890
Fixed Expenses	77,642
Other Expenses	143,116
TOTAL EXPENSES	310,648
NET LOSS	$ (91,352)

When construction is complete, the L.L.C. expects to finance the construction project with long-term debt guaranteed by each member in the amount of $8,000,000. The balance of the remaining costs of construction are expected to be financed by the members of the L.L.C. The Cooperative expects to finance its portion of the remaining construction costs with long term debt and insurance proceeds.

During the year ended March 31, 2019, the Cooperative incurred payroll costs of [illegible] and interest costs of $285,673 that were related to construction of the Western Planters, L.L.C. gin. These amounts are included in advances receivable on the accompanying balance sheet.

Figure 23-4

CHAPTER XXIV

You'll Need a Scorecard

As YOU LOOK back, we have discussed questionable characters and how people died for unknown or misidentified reasons. As we saw in the previous three chapters, what appeared to be a well-organized but vague plot to steal some monies from family members appeared in affect to be a lethal murder plot and a bank conspiring with a ruthless money-hungry mob (of family). If you look at the flow chart below (Fig. 24-1), you will see names and persons who conspired to and took monies that were not their own. The people are real, and documents follow to validate each. The one issue we can specifically state, was that Clifford Newberry was the sole beneficiary of Robert Dean Newberry, his father and Clifford never received any of the FEDEX Settlement. We have an attorney who agreed to represent a lady, and for whatever reason, he guided her effectively to the gallows. We have documents that show that immediately after a large settlement payment was received, direct and indirect family members began purchasing land and homes with no liens on the property. About this same time, the monies in R. D. Newberry's account vanished. Parts were deposited in BancFirst under the name of Robert Dean Newberry, with Andrea having signature authority, kind of! Four days later, a power of attorney for her was received on BancFirst letterhead (Fig. 24-2). You have to ask yourself, (1) What bank would allow a fraudulent bank account to be opened with a fraudulent power of attorney that used a distant, out-of-area notary?

(2) What bank would accept a fraudulent power of attorney four days after said fraudulent account was opened? (3) And what bank would allow a fraudulent mortgage to be filed using the same distant notary without the owner of the property being notified and without the signature of the owner?

Should Mr. Cummins have been acting in any capacity of a legitimate attorney, he would have never accepted the case when he accepted Clifford's $5,000 retainer. More appropriately, he should have considered his actions long before he got into this mess.

The attachment 24-1 shows the association of the family. You be the judge and be sure on attachment 24-3 to read item 19 on the attorney-client agreement.

As stated, David L. Cummins represented (even though very questionably) Jennifer Caswell at the time he was representing his stepson Jamie Boone, who had just received his fourth DUI and left the scene of an accident. Through the family connection in 24-1, you see that when he accepted the case from Clifford to recover his inheritance, he did so and asked for a 40 percent return for all recovered. Looking at number 19 in 24-3 to do such, he would, in effect, be suing himself. This would explain why, for three years, he had done nothing other than hire another firm and file nothing. It might be noted that after a year and a half, the other firm did file a civil case.

Looking at 24-4, you will see home and land purchases with no liens at about the time of Robert Dean Newberry's settlement by those assigned to care for it and also those related to Mr. Newberry. Note also the date he passed; all of his settlement was already gone. How is it that he can receive millions on a settlement in August 2015 and by October 30, 2016, have his accounts be drained with little to show for such for being a quadriplegic? In Clifford's case, the only thing I can prove is after the crash and in the event of his father's death and his will vanishing, his stepmother would have received everything. After his stepmother got everything, it would go to his stepsister, Rhonda Bourland. However, his stepmother died first after signing the contingency fee agreement, which would not be legally binding since Robert Dean Newberry was still alive and it was his settlement. David Cummins's stepson is also Donna Bourland's stepson. The Bourland family would have gotten everything had Robert Dean Newberry died first. It appears Clifford's aunt Andrea Newberry did not like any of those scenarios and perhaps weighed the odds, because she wanted it all. It appears that through the actions of David Cummins, Andrea Newberry, and possibly the Bourlands, that Andrea may have conspired with them to ensure the plans for success. David Cummins's actions or lack thereof prove a conflict especially when Andrea Newberry was boasting about her instructing Cummins to back off through her legal counsel, according to a witness.

Recall that we saw that one of these caregivers, named Sue Livermore who had taken a total of $45,000, of which only $10,000 had been approved by Robert Dean Newberry. That leaves only, let's say, millions unaccounted for.

Look back at 24-1, and let's start analyzing each step. We have shown that Andrea had been quite busy with the power of attorney (a bit late of course) and such but now, look at Rhonda Bourland, Clifford's stepsister. She is married to David Bourland, and he has a sister named Donna Bourland who is married to Nicky Boone, whose son Jamie we spoke of earlier. Nicky's ex-wife is Marsha, who is now married to David Cummins. She was very sweet to Clifford in the office until he fired David L. Cummins for lack of attention and action on his case. That could have been due only to the lack of now being a client, or more likely as he was with Chris Poindexter who was investigating this mess. She, as did her husband know that the money that had been stolen would soon lead back to their door. Strangely enough, people seem to become quite hostile when they are caught with their hands in the cookie jar! Strange?

Look carefully at paragraph 19 in 24-3.

> 19. Attorney is authorized to select and retain such additional legal counsel as Attorney may deem beneficial to assist Attorney in handling

> motions, and/or doing research on legal arguments which may arise after the filing of any lawsuit for the return and collection of the above described monies, accounts, and assets.

Note after saying in here "after filing of any lawsuits," he apparently contacted additional counsel even though he never filed anything. Why, is suing yourself that difficult or is suing yourself and not getting caught that complex? Again, as earlier in the book, we've got a real mystery on our hands here. More appropriately, Mr. David L. Cummins has a real problem on his hands!

Here is how I see it. I would say "in a nutshell," but you couldn't put this mess in a ten-gallon hat.

Andrea set up that meeting back in the fall of 2012 and had an attorney, Mr. Bell, an investigator for the Iron Workers Union, and Sharon Newberry in attendance. Robert Newberry was close by but not brought into the discussion nor was Clifford, his son, or Sharon Newberry's daughter, Rhonda. Why were they not included? Two months later, Sharon was dead! Andrea deposited money for Robert Newberry to BancFirst from the settlement and awarded herself as a signer and had the power of attorney. Oops! Four days later, on the BancFirst stationary, that showed up. She also claimed that she had been given the power of attorney to sign for his care and all affairs. The problem is that she has never provided such, and there is a strong possibility that that document does not exist. She claims that Attorney Bell has such, but that has never surfaced either!

In October 2016, Robert Newberry goes for the ride of his life, which ended his life. After the settlement arrives in 2015, a string of land and home purchases with no liens are accomplished that has a group of relatives included on the purchasers list along with David and Marsha Cummins. Robert Newberry's brother also purchased two homes in Henderson, Nevada, as well as one in Virginia for cash. One that really stands out is, Andrea actually wrote out a check for over $200,000 (24-5) to buy her home and furniture and an upgraded heating and cooling system (24-6). Looking at all of these procurements, one must ask, Where did the money come from?

Here we go again; you get to be the judge. From my experiences, banks and the like enjoy holding a lien until the property is paid in full! Gee, I wonder why that is? Perhaps this bunch just looked trust-worthy and the banks did not want to question such? If you believe that, please contact me immediately, as I have land for sale just off to the southeast side of South Padre Island. I will furnish a tide table, and we can view the property on low tide.

I realize that I am a bit sarcastic, but when one begins to follow the money trail, one becomes that way!

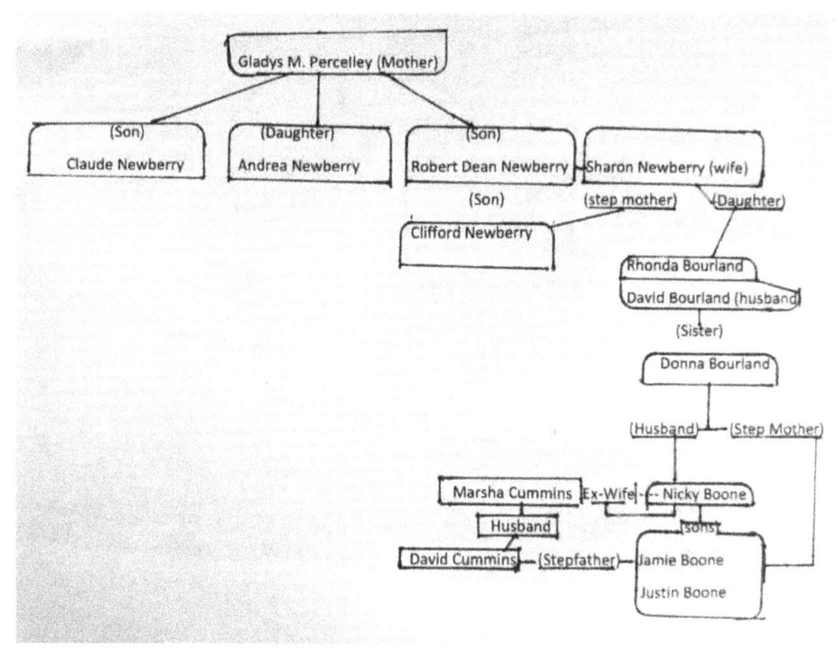
Gladys M. Percelley (Mother)
(Son)
Claude Newberry
(Daughter)
Andrea Newberry
(Son)
Robert Dean Newberry
Sharon Newberry (wife)
(Son)
(step mother)
(Daughter)
Clifford Newberry
Rhonda Bourland
David Bourland (husband)
(Sister)
Donna Bourland
(Husband)
(Step Mother)
Marsha Cummins
Ex-Wife
Nicky Boone
Husband
(sons)
David Cummins
(Stepfather)
Jamie Boone
Justin Boone

Figure 24-1

BancFirst

Statutory Durable Power of Attorney

To Act with Respect to Account
(15 O.S. Supp. 2004, 1001 et seq.)

ROBERT DEAN NEWBERRY — Principal's Name
4208054785 — Principal's Account Number

NOTICE: THE POWERS GRANTED BY THIS DOCUMENT ARE BROAD AND SWEEPING. THEY ARE EXPLAINED IN THE UNIFORM STATUTORY FORM POWER OF ATTORNEY ACT. IF YOU HAVE ANY QUESTIONS ABOUT THESE POWERS, OBTAIN COMPETENT LEGAL ADVICE. THIS DOCUMENT DOES NOT AUTHORIZE ANYONE TO MAKE MEDICAL AND OTHER HEALTH-CARE DECISIONS FOR YOU. YOU MAY REVOKE THIS POWER OF ATTORNEY IF YOU LATER WISH TO DO SO.

I, ROBERT DEAN NEWBERRY pursuant to Section 1003 of Title 15 of the Oklahoma Statues, have made, constituted, and appointed, and by these presents do make, constitute and appoint ANDRA KAY NEWBERRY, whose address is ________, and whose signature appears below, as my true and lawful attorney, to act for me in my name, place and stead, and with full power and authority, to do and perform all and every act and thing whatsoever in connection with the above referenced account with BancFirst as fully and to all intents and purposes as I might and could do if personally present, including, but not limited to, the following initialed subjects:

TO GRANT THE FOLLOWING POWER, INITIAL IN THE LINE IN FRONT OF THE POWER TO BE GRANTED.

AN (A) Banking and other financial institution transactions as defined in 15 O.S. (Supp. 2004), Section 1010.
____ (B) Retirement plan transactions as defined in 15 O.S. (Supp. 2004), Section 1017.

SPECIAL INSTRUCTIONS: ON THE FOLLOWING LINES YOU MAY GIVE SPECIAL INSTRUCTIONS LIMITING OR EXTENDING THE POWERS GRANTED TO YOUR ATTORNEY-IN-FACT. PLACE YOUR INITIALS IN THE SPACE IN FRONT OF THE APPLICABLE PROVISION.
This power of attorney:

____ Is limited to transactions involving the reference account described above, maintained at BancFirst.
RDN Is applicable to all of my account relationships with BancFirst.

My attorney-in-fact shall NOT h[illegible] wers granted under Section 1010.8 of Title 15, to borrow in my name as Principal.
(Attach additional pages if n[illegible])

UNLESS YOU DIRECT OTHERWISE ABOVE, THIS POWER OF ATTORNEY IS EFFECTIVE IMMEDIATELY AND WILL CONTINUE UNTIL IT IS REVOKED.

THIS POWER OF ATTORNEY WILL CONTINUE TO BE EFFECTIVE EVEN THOUGH I MAY BECOME DISABLED, INCAPACITATED, OR INCOMPETENT IN THE FUTURE.

This power of attorney shall remain in full force and effect until such time as written notice of revocation of the same, signed by me, has been received by BancFirst at the branch where my account is maintained. Each and every act performed by my said attorney-in-fact pursuant to the provisions and authority of this power of attorney shall be binding on me, my estate and my heirs, and I hereby ratify and confirm all that my said attorney-in-fact shall do or cause to be done by virtue of this power of attorney.

Neither BancFirst nor any of its officers, employees, or agents shall be under any obligation to make any inquiry as to the purpose or propriety of any act of my said attorney-in-fact or of the use or application by my said attorney-in-fact of any of my assets.

The following is a specimen of the signature of the attorney appointed hereby: Andrea Newberry — Signature of Attorney-in-Fact

I agree that any third party who receives a copy of this document may act under it. I agree to indemnify the third party for any claims that arise against the third party because of reliance on this power of attorney.

Signed this 30 day of Aug. 2015 — Signature of Principal

443-46-2280 — Social Security Number

ACKNOWLEDGEMENT

STATE OF Oklahoma)
) SS:
COUNTY OF Cleveland)

The foregoing instrument was acknowledged before me on this 30 day of August, 2015, by ____

My Commission Expires: 6/28/19

Jo Ann Campbell — Notary Public

Commission Number: 03008314

BY ACCEPTING OR ACTING UNDER THE APPOINTMENT, THE ATTORNEY-IN-FACT ASSUMES THE FIDUCIARY AND OTHER LEGAL RESPONSIBILITIES OF AN ATTORNEY-IN-FACT.

BFA0023 (revised July 08)

Page 1 of 2

Figure 24-2

BancFirst. Signature Card

Product: SENIORITY CHECKING
Date: 08/26/2015 HOM Phone: 405-627-0032
Plan ID#: 000 Phone:
New ☒ Rev ☐ CSR BWEESE
Comments:

Account Ownership Description:

Account #: 4208054785

☐ Check if Signature Card Addendum is attached.

Account Owner(s) and Mailing Address:
ROBERT DEAN NEWBERRY
ANDREA K NEWBERRY
SETTLEMENT ACCOUNT
2505 NW 39TH TER
OKLAHOMA CITY, OK 73112-3729

The undersigned acknowledges receipt of Bank's Deposit Agreement, Funds Availability Schedule, Electronic Funds Transfer Disclosure, Account Disclosure, and Privacy Disclosure and agrees to their terms. If not signed in the presence of a BancFirst employee, signatures must be notarized on the back of this card.

Name of Signatory	Signature Specimens
1. ROBERT DEAN NEWBERRY ID#: 081252930 Issuer: OK DOB: 8/10/1944 TIN: 443-46-2280 Relationship: Joint Tenancy/Or	
2. ANDREA K NEWBERRY ID#: 081378392 Issuer: OK DOB: 11/22/1954 TIN: 443-46-1420 Relationship: Joint Tenancy/Or	
3. ANDREA K NEWBERRY ID#: 081378392 Issuer: OK DOB: 11/22/1954 TIN: 443-46-1420 Relationship: Power of Attorney	
4. ID#: Issuer: DOB: TIN: Relationship:	
5. ID#: Issuer: DOB: TIN: Relationship:	
6. ID#: Issuer: DOB: TIN: Relationship:	
7. ID#: Issuer: DOB: TIN: Relationship:	
8. ID#: Issuer: DOB: TIN: Relationship:	
9. ID#: Issuer: DOB: TIN: Relationship:	
10. ID#: Issuer: DOB: TIN: Relationship:	

Payor's Request for Taxpayer's Identification Number and Certification

Taxpayer Identification Number: 443-46-2280

Certification • Under penalties of perjury, I certify that:

(1) The number shown on this form is my correct taxpayer identification number and

(2) I am not subject to backup withholding because: (a) I am exempt from backup withholding, or (b) I have not been notified by the Internal Revenue Service (IRS) that I am subject to backup withholding as a result of a failure to report all interest or dividends, or (c) the IRS has notified me that I am no longer subject to backup withholding.

(3) I am a U.S. Person (Including a U.S. resident alien)

Certification Instructions – You must cross out item 2 above if you have been notified by the IRS that you are currently subject to backup withholding because you have failed to report all interest and dividends on your tax return. For real estate transactions, item 2 does not apply. For mortgage interest paid, the acquisition or abandonment of security property, cancellation of debt, contributions to an individual retirement arrangement (IRA), and generally payments other than interest and dividends, you are not required to sign the Certification, but you must provide your correct TIN.

Signature ROBERT DEAN NEWBERRY Date

Figure 24-2a

CONTINGENT FEE CONTRACT

This contract made and entered into this 15th day of March, 2018, by and between DAVID L. CUMMINS, Attorney at Law, (hereinafter called Attorney), and CLIFORD DEAN NEWBERRY (hereinafter called CLIENT),

WITNESSETH:

1. Client on or about August 23, 2017, Client retained Attorney to Petition for the appointment of Client as Personal Representative of the estate of Client's father, Robert Dean Newberry, Deceased, (the Decedent) in Kiowa County probate case #PB-2017-21. A prior Petition for Letters of Administration was then pending in said probate, filed by Andrea Kay Newberry, sister of the Decedent. Client is the sole and only heir at law of the Decedent, and on August 28, 2017, Client was appointed by the Court as Personal Representative of said estate.

2. Client has paid Attorney the sum of $5,000.00 as retainer to represent Client in the probate matter, which attorney will earn at the rate of $200.00 per hour, and utilize to pay probate costs incurred. Said $5,000.00 is not a fixed fee for the handling of said probate, but is anticipated to be sufficient for that legal service.

3. Client acknowledges that a probate is a legal proceeding to identify the assets held in the name of Decedent to be conveyed by the Personal Representative to the heirs, and to pay the debts of the decedent, and to distribute the remainder of the assets to the person or persons determined as the heir or heirs of the Decedent. Assets of the probate do not include assets which are transferred at death by other means, for example, prior transfers by Transfer on Death Deed, property held in joint tenancy, transfer of accounts which are Payable on Death (POD) accounts, and transfer of insurance proceeds which are payable to a named beneficiary.

4. The parties believe that a sizable sum of money was paid to the Decedent from the settlement of claims of the Decedent derived from settlement of Kiowa County civil action #CJ-2103-31, both as an heir to an undivided 1/3 of the estate of his mother, Gladys Purscelley, Deceased, and individually. Such civil action sought damages for the death of Gladys Purscelley and personal injury to the Decedent, Robert Dean Newberry.

5. Upon inquiry by Attorney following examination of records provided by Client, Attorney learned that Decedent had an account with BancFirst of Hobart styled "Robert Dean Newberry Andrea K. Newberry Settlement Account." Attorney requested that BancFirst provide copies of the statements and items of said account from its inception to date. BancFirst, by Mark Bobo, replied that the records requested would not be provided due to the refusal of Andrea K. Newberry to permit release of said records, unless sought by subpoena.

6. Attorney made inquiry of Bryan K. Walkley and Ginger K. Maxted, attorneys of record for Plaintiffs in the civil action CJ-2013-31, for a copy of the Settlement Agreement(s) in said civil lawsuit. Said attorneys have failed to answer such request.

7. Attorney spoke with attorney Bill Gentry of Hobart, OK, who was attorney of record

Figure 24-3

for Andrea K. Newberry in her Petition for appointment of herself as Personal Representative of the estate of Robert Dean Newberry, and as attorney of record for Andrea Kay Newberry in her capacity as Personal Representative of the estate of Gladys Purscelley, Kiowa County #PB-2012-19. Gentry provided Attorney with a list of assets of the estate of Robert Dean Newberry, which attorney Gentry represented as having been provided by Andrea K. Newberry, and which contained only real property held in the name of Robert Dean Newberry in whole or part. Attorney inquired of Gentry as to bank accounts and/or other similar assets of Robert Dean Newberry, and was told that Andrea K. Newberry had represented to him that there were no bank accounts to be included in the probate of Robert Dean Newberry's estate.

8. Records provided to Attorney by Client further reveal an undisclosed Annuity issued by Great American Insurance Group in the initial sum of $150,000.00. Other records reveal a portfolio with BancFirst investments having a value of $301,882.29 as of September 30, 2016, which appears to be subject to a TOD (Transfer on Death) designation. The beneficiary is not identified in the referenced documents.

9. From these inquiries and uncorroborated statements made by other persons, Attorney and Client believe that accounts and monies of Robert Dean Newberry, Deceased, have been transferred outside probate, and that such transfers deprive Client, as sole heir of Robert Dean Newberry, Deceased, of his right to receive the said settlement funds and any other funds.

10. Client has requested that Attorney act to discover and recover the funds to which the estate of Robert Dean Newberry, Deceased, and Client are entitled to receive.

IT IS THEREFORE AGREED BY THE PARTIES:

11. Attorney agrees to represent Client in the pursuit, discovery and collection of said monies and accounts, and other assets if any, in consideration of the terms of this Contingent Fee Contract.

12. Attorney agrees to issue discovery requests, including but not limited to Subpoenas Duces Tecum, to persons believed to have relevant information pertaining to the accounts and assets of Robert Dean Newberry, including but not limited to Subpoenas Duces Tecum issued to obtain the agreement of settlement and/or other documentation identifying the sums paid to the Estate of Gladys Purscelly, and to or in behalf of Robert Dean Newberry, and Subpoenas Duces Tecum or other discovery to obtain records pertaining to the accounts in which Robert Dean Newberry held some right, title or interest.

13. After discovery of the described records and information, and any other documents or information which may appear pertinent, Attorney will demand the return of said funds from the person or persons who received same.

14. Client shall pay or convey to Attorney a sum equal to TWENTY-FIVE PER CEN (25%) of all net sums received by agreed settlement of claims made upon such demands prior t filing of any action to recover such funds.

Figure 24-3a

15. Client shall pay or convey to attorney a sum equal to FORTY PER CENT (40%) of all net sums collected by Attorney after the filing of any lawsuit seeking the accounting and return of any and all such funds.

16. Attorney and Client agree that "net sums" shall be defined as the amount received from such demand(s) after payment of costs incurred for issuance of discovery requests, and for filing fees and court costs, costs of depositions, copying of documents, costs of associate or appellate attorneys, and other similar costs incurred in pursuit and recovery of such funds.

17. Attorney shall advance all necessary discovery and litigation expenses. Client agrees to reimburse Attorney monthly for 75% of all costs expended prior to filing of any lawsuit for the recovery of such monies, accounts and assets. Client shall reimburse Attorney monthly for 60% of all costs expended upon and after filing of any lawsuit for the recovery of said monies, accounts and assets.

18. Attorney and Client shall each be reimbursed for their respective sums paid for the above described and identified costs and expenses prior to division of any "net settlement" obtained from either settlement of demands or after filing of any lawsuit.

19. Attorney is authorized to select and retain such additional legal counsel as Attorney may deem beneficial to assist Attorney in handling motions, and/or doing research on legal arguments which may arise after the filing of any lawsuit for the return and collection of the above described monies, accounts, and assets.

20. In the event of any appeal of any judgment obtained, or of any action by any opposing party presented to any appellate Court, Attorney may, and is authorized to retain an associate attorney for the purpose of representing Client at such appellate level.

WITNESS OUR HANDS this 15th day of March, 2018.

David L. Cummins, OBA 2090
Attorney at Law
215 N. 2nd
P.O. Box 489
Hollis, Okla. 73550
580-688-9276
cumminslaw@pldi.net

Clifford Dean Newberry, Client
708 Evans Avenue
Lone Wolf, OK 73655

Figure 24-3b

Figure 24-5a

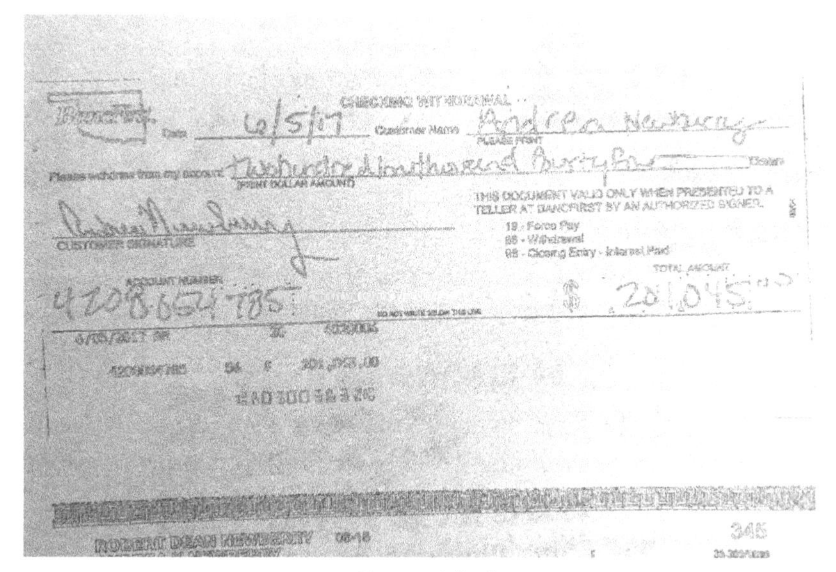

CHECKING WITHDRAWAL

Date 6/5/17 Customer Name Andrea Newbury
PLEASE PRINT

Please withdraw from my account Two hundred one thousand forty five Dollars
(PRINT DOLLAR AMOUNT)

THIS DOCUMENT VALID ONLY WHEN PRESENTED TO A TELLER AT BANCFIRST BY AN AUTHORIZED SIGNER.

18 - Force Pay
86 - Withdrawal
88 - Closing Entry - Interest Paid

CUSTOMER SIGNATURE

ACCOUNT NUMBER
4208654785

TOTAL AMOUNT
$ 201,045.00

DO NOT WRITE BELOW THIS LINE

ROBERT DEAN NEWBERRY 08-18

345

Figure 24-5b

CHAPTER XXV

BancFirst and the Nations

In June of 2013, Mr. Jack Stuteville had his deposition taken in reference to the lawsuit taken with respect to Pridex Construction, of which the Jury unanimously awarded a judgement that Lord Woodward reversed, as discussed earlier in the book. Stuteville was asked in the deposition what he did for a living, and part of his response was most interesting.

> "Basically in the farming operation. I also represent a chemical company. (Question) What capacity do you represent the chemical company? (Answer) Marketing and sales. (Question) What's the name of that company, please? (Answer) On—they've just changed. It's an Australian company. It's called—it's just changed. I'll get it to you in a minute." (25-1)

Now that's the kind of marketing agent that I want! He can't even recall whom he works for! Or in reality, does he simply not want you to know, as the Ponzi scam is in that infantile stage and could still be sacked?

The main thing the citizens of the United States need to understand is that in his deposition, when Jack Stuteville stated he worked for an Australian company but couldn't recall the name, he simply did not want that name released. Jack Stuteville provided marketing and sales services for them but with only one intention in mind. Its purpose was not to create any useful product for the world to use. It just so happens that after No Heat & Earth Heat Resources received hundreds of millions in guaranteed loans to dig geothermal wells in Copahue, Argentina, they changed their name to Rampart. Why would they do such a thing and why did he not want to state the name? Now comes a really good question: why did Rampart loan $7.1 million to a convicted felon named Larry Wright? The answer is quite simple, but its construction is quite complex. Rampart has a judgment against Larry Wright to keep people like Chris Poindexter (Pridex) and others from collecting the $2.7 million (in the case of Pridex) that Larry Wright owes them. The first big question is, How did they make that happen?

If a person or a company has a judgement against them, the state and/or the federal government is responsible to assure the public that that person or company pays up! So how is it that this person isn't paying and continues to do business as usual and write fake bonds for federal government agencies and many others?

Recall that in 2008 that the Oklahoma insurance commissioner Kim Holland issued a cease and desist order for Larry Wright to discontinue doing business in the state of Oklahoma. Then in 2011 came the new guy, John Doak, who simply passed it off as "Well, we can't do anything to him, as he is not licensed to do business in Oklahoma!" Recall we are back to the bank robber who is not licensed to rob banks in Oklahoma; therefore, we cannot go after him.

However, since the State of Oklahoma and the federal government seem to promote Larry Wright's fraudulent insurance sales, they should be held liable along with our state and government leaders. That also includes our state and federal judges that promote insurance fraud in Oklahoma. They know fully well that the funds were being deposited in Native American Bank here in Oklahoma via Ironstone Bank (which, by the way, does not exist) and allow such to continue (Fig. 25-2).

This brings to mind an interesting thought that if certain people are not held accountable for their actions, then legally, since the court is the one that has to predicate its actions on prior cases, then none of us can legally be held accountable if we follow these footprints. In other words, it will return to the days of old when the law was an eye for an eye and a tooth for a tooth! This shows a strong animus leaning toward our justice department and the law enforcement. If no one has noticed in the recent past, we have seen a sharp turn upward in the shootings of police officers in this country. There is one very sad but definitive reason for such, and that is people—let's call them criminals—are snubbing their noses toward our age-old system, and that is due solely to the two-tier system that has grown by the day!

Recall that recently, a senior law enforcement civil servant was let off after lying to the FBI and others. Not that this was the first nor, as we are going, will it be the last. Why did this happen? Well, he was protected by those who worked around and with him. A clear case of our government against us—we the people!

Thomas Jefferson stated, "A government big enough to give you everything you want is strong enough to take everything you have."

Let's now turn our attention to the Australian company called Earth Heat Resources Ltd. Recall how Stuteville could not recall the name. Well, of course, it is a real odd name, Earth. Shortly after the receipt of the guarantees, the company went under and changed its name to Rampart! Where did the money go?

It may be worth noting at this time that a Ronald Pelosi who was on the board for Solyndra was also on the board with Earth Heat Resources Ltd. Purely coincidence that both went bankrupt!

> Ronald Pelosi's political contacts (may) have been a reason why he was hired by PCG, but not from a federal perspective. The firm has been indirectly caught up in a California pay-to-play scandal, which resulted in it getting fired last fall by the state's largest pension fund. If Pelosi

> is supposed to get PCG back in political good graces, it's a local issue.

Now, as we have been going in this direction for quite some time with the initial companies out of the way and Rampart Capital Management LLC, a Delaware limited liability company proceeded to sue Larry James Wright and took his deposition on June 7, 2011. Strangely enough, Rampart prevailed and got a judgement for over $7 million dollars. And to this date, he has not paid—kind of like all other suits against him, unpaid! It may be worth your time to read the entire deposition as it is literally entertainment at its finest!

While PCG, The Underwriters Group (TUG), and other suspicious entities were continuing to operate, Chris Poindexter was still trying to recoup his losses from the fraudulent bonds. He was met with, at the time, a seemingly unrelated event. His construction company, Pridex, was being hit with unbelievable bank charges at BancFirst in Oklahoma. With an open-door meeting with Dwight Waugh, he, Chris, was receiving an unacceptable screaming ass-chewing for effectively doing nothing, or so he thought. Without going into the details, this bank held the note for some of the properties that Chris was working on. The day following this eventful exercise, Chris went in to get the payoff and close out the account. Shortly thereafter, the president of BancFirst got in touch with him to moderate this or to stop Pridex from moving the loan. When that could not be accomplished, the fees really hit, with over $30,000 to just pay off the loan.

Now, with this, Chris contacted his longtime attorney, Clay Christensen, who was, by the way, the brother-in-law of the governor, Mary Fallon, and was contemplating suing the bank. What came next was unbelievable—his attorney told him that if he persisted in this suit against the bank, he would have nothing again to do with him!

If we look at the overall picture, why would this be occurring? Look closer. As I had mentioned earlier, the president at BancFirst in Hobart, Oklahoma, Dwight Waugh, had worked for some eight years under Jack Stuteville at First Capital Bank (FCB) and was quite in tune with what was going on. Mike Frey had worked at FCB for a number of years as well. Both were very knowledgeable as to what was going on with PCG, and I would say that there is great cause to even assume that he may have been on the receiving end of some of the funds from way back in the Solyndra days or events thereafter. At one point, Chris Poindexter went into Mike Frey's office and asked him what he knew about PCG. At first, he put on an act of no knowledge, and then finally, he responded by saying that the company vaguely sounded familiar. It was at the time when Frey worked there that Jack Stuteville loaned PCG via First Capital Bank (FCB) over $8 million. I then asked how Jack Stuteville and Troy Vanbrunt could sign so many bank notes issued to a company Jack Stuteville has ownership in. He immediately said Jack did not have any ownership in PCG, and Chris said that according to these documents, he sure did. Chris asked him how he was able to do that and handed him a document showing ownership and Stuteville as an owner of PCG. It was clear that Chris had just hit a nerve with Frey. Mike Frey stood up red-faced and shouted, "Where did you get these documents!" and Chris replied, "I have obviously struck a nerve." Chris grabbed the document back! Chris stated that he got them in Arkansas and said that he had best be leaving, and he exited Bancfirst in Kingfisher. I find it interesting that both Mike Frey and Dwight Waugh were employed under Jack Stuteville at First Capital Bank while a lot of these PCG Ponzi schemes were going on and then went to BancFirst prior to the First Capital Bank failure.

At the time this was occurring with Chris Poindexter and BancFirst, the County of Kingfisher was in the process of building a new hospital. Jack Stuteville was on the hospital board and was also calling the shots on a lot of the hospital construction. As the construction proceeded, according to a deposition with Mike Kevin Mathews, he was awarded the bid and Jack taketh away. The hospital construction was seeing more and more cost overruns and BancFirst was more than happy to accommodate and advance money to provide the required financing. When the project was nearing completion, Mercy hospital would not takeover management of the hospital until the cost overruns had been remedied. At that time the

Kingfisher Times Newspaper was continually running articles for a bond issue to cover the costs as "We have to have a hospital here please vote yes on the bond measure…!" So, as this wound down, the good citizens of Kingfisher got their hospital but for a severely inflated price. BancFirst was only too happy to hand out cash no matter how far the price overrun would be! This helps to explain the reaction to Mike Frye when he saw the ownership that Jack had in PCG at a time when FCB was loaning Jacks company money by the bucket full!

What was going on was an attempt to quiet Pridex completely by financially breaking Chris and his company. Dwight Waugh even told one BancFirst customer, "Chris Poindexter, Pridex Construction would be going bankrupt." While Chris was digging through court and banking records, Stuteville, PCG, and other bankers and banks were busily attempting to quiet his voice financially.

We have seen this strategy before and have seen how it works. In an anonymous letter that I, the author of this book and others, received after I was a whistleblower to federal corruption, the writer of a four-page diatribe stated that chapter 21, which is where I described the financial breaking process and the destruction of my family, farm, and farming business, is funny! I'm certain she will consider it funny in the future, as she left a nice thumbprint on it!

Above in this chapter, I mentioned the prior governor of the State of Oklahoma, and now it is time to get acquainted with something called compacts. Governor Mary Fallin and some before her had entered into these compacts with the Native American tribes here in Oklahoma and some in other states. You will, in the remainder of this book, see how these legal instruments are associated with PCG and other schemes to collapse our nation financially!

Before we leave this chapter, it is imperative that you, the reader, fully understand what it is, this compact. In general, a compact is described as the following:

> Unlike contracts, compacts are solemn agreements between two sovereigns that remain in force until both parties agree otherwise.

So in plain language, if you and I sign a compact on any issue as two sovereign parties, it will remain in force until such time as we agree to change it. More simply stated, if we sign this compact for you to pay me a million dollars a month, you are required to pay me until I wish to no longer receive a million dollars a month from you and we change such!

Governor Mary Fallin made a number of most interesting agreements (compacts) with the various tribal nations here in Oklahoma, from free hunting and fishing to attempting to roll back compact agreements on class I gaming and class II and III electronic gaming.

> A house divided against itself cannot stand. I believe this government cannot endure, permanently…I do not expect the Union to be dissolved—I do not expect the house to fall—but I do expect it will cease to be divided. It will become all one thing, or all the other. (Abraham Lincoln)

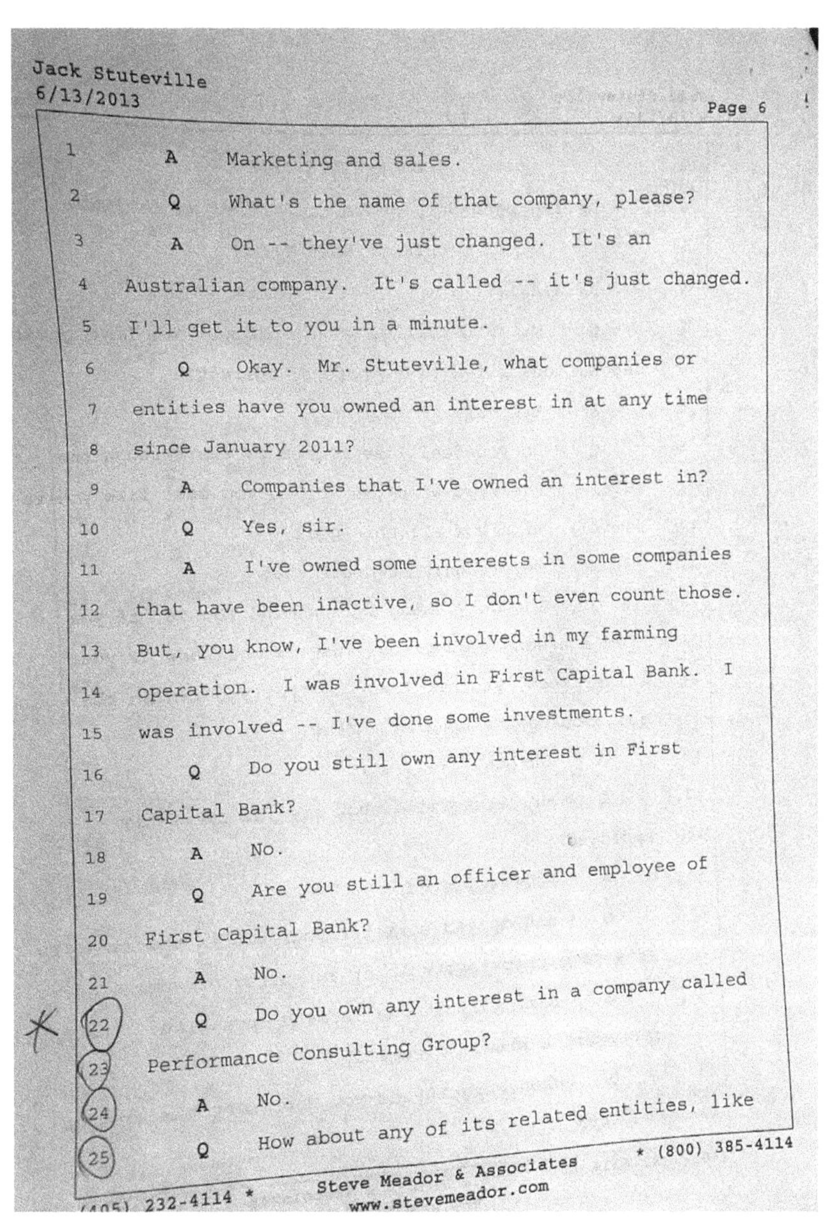

Jack Stuteville
6/13/2013
Page 6

1 A Marketing and sales.
2 Q What's the name of that company, please?
3 A On -- they've just changed. It's an
4 Australian company. It's called -- it's just changed.
5 I'll get it to you in a minute.
6 Q Okay. Mr. Stuteville, what companies or
7 entities have you owned an interest in at any time
8 since January 2011?
9 A Companies that I've owned an interest in?
10 Q Yes, sir.
11 A I've owned some interests in some companies
12 that have been inactive, so I don't even count those.
13 But, you know, I've been involved in my farming
14 operation. I was involved in First Capital Bank. I
15 was involved -- I've done some investments.
16 Q Do you still own any interest in First
17 Capital Bank?
18 A No.
19 Q Are you still an officer and employee of
20 First Capital Bank?
21 A No.
22 Q Do you own any interest in a company called
23 Performance Consulting Group?
24 A No.
25 Q How about any of its related entities, like

(405) 232-4114 * Steve Meador & Associates * (800) 385-4114
www.stevemeador.com

Figure 25-1a

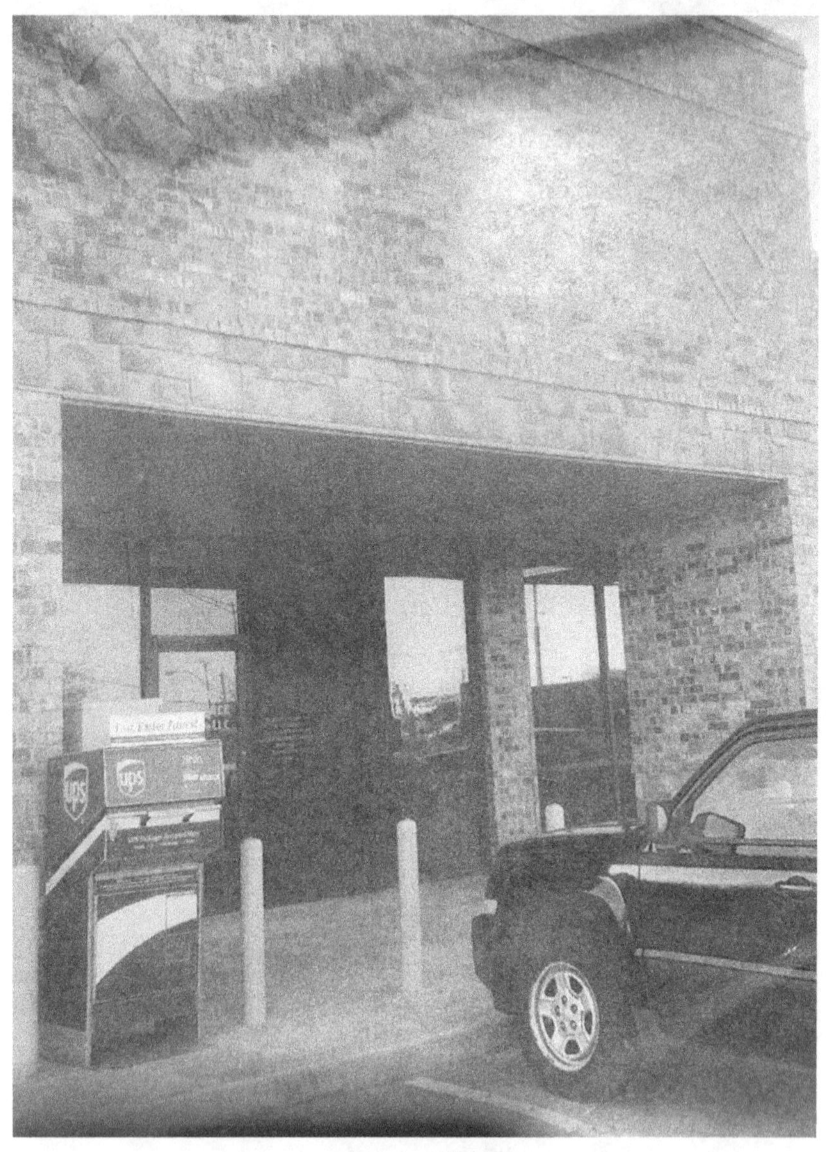

Figure 25-2

CHAPTER XXVI

PCG Ponzi Schemes Go Full Circle

Any bank that can stay in business for 110 years must have been doing something right. First Capital Bank originally founded in 1902 as Guthrie Savings Bank, provided banking services to its customers at a time when Oklahoma was not yet a state and Guthrie was the capital of the Oklahoma Territory.

> The long and colorful history of First Capital Bank came to an unfortunate end today when the Bank was closed by the Oklahoma State Banking Department. The FDIC, acting as receiver, sold the failed bank to F&M Bank, Edmond, OK, which will assume all deposits of First Capital Bank. Despite the Bank's long history, First Capital Bank had only one branch. Total assets of First Capital had declined from $119 million in March 2011 to only $46.1 million on March 31, 2012. A Consent Order issued by the FDIC in October 2010 ordered the Bank to initiate an asset reduction plan to rebuild capital. First Capital Bank was a wholly owned subsidiary of holding company FCB Holdings, Inc. of Guthrie, OK. (https://problembanklist.com/)

The statement in 2012 was most accurate; they must have been doing something right to stay in business for over one hundred years, but with the current management, they must have been doing something really wrong.

As noted by then fire chief of Kingfisher, Oklahoma, for multiple days before the bank was seized by the FDIC, Attorney Randy Mecklenburg's car was parked in front of First Capital Bank, and they were loading files that were taken out of the bank into a cargo transport and then storing them in a locked storage behind the law firm that was owned by Harrison and Mecklenburg. There were many mortgages filed at the Kingfisher County Courthouse having to do with the real estate and development ventures involving the Mecklenburg family. The fire chief tried repeatedly to report to the FDIC investigator, Agent Hernandez, who was unconcerned or, perhaps we should say, well informed (from what we have previously covered) and did not want to hear such. The FDIC did not want to hear from the fire chief as to what was going on. Randy Poindexter, the fire chief, went to the extreme of contacting Representative Todd Russ to have him notify the FDIC, Agent Hernandez, and he, too, took no action. Why, because they already knew and wished to not have anyone else know. It would interrupt their plan on the bank collapse.

Before this, in 2003, a seemingly unconnected event transpired that would begin the ball rolling. Let's call this the Ruby Escapades. Mr. Rick Moore, CEO of the Indigenous Nations Federal Charter Association (INFCA) Tribal Reserve was in contact with Larry Wright or, should I say, in collusion with setting up a guarantee for the Fort Cobb Power Plant hoax. The overall plan was to issue some $4 million worth of tribal shares to six tribes combined with the fraud $4 million in fake rubies along with other unidentified collateral and the fake bonds of Larry Wright; then via the Department of Agriculture loan guarantee wrap, the project was up and running. There never was a real plan to begin this power plant, only seed money to possibly begin the largest casino in the world at that time.

Now I use the term *fake rubies* as these were deposited into the First National Bank in Davis, Oklahoma, and stored in the safe there. A fake statement was generated that gave a value of over $4 million, which guaranteed additional money to be loaned against these and got the ball rolling. In reality, the rocks were nothing more than fossil rocks and had a value from $300 to as high as $1,600 after being appraised. Before the appraisal, the big question was, Where did the money come from for the rubies? That question was quickly answered with the appraisal.

Look deeper. In 2001, a direct link was established between the INFCA and the United States Treasury. Unbeknownst to us, the United States citizens, we were sending monies directly to the Tribal Nations to fund the new and soon-to-be-thriving enterprise of gambling and the construction of numerous casinos in Oklahoma and other states and soon in China. The Cotai Strip in Macao received a $10 billion infusion to grow from the Tribal Nations or, in other words, the United States taxpayer! The popular story was that multimedia gaming footed the bill to get this one casino started, and Summit Structures were contracted to provide the temporary structure for the gaming since, as it stood at that time, the Tribe was not allowed to build a permanent structure. Supposedly, there was an agreement that the gaming company would get 80 percent of the profits until they were repaid, and thereafter, they would receive 20 percent. It seems like a most interesting deal and the big question is this: out of all of the funds that were supposedly set up for the power plant along with the USDA wrap on the loan, nothing was ever done, so where did the money go? The timing seems very interesting. Great food for thought!

One problem I see or, should I say, is a real question is, why was there such an effort to push Robert Stone to prison (flash drive exhibits: EX-86, 87, 88, 92, 94), as from all outward indications, he was innocent and set up only as the fall guy. We discussed this earlier, and still I can see no reason. Jack Stuteville worked day and night to tie Robert Stone into this state representative Todd Russ and Tom Parrish as well as OSBI agent Steve Neuman and assistant district attorney Brian Slabotsky worked feverishly to make this happen. It certainly appears to be tied to the collapse of First Capital Bank (FCB). Recall that it was shut down by June 8, 2012, by the Oklahoma State Banking Department. As we saw earlier, there were e-mails where Stuteville, Ed, and Susie Pritchett (who was also the judge that issued an arrest warrant from Kingfisher County on Stone) worked night and day shoring up a case just prior to the FCB collapse with the district attorney in Missouri, Fusselman. As noted, initially, Stone was to serve his sentence here in Oklahoma then be returned to Missouri and be charged and tried there. As you also recall, due to the lack of a credible witness (Stuteville), he was never charged in Missouri, and all was dropped against him. We know that they, Chisolm Trail Construction, i.e., Stuteville and Terry Kutcher, were the owners of that and that there was a USDA-guaranteed wrap on the price tag of the vicinity of $45 million for this racetrack near Columbia, Missouri, that never materialized, but the loans apparently did. Reading from this case, the following may be helpful as to why they always look to a government-backed loan.

> This group seeks to provide the remaining $40.134 million capital requirement through debt instruments. If needed, the company will ask lending institutions to seek government loan guarantees available through the Small Business Administration or the U.S. Department of Agriculture-Rural Development.

The above statement, in a more general form, was/is the mentality of the PCG management (Stuteville, Ron Murray to name a few) as a way to ensure that with the fraud TUG bonds, they would and could always get paid. Let's make this simple enough for me to understand: the project was backed by fraud bonds to guarantee that the project would be completed, but the bonds were worthless and wouldn't pay for the postage stamp that mailed them. So the bank was satisfied, as they could loan the money with the guaranteed wrap, the company (if one existed other than PCG) to do the job had no worries, as the loan monies were there and PCG/Stuteville would do nothing other than collect the monies.

Beginning shortly after its conception and before, PCG has run a large series of schemes and then collapsed whatever it was, took the guaranteed loan monies, and moved on. Through this chapter, we will look at a sampling of other scams and what the company yielded from each when I could locate an approximate yield.

Get ready for a few additional briefs, as it will be an interesting ride. With each of these, I will list next to the entry a EX-"XX" to show what exhibit this reference is associated with on the flash drive that was logged in as evidence when Chris Poindexter was arrested and charged with home repair fraud in Beckham County Courthouse, Sayre, Oklahoma, in January 2018 (case number SF-2018-000014). The charges were shortly dropped, and in a trial in 2020, the person who filed this, Mr. Beck, was ordered to pay and pay all the attorney fees that it had cost Mr. Poindexter to eventually get paid for all the work he had done! All this is public information and can be accessed in one step by requesting the drive as described in the conclusion of this book.

Round 1

Tinker AFB, NORESCO Job # 440038 (EX-08)

Energy Efficient Upgrade Lighting, March 7, 2008

"Performance Consulting Group, LLC, (PCG), a Certified Woman Owned Business Enterprise, is pleased to submit our response to NORESCO's RFP…at Tinker Air Force Base." Looking at the ownership documents for PCG at that time, Rita M. Murray was a manager, not an owner. Jack Stuteville was listed as the bank officer's name and First Capital Bank as the primary bank reference where, in effect, he is the owner of the bank. Therefore, unless he has falsified the ownership documents, he unlawfully sought to gain this contract under fraudulent means of claiming female ownership. He is the owner and the banker and was stating that his company was creditworthy!

Next, you will find that The Underwriters Group (TUG) stated their bonding level was $1.5 million a bond, which has been proven fake/worthless! It should be noted that in March 2005, a criminal alert notice (CAN) (EX-56) was issued, and they were to stop issuing bonds to the US government facilities or for their contractors.

Round 2

Hurricane Catrina struck in 2011 and left a path of destruction that would leave substantial work to be accomplished. Jack Stuteville immediately got underway and made a connection with two individuals and so began another Ponzi scheme to be had.

The company, CSR Nationwide, was owned by Chris Coryell and was a new association with Tim Aduddell to gain work with the backing of federally insured loans to do the work. What was to come next was both individuals having to file bankruptcy and Mr. Aduddell living abroad for nearly seven years.

The monies were all federally backed, and only the usual one was to gain from the scam.

Round 3

In September 2005, Marsha Kay Shubert, a former Crescent investment adviser, was sentenced to ten years in prison for a scheme that bilked investors out of as much as $20 million. She and the assistance of a few well-known individuals allowed her to gain the trust of her investors by promising returns of 30 percent or more through day trading and options trading. If one was to stop at this point, that would be the end of the story, but it is far from over. In the run of a normal Ponzi scheme, the first investors make the big money and those after losing all.

One leading factor that makes one wonder was that the crime was in Logan County, Oklahoma, and the court-appointed Robin Hood was from Enid, Oklahoma, in Garfield County. So with that bit of trivia, I began to research records and found that a large number of the first investors were from the Kingfisher and Enid area and/or had borrowed large amounts of money to invest from First Capital Bank, a Jack Stuteville company. Apparently, a very high percentage were friends of Mr. Stuteville, as he had directed them to get into this investment early! One that really stands out was Richard Reynolds, the city manager from Kingfisher, who received all his investment and a healthy return. Not all were so lucky! Seems like this is another example of Mr. Jackson becoming the receiver of such an event even though he did not happen to be in that city or county! I wonder how that works. Perhaps a shingle hanging outside of his office stating "Receiver within?" The following was stated by Mr. Jackson: "If I were to go rob a bank in Enid and walk down the street giving money to people, you wouldn't get to keep it."

Recall in an earlier chapter, I covered how a Ponzi scheme functioned! Fits the ticket, does it not?

Even though the above is only a very short list of all that has been taken, one needs to pay attention to all those who have received prison sentences, and for what? Primarily only to be the fall guy (or girl) so that the true perpetrator can walk off scot-free and take the spoils of the deed with them. It has been eight years since First Capital Bank was shut down, and to date, Jack Stuteville has yet to be charged with anything even vaguely related to his bank's failure! I wonder why. Perhaps Agent Hernandez needs to be questioned and perhaps charged for his lack of actions! Perhaps even look into his bank accounts?

Pridex Is Notified the Restitution Will Be Paid Or Not

ON MAY 8, 2013, Chris Poindexter was informed that Larry Wright had been arrested and that he was going to have to pay restitution to those he had scammed and that he (Chris) would be getting his money back in Jacksonville, Florida. He caught the next flight out of Oklahoma City to Jacksonville, Florida, and proceeded to the state's Department of Financial Services so that he could get paid. In less than twenty-four hours, Chris was meeting with a detective, Seth Schiefer, in his office, and the detective looked a bit surprised and stated that he assumed that Chris would call him before he came down. Chris told him that he had been fighting this for quite some time and wanted to get it resolved. Detective Schiefer looked really nervous and told Chris that Larry Wright had been arrested some six months earlier. What happened once he had met this detective would shock anyone who had their eyes open. After only being told a day earlier that Wright was to pay restitution, he was confronted with an unbelievable statement—"The case is closed!" Chris wanted to speak with his supervisor, and Seth told him that he had been instructed to give him the news. Chris stated that he wanted to know what was going on, as he had been to the Duval County Courthouse and all the files on this case had been removed! Why and who and where had this been allowed to happen? He was finally able to get the case from the state's attorney general, and it was so voluminous that they provided it on a CD.

The supervisor would not meet with him. The detective told Chris that he only made fifty some thousand a year and it wasn't worth the hassle. It was clear that he cared not for the position he had been put in. Seth told Chris that the case had been closed and some (a few) of the victims had been paid. Chris was insistent on knowing where the payment came from, and after a lengthy argument, the detective finally revealed that the payment came from the Middle East! An interesting fact is that around the exact date of the payments, Jack Stuteville was returning from Dubai, which, if one was uncertain, is in the Middle East. Chris received the call from his brother shortly after talking to the investigator for Financial Services, and he told him that Stuteville had just got off the plane from Dubai where he had a new startup company. Coincidence? Not likely!

From here, Chris called the postal inspectors, which put him through to a person named Lindsay Grinstead in Chicago, Illinois. She explained to Chris that she was a contractor in the postal service fraud hotline and the normal process was that one would call in, and from there, the case would be assigned; and at some mystical date in the distant future, someone may call you and work the case! At this point, I need to digress to my own issues with another government agency, the Department of Transportation Inspector General's Office. After filing over seven hundred complaints and nothing accomplished, I was then set up for the kill! People, wake up! Our government is not here to help us in the least, or at least certain factions of such! After filing with the DOT/IG on the FAA, some eight months later, I filed a complete case with the FBI and provided a complete list with documentation of all the items of proof (IOPs). I passed the seven-year mark in September 2019, and to date, there has been no action whatsoever.

These were the exact words of the postal fraud hotline:

> He (Chris Poindexter) was very insistent on coming to the office today or having an Inspector call

> him, so I wanted to give you a heads up in case he finds his way there somehow.

One would think that an inspector would be very interested in getting to the bottom of the problem, not hide from the issues at hand. But as we are seeing from one department to the next, the issue is delay, postpone, and do nothing. Eventually, the complainant will get tired and go away!

> Experience hath shown, that even under the best forms of government those entrusted with power have, in time, and by slow operations, perverted it into tyranny. (Thomas Jefferson)

There was a delay until much later in the day when Chris received a call from a Richard C. Batchelder, as he identified himself. Chris was still at the parking lot of the Department of Financial Services, and this guy did not want to meet him there but would meet at a restaurant downtown. When Chris arrived to meet the postal inspector, he was in sneakers, blue jeans, and a T-shirt. The discussion was this: how could the agency in charge simply close a case where this guy had stolen so much from the people? Now, speaking with the postal service, it appeared to be a clear-cut case of mail fraud, and Larry Wright should be prosecuted! Looking back, he had previously been prosecuted and imprisoned in Jessup, Georgia, for fraud. This was also a setup fix, as while he was in prison, he continued to peddle his fake bonds.

In an interesting note with Jack Stuteville being in Dubai working with his new startup company, Earth Heat Resources and No Heat Resources—which is related to Rampart Capital—through a series of interesting maneuvers, got a $134 million loan and then became Rampart Capital and loaned Larry Wright over $7 million. Really, they are going to lend a known and convicted felon $7 million. Would you? At approximately the same time, Jack Stuteville donated a million dollars to Oklahoma State University. The timing for these events all seemed to be lining up rather well.

One has to ask, Why would a company lend such a colorful person that kind of cash? It gets more interesting; they later sued him to get it back and now have an uncollected judgement against him. Again, why? The answer is simpler than one would think. In so doing and getting a large judgement against him, they would tie up anyone else's chances of collecting. So to speak, they keep the money all in the family!

In the fact that Chris had gone to such extremes to get his money back and that postal or mail fraud was involved, he received Offender Tracking Information System (OTIS) reports for Jack Stuteville, Lori Diaz, and Larry Wright. Additionally, he took from the Kiowa County sheriff listings of felony statutes for Larry Wright and Jack Stuteville to be charged. Chris took this package to the district attorney, Mr. John Wampler, and requested that he file charges against these individuals. Not only did he not do such, he told Chris that he would go one better and have him testify in the state's attorney general's grand jury so that all would come out. If you recall in an earlier chapter, Chris was given an order that he could not testify or even mention anything that had happened with these fraud bonds and all. Shortly after this meeting with Mr. Wampler, he resigned and now works as a city judge in Altus, Oklahoma! That's what we need? Perhaps another voter recall is in order here as well?

So as we look into this further, there is a pattern developing, and it's not just on the use of fraud bonds but in a level of protection occurring within our own justice system. It is quite obvious how these fake bonds are sucking money away from the citizens of this and other countries, but there has been a shield constructed to prevent them from being prosecuted and stopped. It seems that recently we have heard the phrase "two-tier justice system"?

> Rightful liberty is unobstructed action according to our will within limits drawn around us by the equal rights of others. I do not add 'within the limits of the law' because law is often but the tyrant's will, and always so when it violates the rights of the individual. (Thomas Jefferson)

Having said this, let's begin to look at our justice system, specifically where we have supreme court justices who state that they do not agree with or believe in the Bill of Rights. How can we have such a person who is sworn to uphold the laws of the country that does not believe in them? Look at our current system where we have a very large section of our legal community all attached to or within the same organization or fraternity. How is it that such events such as the filing of a RICO statute case be dismissed as there is no sign of organized crime? I suppose that only applies to one side of the equation being organized and not both.

You will find it very interesting how certain names or, should I say, certain people pop up repetitively when it comes to certain scams. Enjoy the upcoming chapter of hardball, as these few scam their way through friendly courts.

> If a nation expects to be ignorant and free, in a state of civilization, it expects what never was and never will be. (Thomas Jefferson)

CHAPTER XXVIII

Setting Up the Defensive Wall

IN 2012 HOPKINS entered into a contract to sell Oklahoma-grown wheat to Turhan's Bay Export & Import Co. (Turhan's Bay) for the purchase price of $269,000.52. Hopkins required a bond to guarantee payment. Turhan's Bay hired defendant Brunswick Companies (Brunswick), a surety broker, to arrange for a bond to guarantee payment to Hopkins. Brunswick contacted defendant Larry Wright and his business entity Phenix Services (Phenix) to provide underwriting services for the payment guarantee. Mr. Wright selected defendant First Mountain Bancorp (FMB) as surety. FMB guaranteed payment of the funds due to Hopkins under the wheat contract up to $300,000.00. Turhan's Bay paid $15,000.00 to Brunswick for surety brokerage services. Brunswick retained a commission of $2,500.00 and transferred the balance to Mr. Wright for payment of a commission to Phenix and the premium for the payment bond to FMB.

> Turhans's Bay paid only $25,000 on the wheat contract, leaving an unpaid balance of $244,001.52. FMB failed to pay the balance under the payment guarantee.

The purpose of this brief is to show how this event got started and what happens as it proceeds. Recall that Mr. Larry Wright, Mr.

George Gowen, and others such as Stuteville always seem to be untouchable. The big question is why.

Going back to the construction project that got Pridex wrapped into this mess, FMB provided Pridex the surety signed by George Gowen. Larry Wright provided the performance bond, and as we saw, both were frauds. Here it is again. Again, as we have seen, Mr. Douglas Jackson was busy defending a company this went through called Advanced Trading (the middleman) and came to an agreement for $50,000 to release any further liability to them. Our old friend Evan Gatewood represented Larry Wright and another company of his called Phenix (EX-149, pp 227–238) (Fig. 28-1). The pages attached of the trial transcript will give you an interesting snapshot at what was to appear. Judge Robin Cauthron, to evade the jury, said (actually the reporter hearing her tell the plaintiff's attorney), "Just don't—you don't need to whisper. Just speak softly." This was the way that the court would exclude the jury if she realized that it would be detrimental to the defendant in the case. The case will be to have the jury make a decision predicated on insufficient and incomplete information. When you read the attached pages, you will see that the defendant has written these fake bonds for up to $18 million and for such events as a sale of guns from the US State Department to Sri Lanka (EX-149 p. 35) (Fig. 28-2).

With respect to these bogus bonds, one has to ask, with as many judgements against this bunch, how do they avoid prison and not be forced to pay what is owed? On the transcript (EX-149 pp. 227), as stated earlier, Mr. Larry Wright was in prison in Jessup, Georgia, convicted of conspiracy to defraud. While in prison, he was referring clients to others to similar bond operators (p. 233).

Mr. Gatewood: "None of these cases have anything to do with First Mountain Bancorp. There's no fraud cases."

In reality, FMB was the same company that had written or, should I say, who signed the bogus bonds for Pridex, Mr. George Gowen. Read the exchange on this page that is attached, and you will see that the judge, with some prompting from Mr. Gatewood, walks the court away from actually telling the jury that there were, in fact, cases where the defendant had been convicted and had never paid the applicable judgement (p. 236).

The court judge Robin Cauthron: "Rather than watch us whisper, we'll just take our morning break. You will not discuss the case or allow others to discuss with you. I hope that we will be able to start again at ten till, but we may still be whispering at ten till. We'll let you know then." Jury exits.

Now comes the really difficult question: why is this not allowed in as evidence, and why are these criminals being allowed to write multimillion-dollar bonds for our government agencies on national and international transactions? At the time this was going on, Larry Wright had $540 million in a bank account in Clayton, Missouri. There are a great number of our federal agencies that are accepting these, but to name a few, Department of State, FAA, FAA SW Region, Department of Defense, Air Force, Army, and the list goes on and on (Exhibit 28-3).

Why with numerous judgements against these people and a criminal alert notice (CAN) put out against these people by the Department of the Army, why and how is this done and how does it continue?

There appears to only be one means by which this continues. Recall earlier that a Judge Friot in the Western District of Oklahoma rejected a case filed under the RICO statute stating that there was insufficient evidence. Note here that the city mayor who started this escapade—or perhaps caper would be a better word—that linked to Steve Standridge in Arkansas, who, in turn, led to Larry Wright in Florida, who actually sold the bogus bond that eventually lead to a unanimous jury verdict that found Larry Wright owing Pridex $2.7 million (with accrued interest). Again, the question needs to be asked—why? Perhaps each and every citizen in each and every state needs to be pounding on the doors or desks of their federal senator, representative, and president demanding answers! I will guarantee that if each and every one of us does such, one of two things will happen: we will either get this changed, or we will no longer be able to locate any of the abovementioned representation.

To conclude this chapter, I would like to mention that since I have used the name of Judge Robin Cauthron numerous times in this book and chapter that it is only fair to also state that in nearly all the cases involving the Tribal Nations that enter the federal court in the Western District of Oklahoma, she oversees the trial, and typically, she has found in favor of the tribes.

Go back to what President Lincoln stated so long ago, "A house divided against itself cannot stand." The statement does not refer to a political divide but rather a division standing as separate nations all within the same borders.

When we have people within our nation who are given a pass on laws broken, it is commonly called a two-tier justice system. The immediate outcome is, some are prosecuted, and some are not for the exact same crimes. The follow-on or, should I say, the long-term effect is a complete loss of concern for any law and, from there, lawlessness! This in its time will lead to revolution or what is commonly called civil war! By definition, *civil war* is "a war between citizens of the same country." This may sound far-fetched but, in reality, closer than most of this country's citizens may know. When the civil servants of our country come to a belief that they are entitled and no longer have laws that apply to them, we are there! "The Regulations Do Not Apply to Us!"

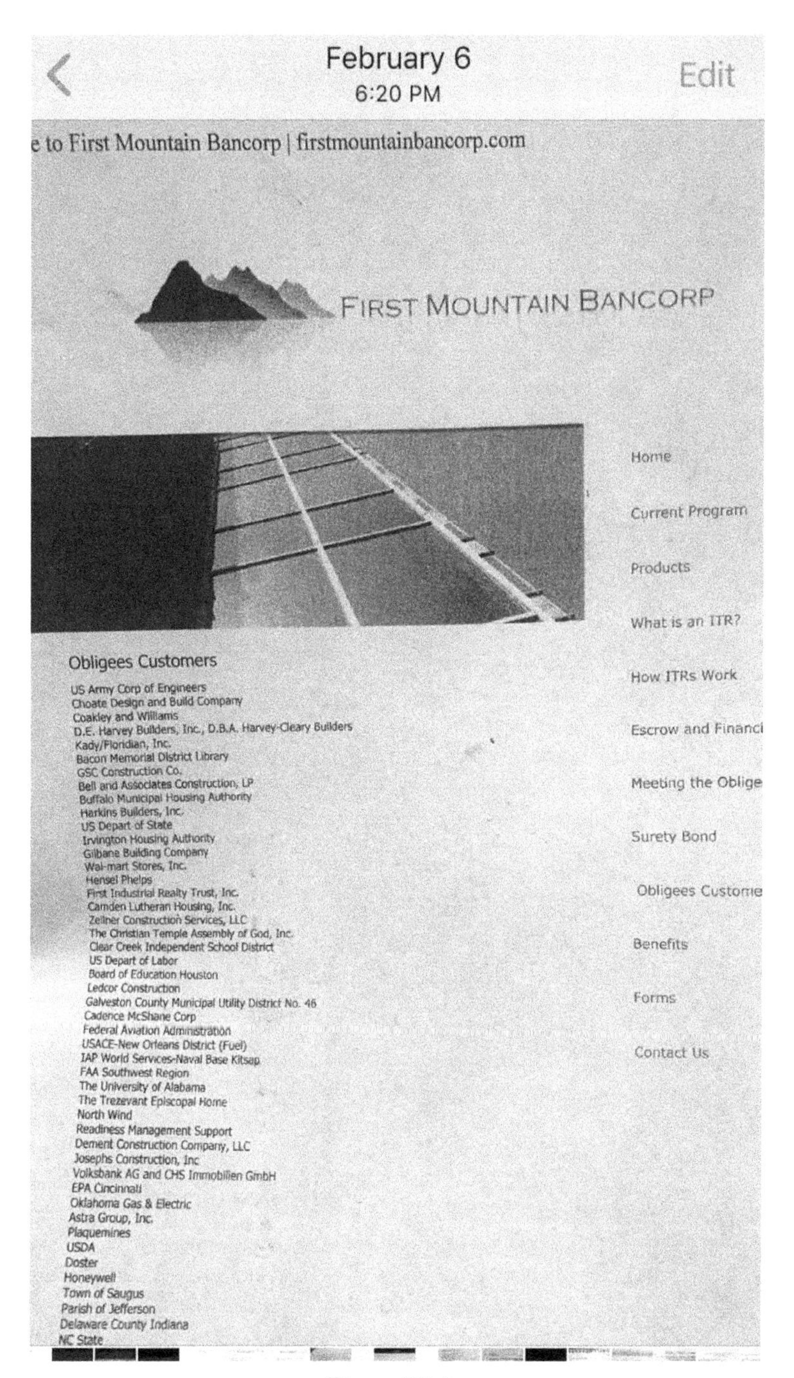
February 6
6:20 PM
Edit
e to First Mountain Bancorp | firstmountainbancorp.com
FIRST MOUNTAIN BANCORP
Home
Current Program
Products
What is an ITR?
How ITRs Work
Escrow and Financi
Meeting the Oblige
Surety Bond
Obligees Custome
Benefits
Forms
Contact Us
Obligees Customers
US Army Corp of Engineers
Choate Design and Build Company
Coakley and Williams
D.E. Harvey Builders, Inc., D.B.A. Harvey-Cleary Builders
Kady/Floridian, Inc.
Bacon Memorial District Library
GSC Construction Co.
Bell and Associates Construction, LP
Buffalo Municipal Housing Authority
Harkins Builders, Inc.
US Depart of State
Irvington Housing Authority
Gilbane Building Company
Wal-mart Stores, Inc.
Hensel Phelps
First Industrial Realty Trust, Inc.
Camden Lutheran Housing, Inc.
Zellner Construction Services, LLC
The Christian Temple Assembly of God, Inc.
Clear Creek Independent School District
US Depart of Labor
Board of Education Houston
Ledcor Construction
Galveston County Municipal Utility District No. 46
Cadence McShane Corp
Federal Aviation Administration
USACE-New Orleans District (Fuel)
IAP World Services-Naval Base Kitsap
FAA Southwest Region
The University of Alabama
The Trezevant Episcopal Home
North Wind
Readiness Management Support
Dement Construction Company, LLC
Josephs Construction, Inc
Volksbank AG and CHS Immobilien GmbH
EPA Cincinnati
Oklahoma Gas & Electric
Astra Group, Inc.
Plaquemines
USDA
Doster
Honeywell
Town of Saugus
Parish of Jefferson
Delaware County Indiana
NC State

Figure 28-1s

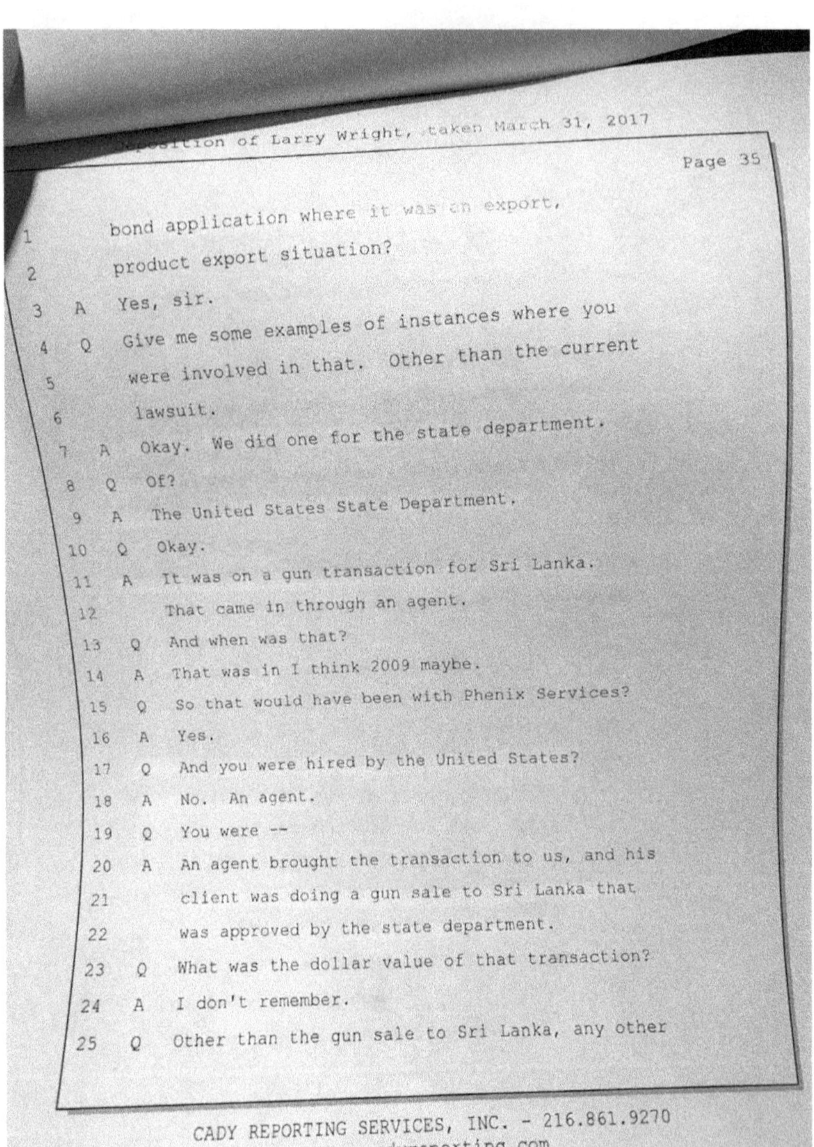

...osition of Larry Wright, taken March 31, 2017

Page 35

1 bond application where it was an export,
2 product export situation?
3 A Yes, sir.
4 Q Give me some examples of instances where you
5 were involved in that. Other than the current
6 lawsuit.
7 A Okay. We did one for the state department.
8 Q Of?
9 A The United States State Department.
10 Q Okay.
11 A It was on a gun transaction for Sri Lanka.
12 That came in through an agent.
13 Q And when was that?
14 A That was in I think 2009 maybe.
15 Q So that would have been with Phenix Services?
16 A Yes.
17 Q And you were hired by the United States?
18 A No. An agent.
19 Q You were --
20 A An agent brought the transaction to us, and his
21 client was doing a gun sale to Sri Lanka that
22 was approved by the state department.
23 Q What was the dollar value of that transaction?
24 A I don't remember.
25 Q Other than the gun sale to Sri Lanka, any other

CADY REPORTING SERVICES, INC. - 216.861.9270
www.cadyreporting.com

Figure 28-2

CHAPTER XXIX

The Final Bell Shall Toll

THROUGHOUT THIS BOOK, you have read of one misdeed to another, each one in itself being atrocious; but imagine if you were so unfortunate as to be related or to know each of these victims.

As I briefly cover each of the people and companies that have been harmed, think of the impact this would have if each of these peoples, friends, brothers, sisters, cousins, neighbors would go directly to these instigators and confront all of these people en masse. This would be something that these criminals who always operate in the shadows fear the most. Take for instance, district attorney Mike Fields, who simply passes those prosecutions that have caused deaths to friends and family members. Take for instance the letter that was written to E. Scott Pruitt, who was the attorney general for the State of Oklahoma. Chris Poindexter wrote him a letter (29-1) in which you can see he stated that murder was being accomplished and not a hand was raised! Why would someone who was sworn to uphold the law take a pass on this? Let me be clear: he did write to Mike Fields and told him of the letter. And Fields took a pass and did absolutely nothing! Excuse me; that is incorrect. He recused himself from any connection with the issue! "This accusation involves my office, so I must recuse myself from any investigation."

Or say, for instance, E. Scott Pruitt, when he was the state's attorney general, conducted a grand jury, and then DA John Wampler threatens in writing to not allow the actual witness to speak. What is the purpose of even bothering if the truth will be hidden away? You will cover a number of these interesting events. Oh, I forgot it looks good when you can report that a multicounty grand jury saw no reason to proceed.

Recall early in this book we covered a gentleman named Robert Stone who was imprisoned after a group composed of (1) Jack Stuteville, (2) Ed Pritchett (longtime friend and associate of Stuteville and husband of Susie Pritchett), (3) Judge Susie Pritchett, who issued a felony arrest warrant for Stone, (4) Attorney Douglas Jackson, (5) district attorney Mike Fusselman, and others all conspiring to falsely imprison Mr. Stone. When he was finally released in Oklahoma, they could not prosecute him in Missouri, as they lacked a credible witness. Want to know who it was? Look at the above list and read the e-mails. An even better way is to simply look at the mug shots attached (29-2). This was truly a conspiracy!

Moving ahead a short distance, Kymberly Marie Hatler Mathews was silenced for what she knew and was publicizing such. OSBI agent Steve Neuman ruled this was a suicide after she was beaten only five days prior by her loving husband! Fake notes were posted (29-3) on Facebook as to what kind of rounds were best for hunting and then quickly taken down immediately after her death. Along with this was a poorly written excuse note (29-4) by the one who most likely was the murderer. How many women do you know choose a violent means of killing themselves? I doubt the answer will surprise you—virtually none! Now that we are discussing the Mathews brothers, recall the text from Mike Mathews, who, in writing, threatened Chris Poindexter: "U better zip your lip, or I will do it for u." Based on the letter (29-4), he perhaps should have taken his own advice and zipped his lip, or at least his fingers. An interesting sideline was when Mr. Doug Jackson represented Randy Mathews!

Going back and looking at the deposition of Mike Mathews (EX-98), he made it known his feelings toward Stuteville, and they were less than great! However, according to the bankruptcy of PCG, Stuteville paid him on a salary. Mathews, in his business, routinely did business with Stuteville. Do you feel that there is a chance that Mathews lied under oath? That's a really tough question.

Going on with our bankers, the prerequisite seems to be, or should I say is a disease to get more and more money. Somewhere down the road, this very illustrious group seemed to fail to understand when enough is enough! This last example of our system failing us is the issue of bankers and, in this case, is a new name to the book but not new to the justice system! In 1982, Mr. Paul Doughty was convicted of the collapse of the Oklahoma National Bank (ONB) in Oklahoma City. Then, again, in 2009, he was convicted by the FBI of fraud and an assortment of other crimes. There was an eighteen-count indictment against him and Mr. Don Anderson. Lo and behold, our own state officials were providing cover for Doughty and Anderson, who were making a reverse Oklahoma land run, which they were now experienced in after a 2007 middle-of-the-night flee out of Colorado on their fraudulent land sales after being informed of the scheme they were operating they would be audited.

As we shall call them, the Altus Gang includes the leader Paul Doughty, who was also president of the failed First State Bank Altus, the Oklahoma National Bank in Oklahoma City, and a land scam in Colorado; Don Anderson; and other employees; Quartz Mountain Aerospace and some fifteen or more sleight of hand LLCs, most notably Altus Ventures (more aptly nicknamed Altus Vultures), Oklahoma Industrial Venture Capital Company, and Oasis Development. The reason I bring this up at this time, as the same folks or government positions that were discussed earlier provided cover for these scams, and they were able to take well over $1 billion. Who footed the bill for the actions of our state and federal elected and nonelected officials? You got it right—YOU DID!

So that you will not worry, Mr. Doughty owns a very nice hotel in Costa Rica, and we, the American taxpayers, don't even get a discount at his hotel when we bought it!

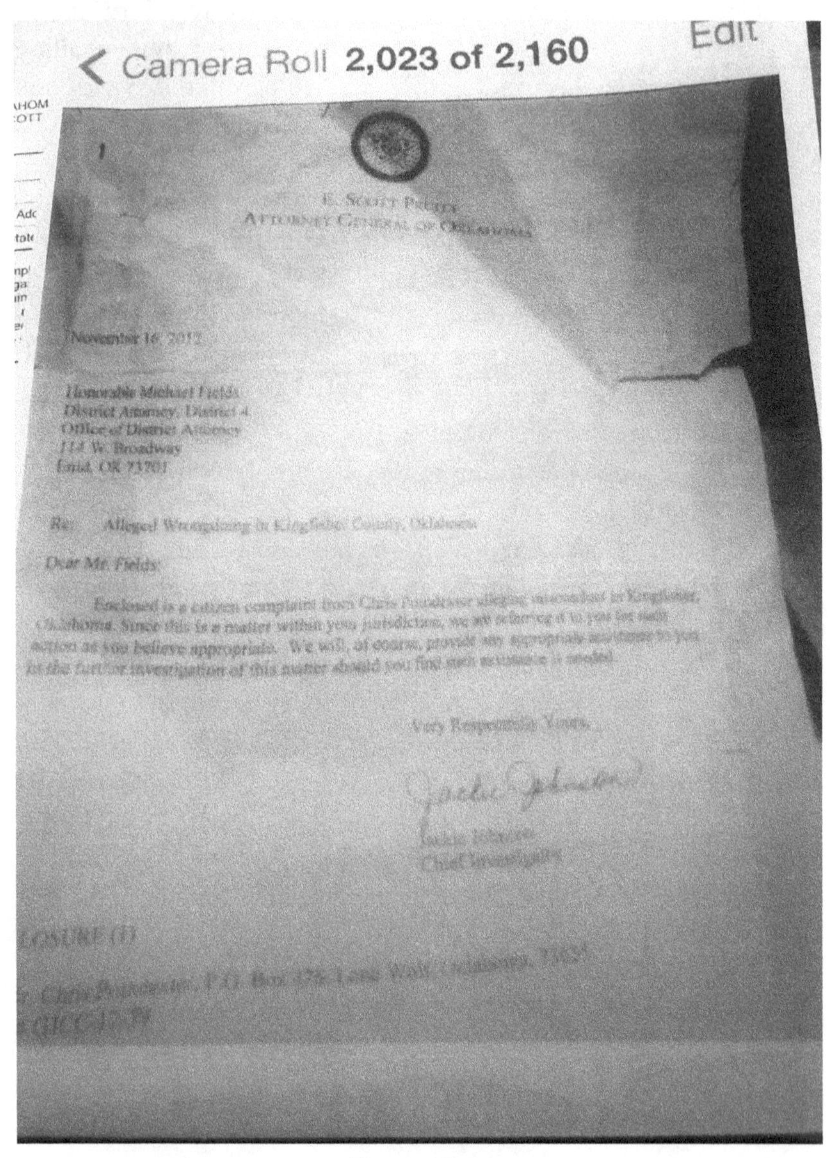

Camera Roll 2,023 of 2,160 Edit

E. Scott Pruitt
Attorney General of Oklahoma

November 16, 2012

Honorable Michael Fields
District Attorney, District 4
Office of District Attorney
114 W. Broadway
Enid, OK 73701

Re: Alleged Wrongdoing in Kingfisher County, Oklahoma

Dear Mr. Fields:

Enclosed is a citizen complaint from Chris Poindexter alleging misconduct in Kingfisher, Oklahoma. Since this is a matter within your jurisdiction, we are referring it to you for such action as you believe appropriate. We will, of course, provide any appropriate assistance to you in the further investigation of this matter should you find such assistance is needed.

Very Respectfully Yours,

Jackie Johnson
Chief Investigator

Figure 29-1a

OKLAHOMA ATTORNEY GENERAL
E. SCOTT PRUITT

CITIZEN COMPLAINT FORM
Website: www.oag.ok.gov

Your Contact Information			
Name	Christopher F Poindexter	Phone Number	580-399-5678
Street Address			
City, State, Zip	Lone Wolf OK 73655	County	Kiowa

By completing this form you are filing a formal complaint against an individual or entity. In order to investigate your complaint, you must provide sufficient information to properly investigate your complaint as well as a summary of evidence available to you at this time to support your claim. Please note that an investigation must be based on facts or circumstances that you personally observed or heard. If you do not have any personal knowledge of a fact or circumstance, you must provide sufficient information to permit us to contact the individual who does have such evidence.

Complaint Information			
Date of Incident	April 6, 2011	Place of Incident	Kingfisher OK
If your complaint is against a public entity, give the name of the agency and any specific individuals within that agency who are connected to the incident.	City of Kingfisher		
If your complaint is against an individual, give their name and relationship to you.	See Case No. CIV-12-31-M		

Describe in detail the incident, any injuries you received and how the Attorney General can aid you in resolving your issue.

See Federal Court
Case No. CIV-12-31-M

(Please continue on other side)

Figure 29-1b

List any evidence you can provide to support your complaint	
Name, Address and Phone Numbers of Witnesses	Brief summary of evidence to be provided by the witness
1. See Attached	
2.	
3.	

List any documents available to you or to any witnesses	Copies are attached	
1. See Federal Case # CIV-12-31-M	Yes ☒	No ☐
2. See Case no CV-2012-3 Kingfisher	Yes ☒	No ☐
3. County	Yes ☒	No ☐

Please attach additional pages if needed

Have you filed a complaint with any other agency or organization? Yes ☒ No ☐

If yes, identify the organization. Oklahoma Insurance Department

What action was taken? Underwriters Group Inc. Dr. Larry Wright was issued a cease + desist order in 2008. OID Verified they have no [illegible] to conduct business in Oklahoma.

I understand that the false reporting of a crime is a criminal offense pursuant to Title 21 O.S. § 589

I swear or affirm the above statement is true and accurate to the best of my knowledge?

Your signature is required: [signature] Date: 2-10-12

The Attorney General does not guarantee an investigation or inquiry. Furthermore you must understand that the Attorney General is not your private attorney. Oklahoma law prohibits us from giving legal advice or opinions or acting as your personal attorney; therefore, if you desire legal advice, we suggest you consider contacting a private attorney to discuss you complaint.

RETURN TO:

OFFICE OF ATTORNEY GENERAL
313 N.E. 21st Street
Oklahoma City, OK 73105

FOR OFFICE USE ONLY

OAG Unit: ____________ **Referred to:** ____________

Disposition of Complaint:

☐ Investigation ☐ Inquiry ☐ Referred to another agency ☐ No action taken

Figure 29-1c

Stone charges dropped due to lack of witness credibility

ROBERT STONE JACK STUTEVILLE

▲ HIDE CAPTION

Robert Stone and Jack Stuteville mugs. - Online mugs

Figure 29-2

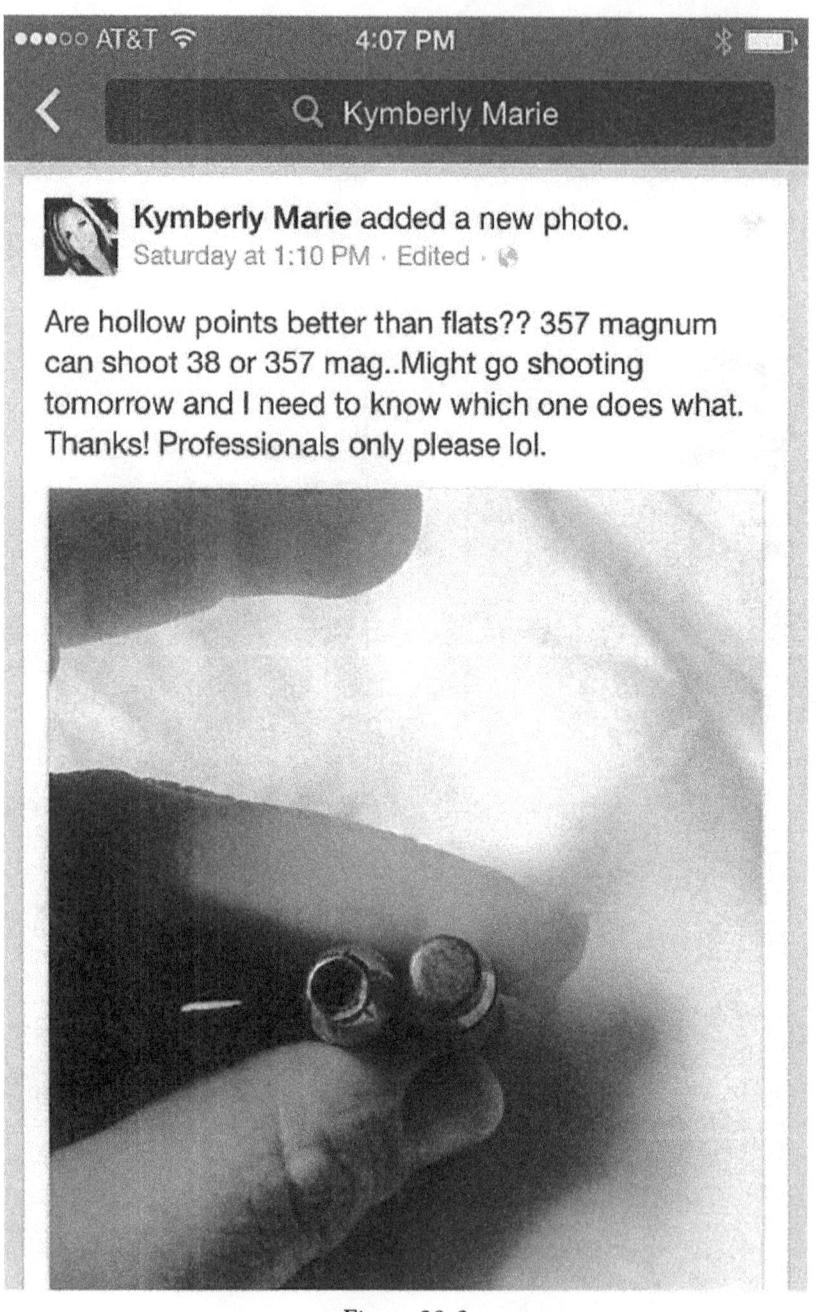
AT&T
4:07 PM
Kymberly Marie
Kymberly Marie added a new photo.
Saturday at 1:10 PM · Edited ·
Are hollow points better than flats?? 357 magnum can shoot 38 or 357 mag..Might go shooting tomorrow and I need to know which one does what. Thanks! Professionals only please lol.

Figure 29-3

Kingfisher Times & Free Press

17348 N 2850 RD
KINGFISHER OK 73750-7066

Fifty Cents | Kingfisher, Kingfisher County, Oklahoma | USPS No. 295-420

OSBI investigates local woman's deatl

A Kingfisher woman was found dead in her home Sunday night of an apparent gunshot wound, but the official cause of death was still pending as of press time Tuesday afternoon.

The body of Kymberly Marie Matthews, 38, was found in the bedroom of her home at 210 S. Eighth St. shortly before 8 p.m. Sunday by the husband of her employer, Kingfisher Police Chief Dennis Baker told the *Times and Free Press.*

Mike Mitchell was checking on Matthews' welfare after his wife, Shawndelle Mitchell, who is Matthews' employer at Hometown Quality Care, hadn't been able to reach Matthews for more than 30 hours, according to the police report.

Mitchell called police from outside Matthews' home and reported that her car was in the garage but she wasn't answering the door.

Kymberly Marie Matthews

While waiting for police to arrive, Mitchell kicked in the northwest door of the residence and discovered Matthews' body, according to the report.

Police secured the residence and contacted the Oklahoma State Bureau of Investigation for assistance.

OSBI agents took control of the scene at approximately 10 p.m. and the body was transported to the state medical examiner's office for autopsy, Baker said.

Baker confirmed that a handgun was found near the body, but did not provide the make and model.

He said law enforcement was estimating the time of death as early Saturday afternoon, but were waiting for a more definitive estimate from the medical examiner's office.

A post on Kymberly Matthews' Facebook page, timestamped 1:10 p.m. Saturday, shows a photogr of a hand holding two different lets and reads:

"Are hollow points better flats?? 357 magnum can shoot 357 mag? Might go shooting to row and I need to know which does what. Thanks! Professio only please."

Both Baker and OSBI Agent Neuman said they were aware Facebook post but couldn't com further at this time.

When asked if evidence had found suggesting foul play o presence of a second party at the of Matthews' death, Baker resp ed: "Not at this time but all case this are investigated as a hom until all evidence proves other

Matthews leaves behind old twins – a son and a daughte

[See Death Page 14]

City calls for tax vote, OKs hotel pa

Figure 29-4

Fifty Cents | Kingfisher, Kingfisher County, Oklahoma | USPS No. 295-420

Foul play ruled out in death investigation

[illegible] Matthews died from an apparently self-inflicted gunshot wound, [illegible] Kingfisher Police Chief Dennis Baker said Friday.

Matthews [illegible] the bedroom of her home at 210 S. Eighth St. shortly before 8 p.m. Sunday by the husband of her employer.

Kingfisher police responded to the scene and called in the Oklahoma State Bureau of Investigation for assistance.

A Rossi revolver with five live rounds and one spent casing was found near the body.

"We are attempting to process one last piece of electronic evidence that may take some time due to the necessity of having to utilize an outside source for assistance," Baker said. "In [illegible]

[illegible] self-inflicted gunshot wound," Baker said. "We have found no evidence suggesting foul play in this case."

Baker said the medical examiner's office did not perform an autopsy.

While the initial police report contained a notation that Kymberly Matthews had told her employer that her estranged husband Randy Matthews had taken their 8-year-old twins out of school in Dover the Monday before her death, Randy Matthews' brother Billy Matthews provided documentation to the *Times and Free Press* showing that the information was inaccurate.

[illegible]

Billy Matthews also told the *Times and Free Press* that he and other family members called the authorities to report that he received threats from Kymberly Matthews that she was coming to Dover to kill his family members.

He said within 20 minutes of his first phone call to authorities, he received a phone call from Kymberly Matthews "chewing him out" for calling the authorities.

Billy Matthews said he called back demanding to know who had notified Kymberly Matthews about his phone call.

Kingfisher County Sheriff Deputy [illegible]

[illegible] at 7:41 p.m. April 7 and reported that Kymberly Matthews was threatening to kill Billy Matthews [illegible] she was suspected to be intoxicated and would be driving a black Chevrolet Traverse.

According to the log, at 7:56 p.m. the dispatcher called Dover Police Chief Jonathan Eason, who said he was at training in [illegible] and he

[See Death Page 15]

Nationals bound

Figure 29-5

Conclusion

Throughout this book, we have discussed various events that most Americans would consider far-fetched. Our own government is acting in unison with people who are bent on the destruction of the very country that has given them every opportunity to succeed. Additionally, attached are documents proving the issues that I have referenced as well as a reference to a more extensive file that contains all the background information for those who desire a more thorough review.

Our founding fathers never had any idea that we would have legislators sitting in their office for thirty, forty, or more years. The crux of the problem is that we are seeing people live longer than ever before and are literally living from one reelection to the next. It matters not what your political preference is; our country has always lived on diversity and change. I'm certain that you can now see, after this book, what the problem has become. Many of our elected and unelected officials have come to a point where connections they have made are criminal; however, with the money flowing to their pockets, they no longer see why they are there and what their actual job is.

With the two-tier justice system, we are reaping what our new system will yield. You have witnessed how these few conspire to imprison and, if that doesn't work, to kill the one who is calling attention to the problem. Recall in my last two books that the effort was to kill the source of the information so that our civil servants could continue to live in the lifestyle that we the people were providing. Rather than to hear and fix the problem, it was easier to shoot the messenger, so to speak.

What we have are career civil servants and career politicians when what we should have are patriots. These people have come to a point where they honestly believe that they are entitled. If they had any sense of what was going on around them, they would bow out and install limits on the time that they could or would stay in office. Considering that in the past few days I have heard that for any single day, there was more ammunition sold in the United States than any day on record, one should note that it is not hunting season at this time of the year but preparation for the time when our government attempts to take away our Second Amendment rights or perhaps the ammunition that we would use to enforce our right.

> A Bill of Rights is what the people are entitled to against every government, and what no just government should refuse, or rest on inference. (Thomas Jefferson)

Looking at each person that was imprisoned or that perished, there was no reason for such other than money and greed alone. Like most of the problems that seem to crop up, they are directed at one issue and one alone—the issue of money and power! We the people are under attack, and the messenger is the first to be shot!

> We are just another player in the tribal battle. (James Comey)

For those who would like to see the information reviewed for the writing of this book, please email: flashdrive@dividingofamerica.com. The price of the information is $89.00 which includes the S&H.

About the Author

Lee McGarr is an aircraft pilot, electrical engineer, and biologist with over thirty thousand hours of flight time. Having worked as an FAA inspector and flight check pilot, he found corruption and violation of federal law and FAA regulations to the extent of tens of millions of dollars annually and nepotism to unseen extremes within the FAA. After testifying, the retaliation was intense, and he finally found it necessary to turn all information over to the FBI in an attempt to bring justice to the corruption within the FAA.

CPSIA information can be obtained
at www.ICGtesting.com
Printed in the USA
LVHW031142070721
691986LV00004B/257